# *Shadows*

## *on a*

# *Stone Wall*

*By Mary Letts*

First published by Lulu.com, 2007

ISBN 978-0-9556929-0-1

For my husband and my three sons

# 1

The wind seemed spiteful. It blew steadily and serenely enough at high altitude, then abruptly nosedived with venomous force and no apparent meteorological reason into the gulley. There it collected every stray pellet of earth in its path only to spray them, like a vicious scattergun, straight at the mourners' faces. If I were more paranoid, Julia could not help thinking, I'd be convinced it had a personal grudge against Frances.

The Cura led the procession, both arms flailing as if repelling an angry mob of wasps. One swatted helplessly at the fusillade of grit, the other slapped at the billowing skirts of his long, black robe, trying to pin them to his thighs. If his legs had been athletic he would have happily exposed them - but they were so painfully thin, and such a ghostly, luminous white that he could hardly bear to look at them himself. Not even somewhere private.

Immediately behind him trudged the pall bearers. They were muttering darkly under their breath, suspicious that the wind had more than doubled the weight of the coffin; struggling too with a wilder, more irrational fear that it was about to burst open, its lid wrenched off by a demonic Frankenstein-type curse and shattered on the rocks.

Once they passed through the wrought iron gates of the cemetery, however, the wind suddenly relented and softened. Much to Julia's relief, for without an interlude of calm she had no hope of absorbing the terrible finality of her mother's death.

The cemetery resembled a miniature toy-town. Each coffin was slotted into its own personal whitewashed 'apartment', but there seemed no way of distinguishing one from another. No names, no numbers. Was there a master diagram somewhere, or would she just have to memorize this spot? She searched anxiously for a landmark, worrying she would lose her mother forever in this death maze, already thinking ahead to when she would bring Alex and Marco. It upset her they had contrived to miss their granny's funeral. Poignant memories of death stay with you... Should she have insisted they came?

But Marco still had the lingering end of whooping cough and the wind would aggravate it, whilst Alex had leapt at the chance of keeping him company. Yet she knew his eagerness to avoid the funeral was mainly the misgivings he had always felt about her mother, who had soured of life long before he was born, and then refused to compromise her normal, everyday irritability by faking some sweet old granny act.

Julia watched the familiar village faces as they drifted in through the gates. Her mother had antagonised them all at one time or another, so they wouldn't be remembering her with any genuine love or respect. But they *had* come to her funeral. Death was strangely ennobling, it would seem - even for someone such a glaring misfit to the quiet, steady rhythms of traditional village life. Or else the group catharsis of a funeral simply had an irresistible appeal.

She began to feel increasingly doubtful that this conventional ceremony was what her mother would have wanted.

"I'll never go back to bloody England - not even as a fucking corpse! Make damn' sure you bury me in Spain," was her only utterance on the subject.

It was, of course, merely a flippant remark provoked by some minor irritation, never remotely intended as a funeral directive - but it was all she had to go by. Actual burial was anyway impossible. No-one dug graves in this hard, stony, unforgiving ground.

She looked up in alarm at the concussive sound of metal jarring brick to see one of the pall bearers hammering furiously at the plastered brick entrance to her mother's awaiting compartment, - unoccupied tombs were always shuttered up to prevent colonies of bats from nesting in them.

The banging then stopped politely for the Cura, who swung the incense burner rhythmically to and fro over the coffin, singing sweetly in a strangely accented Latin. The knot in Julia's stomach tightened as she imagined her mother (an ardent atheist) writhing with loathing at this ritualistic intoning so uncomfortably close to her coffin lid. The four pall bearers then hoisted the coffin up and tried to persuade it through the jagged gap - but it was immediately obvious it would never fit. So Eulogio, who way back had sold Frances his old finca, snatched the pickaxe contemptuously from the feeblest pall bearer and, grunting with each blow, energetically hacked away until he had exposed a larger, neater, squarer entrance.

Renewed silence fell as the coffin was again steered towards it.

She groaned inwardly. All along she had suspected the dimensions of this coffin. She had obstinately opted for the 'Modelo Normal' while Emilio 'Fuster' (the village carpenter) had pushed hard for the 'Modelo Superior' at over twice the price. And evidently he had decided to show her the folly of cutting costs by proving that exact measurements come at a price. She walked away, unable to watch - half-expecting him to plane down the coffin to fit the gap, thick clouds of sawdust drifting over her mother's body.

Behind her she heard animated discussions on what to do next. Eventually some compromise agreement must have been reached, for now the coffin was tilted sideways so that Eulogio could prise off its pitch-pine rebate. This seemed to take forever, but finally some faint degree of solemnity returned while this slimmer, weaker coffin was squeezed with agonizing and squeaky difficulty into its niche. That done, Eulogio mournfully blew his nose into an embroidered handkerchief - then promptly used it to dab his eyes; whilst Dolores from the bakery, who had often shown contemptuous outrage when Frances had one of her periodic drunk and insulting evenings, suddenly gave a piercing wail of pure misery.

Julia's own eyes involuntarily brimmed with tears as she bent to place a wreath against the tomb, which would now need sensitive repairwork to disguise the ugly signs of struggle. Blurred memories swam dizzily before her eyes and her mind felt dislocated; while instead of raw, genuine emotion she felt only a bleak and frozen numbness. Perhaps grieving wholeheartedly was only ever possible if you had unreservedly loved. And perhaps it was only poetic justice after the whole mad circus of her mother's life that her funeral would end up partly a fiasco... Thank God it was nearly over. And that Alex and Marco hadn't had to witness it.


Reggie and Colin were recovering from the ravages of the wind in the corner bar.

"Stiff one for me," Reggie reminded Colin, whose round it was. "Didn't see you at Frances' send off. There was a surprisingly healthy turnout nonetheless."

"I'm not a funeral man. Damn' cypress trees give me the rash," (he checked suspiciously under his shirt) "and I won't pretend we saw eye-to-eye, as you well know Reggie."

Reggie sipped his brandy thoughtfully. Looking up, he noticed Julia come through the door with her two boys. He swiftly gave Colin a warning dig in the ribs in case he was warming up to a more virulent attack on Frances. He had never discovered exactly what first sparked off their enmity. Perhaps Colin had made a try for her, and, appraising Colin's beer gut, retreating hairline and lobster pink complexion, he guessed Frances would certainly have cruelly humiliated him. Noting a spare chair at the table where Julia, Alex and Marco were sitting, Reggie patted Colin pityingly on the back and left him to drink alone.


As he approached Julia his expression shifted to one of more suitable gravity, and he sank dolefully onto the chair.

3

"Please accept my condolences. And I'm so sorry to have let you know by telegramme - ridiculous these days. But I only found your address, no phone number, and (he blushed slightly) didn't even know what name you use. It must have been a terrible shock."

"In the back of my mind I guess I always knew it might happen. She should never have driven at night."

Marco looked curiously at Reggie. "Were you a *friend* of gran's?" Then he turned challengingly to Alex, "You said she didn't have any."

Alex glared at Marco, who had no sense of discretion even though he was nearly nine. Reggie laughed raucously, then, suddenly remembering his role as fellow mourner, leaned more soberly towards Julia.

"I know this isn't the time or place but - sometimes practicalities help us cope." He folded his handkerchief into a neat little triangle, darting a furtive look at Julia. "Any thoughts about selling the property, once probate's sorted?" He tried hard to look concerned rather than eager.

"I've not given it any thought, not yet."

"Well if you do, I'm your man. 'Course you know the ropes around here as well as anyone, and speak the lingo infinitely better than me. But you'll still need an agent with contacts." He produced a peach coloured businesscard with a line drawing of a finca and leaning palm tree. "One you can trust a hundred percent."

She smiled disarmingly. "I wouldn't trust anyone a hundred percent."

"Not even old uncle Reggie?" he sniffed plaintively. "Your mother's only friend."

She listened politely, the ghost of a smile still playing on her lips. He didn't easily inspire confidence, but there was something endearing about him all the same. She tried to concentrate, aware that his voice was still rambling on.

"*I* at least spread the word she was on medication, so one drink was all it needed to affect her judgment, making her understeer that corner. I've tried my hardest," he sniffed again "to fend off the inevitable aspersions."

Her smile vanished instantly. "I'm sorry." She gave his hand a slight squeeze, scooped up the card and slid it into her wallet. "I'll let you know whatever I decide. And thank you," she stood up to go, giving Alex a meaningful nod, "my mother was no easy friend, I know that."


She spent a sleepless night on a thin strip of foam on the living room floor. Alex and Marco were in sleeping bags on the sofa, and their feet clashed in the middle so they, too, continually woke each other up. Her mother's little rented house in the village had only one bedroom and Julia was determined not to use it. It was too personal - her mother's perfume still lingered in the air, and she especially wanted to avoid the temptation to hunt for traces of Reggie. As a child she had secretly ferreted through her mother's top drawer hunting for exotic treasures of mysterious purpose: creams, a rubbery diaphragm, nude photos, and dark chocolate lumps of cannabis, and of course anything attributable to a man. Then it had been nerve-wrackingly exciting, a thrilling peephole into adulthood enhanced by the sheer terror of being caught in the act of spying.

Now she still felt twinges of curiosity, she could admit, but there was an overriding sense of dread that she would uncover undignified intimacies like false teeth, a chestnut wig, or - almost worst of all - a pair of Reggie's boxer shorts.

Soon she would have to face the task of sorting through Frances' personal possessions, but not yet.


Next morning they went to the farmhouse. The boys made her slow to a crawl around the bend where Frances had driven off, and they stared in silent awe at the tyre burns on the road, the crushed bushes and flattened weeds down the steep embankment, and the line of vines ripped out by her slewing wheels. A little later, when Dolores from the bakery judged that the pain of bereavement could give way to practicalities, she presented Julia with a bill for those vines. It was only so high, she explained, sighing deeply, so as to compensate for the future lean years while the new vines matured. But it was the way it was presented more than its priciness that offended Julia, for she had noted it down, so matter of factly, amongst the normal items of her bakery bill on an old scrap of greaseproof paper: pan - 2.30 euros, harina integral - 3.25 euros, 7 vinas - 300 euros.

"You can pay by cheque if you want," Dolores assured her, "since it's rather a lot."

She thought back to the Dolores dressed in sombre black at the funeral who had howled so woefully, sobbing, sighing and praying for Frances' deliverance, and in doing so exhaling so much simultaneous sound and air that she had tripped twice and nearly fainted, and then needed the support of her son all the way down the rocky path back to the village. She knew that the cost of her mother's death being itemized like a loaf of bread more accurately reflected Dolores' true feelings, yet family honour demanded some sort of riposte. Thus she deliberately left the cheque in the bank for Dolores to be forced into going there and asking for it publically.

Bump, bump, bump, up the dirt track to the farmhouse her mother had bought thirty five years ago now. It was built from the same warm yellow-grey stone as the terrace walls that climbed the mountain slopes like flights of stairs, curving and snaking around the natural contours; and it had a dramatic view of the valley, with the village of Milagra in the foreground.

Frances had moved down to the village about a year ago, when her arthritis forced her to accept she could no longer live alone without close neighbours. In her prime she had rarely been alone, of course, but Julia's thoughts were so awash with childhood memories right now that she could not pin names, faces or personalities to any of the many lovers - they simply merged into a single shadowy presence that was never, ever, her father.

Frances had lately only managed to visit the house on occasional afternoons, taking a cane chair into the garden to read a book or, much less often, write a scathing or self-pitying letter to Julia, and she always returned to the village before dark. That was why it was strange she had been heading in the direction of the house on the night of her fatal accident. Reggie found the house keys and an old torch on the floor of the car, evidently flung from the passenger seat when she lunged off the road. It puzzled him - but he did not tell Julia.

Arriving at the house she opened the heavy carved door with those self-same keys, and hurried from room to room unbolting shutters and flinging wide the windows. Winter sun flooded in, and thrown into a panic by the sudden light, geckos scurried across the walls to find refuge in the dark shadows of beams. They had suction pads on their toes so that if you pulled them off it sounded like a cork being plucked from a bottle. She used to detach them sometimes when she was little, but they went rigid with fright so she freed them up the chimney shaft.

'Whitewashed walls, terracotta tiles, exposed beams, coved ceilings bla, bla, bla'… She rehearsed the real estate clichés as she wandered into the kitchen, trying to suppress the tidal wave of emotions by imagining herself a prospective buyer setting eyes on the house for the first time. *Should* she sell it? Reggie was certainly itching to get his hands on the commission, and nothing suggested he did not deserve it. Then she eyed the film of dust and proliferation of cobwebs and realised just how frail and helpless her mother had become; even the welcoming atmosphere of a supposedly family house seemed a cruel contradiction of the lonely reality of Frances' life. Suddenly it spoke of all her unrealised dreams, and Julia felt a spurt of pure hatred for her father. Years of watching Frances fuming over his cowardice, then drinking to forget him – and in the meantime revenging herself on a succession of substitute men, had at least convinced Julia there was no joy in living a life that you blamed someone else for.

And she felt guilty for her own role in their estrangement. She had left home in anger so long ago, always imagining, optimistically, unrealistically, that one day Frances would mellow enough for them to forget their differences.

6

Or, at least, make *some* form of peace before she died. She should have known Frances would never make the first move towards reconciliation.

A glance at the row of photos fading on the mantelpiece reminded her that Frances had had one close friendship once, with a German woman called Marte; a lesbian one according to the sort of scurrilous bar gossip that was as predictable as it was untrustworthy.

Marte was a friend from way back who had embraced the hippie culture much more wholeheartedly than Frances. Marte had done everything properly according to the ideals of the time. She dropped out of Art School and, to put distance between herself and the numbing conformity of middle class Germany, headed for a small and primitive village in the Moroccan Rif. Her journey companion was a pin-thin potter who had gone prematurely bald (he blamed Marte's strictly macrobiotic cooking), and while he lay on the hot, melting tarmac beneath the undercarriage of their VW van struggling vainly to repair a broken axle, Marte wandered off to the nearest bar to wait in greater comfort. There she fell instantly in love with a golden haired Apollo called Manfred Schneider who had just phoned home for his return fare to Hamburg, and when the money arrived they made an impulse buy of a slice of mountain scree with a clump of pines.

There they lived in a homemade hut until Manfred left for Poona expecting Marte to follow, but she never did. Instead she stayed on that mountain in that temporary structure always about to be properly built for what must now be - Julia made a quick calculation - twenty five years or more. And as it turned out it was just as well that she never strayed far from German soil, since none of her careers (in handmade home-dyed knitwear, glass leading, patchwork, and aromatherapy) ever quite jelled financially. Hence she had to make frequent journeys back to Germany to safeguard the regular payments of Child Benefit, her only reliable source of income.

Julia wondered if she was back there now, since she had not come to the funeral. In amongst the confusion of her emotions, the swirling feelings of sadness, anger, regret and terrible guilt, she suddenly became aware of the beginnings of a lighter mood, a growing and gathering sense of release that the past was finally over and Frances no longer there to vent her fury or complain.

She was jolted from her introspections by the cheerful voices of Alex and Marco out in the garden. They had returned from their foray up the mountain to hunt for anything ripe or edible.

"Dried figs 'n raisins." Marco proudly spread them on the leaf strewn table. They were revoltingly discoloured.

"Don't eat them!" warned Alex "*Look* at the mould!"

"Isn't *anything* ripe now?"

Marco's eyes scanned the hillside with the anguish of someone forced to live exclusively from the pickings of the land. His toddler's memory of Spain was of a paradise of plenty, where the sun always shone upon perpetually ripening fruit, swarms of bees supped nectar from exotic flowers and the air smelled sweetly of jasmine. Alex, at nearly thirteen, had a wider perspective on things, and a more realistic grasp of the seasons.

"Oranges. Not here though. Only near the coast around Villahermosa."


She could feel the warmth of the sun on her cheek. The house had been cold and dank, shuttered up and breathing its own stale air, tomblike. These houses were ideally built for the summer heat, with all their surfaces cold to the touch. Thick stone walls, tiled floors, marble slabs, the cool colours of whitewash delicately tinged with blue. She had felt tempted to find firewood and light a fire in the huge open grate, but now the sun revived her. That relentless wind on the day of the funeral, with its ice blue sky and wintry colours of stone, brown leaves, and the dead-looking branches of dormant vines protruding from the rusty earth, suddenly seemed from another lifetime.

As she looked now at the cloudless blue sky, the blades of bright new grass sprouting in the almond orchard, the swollen almond buds beginning to blossom, and the backdrop of shadowy blue mountains, she had the sensation of being suspended in time and living inside a Japanese watercolour. Sometimes it was hard to remember why she had been so determined to turn her back on this beautiful place.

"Can't we stay for a while?" Alex's thoughts were running parallel. "Who'd buy this place now – it looks a total wreck."

His critical glance strayed over the weed-filled garden, the malingering lemon tree which was the final survivor of Frances' citrus grove, the bilious green smudges of lichen on the mosaic tiles of the patio, and came to rest on a broken shutter suspended dangerously from a single rusting hinge. Julia's expression seemed sympathetic but his question hung in the air, unanswered.


The following day she took them to the cemetery. They had no problem identifying the location. Although she had delayed taking them to allow time for the tomb to be properly bricked in, as promised, absolutely nothing had been touched - even the pick-axe lay exactly where Eulogio had thrown it. However as they drew closer Julia did detect a change - but certainly *not* for the better. The coffin, from being so crudely trimmed down, now lay with its sides partially caved in and its lid slumping at an angle so that Julia, with a

8

feeling of horror constricting her throat, could just glimpse her mother's white, scarred and lifeless hand through the resultant gap.

Luckily the boys were not tall enough to see from the same angle, but they did notice that the coffin had imploded. Alex said nothing. He tried to distract Marco into finding something to prop up the almond blossom they had brought, but Marco was fascinated by the signs of apparent vandalism.

"I bet she's gone. Trust ol' gran to hate where she was put…"

He stared suspiciously along the ground, as if expecting to find depressed footprints or those arrows built from broken twigs that he and Alex constructed when playing 'tracking'.

Alex turned pale. Julia grabbed Marco's hand and spoke hurriedly,

"Lay the blossom there, Marco. And let's go."


She was deeply regretting not having come beforehand to check that the work had indeed been done. It showed her to what extent she had lost touch with this place, for she should have expected it. Moreover it was all absolutely consistent with the entire pattern of her mother's life. Is there really such a thing as destiny she thought, or does one create one's own luck? Marte used to be a firm believer in karma, back in those days when spirituality was more popular and far too many people fancied themselves in the role of the guru.

Julia had always been uncomfortable with those notions (especially after Sylvia, a friend of Marte's who chewed betel nut and hennaed every part of her body, suggested that she, Julia, had actively chosen Frances to be her mother!).

By the time she had locked the cemetery gate and they were halfway down the cypress path, Alex had recovered. But Marco remained completely enthralled, convinced he had spied an empty coffin and certain the tomb could only have been ruptured by a dramatic escape.

"If you don't go to heaven…do you (his voice sank to an excited whisper) get kidnapped by the devil?"

Alex turned on him angrily. "You know that's crap! The devil's just a stupid myth."

"Then what *does* happen when you die?"

Julia was in no mood for philosophical discussion but knew Marco would persist until satisfied. Reluctantly she offered him a comforting postulate;

"Some people believe in reincarnation, meaning being born again - only as someone else. But you've forgotten your past life."

Marco fell silent, deeply thoughtful. Alex, suddenly brightening, enlightened him further;

"And you might not be a person. You could be an animal, or an insect. That's why people tell you not to kill spiders, remember? – In case they're your gra...."

"Alex! Run ahead. I'll catch you up in the bar."

The next day the tomb was finally repaired. And although Emilio Fuster swore he had also reassembled the coffin she privately doubted it. But there was now, thankfully, no way of knowing. At last, to the best of her ability, she had laid her mother to rest.

Marco, however, remained convinced she had burst from her coffin and fled the cemetery. Either she would now haunt the village mercilessly, an idea uncomfortably plausible considering relevant factors, or she had taken on a new existence as something completely different. Although a fan of fictitious ghost and horror stories he had no desire to confront a vindictive ghost in real life, so the rebirth option was preferable. He in fact felt supremely confident that he would find her, in whatever new form she had taken on, somewhere in or around the farmhouse.

But his confidence ebbed and he began to lose heart after a long morning trawling through webs and discounting spider after spider, especially as Alex was repeatedly praised for his constructive work on the garden and Julia seemed unimpressed by his own indoor agenda. One thing he did not doubt though was his ability to recognize her in whatever physical form she reappeared. Her kind of crabbiness *had* to be unique.

It was late afternoon when he was finally rewarded. Alex and he had gone to the Fuente (the Spring), where wild mint grew and a flow of water emerged through a rock fissure throughout the winter months, but dried to a trickle in summer. As Alex plucked a handful of mint Marco spied a green slimey speckled body shrink against the rock, and then the two bright eyes of an enormous toad watching them curiously. Marco was entranced. The toad was even friendly enough to be touched, rather squeamishly, on its cold, wet back. But Alex reacted with vehement hostility to Marco's telepathic recognition.

"Believe what idiotic things you want, but *don't* tell Julia..."

Marco could not imagine any humiliation attached to rebirth as a toad, but when Alex was emphatic it was wisest not to argue. Julia noticed his shining eyes when they returned to the farmhouse.

"We found one ginormous toad," was all he said.

"So you can kiss goodbye to that commission then." Colin wiped the effervescing beer froth from his left nostril and beamed at Reggie.

Reggie looked back wearily. He sometimes thought there was more to Colin than met the eye, but often had to concede that there wasn't.

"Still, buyers wouldn't be falling over theirselves. No mod-cons, cold as a witch's tit in winter but... beautiful spot, mind you."

"Strangely enough there *was* a buyer sniffing around, that's why I asked her in the first place. That Yankie chap. Stinking rich, owns half the coast already, and is now eyeing up the hinterland - but he wanted to be kept well in the background."

Colin shook his head in bewilderment. That, beaming, and periodically inspecting his midriff for signs of allergy rashes were his main mannerisms.

"But surely she knows him? Probably in the biblical sense too (he chuckled merrily) so why did he try to go through you?"

"For that reason I guess. If you're rich and want to buy, the price stays high. Or - he has good reason to be secretive."

"You're a bit stuck on the mystery element these days. 'Reggie Rendell' hah, hah! What about those dark hints Frances' death wasn't accidental?"

Reggie signalled him to silence. He checked hurriedly that they could not be overheard, but as they were in the Bar de los Pensionistas, not a foreigners' haunt, there were only old men intent on dominos. He leaned closer to Colin.

"I never said it wasn't an accident. Just that it looked as if there'd been another car on the road and she'd swerved to avoid it. It can be someone's fault, but still an accident."

"Well that's a relief - I thought you implied she was bumped off on purpose. Let's face it, the old girl was no bloody saint. Didn't the Guardia Civil notice anything?"

"It was dark Colin, and she wasn't exactly known for being abstemious. Plus she didn't have her glasses with her, so, well, the Guardia didn't even *look* at the road."

"Have you shared this with the daughter?"

Reggie shook his head. "What good would that do? It doesn't alter the fact that she's dead. It'd only make it more painful, like a hit and run."

"Well..." Colin shrugged. For a fleeting moment he looked intelligent as he scanned Reggie's face for signs of pain, still unsure of the true nature of the relationship he had had with Frances. "I guess you're right. But there she is, wondering whether to sell or stay and renovate, and you keep quiet on relevant info. Like that Yank – could've influenced her you know. It would me."

"She isn't you, Colin, she's a beauty. And this place could do with the likes of her."

# 2

Julia side-stepped through the bead curtain into total darkness, nearly tripping on the stone step. Inside there was an enticing smell of freshly baked bread and roasting rosemary but the shelves behind the counter - once her eyes adjusted to the dimly lit room - were disappointingly bare. This proved nothing though, because Dolores loved to keep things hidden. That way, if she disliked the look of a customer, she could pretend to have sold out. Being the sole village baker was a position of power she revelled in.

Julia called 'Hola!' to the dark interior room where the horno was, having detected some scratching, scraping, scuffling noises. Dolores materialized like a plump genie, seeming genuinely pleased to see her. And Julia, although she had not forgotten the matter of the vines, was trying to be more philosophical, less personal about it. While Dolores hunted through her cupboards for her secret stash of loaves, her copious rear thrust towards Julia and the skirt lifting alarmingly to reveal the tops of elasticated knee stockings biting into her pudgy thighs, Julia examined a garishly framed photo of a man posing with his gold Mayor's medallion and chain of office. It was propped beside a cut glass vase with a bunch of plastic African lilies and the old bronze set of scales used to weigh the flour very generously in Dolores' favour.

"Your son's the new Mayor?"

Julia made it sound as impressive as being President, but privately she was wondering if Dolores' family owned any land that could be reached from the track to her finca, since it badly needed resurfacing. The system of highly localized government where every village had a Mayor and local governing council, although avoiding the dangers of massive corruption and tyranny posed by a monolithic structure, simply meant there was much more opportunity for corruption on a smaller scale. Very occasionally Mayors did get prosecuted for embezzlement, or receiving backhanders for turning a blind eye on building irregularities, but it was very rare. After all, in a close knit village community, whoever blows the whistle on corruption makes some lifelong enemies. And if a corrupt Mayor goes, chances are he will only be replaced by another equally as corrupt.

"He was elected last April," Dolores replied, her smooth round bosom inflating with pride. "The responsibility's grown so big…but not the pay, of course," and she gave a little grimace of disgust.

Absentmindedly Julia nibbled at the warm bread while she waited for Alex and Marco to tire of testing how long they could hang upside down from the railings in the plaza. She remembered doing exactly the same herself; and at the time Eulogio had told her, approvingly, that the village only made sense viewed from upside-down - owing to the usual mix of religious subterfuge and delusion, he added. It had very foolishly been renamed 'Milagra' (Miracle - except that the word had been incorrectly spelt with a feminine 'a' instead of the proper masculine 'o' ending; an error no-one would take the blame for, and no-one could be bothered to correct) in place of its previous Moorish name, Benicassim. It was to his undying shame that his wife's family were responsible...

Vicente, his wife's great-great grandfather, had been snoozing in the midday heat while his mules passed the time foraging for ripe carobs (perhaps even from the very tree still in Julia's garden) while he slept. Carob trees, as well as sprouting the flowers with that sexually evocative smell, produce beans which are wonderfully nourishing but in excess, and particularly when mildewed from damp Autumn nights, have mysterious hallucinogenic properties. Perhaps Vicente had eaten some too, for they have a taste that tempts like rich, dark chocolate. Whatever the case, Vicente was goading his mules up the steep path to his terrace of olives when the pair of them stopped, dug in their heels and refused to budge. They then sank to their knees, rolled their eyes and foamed at the mouth.

Vicente was at first too busy thwacking them with his stick and swearing obscenities to notice anything untoward, but he gradually became aware of angelic voices singing, and looking up he saw a golden radiance in which floated the weeping face of the Virgin Mary. For a fleeting second she looked down at him and smiled, then returned to her steady weeping.

That, anyway, was how he recounted it hours later in the bar, after several brandies which he needed in order to recover from the shock of such a Holy Encounter. Of course his drinking companions were highly sceptical, suggesting plenty of witty and salacious theories as to why the mules had frothed at the mouth, but when Vicente sobered up enough to lead them to the site of his vision there could be no contradicting his tale. Out of a crevice in the rocky gulley which served as the path, exactly where he had described the pool of celestial light into which the Virgin's tears fell, welled a small but persistent trickle of water. Now called simply 'La Fuente' but until recently 'La Fuente del Virgen', it was now home to Marco's friend the toad.

Eulogio had his own slant to this story. Old Vicente's wife was a tricky one, deeply pious and bitterly contemptious of Vicente whom she thought her inferior. But if the Virgin appeared to him not her that would give him a lifetime advantage over her, plus guarantee him the undying respect of the entire village - and that was why he clung so emphatically to the myth of his vision. The church even agreed to provide money for a shrine on the holy place, which should have made the land more valuable (spiritually, at least), but neither money nor shrine materialised. Eulogio did admit he had good reason for his cynical interpretation - apart from his natural atheism, that his, for he had married into this self-serving family, much to his subsequent regret. Unluckily his wife had inherited her genes directly from her odious great-great-grandmother. She had the same superior attitude to her husband (himself), and had highhandedly named their son 'Vicente' in total disregard of his wishes.

According to Frances, however, his marriage was never anything but tactical. He had been known as 'El Rojo' (the Communist) ever since the Civil War when he was Marco's age and used to vandalise the church by daily defecations into an elegant silver urn behind the altar. One older brother mysteriously 'disappeared', and when another two died from a surprise 'fall' in the mountains when Eulogio was eighteen, he hastily ensured his survival by pragmatically marrying the 'enemy'.

He still carried on despising both government and church however, at least enough not to seem too much of a turncoat in his own eyes. Whenever he passed the Cura driving the road between Milagra and Montejoven, he would - as a matter of fiercely observed custom - instantly unzip and relieve himself onto whatever patch of tarmac the Cura's tyres had sullied. Julia had been apprehensive about what mode of personal protest he might choose at Frances' funeral, where he came so uncomfortably close to the Cura. But, whatever it was, he had been most discreet.

His only son Vicente was a bitter disappointment to him. Fastidious, prudish and, even worse, a practising Roman Catholic. Even worse *still*, he had recently taken up a post on the Milagra Town Council, as part of the right wing Partido Popular that Eulogio hated just as heartily as the church.

Once the boys were in bed that evening Julia sat outside. Being alone at night in the Spanish countryside had never felt threatening, not even when she was little. On a clear night the sky glimmered with a million stars, and often audible above the regular hoot of an owl or throb of a nightjar was the spine-chilling, blood curdling cry of a vixen on the prowl. Yet even that unearthly scream only gave her a momentary stab of fear, quickly overridden by the more comforting notion that animals were plodding about on their normal nightly business. She would often sleep outside in the early summer before the mosquitoes hatched, listening to the cicadas and hoping for the rare, exquisite song of a nightingale. Dark, moonless nights held no sinister shadows, either. If anything, the illusory extra chill in the air and the ink-blue tinges of the landscape merely added to the whole feeling of exhilaration.

But tonight she felt truly alone. She consoled herself she did not *have* to stay here, struggling to untie the tangled knots of her mother's life. She could go back to England, leaving Reggie to handle everything; he would undoubtedly be capable. Coming here had only opened the pandora's box of memories, bewildering her again with her hurtful, ambiguous feelings towards her mother. Frances was always so inflexible, so sure that her views were right - but her pride had merely gifted her lifelong disappointment. She had only loved one man, was so unshakeable in her conviction he had loved her too, that she never could accept he was able to leave her, to continue to live a lie and persist with his sham marriage.

Even as a very young child she had had to mother her own mother through an endless series of emotional crises, not to mention the frequent smoothings of troubled waters. At that time, though, she still unquestioningly loved her; it was only when she was twelve that she became embarrassed by her. And soon began to actively hate her. Sometimes, then, she had even prayed Frances would die quickly of alcohol poisoning so she could be adopted by calm, tranquil, *normal* parents. She had looked up a description of cirrhosis of the liver in Frances' medical encyclopaedia, then stared long and hard at her as she read under the lamplight, wondering if her skin was developing a telltale jaundiced hue, actively, cruelly willing it to do so...

Perhaps the truth was that Frances had only begun to drink heavily around this time, not before, but Julia's memory had unfairly elided all the ugly scenes into a massive concentration of negativity in order to justify their subsequent enmity. Maybe it was a gross distortion to remember her mother as always drunk, always bad tempered, always deservedly friendless.

At fourteen she pleaded to go to Dance School as much to get away from Frances as to fulfil her desire to dance. She was also secretly hoping Frances might miss her, but it had the opposite effect. Possibly, she only *now* realised, with her dark blonde hair and deep blue eyes she embodied far too closely the physical memory of her father, and her escape to England too exactly paralleled his own betrayal.

When she was seventeen they had a bitter disagreement over Julia's pregnancy. Frances saw it as ill-omened and disastrously ill-timed. Which undoubtedly it was, from any objective viewpoint. But when had Frances ever been objective before?

"Why on earth go through three hard years of dance school plus all your extra academic work on top, only to then fall pregnant the minute your career takes off? Abortion is not a mortal sin, Julia. Given all the circumstances, including the father being a goddam gay and nearing forty - who *cares* if he's brilliant, famous dancer - no-one would condemn you."

"No. I'll love this child. And for who it is, not whose it is. Not as a souvenir of a father I've grown to *hate*. And I'd rather be too young than too old," she'd retorted, staring pointedly at Frances' scrawny, shrivelled breasts.

She convinced herself she hated Frances and determinedly kept her distance from then on. But it did not prevent her being distressed by Frances' ever lonelier life troubled by failing health and the constant pain of arthritis. She never managed to be as hard on her mother as she longed to be, her indifference always less wholehearted than Frances'. And when she learned about Reggie's friendship, she felt pathetically half-grateful that she need worry less, half-resentful that Frances was not as miserable as she deserved to be.

Sitting now: at night, alone, cold, uncomfortable, seemed suddenly an uncanny re-run of her childhood. She thinking and worrying over the future and what to do, while her mother lay blotto without a care in the world! Frances, by dying, had freed herself from all pain and responsibility, leaving Julia yet again to pick up the pieces, mull over the memories and lay the ghosts to rest.

And now Marco too seemed inexplicably caught in Frances' web. She had all but ignored his existence, more so even than Alex's, yet recently he had begun to talk about her. Perhaps it was only a strategy for overcoming his earlier fear - but he now spoke as if they had some intimate buddy relationship. At least his manifestation of Frances, presumably some kind of imaginary friend, appeared to be alive.

Thinking of Marco awakened thoughts of his dad. Another relationship of ambiguous feelings, confused emotions, circular problems. Some say we seek out the familiar – God forbid she was trapped forever into living with a Frances-type!

He was in many ways a sympathetic, caring man - so not like Frances there, but they had grown far apart now. He had been both unable and unwilling to deal with Marco. Had been expecting him to be an improved younger version of Alex; calm, self-contained, mature for his age. It irked him beyond belief that his own son failed to match up to the son of a crazy Romanian ballet dancer, for God's sake! Marco had been a hyperactive baby who rarely slept, a wild toddler who would not speak, then finally diagnosed as having asperges syndrome, on the mild end of the spectrum of autism. Possibly mistakenly, for she saw a lot of her own childhood antics in Marco. And, oddly enough, he was at his most difficult around his father. He had become much calmer since arriving in Spain, able to concentrate and converse, no longer obsessively asking a thousand million questions and never bothering to listen to any answers.

Leave it alone, she urged herself. Stop this constant rewinding, replaying - you can never change what has happened, never manipulate a happy ending to it. The past is a dangerous place unless you treat it with due respect, you should have learnt that from Frances, whose life was swamped by it.

Aware that the cold night air had seeped into her bones, she rose stiffly and went upstairs to the warm comfort of her duvet...

Two blindingly powerful lights were directed straight at her eyes. She blinked, trying to look beyond them, to get her bearings from the pools of darkness to either side of the glare but she had been momentarily blinded, all she could see was a daze of hot white light. Sun blindness...had she looked at the eclipse without properly smoking the fragment of glass she had been given? She was confused and lost her bearings, hypnotised like a rabbit in the glare...that was it, she must keep control of the car and steer by memory. Her hands gripped the steering wheel as she edged it round the curve, steering just to the right of the oncoming lights, avoiding the trap of being drawn directly towards them for that was the temptation, being hypnotised, losing free will. She could hear a squeal of brakes although that might be her imagination, certainly the lights jerked and swayed so that her eyes could pull free of the connecting beams of light and maybe even steer a narrow course to one side and avoid the crunching blow of a head-on collision, or scraping the side of the car, or ricocheting off the left front wing.

Almost level with the lights now. Perhaps she might manage... She could feel cold sweat on her forehead and the palms of her hands. She gripped the steering wheel more tightly but there was no response this time from the tyres, just an eerie floating feeling that the road was no longer there beneath her. Still the lights burned her eyeballs and her brain floundered, but now sounds battered her consciousness. She tried with an oddly detached curiosity to locate them, identify them. Something was ripping at the metal undercarriage, and that higher, sharper, shorter sound might be the shattering explosion of glass, and that might be a tree tearing its roots and slithering over the rocks. She held her breath to brace herself for the rushing sound of burning petrol, wondering how loud the explosion would be, or whether the force would catapult her clear. Something must have made her deaf because she knew her mouth was wide open in a scream of terror, but no sound at all came out...

She threw off the duvet and sat bolt upright. Her throat was so sore she must have been screaming for some time, while her body was drenched in sweat. Even in sleep, it seemed, she was still plagued by her mother's suffering. She

18

was panting heavily, and had to wait for her breathing and heartbeat to slow down before she dared stand up. It was some time before the shivering subsided and she finally went back to sleep.

She was woken by Alex bringing a mug of tea and Marco a slice of dry toast with only the faintest smear of butter.

"You overslept. It's after ten." Alex looked at her white face curiously, tactfully speaking at low volume in case she had a headache.

"You must've been drunk." Marco's voice was cheerfully loud.

She smiled wanly, feeling tempted to play along with his theory. "No," she sighed, "I had a nightmare. Open the curtains. Please."

"Get eaten by a bear?" Marco was solicitous, "That often happens to me."

"You always wake up before you die," Alex informed them, "'cos if you dream you're dead, you really *are* dead."

"I wake up when he's finished swallowing my legs. Before he starts on my body, I stun him on the nose."

"Why not *before* he eats anything?"

"I can't - I'm kind of in the grip of the dream at that stage."

"Can't we talk about something other than death," Julia swallowed uncomfortably.

There was a pregnant silence. No other topics seemed of any interest.

"Toads are dead clever," Marco said at last, "There's a South American desert one what stays asleep, not eating, for years and years. Only when it rains it zaps into life and eats, drinks and prances about until the rain stops. Then back to sleep for the next nine years."

"Sounds a deadly boring life to me," Alex sounded impatient. "Think how much it misses out on."

"Toads don't see it that way," Marco declared with a note of authority.

19

Determined not to stay at home wallowing and drowning in memories, Julia set out early that evening for the social mecca of the valley, a tacky bar called El Molino Divino. It would force her out of her introspections and give the boys a chance to play pool.

She arrived to find an enormous technicolour coach garishly labelled MISTERVISTA TOURS straddling the bar car park, so left her car perched lopsidedly on the riverside verge. In summer there was no flowing water, the river reduced to a few foul smelling, stagnant pools, but now, in winter, a small, appetizingly clear stream burbled over smooth white stones between tall banks of wild bamboo. Marco pulled away from her hand, feeling the lure of the river more keenly than the pleasures of a fizzy lemon. He was going through this strange reptilian phase. Instead of nursing a batch of tadpoles in a bucket, however, he spent hours hunting for a toad. She could not see real harm in it, apart from his mounting distress at the damn' toad's prolonged absence, but the situation clearly irritated Alex, who (sometimes justifiably) felt that by being hyper-active, more demanding and younger Marco all too often dominated their life. So she resisted Marco's pleading. The river could wait.

When they reached the door of the bar it suddenly swung open to liberate the entire coachload of tourists, all transparently British. They emerged en-masse like some monstrously conjoined centipede waddling on uniformly pink legs, proudly nursing their souvenir booty of identical mini wine barrels, 'El Molino' T-shirts, straw sombreros and string bags of oranges which they clutched possessively in their pink upper limbs. This homogenous column almost trampled them underfoot as it swept across the tarmac and up the coach steps, only splitting into individual humans when the inevitable fight over who got the best window seats began.

Once Julia's eyes adjusted from the vivid sunset colours outside to the dim lighting and eddying swirls of cigarette smoke inside she could see Scotty flipping round his tariff sign so, now that the weekly tourist troupe had gone, normal, everyday prices could resume. Scotty wore a plaid shirt and baseball cap, homage to his twin identities as a Scots Canadian (though the only relative to drop in on Milagra was a sister, who claimed to be an ex-Latvian Jew from Ealing, and since there was no obvious kudos in that, chances are it was the truth).

Spain was a country that attracted ex-pats of dubious provenance to reinvent themselves. Of course Rio, in fact South America in general, had always been more exotic hideaways for criminals, but Spain was still the favoured destination for those who were homebodies and felt homesick outside Europe: chiefly petty embezzlers, car robbers, tax evaders, fraudsters, and perpetrators of various crimes of violence ranging from pub brawls to even murder itself. The most recent to flock in were the Russian mafia, keen to launder their money in football, property or vice.

Those on the run had an understandable, practical need to invent a fictitious past of course, but the trend of embellishment, of representing oneself as a more enticing creature, was so extremely widespread that hardly anyone seriously believed anyone else's personal tale. If Frances had lived somewhere other than Spain, Julia wondered, would she have been more trusting of humanity?


Scotty exuded bonhomie, but above the permanent grin was a furrowed brow worrying that business was perilous, the profit margin papery thin, and most of his clientele a sleazy lot trying their best to put one over him. He suffered miserably from the Spanish custom of serving on trust. Everyone ordered what they wanted and paid when they left, whereas elsewhere you paid up front. Scotty had never learnt to be at ease with the Spanish way; he would stand behind the bar in a state of nervous apoplexy, his eye darting from the emptying glasses to the doorway, wondering who might try to escape.

Even worse was the accepted norm that regulars could mount up bills. The village shops operated on this same principal of trust, centuries old, that if one could not pay one day then perhaps the next, or not until after a good harvest. The system worked in a local, farming community where continuity reigned and everyone knew each other, generation after generation. But now that so many foreigners had intruded this trust was eroding.

Twenty five years ago the foreign contingent had been mainly hippies, artists, potters and such-like, who would mount up bills claiming they would pay 'after the exhibition'. Well, that had been a less nervy time because most of them actually meant it. But now there were suspicious new breeds of intruder exploring the valley in flashy four wheel drive off-roaders: satellite engineers, salesmen, cowboy builders, computer technicians and heaven knows what, all highly unworthy of trust and undeserving of credit.


Colin and Reggie sat directly in front of the bar, slouched on the only two stools. Julia felt Reggie looked wistful and wondered if he could truly be missing Frances, but decided this was fanciful - more likely he was low on funds, for she had noted his disappointment when she told him she didn't want to sell the house immediately. Colin, by contrast, seemed in high spirits. He was true to type of a particular breed (a dying breed) of Brit with post-Empire nostalgia, who had chosen Spain as a retirement ground because he could feel comfortably blonder, pinker and taller than the natives.

"I say Scotty, d'you want to sell more beer?" he blustered.

"Right on!" Scotty was always happy to listen to Colin because he was meticulous in settling his bill.

But Colin pointed gleefully at the fast evaporating foam. "Then fill the bloody glasses ...hooar, hooar, hooargh!"

Reggie mournfully held out his glass for a top up along with Colin. Yet when a gaunt, grey-haired man squeezed in alongside him his spirits suddenly revived. "You're new here aren't you?"

Reggie was of course not blind to the worn trousers and the pair of ultra-cheap reading glasses that had been clumsily repaired with a twist of rusty wire, but the man apparently wrote for Der Spiegel and was rumoured to be working on a bestseller, plus there was a breed of writer who got their kicks out of looking poor and dishevelled. Also, in his experience, Germans were never truly poverty stricken. The man gave Reggie a retaliatory inspection. They were like two dogs sniffing out each other's secrets, Julia thought, but focused on the wallet rather than the arsehole.

"Yah. I hope zat's not a problem?"

"'Course not - though I know some do apply that ridiculous kind of pecking order... Not looking for a house, by any chance?"

The man glanced furtively around, then leaned closer to Reggie. "Actually, my present house is a little *too* simple..."

"You've come to the right man, then," (out flashed the peach card) "good houses are hard to find - keep getting snapped by the Hun...Belgians."


Julia was staring at a woman whose statuesque body had been tightly squeezed into black leather trousers and chest-hugging charcoal top, and whose hair aflame with hennaed highlights framed a face that was definitely familiar. Their eyes met.

"Marte?"

"Yah Julia!"

Marte lunged forward, pressing her body so forcefully against Julia's that she felt it must leave a permanent imprint.

"Oof, *such* a long time" she crooned into Julia's ear, then stepped back so their bodies could reinflate to their original, individual shapes. She studied

Julia critically, "You look gute. When last I saw you you were still so young – now I see Frances in your mouth and eyebrows…Oh, how terrible to die like that! *Such* a shock! We weren't so close these last years and I only just heard."

"She wasn't close to anyone, except possibly Reggie."

"Ze short one there, wiz Otto? I must introduce you… But death can also be liberating, you know. Sometimes I sink my father only stays alive so's to carry on scolding me for wasting my life wizout a good career." She massaged her temples tenderly, "Oof, such terrible tensions - Otto must be poisoning my mind with his violent images of war!"

"*War?* Which war?" Julia's thoughts drifted guiltily to the carpet bombing of Dresden.

"For him zere is only one. Ze Spanish Civil War. Gott how I wish he could write something positive, some beautiful fantasy. But no, always ze brutal things."

Otto's ears were evidently finely tuned to pick out key words above the general hubbub of bar conversation. He joined them eagerly, "Well, like it or not mine liebling, violence sells. Zese village murders are ze perfect hook. I like to uncover ze truth, and someone from here betrayed my poor bandolero."

Julia had never heard of any local murders, let alone bandoleros – a shadowy type of war racketeer; but she could believe anything possible in war. She had an uneasy feeling he might enjoy stirring old troubles.

"I always understood the village was united against Franco,"she suggested, over optimistically. "They certainly spent most of their time fighting Nationalistas in Montejoven."

"Huh, no village is *ever* united, you can be sure of zat!" he stroked his beard and looked artfully at her. "So, you must be Julia, who Marte talks so much of." His eyes roved across the contours of her body. "And it is clear to see you are a dancer from ze artful way you move."

Marte swiped at him half playfully, and Julia made her escape down to the pool den to check on Alex and Marco. It was a semi-basement room with the lower half of the wall chiselled out of solid rock to resemble a subterranean cave. Scotty pursued a policy of neglect on all dusting and cleaning of this room to improve its grotto-like effect, so the cobwebs had proliferated out of control. His ex-wife used to sell macramé from the bar, but after she ran off with a Dutch dentist Scotty angrily stuffed all her macramé 'objets' into chinks or rock ledges down in this den. Over time they became indistinguishable from the cobwebs, and rumour claimed that Scotty had once sold a large cobweb to an unsuspecting tourist for a very healthy price.

By the time Julia tired of watching a jubilant Alex, who had teamed up with Emilio Fuster (the carpenter responsible for her mother's coffin fiasco), repeatedly defeat a glowering Pepe (the builder who had failed to repair her mother's fractured grave in time for the boys' visit) who had drawn the short straw and was thus reluctantly partnering Marco, she climbed back upstairs to find the scene unrecognizably transformed.

An old pink Cadillac had just lurched into the car park, followed by a fleet of Shoguns and Humvees, and through the door in bright lime green beer-belly-hugging vest, tight black jeans and heeled cowboy boots came Degsy Lean in the flesh. And boy was there plenty of flesh! What was more, he had evidently come to party. Two hunklike minders hovered at his heels, behind whom swarmed an entourage of forty-to-fifty somethings with uniformly bald heads and yards of tattooing on their pudgy biceps, all with full-blown, once-luscious ladies hanging off the folds that should have been their necks. Degsy had been a name on everyone's lips - everyone who followed the rock music scene that is - some sixteen to twenty years ago, but had vanished outa sight due to one of those typical aging rock star ailments; drug abuse, alcohol abuse, or perhaps simply wife abuse.


Scotty had always fancied himself a promoter. Years ago, when a student at Gwelph University and still optimistic about life, he had been vice president of entertainment, but it all came to an abrupt end when he failed his summer exams and was thrown off the course. Thus his dreams of being a famous rock impresario and respected academic evaporated, and he had to settle for third choice: a bar of his own where the night life was buzzing. New York, London, Paris, Bali....funny how things turn out. For the very last thing he expected back then was that out there was a smalltime Spanish mountain village not properly on the Mediterranean, with an unconverted muleshed abutting a B road, just waiting for him.

And now, out of nowhere, a second chance! He had always encouraged live music; a gyspy violinist from Amsterdam, a Flamenco guitarist from Menorca, an Argentinian crooner - but this Degsy guy was in an altogether classier league. Suddenly the lines of worry, anxious stare and nervous twitches vanished and a broad grin spread from ear to ear as he squatted under the bar counter to hunt through his reserves for the crate of dirt cheap, rotgut Korean Whisky cunningly disguised as Glenfiddich, in case the situation demanded drinks on the house. He had to bob up and down like a yo-yo, because every time a camera flashed he lunged forward to get in the frame in case the photographer was from a high profile newspaper.

Colin and Reggie waged a losing battle for control of their customary stools, and were soon squeezed from the front row out into the wings by a flurry of activity focused on setting up a PA system and distributing drinks. Colin was visibly upset by the invasion. He never felt comfortable in a crowd in any case, it revived dormant memories of his babyhood in India where his parents must have communicated their own fear of mobs; volatile, unpredictable and spelling serious trouble for whitey. Reggie was far more sanguine, oiks did not worry him at all so long as they had money, and he could see immediately that these were the flashy sort who indulged in unrestrained holiday spending. He might even find a potential client among them, perhaps an ideal victim for a Time-share in that new apricot villa with the dodgy foundations that was plumb on the seafront (and plumber by the minute!). As Colin retreated towards the door Reggie made friendly overtures to the larger of the two minders, but all talk was suddenly drowned by the piercing whine of feedback, and the audience flinched in unison.

Someone began testing the PA system "1,2,1,2, (hoarse coughing) 1,2,1,2,1,2,..." Apparently it was satisfactory, so Degsy vaulted surprisingly athletically onto the bar and executed a quick bout of tap dancing whilst Scotty rescued the slices of lemon and ash trays from beneath his twinkling toes. Then a body builder with skin gleaming like polished leather passed him the microphone and he settled into a nostalgia number, walking the bar slowly, his body heaving with passion. Each time he changed direction he twitched his bottom seductively, and the assorted entourage howled and wolf-whistled in delight. Colin had reached the end of his tether, he could sense an impending asthma attack and groped for his inhaler, but Reggie had seen the warning signs and was already steering him to the door.

"Scotty might have warned us reg'lars this was in the offing," Colin gasped.

"Don't worry, hang about outside. I can see by the sweating he lacks stamina. He'll be flaked out after a couple of numbers."

Julia watched Reggie with curiosity. He seemed to be perenially in the midst of some disastrous business deal, penniless, scrounging what drinks he could, yet cheerful in the face of repeated failures. Was it his optimism that had endeared him to Frances? She had uncharitably assumed that he befriended Colin solely for the free drinks (just as she had originally suspected with Frances, whose cellar was superbly stocked), yet he seemed a man genuinely at ease with himself, not driven by any motive, ulterior or otherwise.

Julia also noticed Otto up front with the minders. He almost matched them in height but was noticeably less nourished, and had more hair in his neatly trimmed Castilian goatee than they had anywhere on their musclebound bodies. There was a glint of battle glory in his eyes, and she hoped he would not provoke things whilst so strategically placed between them and the ammunition stockpile of Scotty's glasses and bottles. Fortunately Marte, who would exert a pacifist influence, was not too far away.

As Reggie had guessed, Degsy soon needed a break. Like a boxer receiving attention after a gruelling eighth round he puffed and rolled his eyes, sweat darkening his vest from lime to deep emerald green. Steam rose in wafting spirals from his body as two minders stroked and pummelled his shoulders with napkins of ice cubes. With luck he had already lost four of his fourteen superfluous kilos, but he had to swallow a litre of mineral water to lubricate his rusty vocal chords. Appreciative squawks of "Great stuff Degsy" "Bleedin' brilliant" "Wow man" and "Encore mate" revived his flagging energy so that, after a final glug from the bottle, he braced himself to vault, much less nimbly this time, onto the bar. He peeled off his dripping vest, now darkest jungle green, and tossed it in the time honoured fashion into the audience where it was shredded within seconds.

Ripples of anticipation ran through his special support group. Ladies squealed, men hollered, and Scotty carried on grinning and passing the drinks through Degsy's splayed legs.

"Gui-ay-ding angel, to point the wa-ay, I-ay-I'll know her by the colour of her hair-air, I'ay'd know her a-anywhere-ere..."

Degsy continued but his audience's attention abruptly switched to a central spot in the room, where a pair of large bare pendulous breasts were bopping and swinging along in time to the music. An old time raver had caught the nostalgia bug and gleefully returned in spirit and nakedness to those rock festivals of old. Her eyes were closed in rapture and her tongue encircled her lips in a slow, savouring motion.

Julia looked anxiously for Marco and Alex. Thankfully they must still be downstairs, although Juanito, Pepe the builder's sidekick, had bounded up the stairs and was watching mesmerized, his eyes following every nuance of the sagging, circular movement of those dancing mammaries. Scotty's laugh jangled nervously but everyone else took the spectacle in their stride except for a tall girl in her early twenties who stuck out her boot to trip the topless groover, spitting out "Abuela!" (Granny) as she did so. They were instantly locked in vicious combat, a bewildering melée of hair, teeth and claws. Not even the two bullish minders could separate them, and one was dealt a sharp knee in the groin.

"Lay off fattyboy, it's me bloody daughter!"

It was a tribute to Degsy's professionalism that he sang on regardless, not for a moment losing concentration, despite the fact that a sizeable sector of his audience had defected to the wrestling and were yelling juicy comments of encouragement. It finally took Scotty to separate them with a bucket of ice-cold water. He was prepared to sacrifice valuable ice cubes, drench his floor and add a half hour to his cleaning up time to salvage some of the honour of hosting Degsy Lean's comeback. The ensuing confusion meant that no-one, not even Scotty, heard the stamp of heavy boots outside the door.

The door swung open abruptly and three armed Guardia Civil marched in. Everyone fell silent. Except for Degsy, whose eyes were squeezed in passion and who attributed the silence to the sheer power of his musicality finally winning through. His last line was delivered with real potency:

"Tried to remember-er the bartender's fa-ace, but's jus' vanish't into the du-ust."

No-one moved (except a few, very surreptitiously, who needed to secrete their drugs). All eyes fixed on the Guardia Civil. The Cabo (officer in charge), impressed by the reaction offered Degsy a sarcastic "Olé" then turned on Scotty, who was desperately disassociating himself from the bucket still dangling in his hand.

"Hoy es Viernes? (Is today Friday?) the Cabo queried teasingly.

"No." Scotty answered tremulously, his Spanish mangled by both Scots and Canadian accents. "But this is a private party," he pleaded, "it's my birthday and Degsy here offered to sing us a song."

But the Cabo had no urge to be merciful. He had his monthly quota of fines to levy and was a little behind target. "For this" he swung his baton in a derisive semicircle, coming to rest on the female wrestlers who now lay in a pool of water artistically garnished by ice cubes, "You have no permit. Be at the Cuartel nine o'clock sharp tomorrow morning."

And out he marched with the two underlings hard on his heels.

Degsy's expression was a mixture of awe and relief. "Jeeesuuus, those guys are heavy! 'n I was just gettin' warmed up..." He wiped his brow and loosened his belt several notches. "Hey folks - let's go boogie someplace else!"

He looked at his audience for response, and Julia wondered if he realised how depleted it had become. Most of his close personal entourage - the minders in particular - had dematerialized (doubtless they were on some Interpol file), while others anxious not to be caught without their documents had silently slunk off into the night.

The mother and daughter duo were now decently clothed and clinging affectionately to each other, while Scotty's arms stretched everywhere at once, voracious tentacles pulling in the empties and frantically cleaning up, and he kept muttering miserably to no-one in particular that they were bound to land him one helluva fine. Reggie and Otto were quick to notice that, with business so brisk and his euphoric condition, Scotty had uncharacteristically failed to note down the orders. Swapping comparative tales of high-handedness amongst the various European police forces they made a rapid beeline for the door. Marte followed. As she was quick to point out, her conscience was clear. Scotty had been overcharging them for years, so a free evening once in a while was simply natural justice.

Alex, Marco, Emilio Fuster and Pepe finally emerged from their marathon tournament in the cellar, surprised that the bar was closing at such an early hour. Alex looked curiously from the flotilla of icecubes on the floor to the retreating figure of Degsy, awash with sweat, being bodily supported through the doorway. Degsy had obviously kept going on pure adrenalin (oh yeah!), because now that the need to stay upright was gone, his legs had buckled. Julia, along with the remainder of the bar regulars, left their own more or less honest assessment of what they had consumed in a brass tray. As they reached their car Marco sighed long sufferingly,

"Pepe swears he only lost 'cos of me, - but actually Alex and Fuster both played better than him."

"Don't take it so seriously" Alex tried not to sound too triumphant. "*Somebody* has to lose."

"I know that." Marco frowned, "But why's it always *me*?"

# 4

Julia drove warily through Milagra. She guessed the Cabo might be on a roll with collecting fines and have set up a road block to breathalise the Degsy crowd. If he could achieve his total quota in one jackpot of a night he could lie back for the remainder of the month, or concentrate on the brothels and drug dens of Montejoven which were his preference. With that incentive she could be fined for incorrect use of a seatbelt, since Marco lay spreadeagled on the back seat, fast asleep.

But her only danger was in fact the turn into her own driveway, when she had to brake violently to avoid ploughing into a red Mercedes with German plates clumsily parked on the diagonal. Its doors hung open like a gangstermobile at which the police had aimed a fusillade of bullets, - but thankfully without any slumped and bleeding bodies gunned down as they tried to escape. It could only be Marte.

A teenage girl was perched on a kitchen stool shelling almonds with a stone the size of a clenched fist. She kept glancing admiringly at a young man who was expertly juggling five oranges. Marte stood at the stove, toasting and tossing the almonds, eargerly sampling the plumpest to gauge their readiness.

"You don't recognise Lise? Fifteen already! And zis vun is Jorgen, you surely met him before when he was small, because he remembers zis place. Wolfgang's son. You *don't* remember?"

Marte had a knack of making herself at home in other people's houses. It had enraged many an ex-boyfriend's parents, but it did not bother Julia because she still sometimes felt a stranger herself, a trespasser in Frances' house. Jorgen tactfully returned the oranges to their bowl and withdrew three luminous green batons from the grip of his belt, then slipped out into the garden where they would glow in the dark.

Otto had temporarily been lost, but was soon located by the growling, whistling sounds of his snores. He had stretched flat out on the living room floor, and in this inert state looked up to twenty years older. He soon revived, however, when Julia discovered a bottle of Torres conac secreted in Frances' needlework basket, and livened up still more as he began to visualise her house in 1937. His eyes roved the ceiling for signs that torture victims had been hung from its beams, and he stared suspiciously at every mottled stain on the worn terracotta tiles, certain he spied blood. He frowned darkly at the section of wooden flooring.

"Have you never searched beneath zose boards?" he asked sharply, looking ready to rip them up with bare hands.

29

Julia laughed cheerily. "They've not been there long! My mother had them laid when I was seven and needed a surface that didn't break my toes when dancing."

"Of course," he mumbled mournfully.


Marco had jerked awake, but thankfully relapsed almost immediately back to sleep. Alex would have preferred him to have chosen his own bed, but at least he was better comatose, no longer able to show off in front of Lise. Apparently they had met before, he and Lise, when he was only two and she a mature five - as Marte had repeatedly told him, illustrating their encounter with some excruciating anecdotes designed to embarrass.

Lise was rather overpowering. She had streaky blonde hair intricately braided into a central plait, blue eyes that were humorous yet had serious depths, was considerably taller than him and had fully formed, gently rounded breasts. For the first time ever, Alex found both his person and his music collection disappointingly inadequate. He handed her the CD they had been listening to, but she lobbed it straight back onto his lap.

"Keep it. I brought so many from Germany."

Alex raised his eyebrows. "Lucky you. I mostly left mine in London."

"Well, I saw my father and he was real generous. Don't tell Marte though, or she'll wheedle it out of me. He's never paid her maintenance!"

Alex could think of nothing to add, especially on the awkward subject of fathers.

"Hey, what d'you think of Otto?"

"I didn't really notice him - apart from the snoring."

"Yah," Lise laughed, "But he's old and works at night. He's OK, and good for Marte. She's always gone for such dumbos up 'till now, thinking they were artists."

Alex studied his crudely bitten nails. It was a cruel quirk of fate that kept him forever three years younger than Lise, although some instinct told him this might not debar him later on, unless she went out of her way *not* to follow in her mother's footsteps.

"And Jorgen - what d'you think of him?" Was there a tremble in her voice, a breathless yearning?

"He's brilliant at juggling," Alex admitted, grudgingly.

"That's just a smokescreen, I reckon. I caught him sewing up a juggling ball and it was filled with white powder. He even tried to block my view! I'm sure he's dealing drugs."

"Jesus! Then we should check it out..." Alex leapt to his feet, eager for action.

"Not now - are you *crazy*? Later on. Wait 'till they get talking."

If Lise preferred to stay on in his room Alex had no desire to leave it.


Julia was feeling increasingly drowsy. Recently she had lived without alcohol or any protracted adult conversation, misguidedly perhaps - for their beneficial effect was to mercifully obliterate both Frances and the past. The clock mocked her by insisting it was only midnight, and still the same day she had set out for El Molino Divino, whereas her exhaustion argued that the combined sessions of the bar and here had stretched through several days. Jorgen sat quietly, his eyes resting on her profile, while Otto and Marte exchanged such a volume of words it was a wonder they had space to breathe.

"If you poke, all you get is reaction, which tells you nussing. If you want to learn you must be patient and let people reveal zemselves."

They had been talking about modern investigative journalism and whether it ever unearthed the truth or merely reflected the journalist's viewpoint, or else the official line, or plugged some pro-Government piece of propaganda. Also, more specifically, how Otto should best research his current book. Marte, like Julia, did not relish him setting the cat among the pigeons. After twenty five years of moral disapproval from the more conservative elements of the village she was rather hoping Otto's age and respectability (he was a genuine Professor of History, no less) would restore her reputation. She infinitely preferred her own mode of operating: to disarm by cajolement, flattery or the oozing of love. This way she had an uncanny ability to get what she wanted, be it a confidential secret from a friend or a tidy sum from German Social Services.

When he had drained the last drop from the bottle, Otto looked at Julia,

"Marte's room is too damp for my rheumatism. Perhaps you have some spare corner here, where I could stretch my bones?"

Marte did not deign to comment but leapt to pummel him quasi-affectionately on the shoulder blades, switching swiftly to a more aggressive massage of the neck. And fortuitously Lise emerged from the shadows to slip into Marte's vacated seat. Marte nodded to her.

"Komm, nach Hause." Then, landing Otto a brusque tap on the head, she snorted, "You are zer ridiculous. We can sleep in ze living room where it's drier... Ah, but Jorgen..." She turned to Julia, sweetly pleading, "He has to leave tomorrow morning, Julia. Remember, he is Wolfgang's son – almost family. Couldn't he stay here tonight, *please*?"

Julia felt the urgent pressure of Marte's hand gripping her arm.

"OK," she agreed, too tired to resist. "One night won't be a problem."

Such misguided words! And she had only herself to blame…

Some hours previously, in fact the very moment Julia's tail lights had vanished round the bend beyond the village and she breathed a sigh of relief that no Guardia Civil were on duty there, Eulogio's only son Vicente reached the Ayuntamiento.

He mounted the steps warily, for the meeting was 'unscheduled', and his footsteps echoed alarmingly down the marble hallway. Still, he did feel an onrushing surge of pride once he swung open the exaggeratedly carved door into the rococco style council chamber. Painted in gleaming white and gold it looked like an ostentatious wedding cake, apart from one wall which was untidily festooned with shields, emblems, national plus provincial flags, and a vilely garish reproduction portrait of a much younger King Juan Carlos.

The Mayor was already there, bursting from his new grey suit after some celebratory sessions eating his mother Dolores' surplus pastries. Also Grant, el milionario Yanqui, whose white designer suit and blond hair blended perfectly with the sickly décor. Although Vicente nodded to him his smile lacked warmth. He would have much preferred an all-Spanish consortium, but sadly both euro funding and eventual buyers were more easily attracted to multinational concerns.

On the polished oval table lay a carefully crafted miniature 3D landscape where densely packed white villas with identical balconies, terraces, swimming pools and satellite dishes smothered the mountainside. The name of the development was painted in large blue and gold letters: HOLIDAYLANDIA. Vicente walked his fingers up the mountain path he had known from early childhood, when he had battled to keep up with a younger, fitter, leaner Eulogio. It was a strange feeling; he had experienced this landscape all his life but the model was oddly grotesque, the colours artificially bright and shiny, the proportions of the mountain wrong and the village of Milagra disturbingly dwarfed by the profusion of new houses. It was like looking into the future through distorting binoculars. But any change, he consoled himself, was bound to be disturbing. This was true progresso!

Grant and the Mayor had already signed and stamped the paperwork to date, so he merely had to append his signature on a few dotted lines and they were poised for the next phase. The gilt edged pen felt cold and foreign to Vicente's fingers and his heart began to race, for the legitimacy of his signature was questionable. Although his official council status gave him authority (he was, after all, in sole charge of 'culture, fiestas, sanitation and rural development') nevertheless for such momentous decisions a quorum of four was strictly required. He hesitated; should it all go horribly wrong he would be implicated - but the Mayor would be the ultimate scapegoat. Also, surely, the potential wealth for the village would effectively silence all criticism, apart from a pathetically small bunch of environmentalist nutters who bleated at every proposed development but never made headway. Vicente rotated the pen until it felt comfortable in his grasp, and, with his tongue probing at a troublesome sinew of lamb chuleta that had lodged between his teeth and bothered him since suppertime, let the ink flow through his name.

"But what about the Fuente?" Vicente suddenly felt proprietorial.

"The Fuente'll be protected. It's of historic importance – and we can make it a *huge* tourist attraction. Like Lourdes. Or Santiago," Grant reassured him. But, despite the fluency of his thoughts and his Spanish, his hybrid accent, with overtones of American and undercurrents of German, was in no syllable reassuring to Vicente's ears.

"Do we *really* want coachloads of invalids coming to get cured? Won't it clash with the image of luxury housing and a healthy life in the sun?"

"No harm making it multi-attractive," Grant persisted.

"And what about the old finca that belonged to la Inglesa?"

"I know her daughter - I'll deal with that."

But Vicente still glared apprehensively at the architect's model, and Grant wrongly attributed the source of his unease to its amateurish, low-tech qualities.

"Don't worry - if you want to see it more realistically come to my office in Villahermosa. It's computer generated but looks just amazingly real. If you guys were hooked into twenny first century technology I'd have brought the DVD for you all to admire."

He smiled affably at the Mayor, who was also looking perturbed, for he had suddenly been struck by a terrible doubt which sent the shock waves churning to the pit of his copious stomach. Had his mother told him to say 'No' or 'Yes' to the development? *Why* couldn't he remember? Two tiny, monsyllabic words, yet such a crucial difference in their meanings! When he'd agreed earlier on he'd felt certain he was doing the right thing. Now, now that it was too late to do anything about it, too late to turn back the clock, a terrifying stab of doubt lay like a cold finger on his flab-protected heart.

He shrugged his shoulders. Oh well. If it's too late there's no use worrying about it, what's done is done. A cake eaten is no longer there for the eating. He'd have to put a brave face on it - chances are he'd made the right decision anyway. He returned Grant's smile with sudden true generosity, and enveloped him in a massive bear hug of an embrace.

Julia had had a brief flirtation with Grant in her late teens. It was probably only to annoy Frances who disliked him on sight, with all the customary contempt of old money (diminished to nearly nothing) for new money (brash and accumulating at a gallop).

Frances' family had themselves been 'new money' not so very many generations previously, when her great-great-grandfather had founded a malt whisky distillery in Glencoe. She was brought up grandly and in grandiose surroundings, so was somewhat stunned when her father informed her she'd have to marry rich if she wished to maintain her lifestyle, as he would be leaving his entire business and all his money to his two sons since they alone would bear the family name. Gender equality was a modern nonsense to him.

That was back in 1960 when she was twenty one and had an agreably cavalier attitude to life, embracing the ideals of freedom, love and self-expression - along with a full and excitingly varied exploration of both sex and drugs.

At that time she quickly recovered from the initial shock and thereafter loudly decried all aspects of evil capitalism, including the curse of inherited money. Much later on, however, when Julia was turning into a tricky teenager and she herself no longer quite such a stunner, the bitterness of her family rejection began to slowly filter through. The fact that she had never married, therefore never changed her name of McIntyre, and had even handed it on to Julia, was perhaps a deliberate act to prove her father wrong. Her estrangement from her family also meant she never would touch a drop of malt whisky throughout her life, although it had not of course diminished her appetite for good wine or other spirits.

Grant was her natural enemy; young, male, transparently ambitious and odiously over-confident. Where Frances saw beauty in the bloom on the purple grapes and the delicate soft green leaves of a vineyard, he saw only a mathematical equation of so many bottles at so much profit; her beloved rugged landscape of shifting sunlight and hovering shadows for him was differing tracts of real estate, with or without a view, the value up or down accordingly.

Ever since then his mini business empire had continued expanding, so he had power and fame on a localized scale and a life in the sun with plenty of money. But he was not BIGTIME. Not yet in the league of the famous rich, and he must know there was a loftier, much more secretive league several echelons above that one, where people were so rich they kept it quiet, happy to be the silent movers and shakers, the invisible power brokers behind governments, owning and controlling...

He had recently had a vasectomy. Irritated by a succession of trumped up paternity suits in the German courts filed by students returning from summer vacation and hoping to recoup their holiday expenses, and bored by his current girlfriend's phantom pregnancies, he had decided to exculpate himself once and for all.

He had never enjoyed losing sperm even when Julia knew him. Prior to ejaculation he emitted a strangled cry of regret, followed by a long gasp like a death rattle. It sounded like no other orgasm she had ever heard. Then he would stretch out immobile for a period of recovery, bemoaning all the thousands of sperm he had lost and was now obliged to replace. One tiny little egg a month, he grumbled, is all you women have to part with. And even *that* is a big deal for some, sanctioning all manner of irritable, bitchy behaviour.

Sex never had been his main motivation. Power was a massive blast, but not essential either. It was exclusively business, pure and complicated, that excited him. Its unexpected manoeuvres, competitiveness and risks. In truth, if he could have made it with chess and been Grandmaster of the Universe he would not even have bothered with business, but business easily came second best.


Meanwhile, Julia was sitting with Jorgen in her mother's erstwhile studio. They shared the cushioned bench by the long window, from where the shimmering lights of Milagra were visible and the stars mirrored them in a way that was intoxicating yet deeply disorientating.

The sensible solution, she knew, was to retire to bed. Her reluctance - the utter dread of re-entering last night's nightmare of her mother's accident. It had prompted her resolve to avoid the past, to not dwell either on thought or emotion. Well, *one* way to avoid them both, of course, was simply to act, be physical and thoughtless, although she did not deceive herself it was a noble method. There were other exonerationg factors too: she had drunk more than she was used to, her sexual drive had not been fulfilled for months, Jorgen was young, relatively attractive and did not seem capable of communicating with words, not even German ones. He lived exclusively through his body; a juggler, gymnast and athlete (he had given her a bizarre little private performance directly after Marte's departure). He had also been watching her pointedly all evening, very obviously waiting for his chance.

She was exhausted; yet only her mind fell asleep whereas her body experienced a kind of second wind. Her mouth suddenly became so parched that the almonds rasped her throat, all the warmth and moisture in her torso seemingly flowed downwards to between her thighs and her skin turned electrified, so that all the little downy hairs stood on end. There was no denying that she wanted to be bodily close to someone, to feel alive again, to be kissed and touched. It happened so automatically, predictably, that she was not fully aware who actually made the first move.

She must have shown too much desperation, she thought afterwards, or else been too absorbed by her own sensations of arousal that she greedily took and gave little back - certainly little affection or love. She assumed that for him it was equally primarily a sexual experience, only likely to last the single night, an unspoken pact between them that deep emotions would not be engaged. Maybe what happened next was his instinctive reaction to her using him that way, a subconscious punishment for her selfishness. His way of forcing her to remember him. Or else, he was just a sadist.

Suddenly, knifing through her sensations of pleasure and arousal there shot an agonising pain, so sharp that she grabbed his hair and wrenched his head viciously back. Her hand leapt straight to her breast and she could feel the warm, sticky flow of blood. Shakily, momentarily forgetting the geography of the room, or even where she was, her fingers at last closed on a box of matches and she relit the candle that had been meant to cast a subtle, romantic light on their lust but had sputtered out in the whirlwind of energy.

As the flame steadied her eyes confirmed what her horrified fingers had felt - he had bitten so viciously into the aureoli and nipple of her left breast that they looked distorted, and blood was welling from deep gashed teethmarks. She made a sound between a sob of pain and a gasp of fear. Then ran to the bathroom, locked and bolted the door, and wrapped her now shivering body in a bath towel. Biting her lip, she rummaged through the first aid paraphernalia for a bottle of mercurocrome. Sitting forlornly on the rim of the bathtub, she subdued the trembling of her hand to paint a bright vermilion stain onto the wound. The colour had probably been chosen to distract children from the sight of blood, but it only seemed to exaggerate the pattern of the teeth marks. God what a fool she'd been! Almost a complete stranger. Someone she knew nothing about - who the hell was Wolfgang anyway? How could she have been such so casually stupid? She mustn't cry, mustn't wake Alex or Marco.

How long she remained there she had no idea. She heard the distant church clock strike each quarter hour, but was too numbed to keep a tally. She might have lost faith in her feminine impulses, but she still felt confident in her maternal instinct, and it told her he posed no danger to the boys. Finally, a surge of anger supplanted the pain and she strode from the bathroom, still nursing a wad of bloodstained gauze to her breast. As she flicked on the harsh, overhead light in the studio she saw Jorgen groping for his boxer shorts. It incensed her all the more.

"Get out!" she yelled "I don't care what stone you slink under, just don't *dare* go near my children!" Then, stumbling over his clumsily discarded shoes, she scooped them up and hurled them at his ankles. "You need your fucking rottweiler head examined! In any other situation, any place but here, I'd have have phoned the police by now."

She stared at him with loathing and he guardedly returned the gaze. Then, almost in slow motion, plucked up his clothes and slung them casually over his shoulder. He halted in the doorway, half-turning, but since he would not look her in the eyes it was impossible to tell if he was ashamed or proud of what he had done. Her final words were subdued more than angry.

"I don't understand why. Nor do I remotely want to…I only wish to God it hadn't happened."

He tiptoed down the corridor. She could hear him clearing his throat repeatedly (but doubted it was from remorse) as he dragged the carpet under the table to form a kind of mock four poster bed. Perhaps he thought she might bombard him with missiles and the table afford protection, a sort of safety roof over his head. She longed for the forgetfulness of sleep. But sleep of course eluded her. She lay with eyes closed, trying to ignore the pain, feeling icy cold and unclean, and especially hating the awareness of the juices of arousal still lingering in her vagina. She doubled up her duvet to generate more heat then, still shivering, burrowed beneath the bedclothes partly for extra warmth, but mainly to drown out the sound of Jorgen swallowing nervously in the next room.

The following morning she ensured he left immediately by taxiing him to the Montejoven road, where she left him to hitch his way south. Only Marco was sorry to see the back of him. He had been eagerly looking forward to an exciting morning of fire eating and ingenious escapology, followed by a bout of barefoot dancing on broken glass, and was even optimistic that a spot of chainsaw juggling might round off the act…

Julia did not speak beyond ordering him to get his bags. There then followed a long, tense ten minutes while they waited in the car but he failed to reappear. Eventually he came, visibly on edge, claiming in indistinct, halting English that a valued juggling ball had mysteriously gone missing. He looked accusingly at Marco, who indignantly protested his innocence. Alex thought he had rarely seen Julia act so icily towards anyone, while Julia noticed that Alex wore a faint, secretive smile, like a cat who had savoured too much cream. It might have given her cause for alarm, except there was really no reason why she should suspect that the ball he had obviously sequestered was in any way out of the ordinary.

## 5

Julia would have loved to obliterate that night from her memory, but the nagging pain was a constant reminder. She knew she should have a tetanus shot, and stitches, but how could she possibly explain away that bite wound to a doctor? No, she would have to monitor it herself - and feel relief that at least she had not contracted rabies from that *animal*. Although it was still sore and inflamed she decided by the next afternoon that it was not dangerously septic. But she would have a tellingly ugly scar for the rest of her life.

*Why* had it happened? Was it her fault? She had often thought her mother made random, erratic choices in her sexual partners; she would avoid some thoroughly agreable man for no apparent reason, regret it, and then respond to whatever rat made the next advance only to throw him out in disgust as soon as she sobered up next morning. And she had always tried *not* to be like her mother; not to have meaningless, one-night stands, not to use sex as a panacea to cure loneliness, satisfy self-esteem, or exact revenge. Well, she had now been brutally punished.

From examining her own motives she fell to questioning Jorgen's. Was he a moral extremist bent on attacking single mothers? Had he computed Alex's age and punished her teenage promiscuity? Or did he go in for S&M and habitually bite women, believing they enjoyed it? Maybe some even did. Perhaps she was lucky he had only bitten her on the breast... It was only when she found herself wondering if juggling balls were such an obsession that he would bite protuberances off *any* rounded object, that she at last managed a wry laugh at her stupidity.

The village was busy gearing up for Reyes (Twelfth Night). An artificial neon star of Bethlehem dangled from the central tree in the plaza, and a plywood stable was being violently hammered into place by Juanito, bloated with pride at being left in charge of any building, - even one that was expected to collapse by the end of the day. Suddenly he bent double in a frenzied coughing fit when Julia passed by, having tried his habitual wolf whistle but forgetting the carpentry nails were still gripped between his teeth.

When darkness fell the Three Kings always rode into the village to distribute presents to the younger children, and Eulogio invariably landed a key role, since in this mechanised era he was one of very few who still looked natural on a mule.

Julia could clearly remember her first experience of Reyes. The custom was for every child to receive their presents personally from the Kings, but

Frances had inevitably forgotten to hand hers in by 11am on the previous day, so whispered negotiations between herself and Eulogio had to precede the hand-over of the gift she had just handed him, thus destroying the whole magical spell for everyone.

When Julia entered Bar del Bigot the door jingled behind her, followed by the piercing cry of "Putamadre!" (Motherfucker!) from a magnificent green cockatiel in its cage amongst the liqueur bottles. Colin and Reggie sat at the window table, puzzling over the crossword puzzle in the free local newspaper.

Colin had lived in Milagra for the same timespan as Frances. He, too, could remember significant milestones like the death of Franco and the day the telephone line was at last extended beyond Montejoven. Although his natural social milieu should have been the retired set who lived nearer the coast, played golf and drank sundowners, he could not in the least way relate to them. He much preferred Reggie, even though Reggie worried him by rubbing shoulders with danger. Scotty's bar spelt danger. Drugs were there - marijuana smoked openly, cocaine sold surreptitiously after 10pm in the men's toilet, forcing Colin to reieve himself outside behind the oleander bushes. Also, there were sometimes embarrassingly brazen erotic displays, especially in the summer heat, and adultery (a scourge amongst middle-aged ex-pats who drew everyone into their predictable melodramas). Plus he despised people who tried to borrow money or cadge a drink, and had never felt comfortable with Germans or French (the war) or Scandinavians (nudity). He had once contemplated exorcising his xenophobic tendencies by hypnotism, but was dissuaded by the size of Marte's proposed fee.

The new wave of Euro-Brits was his other headache. He hated their loud, ostentatious lifestyle; round the clock satellite TV, endless BBQs, dyed blond wives whose skins leathered rapidly from the hours lain out on poolside sunloungers, rude and indolent kids ferried from gokart track to theme park extravaganza to gokart track again. A life in Spain - God, most of them did not even register where on the planet they had ended up! They paid with euros, for sure, but the supermarkets stocked all their favourite must-have goodies: hot dogs, pickles, bacon, salad cream and tea bags, so same difference. He would now happily roll back the years to the old Spain, when foreigners were still a minority on the coast, and almost an exotic rarity inland.

Then, at least, they had inspired *some* respect for being mainly educated, with sometimes even a hint of talent: artists, writers, craftspeople - although there were of course a lot of dubious hippies too, partying naked whilst smoking, chewing and swallowing drugs with gay abandon. But maybe the seeds of disaster had already been sown then, when he and Frances first arrived in

Milagra. Ah…Frances, - what a vicious, arrogant, compelling, beautiful, terrifying, outrageous woman she had been.

Suddenly his glasses steamed up with angst and the crossword puzzle dissolved in a swirling mist, as with a frightened gasp he veered away from Frances' accusing face peering at him out of the gloom…

"D'you mind if I join you?" Julia asked, hesitating because Colin's reaction was so strangely hostile that her own early memories of his weird behaviour returned to nudge at her uneasily.

" 'Course not." Reggie was immediately reassuring and pulled out a chair. Colin blushed crimson and managed a tortured smile. "Don't mind Colin, anagrams always get him hot and bothered. So, how's it going?"

"OK. I've nearly cleared her rooms in the village. But the paperwork's still a huge muddle and I don't actually know how to deal with some of the official forms. Don't I need a solicitor?"

"Whoops - I should have told you. Being her executor I've hired one already, just for rubber stamping. But," he dropped the bantering tone, "I do need to talk about another issue. When'd be a good time?"

"Six this evening?" Julia was mildly intrigued.

The door jingle struck up again, the cockatiel jeered, "Communismo o muerte?!" in a Cuban accent as Otto trudged into the bar, and Reggie once more regained his cheerful persona. Marte sauntered in a few steps behind, so the cockatiel reverted to. "Putamadre, mas puta que madre!" (more a tart than mother), a variation he seemed to have composed in that instant for he cocked his head to one side as if listening in amazement as the new sound decayed into silence. Marte was wearing a brand new pair of shiny, calf length boots with high heels and pointy toes, and had thrown aside black in favour of purple and poisonous green. If slung behind bars and shrunk to size she could easily be mistaken for another cockatiel.

"Oof, my feet are killing me," she announced, sinking into a chair as she darted an aggrieved look at the cockatiel.

Otto found a gap between Reggie and Julia, accidentally thumping Reggie in the chest as he struggled out of his jacket.

"Hey," Reggie gasped, mildly winded, "give a chap his Lebensraum!"

Otto's eyebrows rose playfully to acknowledge the age-old challenge. "Hah! You English have lost your Lebensraum - plus most of your Commonwealth too. Though I notice you are colonizing Spain these days."

"Oh I say…" Colin knew all about colonisation and didn't like inaccuracy, even in jest, "that's a bit thick…"

Otto peeled off his glasses to look Colin sternly in the eye, "I am many things, but not thick." He swivelled towards Reggie, "Have you heard zis one - it is even a *German* joke: 'How do you make a small fortune?'"

Reggie wracked his brains, hating to lose a battle of wits. "Er...spot of bribery?"

"Come to Spain wiz a big one!" Otto boomed, grinning victoriously, and Reggie's laugh ackowledged it without rancour.

"You look *not* gute," Marte confided to Julia, casting a satisfied glance at the green sheen of her own trousered thighs. "I have some oil for stress. You must komm to my house." She placed her massage hand on Julia's arm as a foretaste of its subtle powers, and Julia instinctively manoeuvred her arm to protect her achingly tender breast.

"I've let things get to me," she admitted.

Her thoughts drifted back to earlier encounters with Marte. Her childhood memories were hazy, although she knew Marte had come to party many times at Frances' house while she was a little girl, but frankly there were so many intertwined bodies and tangled relationships back then that Julia could not recall individual faces or attach them to their appropriate body. What her memory served up was an amorphous morass of writhing, copulating limbs and torsos, a kind of giant octopus-creature, with the occasional jewelled ankle bracelet waving and sparkling in the candlelight. And the sounds of sighs, moans, yelps or gasps coming either from its suction pads on its tentacles, or from the waves breaking and sucking back the pebbles of the beach where it basked. The vision had a surreal, dreamy quality because she only used to encounter these scenes if she happened to wake in the middle of the night and, three-quarters still asleep, had to tiptoe over and around the bodies on her way to the bathroom. Frances' body was never there because she was no enthusiast of group anything, preferring hers intense and personal in the privacy of her own bedroom.

A later meeting did stick in her mind, however. Marte had been warm and friendly, her bosoms curvaceously recovered from their shrunken macrobiotic state under the ascetic régime of Tomas the potter, whom she had dumped in favour of Manfred and a life of glorifying in the pleasures of the flesh; vital statistical facts she immediately told a startled young Julia at their chance meeting in Villahermosa. Marte was selling handmade clothes from a colourful market stall on the beach front, for in those days she had not fully worked out the best system of manipulating KinderGeld, being not yet a mother but only heavily pregnant with a future little Lise.

She had invited Julia back to her bamboo hut on the mountain, where wafting steam rose from many bubbling cauldrons as she stirred the bales of raw oatmealy cotton in her concoctions of homebrewed vegetable dye. Julia was enchanted. She was fifteen at the time, on holiday from dance school in England, if time spent with Frances at that period could conceivably be described as a holiday. The contrast between the dark brooding oppression she experienced with Frances and the magically light atmosphere of this spectacular mountain eyrie was as stark as prison and freedom. Yet geographically they were separated only by a small boulderstrewn hill, Frances' farmhouse above and to the north east of Milagra, Marte's hut due north from Milagra and overlooking the gorge. Then, Marte had seemed like the mother she wished she had.

But time ticks on. Both the bamboo hut and Marte's body showed signs of wear, so she turned her skills to other healing arts. No longer with the softly seductive touch of lips or hands, but indirectly using herbs, tree bark, pollens or petals found growing on the southern slopes of the hill. Had Frances, eighteen years older than her, and with a far more formidable reputation for pulling men and metaphorically eating them for breakfast, been a source of inspiration or of envy for Marte?

Julia decided to go to Marte's, but to be on her guard. She had not spoken a word about the encounter with Jorgen, but, irrational or not, in the back of her mind she partly blamed Marte for it. Her breast wound even reinflamed and throbbed from proximity to Marte.

As she drove home she saw Eulogio outside his casita, uproariously entertaining Jaime the doctor and Pedro the plumber to one of his salacious stories, judging by the rapidity and obscenity of his gestures. Eulogio wore a striped kaftan, Roman sandals, woolly socks and a white turban, while Jaime had a gold and green velvet cloak and impossibly tight cream breeches. Pedro sat while they smeared thick globs of black axle grease over his face – it was his turn to be Balthasar. Their three gilt crowns hung incongruously in the bare branches of an apricot tree, while their gifts of 'frankincense, gold and myrrh' lay casually amongst the débris of their lunch.


Reggie arrived at quarter past six, a compromise between his natural punctuality and the Spanish obligation to be late. With a tinge of amusement she noted the effort he had put effort into his appearance, having run a comb through his hair and untidily applied polish to the toes of his shoes. Protectively clutching a beribboned sheath of papers he toured the downstairs rooms with boyish curiosity, grunting in surprise at some of the changes she had made. Eventually they settled in the small study room with Frances' books, where they could hear themselves speak above the laughter from the boys playing a game of 'truth or dare'.

"I don't know if you're aware what she was up to in the last months?"

Julia shook her head, "We weren't in contact. You know that."

"Well, she'd always been interested in the local area. She'd been researching and, it seems, become absorbed in the history of the Fuente, because she wrote to various religious bigwigs in an attempt to have it officially protected as a shrine, even claiming it had miraculous properties and had cured her arthritis! Here are copies of her letters..."

Julia glanced down in amazement. Not only had Frances always been an atheist, but her arthritis had worsened, not improved.

"She also wrote to the Provincial Diputacion requesting they list the farmhouse as a building of historic importance, worthy of protection." Again Reggie supplied Julia with letters. "She cited a find of Roman amphora shards in her well as evidence the site was of ancient habitation." He looked almost embarrassed, "The question is, was she genuinely onto something, or had she simply gone bonkers?"

Julia looked out at the fading evening light, which faintly illuminated the bilious green of the moss smothering the old grey stones of the terrace walls. The place did have an ancient feel to it, a timelessness. It was not hard to imagine early Stone Age man living in these mountains, especially in the natural caves along the gorge. And the Romans had criss-crossed the Iberian peninsular scattering traces of their settlements, so why not here? Also, Frances knew her pots better than almost any other academic expert, having made a professional career out of painstakingly reassembling them for archeological museums all over Europe. Her opinion would carry weight, for she was considered an authority on early ceramic glazes and earthen potteryware - as she was well aware.

She had shown such little patience towards people, but Julia remembered her sitting in her workshop gazing at the table surface covered by thousands of tiny fragments, and, as Julia watched, slowly, bit by bit, a beautifully turned pot would be reborn by the careful manipulations of those deft fingers. It was much harder than any jigsaw puzzle; no picture to guide one to the finished article and no initial hint of the overall shape and contours. How bizarre that a woman who lived on such a short fuse and could explode into rages and smash her own china into smithereens, would choose to labour so intricately to mend damage from a distant past. In that moment Julia suddenly felt keenly the despair her mother must have suffered when her arthritis made it impossible for her to work anymore. And it was, of course, the work that had made her susceptible to arthritis in the first place.

"Where are these 'Roman' shards then?"

Reggie shrugged, "Her letter doesn't say. You've not found any, have you?"

43

Julia shook her head. "Nothing that wasn't here before."

Perhaps her mother had entertained delusions near the end. She had always hovered on the brink of sanity, after all.

"You needn't answer, since I know it's not my business, but I'd love to know how you saw Frances - what you really thought about her."

Reggie looked surprised. His response was not immediate.

"She was…hmm, probably the most fascinating person I ever met. I grant you this place isn't exactly swarming with intelligence, profundity or talent, but all the same she was unique, and would have been anywhere. Trouble was - too extreme. Couldn't stand subterfuge or insincerity and never applied diplomacy, so made enemies left, right and centre. A hopeless case really. But of course let down by both her own father *and* yours." Reggie smiled wistfully. Then his more usual, light-hearted self resurfaced. "And you've got to remember she was a Scot, with the temper of a Viking. She had to make do without family money or whisky, both dear to a Scots' heart, so the only thing left was oats. It's no wonder she went a bit overboard in the manner of sowing them, though frankly some of the stories are grossly exaggerated."

So Reggie was not the bumbling clown he often pretended to be, and she could now appreciate more readily why Frances could relate to him. Although Otto was Marte's equivalent of Reggie, Reggie was alone in being non-judgmental and deft at pouring oil on troubled waters. But neither were remotely the Lothario type Frances and Marte used to go for in their heyday.


After Reggie left Julia wandered down to the old well. Above ground it was shaped like a large stone rain butt, its opening capped by a chiselled lintel. Inside, its curving walls of dry stone formed a perfect circle, narrow at the top like the neck of a bottle, but widening to a diameter of three or four metres below ground level. Like a giant amphora. She leaned over to whistle softly, as she used to long ago, and listen to the pindrop accoustics and the slight delay but perfect tone of the returning echo, catching sight of her pale face, whitened by moonlight, reflected on the dark, mercurial surface of the water.

Some crazy flute player had once sat on this stone ledge for a marathon session of playing Indian ragas into the well, and got so wound up by the hypnotically haunting sound that he nearly passed out. In this trancelike state his flute slithered through his benumbed fingers and fell into the water with a scarcely perceptible 'plop'.

He ranted and raved and hung around for days trying to retrieve it. First with a fishing line and hook, and finally by bodily lowering himself into the murky depths clad in a wet suit, flippers and goggles, with an underwater lamp strapped to his forehead. He fought his way through the layers of silt and sludge, past the mosquito lava, resident eel, two green water snakes and a drowned rat, more jumbled layers of lost metal and plastic buckets to the earlier clay water carriers of a more ancient era - but still no flute!

He was about to buy oxygen tanks and a mud suction pump, but a brief interlude of sanity prevailed in which his mathematical brain (a feature of musicians) sprang into life, and computed for him that the price of a new flute was easily the cheaper option. He therefore left with scarcely a goodbye, to Frances' immense relief, and afterwards Julia played happily with the underwater lamp until its battery expired.

She would not touch the wet suit though, because he was an ardent believer in the beneficial powers of his own urine. As a daily ritual he massaged his face with it (aimed via a funnel into a green stoppered bottle) whilst it was still hot and steaming, in the belief his complexion was thus rendered clean, ageless and acne free. She remembered aiming onto the wet suit herself, until its smell turned utterly nauseous; and she could thankfully abandon the habit altogether when it was finally gobbled up by a ravenous stray dog.


Now the bucket hung precariously from the last thread of fraying rope, weakened by years spent in the updraught of cold, damp air. It was transparently obvious it had not been used recently, and that no-one had walked on the clumps of healthy weeds amongst the flagstones. So why had Frances lied? She had hated lies so fervently that there must be some very potent reason for her to embroil herself. Unless she was no longer of sound mind near the end, and her amphora story pure fantasy.

Or…she had only *pretended* to hate lies, but had in fact lied more often than anyone realised. And this was merely the first lie to be exposed…

Julia felt an urge to interrogate the well itself, sunk deep in the earth like the oracle at Delphi, but she knew there had been no real word from the Gods at Delphi either. The 'miracle' was just an ingenious combination of subterranean accoustics and a tricky old witch forced into the role of oracle as a punishment. But despite her uneasiness over Frances' truthfulness, or lack of it, Reggie had at last reawakened in her a more positive attitude towards her mother.

# 6

She opened her eyes to catch the first glow of sun strike the ridge of mountains across the valley, while elsewhere remained steeped in dark shadow. It was mid January now, and each morning the sun rose slightly earlier so its first rays struck the western mountains at a different angle, illuminating a different ridge or gulley. It was like a natural, geological sundial.

Her ears puzzled over a rumbling emerging from the bowels of the earth. At first she considered an earth tremor, then suspected Alex and Marco were watching one of their catastrophic disaster movies, but when she sat up in bed she realised it was something mechanical in the Milagra direction. Assuming a tractor was struggling to plough a neglected terrace she dozed off again, but when she got up thirty minutes later to make tea the sound was so persistent that she hurried to Frances' old studio for its view onto Milagra.

Three enormous mechanical diggers with caterpillar wheels were scudding to and fro across what used to be Begonia Roca's olive groves. They had already tossed aside trees and sliced into the dry stone terrace walls; now they seemed to be pounding, battering and flattening the earth in a frenzy, as if someone had ordered a football stadium of international standards to be constructed there in a matter of mere days.

Alex and Marco joined her on the window seat. They watched in fascinated horror, aroused by the same ghoulish magnetism that drew spectators to a public beheading or Romans to a gladiatorial contest. Julia knew in her heart this was a stupid comparison; trees, plants and grasses were essentially different to humans and animals, so cutting them down could hardly be aligned with sadism and murder. But she felt a deep rooted unease to witness this sudden carve up of a mountain she had known and loved from birth.

A younger Marco would have been circling in frenzy, revved to fever pitch by the repetitive noise and mechanised energy. Instead he stayed by the window, his mouth close enough to cloud the glass with his breath, his fingers tweaking anxiously at a loose thread in the cushions, saying nothing.

She drove to the village to find out what was afoot. As she neared the pancake flat rectangle sliced from the mountain a fine coating of pale dust, like a Saharan sandstorm, settled over the car. Through this swirling dustcloud they saw that Juanito was the driver of the smallest digger - despite the fact that he'd yet to pass his driving test. On seeing them he executed a clumsy three point turn, changing gear too fast for the lumbering vehicle which shuddered in protest, and dug out a new swathe of destruction as he sped towards them, skidding to a halt just short of the gulley. Julia wound down the window, coughing as a fresh whirl of dust clogged her nostrils and throat, so that Alex had to ask, "What *are* you doing?" on her behalf.

Juanito grinned, slapping the door panel of his yellow steed with proprietorial pride. "Driving this digger" his voice cracked with the honour of it, and he waved a green sheet of paper that he'd found on the dashboard. "My permit's here!" he shouted, but with such volume and defensiveness that she knew it wasn't.

Hastily she wound up the window before his sudden retreat pelted them with clods of earth.


The villagers seemed as confused as she was. Each one had a different theory: a new supermarket, a cinema, a hotel, a disco, a gokart track, a golf course, a tennis club, a municipal swimming pool, a water deposit, a replica castle for medieval jousting tournaments, a hospital, a maternity clinic, a helicopter landing pad, a ganster's hideaway, another mountain retreat for King Juan Carlos, a paddy field for growing the best Basmati rice, a giant avocado greenhouse, and, last of all - a huge tent for the sweetest Egyptian mangoes like Manolo Pons made near Pontereal, which turned him into a millionaire overnight...

There was a shared excitement, a conspiratorial feeling that something big was about to happen. But there were also dissident mutterers. Some who whispered darkly that nothing good would come of it, for change was never for the better.

Dolores belonged to the latter camp. "Mi hijo es imbecile," (my son's an idiot) was all she said, clinging to her worry beads, a strange, non-Catholic Greek practice she had abandoned years ago. "You should have had daughters, like your mother," and she sighed so profoundly that her breasts gyrated against the bakery counter, making the portrait of her son tremble so violently that it fell in an explosion of shattered glass.

Julia helped her sweep it up before joining the boys in Bar del Bigot.


"Commercialismo o muerte," shrieked the cockateel as she came through the door.

She wondered for the umpteenth time who coached him with his repertoire, and what, or who, cued him in to a particular utterance. But Sra Bigot, plump, cheerful and always polishing the wine glasses then holding them up to the light to check their sheen, would only smile and insist, "Es un pajaro superinteligente." Her husband, called 'el Bigot' because of his wonderfully thick, drooping moustache, had a mournful face and pained expression and rarely ever spoke, so no-one bothered to ask him.

His brother was known as 'Manos arriba' and he suffered from involuntary limb spasms - but the adolescent girls of the village knew that his hands could wander in strangely predictable ways that were unlikely to be truly involuntary. Once, when Julia was about thirteen, she found him sitting on an old cane chair near the communal washbasin, where the route to the Ladies and Gentlemens' toilets divided. As she washed her hands he suddenly bobbed up behind her and clamped his fingers over her firm young budding breasts, and it took all her strength with fists, nails and sharp kicks to his shins before she was free of his limpet grasp. Frances advised, 'a sock in the puss and a knee in the groin' was a far more effective tactic, should there be a next time.


Colin and Reggie were in their accustomed seats but today the crossword puzzle played second fiddle to the hot topic of the day.

"It's an asylum centre," Colin opined wistfully. He had been growing uneasy at the numbers of Moroccans who accosted drivers at the traffic lights in Villahermosa with a yearning expression, pointing in slow motion to their empty pockets. "I know the Spanish government is edgy about this influx of illegal immigrants. Europe's a new bloody Mecca."

"Oh come on Colin, let's not be hysterical. The only uncontrollable influx is fat bastards from the north who want to stuff as much greasy barbecued pig and cheap beer into their bellies as their bloated bodies will allow. Then stuff the wife..."

"I say - watch out!" warned Colin as he saw Julia approaching, relieved to find a pretext to silence Reggie's uncharacteristic vehemence.

"What d'you reckon's going on?" Julia asked Reggie. "Dolores definitely knows, but is keeping tight lipped."

Reggie was not his carefree self. Troubled doubts and dark suspicions lurked like cloudy stains in his normally smiling eyes.

"Dunno, but my guess is that Grant, the rich Yank, - you know him I think, has a few fingers in this pie. I tried to see the Mayor but he's indisposed...too many empanadas."

"*Grant?* In this *rural backwater* as he always called it? Must be a big investment then..."

"Well - that rules out my preference, cultural centre complete with library and museum." Reggie smiled wanly, his spirits and sarcasm beginning to revive. "Colin here has voted for a high security jail with floodlights, high wire fencing and bloodhound patrols; Otto wants a concentration camp for the Germans now in Paraguay and the Zionists now in Washington; Marte favours a sanitorium and Juanito's just bursting for a brothel. No wonder the Mayor's been taken sick from the burden of trying to please us all. - Oh, and most of the villagers are pinning their hopes on a boating lake with mallard duck, crested grebes and pink flamingos, to be officially opened by Placido Domingo. We're an eclectic lot, us of the village. A corrupt, Florida-style referendum is the only viable solution."

Colin was agitated, he had been trying to interrupt Reggie throughout his monologue and was the more irritated because Julia found it amusing.

"You do talk a load of piffle," he muttered feebly. Then he got up suddenly, an unheard of act in the middle of the day, with beer still waiting in his glass. "Must dash, catch up with you later!" and he had gone.

Julia had wanted to find Eulogio, who would surely be better informed than most on the activity above the village since his land adjoined it, but when she failed to find him in any of his usual haunts she gave up and drove to Marte's.

Marte's flank of the hill had a different personality, despite its physical proximity. Frances' farmhouse was set amongst the silver green of olive groves and the sharp, angular branches of almonds softened by their pale green foliage, the colours all soft, cool and muted. The stones of the terrace walls and the pillars of solid rock - what Eulogio called the roots of the mountains - were a beige or soft grey in colour, with a dusting of green where moss sprouted in the areas of perpetual shade. There was an area of livelier, denser green where the Fuente emerged and moisture permeated not just the soil but the surrounding air, so that the sounds of birdsong from there were more limpid, more beautiful, and rare orchids grew amongst the water irises.

Marte's side had redder, earthier colours and more contrasts. A sweep of pine forest stretched from the mountain crest down to the head of the gorge, and the hillside was less terraced, wilder and strewn with boulders amongst which grew prickly bushes interspersed with heather, gorse, wild thyme, rosemary, sage and a million other breeds, some exotic, some healing, some poisonous, and some - like saffron - surprisingly valuable. The phalanx of rocks falling into the gorge had a speckled grey colour on the top surface, but progressed through rust, pale orange and tawny cream to finally almost bleached white at the foot of the gorge where dinner plate sized pebbles marked the river bed and wild bamboo grew alongside pungent clumps of mint and arrowroot.

If Frances' side was the French Pyrenees, Marte's was Africa, and in time it was hard to tell whether they had chosen their homes to suit their personalities, or whether their locations had moulded their characters.

Just short of Marte's hut, in the elbow of the final bend, there was a rutted field with more than a dozen dented, rusty and decrepit cars, or parts of cars. It was known as 'Marte's graveyard', and they were the wrecks of vehicles once proudly driven by Marte's different lovers. Like the chicken and egg quandary it was unclear which died first, car or relationship, but the two deaths always coincided and the ex-lover departed leaving his defunct car as a perpetual memento, rusting, peeling and disintegrating year by year. Marte naturally denied responsibility for this hideous junk heap, claiming only one and a half of its wrecks had ever been owned by any lover of hers. But word had got around and the rest had just been dumped there, secretly in the night by total strangers because the cost of officially scrapping cars was so exorbitant.

While Julia parked the car Marco and Alex ran headlong for the pine copse, where a former lover had erected a magnificent series of ropes, pulleys and ladders, modelled on the rigging on an old schooner but with the added joy of swings, seesaws and 'flying foxes'.

"Take care," Julia advised, but they had already vanished.

She could hear a heated discussion coming from Marte's kitchen area. Being angry in German sounded wonderfully operatic. Otto had descended to a deep throated tenor of roars and Marte, normally sexily husky, had risen to soprano heights, raining down consonants and howling out vowels in a Wagnerian crescendo. There was no point Julia announcing her arrival with a cheery call, so she walked in on them without warning.

The effect was dramatic. She experienced, for the first time ever, the power of a conductor controlling the finale. At the sight of her all sound and action ceased instantly; it was like in drama class when the teacher yells 'freeze!', or the game when the music stops and you are out if you twitch a whisker. They stared at her open mouthed, petrified statues with rigid hands on hips and stiff fingers pointing with menace, until Marte broke the spell and began to giggle, and Otto relaxed his frown and wrinkled his nose, at last appreciating the smell of fresh coffee from the stove he was leaning against.

"Oof," said Marte cheerfully. "So gute you came, for I think we might otherwise have killed each other."

She flexed her legs gingerly, one by one, to reengage the circulation and set the juices flowing properly. Then she gave Julia an all embracing hug, stroking and caressing her back so that the movement ended, lingeringly, on her buttocks. Julia laughed good naturedly but clenched her buttocks and side-stepped out of reach.

"He says my German is not truly...how do you say in English? We say 'hoch'. Maybe it is 'high class'..." Her voice was steadier, but the vestiges of flames still flared from her nostrils.

"She takes it too seriously I tell you." Otto tried to sound both placatory and professorial, as if fresh from an elocution seminary. "She has this regional accent from Worms but it is no problem. It only becomes a problem if you deny it." He gave her a haughty, no nonsense stare.

"Anyway, is it not more important what you say than how you say it?"

"What you do is also important. It's easy to talk."

"Ha! We all know what *you* do is just *so* important."

Julia sensed they were on a slippery slope back into the realms of marital-style warfare.

"Do you know what's happening on Begonia Roca's land above the village? Apparently Grant's behind it - I thought his mother might have told you something."

"Oof, I've not set eyes on ze bitch since ages. I could not shift her cellulitis, so she tries some new detox system now, thanks Gott."

Marte at last noticed the smell of burnt coffee and rescued the pan before it fused with the hot plate of her cooker. Her kitchen was an amazing apothecary's den, the shelves from floor to ceiling stacked with jars and vials neatly labelled in a Gothic script, although the organisation was less systematic. Herbs, spices, potions, creams, lotions and oils were indiscriminately ranged amongst powders, make-up, henna, shampoo, cotton wool, candles, razors and rat poison, and although Marte claimed she knew her way around she had apparently once spiced a succulent ghoulash with henna instead of hot paprika.

A ginger cat slept curled on a blue silk cushion cradling a tub of margerine that he had licked shiny clean, and two large hairy moths lay drowning in a pool of eucalyptus honey.


It was obvious that for all his intellectual clout Otto was no handyman; the ladder was nowhere to be seen, and an array of buckets and bowls had been placed strategically under the cracks in the ceiling where chinks of daylight showed through. Even those lovers most skilled in DIY had been stumped for a solution to keep the roof weatherproof. It leaked like a sieve in a heavy downpour and Lise, whose bedroom was worst affected, had to sleep on a raised island underneath an enormous yellow golfing umbrella.

"How's your bandolero book going?" Julia asked politely.

"Don't ask," Marte jumped in, "the reason he is so nasty today is because he is stuck. Or is it 'blocked'? You see..." she turned accusingly on Otto, "now that you criticize my way of speaking I lose confidence. Just because you cannot write your stupid man's book you take away my speech."

Otto sighed wearily as he threw the deformed coffee pan into the wastebin and found a dented kettle in which to boil more water.

"Tell me," he addressed Julia, "is zis man Eulogio a reliable source?"

"His family have owned land here since the beginning of time and he has plenty of stories. Still, I wouldn't be *too sure* about his memories of the Civil War. He was only seven when it ended. Younger than Marco."

"That's when ze mind is clearest. No doubt you, too, have interesting memories from zis age?"

"Don't fall into his trap Julia," Marte cut in urgently, "he should be sticking to his war, not poking his nose into zose days."

"The Spanish are a forgiving people, they get on with old enemies," Otto remarked with quiet dignity, giving Marte a reproachful look. "They were killing each other seventy years ago, but who would know it now?"

Marco ran in twirling his dismembered T-shirt above his head, while Alex followed at a subdued walk, holding its torn-off sleeve to his forehead to staunch the flow of blood that had already spattered his jeans.

"It looks worse than it is," Marco reassured Julia.

"Remind me to stay away from Marco and swings," Alex said, wincing painfully as he sat on an old oak pew that had surely belonged in a church.

"Face this way," Marte inspected Alex's wound with an expert eye, "for Otto goes faint at ze sight of blood, yet he can write about it all night long."

"Zat must be why," Otto said solemnly "I waited to know you until after your menopause. Take care," he warned Julia, "she is jealous of those who menstruate."

"*I* still do," Marte corrected huffily, "but no longer in tune with the moon, zat is all."


Julia drove home slowly in deference to Alex's bandaged head. He had been generously plied with arnica cream and dosed with a strange, knobbly root like a white truffle freshly dug from Marte's pine copse. He was drowsy, but Marte assured her this was normal after a head wound. He was also very obviously disappointed by Lise's absence. She had gone off for the day with a girlfriend, and if she had been there he would never have wasted time on a swing with Marco.

As she mounted the hill from Milagra she instinctively braced herself for the shock of the newly felled trees, and the gouged out topsoil with its layer of grass and wild flowers tossed contemptuously aside.

She told herself not to overreact. Buildings were erected in many, many beautiful places all over the world; near Bilbao they had to cope with nuclear power stations blocking out the beaches; while elsewhere oil rigs sprung out of the desert breathing fire, and whole valleys were drowned for the sake of hydro-electric plants. But she had an uneasy feeling all the same. The rich red earth, now exposed to a depth where it had lost all colour, appeared like a flesh wound which had reached the bone.


Did her mother somehow get advance wind of this destruction? Might her pretence about the Roman shards have been simply a manouvre to fend it off? And what could Grant possibly want to build here in the midst of agricultural Spain that he couldn't build in his natural milieu on the coast?

She thought of the war in Iraq, and then she thought of oil. But it was hardly the terrain for oil, and the heavy machinery she'd seen was for flattening and gouging, not for deep drilling.


Marco sat silent in the back seat, lost in thought and perhaps also plagued by guilt.

"*Why* doesn't it rain?" he suddenly demanded.

"'Cos we're not in England, dumbo," Alex answered groggily.

Marco sighed, "Everyone's ratty today. Martyr and Himmler were having a right go and you blame me but it wasn't my fault." He paused, "Can I look for toad?"

"I guess so, but don't be long."

"You wouldn't be so damn' easy going if you knew who toad was" Alex said peevishly after Marco had vanished.

"What on earth d'you mean?"

"Oh... never mind. Maybe I did get concussed. Forget it," and he went off to his room to rest.

His irritation was in reality more to do with Lise than Marco. He had readily agreed to hide Jorgen's ball of cocaine (if it was cocaine, not heroin) for a few weeks, but not for ever. Now he felt torn. On the one hand he longed to be rid of it, but on the other he worried that once she had it in her possession her interest in him might suddenly evaporate.

Julia lay awake long into the night, her mind drifting through layers of reality. Her brutalised nipple felt raw and newly wounded, as if the sight of Alex's blood had torn it afresh and dug beneath its scar. She caressed it gently, trying to soothe, but her fingers recoiled at the lumpy, ugly feel of knotted distortion so she ventured lower, stroking the smooth skin of her stomach, then lower still, seeking out the moist warmth between her thighs. She tried to summon the physical presence of Marco's dad, to picture his overhanging face, to sense his breathing in time with her accelerated pulse, to imagine her fingers were his, that it was his warmth flooding towards her, her tongue was his tongue, her lips his lips...

He had always resented her sexual drive, she realised, suspecting it was an inherited, aberrational libido, unhealthy, although conversely he had enjoyed it too. The sensuality of her being a dancer, having a professional body, had aroused strange, prudish reservations despite being a source of pride in the beginning. Initially he felt protective of her, a talented young dancer struggling to balance a promising career with being a mother of an energetic three year old. But in time it irked him that she had been pregnant with someone else's child at only seventeen, and then he became alarmed thinking of her unorthodox childhood, her loss of innocence when very young.

Was it her fault he had hated Frances so much? Perhaps she had misrepresented her childhood experiences, or deliberately poisoned him against Frances to bolster her own antagonism. Or maybe he simply needed an excuse to justify his own unpaternal rejection of Marco, and had decided that she, from lacking a father, a male role model early on, had totally failed in the delicate balancing act between male partner and sons.

She wondered idly whether Frances used to touch herself whilst imagining her father's presence. Or whether she was always so totally immersed in self-love that she had no need. Or whether she never needed to touch herself because she always had a man to turn her on.

## 7

This could be Palestine, Julia thought as she watched the daily encroachment of the earth movers, grinding to dust the growth of centuries and the toil of generations of farmers beneath their caterpillar tracks. Except that there the tanks took over the high ground, parading their strength on the ridges and hill tops, venturing a little further each day, swallowing more land, knocking down houses to build better ones for themselves – or to construct illegal boundary walls and plant orange trees on the one side only. Here it was done in reverse; the vehicles of destruction came from downhill since there was no resistance, trees were knocked down to build houses, and really she was being ignorant and insensitive because whereas Palestinians had to watch their land being eaten bit by bit, and lives were lost in the process, she was being robbed of nothing more than the beauty of her view, and without bloodshed.

The comparison dawned on her, though, because Marco had run out impulsively and thrown stones at a JCB. Juanito happened to be its driver, and a stone hit him in a vulnerable spot, so a furious chase ensued until Marco was hunted down like a rabbit and eventually caught when he tripped in the gulley. Julia ran fast, arriving just in time to prevent Juanito having to justify why he was man enough to outwrestle a slightly built eight year old. His face was flushed and mottled with anger.

"Why can't you control the brat? He nearly crushed mis cojones..." He picked Marco bodily up and held him dangling in the air like a limp rag, before passing him to Julia. "He needs a fucking father to knock sense into him!"

Juanito had been in a class three years below her at the village school, and five below by the time she left (failing the end of year test meant repeating that year), and even then he was a bully in the making. Too frightened to challenge her on his own because of her reputation as a kick boxer, but happy to stick the boot in if others would back him up, and quite able to steal bocadillos from the tiny infants.

Later on he had leered and slobbered as an alternative form of provocation; so now she felt tempted to retort that *had* there been a father, he, Juanito would have been the first to have had sense knocked into him.

However she kept quiet. Conscious that Marco should not have thrown the stone; that Spain was a non-violent society, relatively speaking, and finally

Juanito, though exasperating, was not unduly aggressive. Not compared to those who deemed it justifiable to kill children for throwing stones.

By now the mystery building was no longer a game of guesswork. Everyone knew a grandiose development was afoot, although the Mayor still played down its proportions.

"Pfff - a few houses on the slopes above the village, for old, retired couples to end their days in peace," he told Reggie when he finally recovered from his indigestion. "What can we do? How is it *our* fault that the foreigners want to come?"

Dolores remained tight lipped and withdrawn. Her lifelong skill with dough and short crust pastry deserted her, and soon even her most faithful customers kneaded their own bread and prepared their own puffs, pies and sweetmeats, which they brought to her twice daily to bake in her cavernous brick oven. She refused to restore her son's portrait to its place of honour on the counter; instead her childhood tapestry, with the message *Jesus Pobre* in red silk chain stitch which she had patiently worked on in third grade, replaced it in the reglued gilt frame.

Occasionally she did - temporarily - recover her old zest for life and its melodramas. On these days she would rise once again before dawn and kindle a fearsome blaze in the oven, then set about making cocas. They were delicious, hot, aromatic and perfectly crisped on the underside, but the careful positioning of tomato pulp, two black olives and a strip of anchovy bore an uncanny resemblance to the rounded, doughy face of her disgraced son, and there was always a vicious diagonal slash of a knife blade across the salty anchovy smile. She avoided touching them with her fingers. Instead she balanced them deftly on her long wooden paddle, then, with a wild cry of 'Caramba!' lobbed them with venomous accuracy onto a sheet of greaseproof paper.

Marco's wish for rain was finally answered. Banks of dark, lowering clouds gathered ominously to the north; the wind freshened, the birds fell silent, the wild flowers wilted as if suddenly aware how desperately they had been missing water, and anything made from paper instantly curled at the edges. The rain struck in the middle of the night, hammering on the roof like a thousand needles, and soon you could hear the gurgling of gutters and drainpipes as the leaf mould, moss and twigs were swilled away in swirling rivulets, some of which were diverted along a feeder pipe to the old stone well.

Julia woke up briefly, imagining the frantic deployment of buckets and bowls in Marte's hut, then dozed off again, lulled by the soothing sounds of flowing water.

They woke up among clouds. Like in a mountain snowstorm, the brain had no orientating perspective and could not distinguish uphill from down. Whichever way you looked clouds drifted past and reduced visibility to under fifty metres, so the rest of the world no longer existed, obliterated by the density of moisture.

All other noises were drowned by watersound. Like passages of music the tempo changed from impassioned drumming and furious percussion to a gentle rhythmic drip, drip from the leaves in the lulls between heavy downpours, and throughout there was a constantly flowing backdrop of gurgling and splashing as the surface water sped downhill in newly formed streams with waterfalls. The dampness was so pervasive that wooden furniture sprouted beads of sweat, vegetables mildewed, matchheads fused, salt and sugar coagulated into blocks.

It felt biblical, transported back to the time of Noah; or much earlier still when the very first drenching rains sucked up the seas and poured them onto the hot steaming earth, desperate to cool the fires sufficiently for life to begin.

"Won't it *ever* stop raining?" Marco asked on the fourth day of incarceration, having grown heartily sick of all his games, books and window watching.

"It might not *be* raining anywhere else but in these mountains," Alex suggested.

"Can't we try to go out?"

"No," Julia was firm, "the track's a mud slide and the car will either get bogged down or slip over the edge. I'm not risking it. We can walk to the village if it doesn't stop tomorrow."

She felt as eager as Marco for the rain to stop. The wooden windows and doors had swollen and refused to open, or, if they did, were then impossible to shut. Her stack of dry firewood was nearly exhausted, food stocks were low and they were running perilously short of clean dry clothes. The boys might feel they had been cooped inside but in reality they had made several forays into the monsoon, each time returning dripping wet and oozily plastered in sticky mud. A clothes horse steamed beside the wood fire and muddy jeans clogged the bathroom. Candles oozed wax and were scattered on ledges in every room, for the electricity supply was unreliable in the rain. Every strike of lightning, every blast of thunder, and every spurt of torrential rain would cause a power cut, and in electric storms the lights flipped on and off like a stroboscope. And apart from all the practicalities of keeping dry Julia was also becoming starved of adult company.

On the fifth day the clouds lifted and the valley was again revealed. A light drizzle alternated with flurries of wind from a new direction, bringing with it the hint of warmer, sunnier climes. Their spirits lifted, and although the car was still not an option and the mud swamp below, where Juanito's JCB listed heavily to one side as if in the grip of a crocodile's jaws, made the journey to the village seem unappealing, they set off on a walk anyway. Alex convinced them that Marte's was the sanest destination, "I ought to have my headwound checked," he said, cunningly playing the guilt card.

This time as they approached they heard sounds of merriment not argument. Marte's throaty laugh reverberated against the bamboo struts of the ceiling and was echoed by the encircling mountains, although the lack of shared laughter suggested a private joke. The first hesitant rays of sunlight filtered through a break in the cloud, and Marte's pine copse was bestrewn with bedclothes, cotton bales, cushion covers and three suits that must be Otto's. Her washing line and all the rope structures of the playground sagged from the combined contents of their wardrobes. In fact the sheer quantity of sodden material was creating its own mini-climate as evaporation rose in puffs from shirt necks and trouser legs, and Marte's laughter then blew it over the ridge into the next valley.

Entering through the kitchen they balanced on planks of wood which bridged the flooded floor. Only Marco had no need to duck to avoid the bags of food that dangled from hooks in the beamed ceiling.

Otto hunched on a high stool wearing woollen mittens and two jackets, tapping at his laptop and toasting his feet on a paraffin stove precariously balanced on the struts of the stool. Lise waded in from her bedroom, sensibly wearing wellington boots and a sheepskin overcoat, smiling as if she had seen no-one in years. She invited Alex and Marco to a miniature speedboat tournament on the waters of her bedroom so Julia, not wanting to interrupt Otto's unblocked writing, bestrode the broad plank which led to Marte's studio.

Marte was encased in an old woollen djellaba from her distant past, with leopardskin leggings and colourful Norwegian socks. She squatted crosslegged on a platform amidst a snowstorm of papery scribblings.

"Eureka!" she cried gleefully, "It is 'eureka', isn't it, when you've done something brilliant? Oh, you cannot imagine how gute I feel, Julia! I have been struggling for ages and now, thanks Gott, I've got it!"

She gazed admiringly at a design for what must be a bottle label. Written in the same slanting Gothic script that identified all her therapeutic and culinary ingredients was the word 'Renacimiento', above which stood a beautiful nude of advancing years clasping a graceful hand mirror and smiling coyly, while in the background a black bull pawed the ground as if preparing to charge.

"What do you think?"

"Is it for a beauty product?"

"You mean I didn't say?" She punched her forehead in self-flagellation. "I've been hunting for the right name for my revolutionary new wonder product since ages. 'Renacimiento' is perfect! You are, of course, too young to understand how our vaginas dry up as we age, but this unguent I've made is so gute they'll stay as juicy as at their peak! Oh, you cannot imagine how schön, how gemütlich I feel!"

"D'you plan to market it?"

"I must." A frown of consternation tempered her ebullience and her tone harshened, "Some sneaking rat in Germany has got my KinderGeld stopped. Now I must take my business seriously."

"It'll sell, I'm sure."

"When I was young like you I used to enjoy to make men excited, now..." she slipped off her Norwegian socks, sliding her feet into leather clogs, "I want only to make women happy. They'll be happy with this, I tell you." Her smile was triumphant, "It is so much more positive than stopping pregnancies."

Julia's memory jolted uneasily. "My mother mentioned you when I was pregnant with Alex. Did she...try that herself?"

"Frances? Huh, she had her own methods."

"Well, they didn't work with me!"

"You think she tried? Of course she didn't! She wanted you more than anything."

This was not what Julia had been led to believe, and she needed time to compose herself. Not wanting Marte to see her emotion, she studied the label with such intensity that it left its imprint on her retina for some while afterwards.

For several more days the JCBs remained idle, waiting for the flooded mud flats they had created to drain and dry.

"Such a pity it's not gonna be a lake," Marco lamented, rescuing his capsized sailboat from the jagged rocky shore.

"It'd be a crazy place for a lake," Alex pointed out, "directly above the village. What if it overflowed?"

"But people *are* silly."

Alex could not argue with that. Juanito's JCB was marooned in water, its neck rearing like the Loch Ness Monster, yet there seemed no rational reason why, if the other two drivers had had the prescience to leave their vehicles on the tarmac near the village, Juanito had failed to take the same precaution. Who was to say that this housing scheme, HOLIDAYLANDIA SL, was not the brainchild of a bunch of Juanitos? He smiled contentedly as he replayed the latest Juanito gaffe in his mind - apparently some English touristas had made sniggering remarks about the fat, bulging cheeks of Juanito's fleshy behind, and he had swaggered off convinced 'builder's bottom' was the apogee of compliments!

Eventually the work restarted. A fleet of lorries arrived ferrying hardcore and gravel, the experience with mud and rain having convinced them that a proper infrastructure of roads was necessary. It was Juanito's task to widen the track leading to Julia's so it could be properly surfaced. He had progressed as far as the high terrace wall which formed the boundary of her land, and she was trying not to be driven mad by the continuous noise of revving, braking, scraping, and thumping - when suddenly she realised there was no noise at all. Just ominous silence.

She raced out, cursing herself for not being more alert to the whereabouts of the boys, for not monitoring exactly how provocatively close Juanito had come to their land. Toad had been spotted there, and it was a danger spot in any case because the terrace wall had collapsed years ago and the steep incline was an unstable scree of rocks, stones and earth held in place by a mere tangle of brambles and convulvulus. As she ran, nightmare visions of Alex's bleeding headwound and Marco trapped beneath the blades of a bulldozer flashed before her eyes, and her legs lost all sensation yet they still propelled her.

When she reached the silent, stationary JCB she found, with a flood of relief, that both boys were unharmed and standing together, bending solicitously over Juanito who was half sitting, half lying on the ground. His face was greyish white, indistinguishable from the colour of the stones he had been tossing aside, and he was gulping for air as if winded by a blow from an iron fist in the abdomen - or an asthma attack. At first she feared the former, since

Alex had been making veiled threats ever since Juanito's manhandling of Marco, but their unequal physiques made this unlikely.

"He's trying to speak," Marco gesticulated at Juanito's gulping mouth.

"A bucket of cold water'll sort him out," Alex proposed.

"He should lie down," Julia said, "He's very pale. He'll faint if the blood can't flow to his brain."

Alex laughed scornfully, "*What* brain?"

They laid him as flat as the uneven terrain allowed. Gradually his breathing steadied, but his complexion remained waxen grey and his eyes flickered uneasily.

"P'rhaps he saw toad. That can be weird - unless you're used to it," Marco admitted. "Some people think they're witches."

A faint groan from Juanito was followed by the less agreable sound of wretching. Instinctively they retreated as the sour smell tainted the air.

"Dolores' empanadas," Marco rolled his eyes.

"Scotty's beer," Alex burped suggestively.

"Let's give him breathing space, he's clearly not fatally ill." Julia was feeling a little shaky now that the drama seemed over.

But Juanito was anxious not to be left alone. A faint whisper of words, and a mild gurgling sound accompanied by weak hand movements were all evident attempts to communicate. Eventually Julia overcame her distaste and bent close enough to hear his uncertain utterings.

"Una calavera....ahi dentro," were his whimpered words.

"He says there's a skull!" Julia translated, for despite their growing fluency skulls were scarcely everyday vocabulary. "He's rambling or hallucinating, and that might mean poison - I know the shepherd puts it down to kill foxes, because he warned me. Alex, I think you'd better call..."


But Marco's keen eyes had seen the source of Juanito's horror. His bulldozer had sliced into the base of the fallen wall, and, level with the bottom stones, still partly submerged in earth, was the unmistakable form of a human skull. It lay sideways on its cheek bone, staring sightlessly at them through hollow eye cavities, and a pale pink worm squirmed slowly through the hollow bridge of what was once a nose. Marco gripped Julia's arm, and for several seconds the three of them remained motionless, stunned by the incongruity and the unreality of it.

At some point in this silent vigil Alex broke away and fetched the more experienced JCB driver. He was not a man to ineffectually stand and stare.

Within minutes he had an old horse rug wrapped around Juanito, had phoned the Guardia Civil on his mobile, and had explained to Marco precisely why he should not touch the skull, let alone remove it to use as a bookend on his bedroom shelf.

Soon the Guardia jeep was racing up the track, bouncing on the ruts and skidding recklessly round the bends as if speed mattered because someone's life was in danger, whereas nothing could really look much deader than that skull. All three leapt from the vehicle with hands to their holsters, the drill they had presumably learnt in Guardia school for tackling the unexpected.

First at the scene was the Cabo who nodded curt recognition of Julia, perhaps remembering her as a face among many in the Degsy audience. He had an air of confident professionalism, but not so the plump young Guardia who ran at the skull like a terrier after a bone, and would have laid hands on it if his superior officer had not grabbed him back by the collar.

"Imbécil! The site must be perfectly preserved."

He lost no time radioing to base for some serious reinforcements; the big guns from Villahermosa. But within five minutes the response came through that Villahermosa had nothing big enough, so the message had been relayed to a higher level still, the Provincial Capital HQ.

The idea of *the* crack team of forensic experts, reverentially called 'los scientificos' visiting their little patch of Milagra and Montejoven so unnerved the young Guardia, who was already mortified by his reprimand, that he spent the long hour of waiting twitching nervously, constantly hitching up his trousers, buckling his belt or straightening his collar. The other two passed the time in relaxation, smoking cigarettes and chatting to the driver of the JCB, until they remembered that they ought to cordon off the area. Since no-one seemed to have any tape Julia, as a last resort, surrendered what was left of her roll covered in little red Santa Clauses, reindeer and sledges that Alex and Marco had used on their Christmas presents, and this was supported on several of Frances' erstwhile runner bean poles. Had the skull been able to witness the scene of his disinterment, he would have found it indeed bizarre.

Naturally the village buzzed with this latest news. It was far and away more exciting than the mystery building, but as with the building, different theories competed. Some supported the idea of the missing link - Milagra Man, but there were arguments in favour of almost any period of history: Stone Age, Iron Age, Bronze Age. There were others, more knowledgeable historically, who preferred to pin him to his location and ethnic origins, calling him Iberian, Phoenician, Roman. And yet another faction who were convinced he was much more recent: a fleeing Moor, a pursuing Christian, a blind bandit, a wandering Jew, a scurrilous highway robber, a lost shepherd, an unfortunate murder victim from the Civil War. Then again there were those who matched him to specific disappearances: a great uncle of Eulogio's who left the village bound for Argentina in 1931 but never arrived, César el loco from Montejoven who used to chase goats and wear women's dresses but vanished one October, and so and so on. The discussions were prolonged but never heated, and that evening everyone sat glued to their television set hoping that the discovery of 'Milagra Man' would feature on the national news. And there was a collective sigh of disappointment when it did not. Strangely enough, no-one seemed to remotely consider the possibility that it might be a woman.


Julia's privacy vanished. The area was cordoned off in a more professional manner, and the painstaking work of forensic investigation went slowly on, day after day, as the rest of the skeletal remains were delicately revealed and every grain of adjoining soil was removed milligramme by milligramme, scraped up, stored and labelled - then transfered to whatever hi-tech laboratory was sifting through the evidence and building up a picture of who, what, when and how.

A canopy of secrecy hung over the site of disinterment, but only Marco really suffered from an unbearable curiosity about the skeleton. He would skirt the area regularly, questioning whichever member of the team happened to be taking a break as to the height, weight, position, likely age and clothing of the recumbent man. All he really learnt was that nothing remained except the bones: no watch, clothing, hat or walking stick, although there was a vague rumour concerning a crumpled pair of leather boots.

"I reckon he's really old, 'cos he didn't even have a watch," he reported back. "D'you think they'll find others under our land? If they find any treasure, will it be there's or our's? I'd like coins, I told them already."

Otto was also an enthusiast, but the team were highly skilled at parrying all his attempts to discover more. He fervently supported the Civil War period faction, and was anticipating a thrilling connection to his bandolero with heavily bated breath, so that the slow progress of retrieval drove him almost to distraction.

"This man was betrayed by his best friend," he declared. "He died in a crouched, foetal position. He could not believe ze disloyalty..."

But Marco disagreed, "No, no, he was way, way older than that. He was a Roman. He didn't have a watch, and your bandolero would have, or how did he keep his appointments?"

And so they argued, on and on, divided by their views but gloriously united in their obsessive fascination.

# 8

After days of noise from the lorries, bulldozers and JCBs drilling, scraping and pounding the earth; and nearer still the silent sifting, extracting and burrowing that was going on around the skeleton, Julia decided they deserved a change of scene and a visit to the coast would be a welcome relief. She also had an ulterior motive for going to Villahermosa; she wanted to see Grant to find out what mischief he had planned with his Holidaylandia development.

Although only February, the coastal climate was more benign. Tulips and other flamboyant flowers were already blooming in the carefully tended formal gardens along the beach front promenades, and the dates were a sticky yellow spray in the waving palm trees. Around the castle ruins and the blue tiled dome of the Gothic church was an old medieval quarter, with cobbled streets and two storey houses whose wrought iron balconies were so close you could shake hands with your neighbour across the street, -or jump into his wife's bedroom if he was out, as the male tour guides liked to claim (with a wink at any unattached ladies in their group). When Frances first came to Spain her artist friends could afford to rent in this area; now all that kind of riff raff had been turned out and the place cleaned up to represent a medieval theme town. Yet without shops, without inhabitants, just end-to-end bars, cafés and restaurants.

Elsewhere the town was unashamedly modern with all the paraphernalia of a Mediterranean resort. Discos, high rise hotels, enough neon lighting to dazzle migrating birds, shops of every type and size from mega department stores to cubicle sized tabacaleras, restaurants from all over the world, and a whole street devoted to pleasing Brits with Irish pubs, fried breakfasts (served all day long), bars with big screens showing Premiership football, cream teas for the pensioners and last but not least, Bingo.

After two months away from London Julia had almost forgotten the skills of driving in traffic. She became uncharacteristically flustered by the flashing orange traffic lights, the cars which suddenly turned across her without signalling because their drivers were conducting heated arguments on their mobile phones or with their passenger, the myriads of scooters and motorbikes who zigzagged between the cars for the sheer fun of it, and the huge advert billboards that were deliberately placed so as to obscure the street names and the signposts.

Her jangled nerves were further bewildered by the constant commentary from Marco on the movements of fellow drivers, in front, alongside and behind, combined with a relentless barrage of contradictory memories and route instructions from both her passengers. Twice she clipped the curb avoiding an inswinging moped with a suicidal technique at roundabouts, and once she was shunted from the rear when she stopped at a red light no other driver bothered to obey.

After she had circled the area of the yacht marina three times looking for the road of bookshops, in search of All About Toads (Marco), Roman Pottery (herself) and Modern Germany (Alex), she had to fight back her tears and admit defeat by parking in the dark depths of an underground car park. Frances had always despised such civic obedience. She would never, ever park where it was legal to do so; instead she would block an entrance, straddle a pavement, or even double park on a busy road, saying half the fun was wondering if your car would be towed away by the time you returned. She might even be proud of the way she had died, crazily, at the wheel. For that was very much the Spanish attitude; dying in a car accident had a strong element of honour, combining just the right mix of bravery, recklessness and chance that was so revered in bull fighting.


After successfully buying the books and avoiding the department stores where Marco had been known to run riot in the past, they went to the beach. In the summer it was a blaze of colour, with ultra violet parasols for those who feared skin cancer, and multi-coloured ones for everyone else, flapping blue awnings on the chiringuitos from which floated appetizing smells of frying seafood, striped deckchairs, orange pedalos, mini-sails of every hue and all the vibrant colours of swimwear on all the different shades and tones of bare flesh lain out to tan on brightly coloured towels. Now though, unlike the sea front promenade, it looked wintry. It was bereft of boats or pedalos, and the chiringuitos had been dismantled leaving only the concrete slabs on which they had stood. Despite the sunlight twinkling on the waves the water was icy cold, and the recent storm had strewn the beach with a wavy line of driftwood, plastic bottles and blanched seaweed.

Hugging the far rocks were a dozen or more nudists, most of them shrivelled and gnarled and well into their eighties, staring at the sea with gimlet eyes and not moving a muscle, so that they looked to have been salted and left to dry like filleted bacalao. Elsewhere small children paddled in the rock pools hoovering the shallow water with their shrimping nets and giggling at the feel of sand between their toes, while plump young mothers spread margerine and cream cheese on cuts of bread.

There was also a small group of teenage girls with long, slim legs and bikini bottom thongs, lustrous hair and firm, topless breasts, sharing secrets and laughter as they sat conspiratorially in a huddle. Alex glanced at them periodically while he dredged the sand for fragments of broken glass that had been smoothd by the sea and the sand, until they had become little cloudy blue or turquoise ovals that Marco was convinced could be passed off as precious gems, privately reassuring himself that they were no match for Lise.

"Why's everyone here so old?" Marco asked, despite being perfectly aware of Alex's wandering eyes.

"I can see babies," Julia contradicted.

"I mean, where are people our age?"

"You know exactly where they are, Marco. In school. You should count yourself extremely lucky not to be there too."

"Oh can't we stay out in Spain? I'd love to be here until the end of summer."

"We'll see."

Julia was amazed to hear herself use those words. The very words she had hated vehemently as a child, knowing they were either meaningless or showed that the decision, the one you didn't want, had already been made. And that truth held good, for she *had* been silently favouring a return to England even though Frances' affairs were far from sorted. Partly because she was weary of being hemmed in by lorries and forensic investigators, partly for professional and financial reasons. The dance company would soon be returning from their winter tour of Japan, so she'd have to be in London come the spring if she wanted to feature in their summer repertoire.

The breath of fresh sea air had temporarily dissolved one knot of trouble, but the casual elegance of the young girls on the beach confronted her with a new anxiety, one that had barely occurred to her until now. As she watched their fluid movements, their naturalness, their pride in their bodies, she realised that her scarred breast had robbed her of that. Until now she had, like them, been unselfconsciously topless on a beach; but from now on she would have to deal with the consciousness of its mutilation. And even thinking like that made her guilty, for her problem was mere vanity compared to the many, far more serious disabilities others had to cope with.

The offices of Holidaylandia S.L. overlooked the new marina and exuded success. The marble foyer was enormous. Rare cacti sprouted from beds of pebbles, fountains tinkled and tropical fish shimmied in blue tinted tanks where bursts of bubbles operated on a timer to oxygenate the water. The ceiling was alive with spotlights and the dark green marble floor polished to reflect them. What was lacking, though, was any indication where to go - even to find Reception.

After quite a few wrong turns and attempts to open locked rooms Julia finally found a desk behind rotating doors, but it was unmanned. The air conditioning must have been stuck on maximum, because the air was so chilled they began to shiver, and Julia wondered if this explained the absence of any workforce. Finally a woman in a wool suit appeared, dabbing her congested red nose with a handkerchief. It took time for Julia to convince her that she did indeed know Grant and intended to see him without a prior appointment, but finally she agreed to phone through.


Grant was sitting in an olive green leather chair looking casual, but Julia noted with amusement the fresh tang of Listerine on his breath as he got up to greet her. He made a show of surprise at her visit, had a stab at sounding upset by Frances' death, and tried to play down his sense of immense well-being as he showed them his panoramic view of the castle ruins. He pointed proudly to the church cupola and the old clock tower, the Sierra del Moro rearing behind it and, sweeping round in an almost full circle, the yachts moored in the marina, the distant lighthouse guarding the bay, the sea front with little ant-like people scurrying far below, and, with a flick of his gold Rolexed wrist, way out to sea where the blue of sky and water merged on the horizon. He even tried to quell his annoyance when Marco spilt an ashtray whilst admiring the view.

"The kids can go on this computer while we talk," he offered magnanimously, and the Listerine again flew out with the words.


Julia was offered a chair that was similar, yet smaller. She tried not to look him up and down too obviously to check on things like hairline, teeth, skin and waistline, all areas that can suffer as thirty turns forty - a rough calculation of his current age. He had managed to hold the visible signs of ageing effectively at bay, - a few frown lines, minor crows' feet, a hint of a future paunch, but nothing extreme. His eyes meanwhile surreptitiously reconnoitered her body, but she had grown from an immature adolescent into a woman in her prime, so she could sense his disappointment that in age, agility and fitness she had the clear advantage. But not in status, as his affluent surroundings and sense of control made him very comfortably aware.

"So, what can I do for you?" There was a teasing note in his voice.

"You can't *do* anything. But I'd like to know the full extent of your Holidaylandia scheme, since it's on my doorstep."

"Hmm. On screen or 2D?"

"On screen I guess. That way I can enjoy the total experience."

But he didn't seem to notice the sarcasm.

Ten minutes later she emerged from his audo-visual booth with surround sound and wrap-around screen in a daze, having experienced a computerised world that could have won oscars for its special effects. She sunk into the chair to regain her sense of equilibrium. Until now she had not imagined any similarity between Florida and Milagra, but the only difference had been the sloping terrain and the lack of everglades and alligators. Milagra was inconveniently hilly, though it was clear they planned to flatten as much as they could.

She sipped the chilled mineral water he handed her with an unsteady hand, not registering the label on the dispenser 'Agua Mineral de Milagra', and clung to a present reality that seemed already supplanted.

"So, whaddaya think?" His Mid-Atlantic drawl had suddenly materialised. "Doan' blame me, they wa-anted me to design this thing."

"It's hard to put into words - polite ones, anyway. Isn't there any call for prior consultation on changes like this? I thought you were obliged these days to consult local residents...and I can't believe there aren't regulations on building materials, ensuring they faintly reflect local tradition."

Grant looked at her pityingly, shaking his head, "You lived here half your life yet you come up with obsolete, crazy words like consult, regulation and tradition. Jesus! Getta grip. This is Euroland Spain, in the twennyfirst century...if you want Tuscany-Italy or Provence-France you came to the wrong place."

"I never came, I was born here. And please - I'm not a prospective buyer, don't talk jargon to me."

"You know perfectly well 'traditional' building's a dirty word round here. Everyone wants modern. Ultra-modern. Just ask your boys" and he waved his hand in the direction of Marco and Alex who were glued like limpets to his computer screen, "if they wanna live in an old world of well buckets and woodfires, or in the modern one of computer technology and central heating."

Julia sighed. "Don't twist my meaning. There are plenty of better ways to combine modern and traditional."

Grant shrugged his shoulders. "Well, should you wa-ant to sell your place you know where to find me. Though to be frank, it'll soon look kinda weird in its new surroundings, but worth a try as an olde worlde restaurant."

While waiting for the traffic lights to turn green Marco suddenly nudged her.

"Hey, isn't that Colin?" He waved at the familiar figure in an open shirt slinking guiltily out of the Bingo Hall. "Hi Colin!" he yelled at street-stopping volume.

It took ten minutes of gentle driving, by which time they were well beyond the outskirts of Villahermosa - or VH as Colin called it - before Colin's face simmered down and lost its flush of embarrassment.

"Awfully good of you to give me a lift," he said, "my car's laid up at the garage and that could be a month. But..." his blush returned "I'd be really obliged if you'd keep mum about the Bingo. Reggie'd never let me hear the end of it."

They dropped Colin on the outskirts of Milagra and continued up their track, the lower section of which was now double its original width and freshly tarmacked. Ever since the investigators had blocked off her entrance she had taken to parking her car some two hundred metres short of the house, but to her surprise this space was now occupied by a MISTERVISTA coach, doubtless the same one that visited Scotty's bar every week.

"Que pasa?" Julia asked the coach driver, who was sprawled on his seat, a large white handkerchief covering his face.

He sat up, looking sheepish, "They just wanted to take photos. It's been in the news, you see - I couldn't really stop them."

The troupe of tourists were already flocking back towards the coach, some quivering with indignation at the brusque manner with which the forensics had ordered them to keep away from the cordoned area. They parted to let her through, staring in curiosity but not daring to ask questions because her annoyance was so palpable. She heard the clicking of cameras and was aware of a barrage of flashlights, but the strangest sensation was this sudden - but unmistakable – awareness of their hostility.

It was as if they had decided *she* bore responsibility for the skeleton's death. Suddenly she felt like some key suspect arriving at a murder trial, flanked by a hostile crowd, but without the normal protection of a police cordon and a blanket thrown over her head to hide her identity.

One of the forensic officers was re-erecting the 'no entry' sign. Shaking his head at the departing coach he greeted her almost accusingly,

"Your compatriots have no respect for anything, or anyone."

"I don't identify with people like that. I prefer - like most of us, I think - to mind my own business and live in peace."

He understood immediately. He added quietly, more compassionately, "Don't worry. We've almost finished here. We'll be gone tomorrow."

"Your skeleton has been so fantastic for my book," revelled Otto, gripping her hand with bone fracturing firmness. "You cannot believe how well it has loosened tongues in ze village. Before, they remembered nothing. Now, I have been informed of seven mysterious disappearances, men from ze village who vanished in '36 or '37 and no trace of them ever found!"

"I'm glad it's brought someone happiness," Julia answered, bleakly rescuing her crushed hand from his grasp and listening anxiously for rattling, broken bones.

"So, Marco, what news of your Roman Gladiator?"

"Same as usual - he's dead." Marco thought for a moment, "But there is an update. His body's finally gone to be cleaned up for the museum."

"Ach so. In that case we will soon learn ze truth."

Otto sounded deflated, almost mournful. He had enjoyed his recent sparring with Marco, in fact their pleasure had been mutual. Marco had never before met someone who, like himself, so thoroughly enjoyed a good quarrel. Alex and Julia got irritated by squabbles and seemed to prefer harmony, and were even willing to compromise to get it. They simply didn't understand or appreciate the delights of all out discord. And they weren't alone. He had discovered to his bewilderment that most kids wanted friends to agree with them, think like them, go along with them. It was weird. So Otto was a rare soulmate; he was showing Marco new methods to wind others up, and how to air outrageous views and unlikely perspectives without risk of violent recrimination. There was a fine line, he had explained. Stepping over it could be fatal.

Privately Marco had lost faith in his Roman theory. Alex had sown the first seeds of doubt. He had pointed out that the skeleton, as far as he could tell from the position of the skull - because he had been prevented by the careful screening from seeing its torso and limbs - was too near the surface to be Roman. Alex, who knew more about these things, said more topsoil would be on top of him if he had been there for two thousand years. But then Alex had backtracked, wondering if topsoil fell on stone walls - perhaps the wind and rain kept them clean - so maybe he could be Roman after all... Then again the lack of coins was compelling evidence that the guy was not Roman, for Romans were known for their carelessness with the contents of their pockets. One thing Marco did know for sure - this guessing was far more enjoyable than knowing, so he privately hoped the news would be long delayed.

Alex had brought his new book on Germany to show Lise. They had to sit with their bodies almost touching as they looked through the pictures together, and he admired the sheen of little golden hairs on her bare shins as she drew her knees up to her chin and laughed at the photo of mud spattered pigs from Schleswig-Holstein. She almost touched his ear with her lips when she whispered,

"For God's sake, you must say nothing to Marte about my meeting with my father. Now that her KinderGeld has been stopped she will think it was him, out of spite, and she will think I must have told him. Not true of course, but it's what she'll think."

"Why would I tell her? You know I can keep secrets, I'm not a fool."

"Of course not - oh, everyone is so touchy these days!" and she laughed again, and Alex in spite of other things was swept along by her gaiety.

Julia told Marte about her visit to Grant and described for her the grid plan streets, and the range of villas from Torremolinos (basic model), to Salamanca (top of the range) via Toledo (standard model). Despite price differences which affected the interior décor, room sizes and extras like the dimensions of the satellite dish and how remotely controlled the double doors to the garage were, they all had identical Grecian porticos, Florentine balustrades, New England wooden decks with hanging baskets of red geraniums overlooking kidney shaped swimming pools and outdoor Jacuzzis; and they would all soon be smothering the slopes above Milagra.

Marte listened with an expression of horror, but Julia sensed a definite hint of Schadenfreude that this monster of Holidaylandia was to be on Julia's flank of the mountain, not hers. Marte also tried to suppress her exultation as she noted that this sudden surge of publicity, due in part to 'Milagra Man' and in part to the future development, would most likely boost the sales of both Otto's book and her new Renacimiento line.

"It would be so gute if you could do me this little favour," she thrust a jar of milk white ointment at Julia, "I need to know if this adds to the sexual pleasure of younger persons, for that of course would mushroom – is zat ze correct word? - ze sales. Perhaps you could try it out."

"I'm not the person to ask. I'm not in a relationship at the moment."

"Ach so. But that would not be a problem, one does not need a man, for sure you ah, pleasure yourself sometimes, isn't it so?"

Julia smiled warily, "You'd be better off with a wider sample. Why not ask Juanito - or Grant - to recruit young lovelies to trial it for you?"

Marte sighed sorrowfully and shoved the rejected bottle back onto the top shelf, where it was unlikely to arouse Lise's curiosity. "Because zey are not discreet, and zey do not take my medicines seriously."

"There's one thing I would like. D'you have something to heal scar tissue?"

"But of course. I have zinc ointment, calendula cream and lavender oil, all my own preparations. Let me see zis scar."

"To be honest I can hardly bear to look at it myself."

Marte stifled an exclamation of dismay and seemed to stumble backwards, but quickly regained her composure and inspected the scarring more thoroughly.

"But zis is a nasty wound Julia! There is still bad inflammation under the aureola, it should perhaps have had stitches. You can even see ze marks of teeth. How in Gott's name did it happen?"

"I knew I should have gone to a doctor, or seen you, but" she shrugged "I didn't. And the reason I didn't is because of the obvious teeth marks. They belong to that bastard Jorgen."

"Madre mia." Marte looked genuinely upset. "Vot a schwein...and he looked so cute."


She searched her shelves and gathered a motley collection of salves whose healing properties she then described in detail to Julia. It was while she was showing her the gently caressing, circular motion in which the calendula cream should be massaged round the damaged aureola so as to restimulate circulation and break down the lumps of scar tissue that Otto poked his head around the door.

"Oh - *excuse me* ladies," and he vanished immediately.

"Don't worry. He can sink what he wants, but he has too many embarrassing habits of his own to make much of this." She patted a clear jellylike substance over the layers of cream.


"Let's see if they admit zis skeleton was murdered," Otto said when they were leaving, "my guess is there'll be a cover up. Zere always is when it comes to reopening brutalities from ze War. So, even if zey say he's more modern, or an ape or a Roman or a Greek, we'll know" and he winked at Marco "zey are deceiving us."

## 9

Reggie had a new regime of alcohol-free mornings. Not a drop was permitted past his lips until after two, and even then only with food. It had successfully drained the excess fluid from his body, most of it centred on the belly, so that he now walked with a positively youthful spring, but Colin felt anxious some of his admirable optimism might have been leeched away. They currently shared a regular mid-morning cafe con leche *without* brandy whilst tackling the crossword.

"I say," Colin's lips quivered with foam from the coffee, "word is this Holidaylandia caper is intended for chaps my age, retirees on pensions. Seems they bring in the dosh without clogging the job market. And don't run riot or cause trouble. Problem is, my doctor says - you know Jaime whatsit - they put a godawful strain on the health system."

"Yeah, I've heard it'll be a kind of retirement park, with en suite golf, medical centre, private hospital wing, nursing home *and* crematorium. Even Bingo."

Colin looked up sharply, but Reggie's comment seemed innocently unbarbed and he resumed, "No-one's more devastated than Juanito. He'd pinned his hopes on having loads of luscious young things right on the doorstep; now he's having to re-adjust to the grim truth they'll be in the fifty to eighty age range."

"Alcalde un ano, que tiempo de gano," announced the cockatiel as Vicente left a coin on the counter to cover his treble shot of local brandy.

"That bird's a socialist," Colin opined, "he always has a go at Vicente."

But Reggie shook his head "He's too clever for politics. Anyway, he has a pop at everyone, you mean you haven't heard yours? Ha, it's apt enough: 'Este gringo, como le gusta el Bingo!' They say he has the highest IQ in Milagra."

"He's a cheeky brat who deserves to be shot!" Colin slammed his fist angrily onto the table so that the coffee cups rattled and the dregs spattered his sleeve. The noise triggered a bloodcurdling shriek from the bird, who stared accusingly at Colin and hissed, "Asesino, asesino!"

Colin shot to his feet and was half-way to the door before Reggie could intervene with a calming pat on the back. "He's not accusing *you* of murder Colin. Look at his expression; he's in a philosophical state, he's merely postulating the idea that a murder has occurred, hence someone is a murderer."

"You mean the skeleton?"

"Well, he *might* have been a murderer, but the murder under investigation is one in which he was clearly the victim."

"You're like that bird Reggie, sometimes I suspect it's you who tutors him."

But even though Colin huffed for a few more minutes, Reggie had succeeded in mollifying him, and they completed the crossword in an affable mood.


Reggie arrived at Julia's shortly before sunset. She noticed his newly trim figure and, like Colin, worried that he had lost his good spirits because he brought an air of troubled seriousness. He volunteered for a spell in goal while the boys thundered penalty kicks at him, then brushed off the mud and mounted the steps to where Julia was waiting.

"Can we talk privately?"

"We'll go to my mother's old studio, same as before."

Julia wanted to remain light hearted, but his smile had a sadness that warned of unwelcome news.


Alex and Marco wandered down to the bend in the camino where the forensic team had dug out the terrace wall, an area cordoned off for so long it now felt unfamiliar. Odd to think that a body had lain there all their lives without anyone knowing. Except that possibly someone did know, someone who had kept it a guilty secret. Alex wondered if some of the nightly creaks or occasional shuddering vibrations that had woken him from time to time had been the ghostly wanderings of the dead man's spirit, trying vainly to attract their attention and encourage them to seek him out. His eyes scanned the descending flight of terraces to where the scars of future Holidaylandia obliterated them, wondering how many bones from the beginning of time lay hidden beneath the layers of soil and would never be found.


They studied the site with curiosity, noting the careful incisions, the stone by stone extraction at the base of the wall and the way it had been secured from further collapse by the insertion of an iron girder. They discovered the wheel marks of Juanito's JCB and the skid mark as he braked in a panic at the first glimpse of those empty eye sockets. Then Alex saw a small pair of heavily lidded living eyes lurking in the shadows of the base stones just to the left of the skeleton's resting place.

"There's toad."

But Marco showed none of his previous enthusiasm at the rare encounter. Instead of the earlier delight that used to dance in his eyes Alex noted a sombre, baleful look, and Marco kicked a stone in toad's direction, but without deliberate aim.

"I've gone off toad lately," he said with an eloquent sigh.

Alex was tactful enough not to celebrate but to wait patiently for Marco to expand on this sudden reversal.

"I know, now, why toad's been hanging round this spot. My book says they like dark, damp hideaways and feed off maggots and insects and stuff. So, he must've got his drink from the Fuente and his food here – 'cos the reason the maggots and worms were here was down to that skeleton.... He's disgusting and I wish I'd never stroked him."

Alex was silent, absorbing the various threads in this outburst. He decided not to question the reincarnation aspect immediately.

"Well you can't really blame toad for his diet. Everything tries to survive as best it can. You can't expect toads to ignore juicy maggots out of respect for a dead human. Maggots are useful 'cos they clean up smelly dead flesh, and toads are useful 'cos they eat up bugs. It's called the food chain Marco."

"I don't *blame* him. I just don't feel keen on him anymore."

"Why d'you keep saying *him*?"

"Oh, I know what you're thinking...what an eejit I was believing he was gran..."

"No. I just wanna' know why you now think it's a male."

This was nearly the truth, but in spite of himself and his better judgment Alex now felt sorry for both Toad and Frances, irrational though he knew it to be. Contrary to all his previous assumptions he realised he would actually miss the passionate intensity of Marco's daily quest for Toad. Three weeks ago he never would have believed that it comforted him to imagine Frances was not entirely dead and gone. - Well, not exactly that, more that death is not final.

"I'm not sure it's male but I'm pretty sure it's old. That's why it can't be gran. 'Cos if reincarnation means being reborn then this toad should only be eleven weeks old now, and only eight days' old when I first saw it! If it *ever* was a person, therefore, it has to be someone who died between ten and twenty years ago."


Reggie, without the comfort of paperwork to occupy his hands, played imaginary piano chords on his upper thighs while he waited for Julia to join him.

"Obviously there's nothing official yet, but working on gut feeling and some credible whisperings I've a grim idea this skeleton died quite recently. Within the timescale of Frances owning this place, anyway."

Julia felt the warmth leave her, "What are you implying? That she *knew* about it?"

Reggie had expected hostility. Julia seemed oversensitive to any perceived criticism levelled at herself or Frances, as if she had singlehandedly fought off waves of attackers and detractors ever since babyhood - which perhaps she had. He had already forearmed himself by consuming all his self-imposed daily quota of alcohol to prepare for what he knew would be a difficult discussion, so a bleak evening of abstinence lay ahead.

"No. You know I trusted and admired your mother. I'm only trying to prepare you for what may turn out an intrusive investigation. It's a legal duty to report a death, Julia. This skeleton was close to her house – that's all I'm saying."

He paused, aware that his throat was dry and his forehead cold. He would have liked to make some physical gesture of comfort to Julia, but resisted, not wanting to be misinterpreted.

"I'm trying to anticipate their tactics so you're not taken by surprise. The Montejoven Guardia are bastards, you know that. If they get to spearhead a murder investigation it'll go to their heads. They'll arrive in the dark, bitter cold of five in the morning to interrogate. You know how it works."

Julia digested the news in silence. She had never subscribed to Marco's Roman fantasies or remotely considered anything earlier. Nor had she seriously entertained romantic scenarios of the time of Moorish rule, but she had been swayed by Otto's ideas concerning the bitter community and family divisions and the many interfactional murders at the time of the Civil War. Most records - of property ownership and population - had been lost or burnt during the war. Many people had therefore disappeared without trace and were never officially on file, but were remembered merely on a personal level by the indelible sadness of close family and friends. Also, the position of the skeleton, slightly below the base stones of the wall, seemed perfectly consistent with a time gap of seventy odd years. And, she had to admit, owing to the close proximity of Eulogio's land, she had been quietly assuming that his elder brothers must have been complicit in the death.

Bandoleros, she now knew, mostly operated for the Republican side, working as gun runners and procurers of equipment or information, and frequently passing over enemy lines. Some of them were into double dealing though, and if Otto's was one of these then Eulogio's brothers would have certainly treated him to a grisly death, followed by a secret burial on the mountainside, and if most of his body was still intact (apparently that was the case) that would be a lucky fate for a traitor.

"I can't think how you get your inside information," she said with mild acidity. "Otto really had me convinced..."

"I did say it's not certain. But there are early whisperings in the village. The middle daughter of Enrique el Fontanero is going out with the young Guardia officer - the one with barely a brain cell - so of course he tells her things he shouldn't, like top secret or highly confidential info." Reggie looked relieved that humour was still permissable.

"Do these 'whisperings' divulge how he died?"

"No." Reggie, now that the worst of the tension seemed over, cast his eye along the shelf where Frances' bottles still lived. "Excuse the presumption, but I rather need something fiery to wash down this mineral water."

Julia was happy for an excuse to leave the room for ice cubes to accompany his stiff measure of vodka. He had very obviously been drinking before he came, and she felt uncomfortable with the way his eyes kept wandering up and down her body, as if he were either mentally undressing her or - almost worse - removing her flesh and imagining her a skeleton! The sight of Alex and Marco approaching the house with a muddy reptilian creature half-wrapped in a towel was almost a welcome diversion.

"*Not* in the kitchen!" she shouted.

Alex came inside to explain. "It's only toad. He's got an injured leg and can't hop - Oh I know that sounds contradictory, seeing as hopping *is* on one leg, but...y' know what I mean."

"Well, I'll have a look while you take Reggie this."

She inspected the leg. It appeared to have been crushed by a stone and had dark brown encrustaceons around the damage. She wondered idly if cold blood was a different colour and coagulated differently to warm. Was she looking at a healthy scab? Or the first, ominous signs of gangrene?

"I'll tape it. Let's hope it's not infected."

"If he can't move properly, will he live?" Marco asked, but with none of the fervour she expected.

"I don't know, *you're* the toad expert. I'd put him where he's close to water and hope for the best."

So a few minutes later Alex and Marco carried a subdued toad, who seemed depressed by the stickiness of the Calendular cream and the whiteness of the tape, up to the Fuente.

"Just supposing he *had* been reincarnated only recently, and was to die again now that he's gotten hurt, do you think he'd get reincarnated again? Or d'you kind of miss a go, as punishment for being careless and getting killed too often, like twice in two months?"

Alex sighed. "Marco! I thought you'd just disproved the whole possibility of toad being gran, on at least two grounds. What *are* you on about now?"

"Nothing. Just wondering."

Alex placed toad gently out of sight behind a clump of foxgloves, and within seconds he had vanished, blending in with the dark, damp shadows and the chill vapours of the Fuente.


When Julia returned to the studio the evening light was already fading and Reggie sitting in near darkness, so that the first indicator of his whereabouts was the noise of crunching as he chewed the ice cubes to squeeze that last beneficial droplet from his vodka.

"I don't want you to get unduly worried about this skeleton business. Frances won't be the only focus of their investigation. They'll trawl through the records of everyone in and around Milagra who's ever had the tiniest scrape with the law. Plus all the odd balls, misfits, eccentrics and anyone whose face they don't like. They'd pick on me if they could, but I'm too recent an arrival here."

"You make it sound like murder. I thought you said the cause of death hadn't been revealed. Couldn't it've just been an accident?"

"Of course. But life in the Cuartel must be deadly. There can't be many thrills to traffic offences, bar licenses, a bit of drunk and disorderliness and the odd petty theft. A skeleton is a field day. They'll make the most of it." Then he lent forward, lowering his voice. "We'd better pray they don't discover she was trying to put a stop to the development, because they'll assume she had a sinister motive for doing so."


After he had gone Julia's eyes rested on the distant lights of Milagra village. At night, with all the disturbed earthworks of future Holidaylandia hidden in darkness, it looked as it always had - a peaceful Spanish mountain village. She thought back to her childhood perceptions of it, and how Frances must have seen it when she first bought the house. She was thirty at the time, the same age as Julia now, and she must have had high hopes for her new life because at that point she had no real responsibilities and was perfectly able to support herself from her Roman pots. She had just cashed in her few malt whisky shares, for although her two brothers were meant to inherit the entire hoard, through some slip of the pen her father inadvertently gave her a small bequest.

This money, smuggled from England inside the cork frame of her favourite bright green stack heeled boots (this was the era of the so-called 'dollar premium', when the legal allowance for Brits travelling abroad was only £50) soon made its way across the Pyrenees, southwards down the old single lane coast road clogged with lorries, eventually veering westwards at Villahermosa and winding through the mountainous hinterland until it reached Milagra.

When she let it be known she was looking for an old ruin, habitable if possible, she was shown almost anything that was one stone piled upon another. Sometimes she would be proudly escorted to a mountain thicket of wild brambles, and told that the ruin lay hidden somewhere within, - once the brambles were burnt she would see it and certainly fall in love with it. Other times she would find what seemed the perfect ruin, only to discover that although most of the family was eager to sell, one obstinate member refused or held out for an outlandish figure, and the delicate negotiations would degenerate into an allout family row which raged through the village for days. Eventually she came across Eulogio who showed her the farmhouse. It had hay in one room, husked almonds in another, and two mules chomping at the manger in the third. She made up her mind immediately, and the money found its way straight into Eulogio's pocket without his wife knowing and subtracting her usual cut.

At that time there were very few foreigners in Milagra. Colin dated from that period, but Julia could not remember exactly how or why he came. She had vague memories of being told he had been honourably discharged from the army due to an incurable skin irritation from handling something secret and sinister. Supposedly this rare cutaneous disorder would improve in a sunny climate, and maybe it had, but not completely because Colin still spent a good deal of his time scratching and itching and breaking out in rashes, avoiding cypress trees, geraniums and too much direct sunlight.

After Colin came a steady flow of hippie types in VW vans who rented empty casitas between Milagra and Montejoven. The men were into crafts like leather work, stained glass, pottery and jewelry; while the women either did more of the same or knitted chunky wool sweaters and bobble hats or, like Marte, explored natural dyes and homemade clothing and even delved into the mysteries of herbal remedies and ancient superstitious cures. Julia could vaguely recall mothering groups of bare bottomed toddlers with muddy hands and honey-smeared faces. She must have been about four or five at the time. She'd enjoyed their sense of fun and the way they followed her everywhere, but was less keen on the thick black clouds of flies that swarmed all over them, attracted by the honey and their total lack of potty training.

Alex interrupted her reverie by slipping quietly into the room to hunt for the R - S volume of Frances' old set of encyclopaedias.

"Did I overhear Reggie say the skeleton died quite recently?"

"Apparently that's the latest news, but it may not be the last."

"That's a bit creepy. I'd much rather he was really old."

Julia took a deep breath and absent mindedly swept the desiccated body of a dead bumble bee from the window sill.

"So would I Alex, believe me." She noticed his anxious face and felt she should change the subject, aware that it was close to bedtime and knowing he was a vivid dreamer. She noticed the encyclopaedia, "What're you looking up?"

"Oh - just 'reincarnation'." He tried to sound offhand.

"In connection with the skeleton?" she asked sharply.

"No, no... Marco's interested too," he answered hurriedly, "in fact you might know enough to satisfy him. Like, does everyone get the chance to be reincarnated? And are you reborn immediately you die? And do you start your next life as a baby, or at the age you died?"

Julia chuckled, "Well, I'm not exactly an authority but...for those who believe in reincarnation, Hindus and Buddhists I think, everyone is reincarnated but you have to wait for forty days after your death. And most definitely you start your next life at the beginning, at birth."

"Thanks."

Alex gave a relieved grin and almost ran out of the room, stopping momentarily to jam the volume carelessly back on the wrong shelf.


An hour or so later Julia was also in bed, her half-conscious mind swirling with ideas of mysticism and reincarnation. The latter brought back to her some of the more bizarre people Frances had had dalliances with. There was one particular weirdo, a Frenchman (or was he Swiss?) who laid claim to a dazzling pedigree of reincarnations which included a few Pharoahs and, in whatever was the correct chronological order: Moses, Jesus, Michaelangelo, Newton, Mozart, Sitting Bull, Gandhi and, most recently, Vilayat Khan. With all those wonderful accumulated skills and intelligences he could have been an acclaimed genius in any number of spheres, but Mozart and Vilayat Khan had swung things in favour of music.

He was in truth a decent violinist. Sometimes he played so fast (prestissimo) that only his Alaskan huskie dog could hear it. It would yowl mournfully in accompaniment, which he called harmony - but Julia was sure was agony. He constantly polished Frances' murkily cloudy mirrors because he said failure to reflect was extremely bad for people's auras, and the shine on a clean mirror was the only way to attract creatures of the spirit world. He also spent an awfully long time in front of these mirrors, checking out their sheen, smiling at his reflection, and sometimes plucking an imperfect eyebrow.

One night - he had only lasted two or three in all - he had an argument with Frances about artistic talent, how to recognise it, and who was genuinely endowed with it. He was tempted to shatter one of her recently reassembled Roman amphora (not a work of art but only a common craft, in his opinion, since it lacked both originality and any spark of inspiration) at the height of his pique, but at the last moment he restrained himself and simply yelled,

> "You stupeed stuck up beetch! You know narthing, you are hardly even four thousand years old, and my speereet is nearly twenty four thousand years on this earth. Only Bob Dylan and Joan Baez are as old as me!" (or words to that effect.)

The reason Julia remembered this so clearly was because she was hiding under the table at the time, terrified at the possible consequences if he did indeed break the amphora, and none too sure how Frances would take the 'stupeed stuck up beetch' part. For Frances was commandingly tall, with strikingly luxurious dark red hair, clear green eyes and the lively Celtic temperament which supposedly goes with them. Normally, if anyone lost their rag and hurled abuse, it was her; she was completely unused to being on the receiving end. But to Julia's intense relief Frances burst out laughing. She wagged her bony index finger at him, shook her head and laughed like a woman possessed. He was so affronted he walked out the door and never returned.

That was Julia's first introduction to the concept of reincarnation.

She turned over sleepily, smiling at the recollection. Then suddenly, like a bolt of summer lightning, the full reality of Reggie's warning words "they might assume she had a sinister motive" struck her. If it proved to be the case that the skeleton's death was dated at a time when her mother owned the farmhouse, then this dead person could be any of the countless men who came to visit her mother, day or night, lover, would-be lover, friend or enemy. With the black horror mood that engulfs one sometimes late at night after an uneasy evening and an unaccustomed couple of vodkas embittered by orange, she played in her mind's eye the sequential scene following on from her mother's crazed laughter.

She saw, from between the fluted table legs, the arrogant strutting departure of Jean Paul - for want of his real name - who strode off without a backward glance of rancour or contempt. She heard more than saw the winding down of her mother's hysterical outburst of unreal mirth, and in slow motion cinematography she focused on the close-up frame of Frances' face, caught by the candlelight as the last reflex movements of dying laughter converted into an ugly, demented snarl of fury.

Then (although the visuals swirled and pulsed with a dreamlike quality) she saw her mother's strong right arm reach for the heavy cast iron saucepan hanging on a brass hook from one of the kitchen rafters. Tremulously she followed her mother's long, purposeful strides along the gravel path, down the flight of stone steps, and across the almond terrace. Scrambling, whimpering as soundlessly as she could, she tried not to lose touch with her mother's faster pace and half climbed, half fell down the lowish five foot wall separating the almond grove from the olive grove below it. The silvery green olive leaves picked up whatever pale moonlight there was, and Jean Paul's retreating white shirt also seemed to shimmer with a strange, nightly fluorescence. She was aware of her mother's shadowy form blotting out the whiteness of the shirt, and imagined more than saw the dark shape of her raised arm, and heard, despite her fists stuck in her ears to muffle all sound, a sickening thump as the saucepan made contact with flesh and bone.

It did not end there. Other sounds reached her as she lay writhing on the ground, a low groaning, sharp muttered words, a curse, and then a deep rumbling sound like an earthquake trapped in the bowels of the mountain, and stones clattering and clanging on top of each other, followed by the slow slithering of descending earth.


Gradually full consciousness returned and her shaky hand reached for the bedside light switch. She sat up in bed. Cold sweat had dampened her hair and lay in a runnel on the fold of her belly; also she had wrenched the sheet away from the bedbase and her legs were so entangled in it that she could barely twitch them, let alone manoeuvre to stand up. So she remained sitting, listening to the rapid beating of her heart and trying to take stock of what had just occurred. She must have fallen asleep without realising it, and her final waking thoughts must have contorted into the horrific version of fictional experiences she had just been through.

In many ways it was similar to the nightmare she had about the car and her mother's death, equally vivid, equally terrifying; but in the grim, haunting suggestibility of it, and her feeble helplessness as an outsider to the horror, it was infinitely, infinitely worse. She had a powerful temptation to wake Alex, just to cuddle somebody, to feel human body warmth, but she resisted it. He needed sleep and he needed peace of mind, she had never foisted her childhood onto him and must not start now. She unwound the sheet and freed her cramped legs, then hobbling from the tingling of returning circulation she struggled to the kitchen and warmed some milk in a pan, adding far more honey than was healthy. Her eyes flickered up to the rafter and she was profoundly relieved to see no cast iron saucepan, and mercifully no sign that a hook had ever been screwed there.

## 10

S he awoke to thick fog. The air was waterlogged and every surface sweated icy beads of moisture. They hung from the leaf tips, elongating into silver lozenges until they could cling no more and fell with the softest plop. It was like an English November morning or a sudden sea fog rolling off the Channel, not a phenomenon she associated with early Spanish spring.

But in the village everyone reminded her it was a regular February occurence. Often, in the final days of almond blossom, when the new leaves sprout and petals fall like snowflakes, the fog arrives stealthily overnight. It attacks the weakest embryonic almonds with a fatal mildew, leaving them stillborn on the branch. It comes to remind us we can't control nature, some said. But others that it was the wrath of God.

Dolores was of the latter persuasion, and, coincidently, always believed God was angry with the exact same people as herself. She revelled in these cold, dark, dank early mornings because then the arduous task of lighting and stoking the wood-burning bread oven became a pleasure. She was in such good spirits, in fact, that she had whipped up a batch of almond mantecas topped with marzipan.

"Aren't you scared up there on the mountain, so near that ghoulish skeleton?" she asked solicitously, sucking a burnt finger and making the sign of the cross.

"Well he's dead so he can't harm me now." Julia laughed it off, then admitted, "You could be right. I've not been sleeping well."

"Put garlic under your bed then, it wards off evil spirits. When someone dies without a proper Christian ceremony on consecrated ground, their spirit is restless and that attracts evil. Lots of garlic. At least fifteen heads."

She darted about almost girlishly as she spoke, rearranging loaves according to her own categories: crusty, well cooked, overcooked; and soft and floury for those with dentures or no teeth at all.

Julia noticed that the photo of her son had not returned. The few in the village who supported son against mother (those whose land had been sold to the developers and who had already been paid) said spitefully that Dolores' return to baking prowess was solely due to the threat of a new rival bakery, a Danish patisserie-bakery, scheduled to open within the year when the first few streets of Holidaylandia would be up and running.

Reggie's forebodings that the skeleton might not be historic were already being aired, but most kept optimistic faith in his Roman ancestry. Emilio Fuster and Arturo el Ferrer (the ironsmith), had even banked money on him being Roman. They had hurriedly designed, and partly executed, a commemorative plaque in wood and metal to be mounted near the village entrance, engraved with the message 'Welcome to Milagra, home to the Romans'. Others suggested another name change. If it could switch from Benicassim to Milagra, then why not Romanise to 'Miraculum' and get rid of the embarrassing error of the 'a' ending?

Juanito was hugely enjoying his celebrity status as the man who made the find. He was rumoured to have paraded secretly in front of his mirror in toga and sandals, or so his sister said for the toga was an old dress that had vanished from her wardrobe to reappear in his. There were detractors, of course, who spread the cruel story that he had cried out 'mama' and fainted like a girl when he first spotted the skeleton, but he had weathered that ignominy and was now waiting to be interviewed by local and national TV when its Roman heritage was officially confirmed. He apparently slept with a clothes peg pinching his chin to give it a more convincing cleft, in case the producers of Gladiator should be watching his TV interview and prefer him to Russell Crowe for future Roman epics.

The owner of the wine Bodega from San Antonio, a village en route to Villahermosa, had also jumped on the bandwagon. He had ordered a change of labels for the forthcoming 2004 harvest so that Roman icons dominated; colosseums, temples, chariots, bacchanalian feastings and warriors in helmets, breastplates and the ubiquitous leather sandals.

For all who sold local products a modern skeleton would be a bitter blow, for there was absolutely nothing evocative or marketable in a dead man from the 1970s.

Essentially the Roman allegiance was so alluring, morale boosting, inspirational and commercial that a mutual understanding was rapidly reached by the village. No other origination would be accepted, they decided, unless it could be proven officially, one hundred percent, by the unified weight of officialdom.

A warm, burgeoning feeling of camaraderie enveloped them. Lifelong grudges were tossed aside and dislocated friendships mended. Even the mayor was coolly acknowledged again.

As well as this goodwill there was a new sense of civic pride, for they would soon be part of the ancient world of civilisations, be mentioned in history books, and be visited by learned tourists instead of the cheap white trash they had been getting lately. They might even be twinned with Herculaneum or Pompeii! Most certainly they could now look down their noses at the tastelessness of the coast, where the closest they came to associating with the classical world was via pretentious and ridiculous theme parks.

Their rose-tinted dreams proliferated delightfully. Now Holidaylandia could be adapted; it could become smaller, classier, and have a Roman flavour. Its proposed golf course could be scrapped in favour of an authentic reconstruction of a Roman amphitheatre. This would appeal to Spanish tastes at long last and be a venue for bullfights, concerts, and give enough space to dance the pasadoble come Fiesta time. Que maravilloso!


Julia felt herself carried along with the buzz of excitement, but not convinced. For she could not shake off the shadow of her dream, and a cautionary voice kept telling her that the skeleton, although in many ways a village feature, was a problem uncomfortably close to her home.


She found Eulogio playing dominos in the bar with Celestino, the only person whose superior age and wisdom he acceded to. They did not converse so much as engage in epigrammatic parrying, a kind of ongoing, never-ending battle of wits that accompanied whatever they did together, amusing them and exhausting them in equal measure. Eulogio had a cold which stupefied his brain and made him wheeze, so he was relieved to take a temporary break from Celestino to concentrate on Julia.

Naturally he deplored Holidaylandia and was personally mortified by Vicente's involvement. But somehow he had lost the rebellious fire of his youth, even the steeliness of his middle age, and, maybe partly due to the weakening effect of his headcold, had adopted a philosophical, almost world weary attitude to it. It was as if he expected to be dead before it happened, so what the hell.

> "What can we do?" he mused feebly. "My generation were thankful just to be alive, considering so many died. We felt proud to work the land, grateful for every harvest, happy not to starve. When I was a chico we ate bread, olives and sardines, and anything else only in season. But it's a different world now. My grandchildren - if that useless Vicente has sperm capable of ever making any - will want their dishwashers, TVs, internet and fast cars just like everyone else. We can't expect them to stay peasants scratching for a living, barely paid a fideo for their produce and travelling by mule and cart. They see all the modern things on TV, so that's what they want."

> "Si, entiendo perfectamente. My sons don't want to live like my mother either, and the world is changing fast for all of us, no-one knows where it's

heading but we all get swept along. But all the same, we should have been forewarned - it's meant to be a modern democracy."

"Ha!" he snorted. "Nothing's what it's meant to be. The church is meant to be holy, Vicente a man and my son, while his mother ought to be my wife."

These sentiments were personal so she had no answer. What she had learned, though, was that despite his view of the invasion of retired northerners as simply part of the relentless march of history, not dissimilar to the invasion of the Visigoths, Romans, or Moors, he had no intention of capitulating by selling his land. This meant that she would not be entirely isolated, should she decide to stay. She would have one ally, one loyal neighbour.

Otto, Marte and Lise came that afternoon, bursting with curiosity to see the skeleton's erstwhile burial place. They stared in awe at the gouged out terrace wall and the carefully sieved mound of earth, and with bated breath traced the tyre tracks inching forward to the moment of discovery. Otto even fancied he saw blood on a discarded stone. But it proved to be no more than a vein of pink quartz embedded in the stone itself, and Marte laughed heartily at his ignorance.

"I knew they would pretend he was not from ze Civil War," Otto said indignantly, when Julia told them the latest theory of 1970s man. "They are ostriches."

"For once I hope you are right," Marte said, unusually pensive, while Lise went quiet as a mouse, absorbing for the first time and at first hand the gravity of death.

Marco cajoled Lise into a quest for Toad at the Fuente. He figured that, with Marte nearby, should the dressing on Toad's wound need changing, now was the time to find out as her hands were more deft and practised than Julia's. He ran ahead up the winding path, where early shoots of bracken were beginning to unfurl and the stones embedded in the path wore a shiny patina from the buffing and polishing of his passing feet. Lise and Alex followed more slowly, Lise still pensive and Alex focused on the intricate flexing and unflexing of her calf muscles as she climbed ahead of him. When they reached the Fuente Marco was crouching on the mossy bank of the small, deep pool where the water collected, intent upon some development that was taking place amongst the reeds. He put his finger to his lips for silence.

As their eyes adjusted to the dark shadowy recess in the rock where the dampness created a perpetual chill, they saw that Toad had straddled another creature, possibly of the same species, certainly warty and a similar greyish green. His eyes were virtually closed but an almost imperceptible lunging motion indicated a state that was not death, but might easily be the very last impulses of life. A logical assumption would be that, having one useless limb, he had chosen to be transported by another toad with the proper use of both. In fact Lise and Marco's whispered conversation showed they had indeed leapt to this conclusion, but Alex, whose mind was already grappling with rising sap and other urges of Spring, guessed immediately that the position was sexual. Neither toad seemed in the throes of ecstasy, but the physical results were soon visible - a foamy stream of jelly flowing out from underneath the double toaded union. It reminded Alex of the head of froth on Scotty's beer, and it flowed profusely, gelling and separating, until it floated on more than a quarter of the surface area of the pond.

"Toad spawn," Alex struggled to steady his voice, "you were right about him being male, Marco."

"Sure," Marco agreed cheerfully, "now there's no way he's gran."

"Gran?" Lise puzzled, "Isn't that 'abuela'?"

Alex sighed at the obtuse tactlessness of younger brothers and their childish, fanciful ideas. "Don't breathe a word to Marte, or it might get to Julia and she'd go bananas. Marco had this idea that gran, since she wasn't all that nice, you know, bad karma and all that, might've got reincarnated as a toad. For God's sake keep it to yourself - he's over it now anyway."

Lise found it hugely amusing. The idea banished all the dismal feelings of death and suffering that the skeleton had planted in her, and her laughter was all the more enthusiastic.

"OK," she smiled, "we make a deal. I keep this secret for you, and you keep my secrets just as safe. If not more, for mine can cause more harm. - It's not for much longer now," she added huskily, a flicker of concern crossing her face so that Marco knew she was talking only to Alex, and wondered what on earth she meant. Then she smiled again, and studied Toad with renewed interest.

"Hey, Frank, having a good wank?"

"Surely wanking's when you....?" Marco sounded aggrieved at the error.

"Shut *up* Marco!" Alex hastily cut him off.


Otto, with all the inborn instincts of a truffle pig in an oakwood, soon found the bottle of vodka she had offered Reggie. He scorned the offer of orange juice and waved aside the mention of ice cubes, drinking it neat out of a tall glass.

"Did you not notice his feet? Ze tarsals and metatarsals especially? Might they, perhaps, have been beaten by iron rods?"

"I told you. The whole long process of freeing the skeleton took place behind screens. We saw nothing."

Otto stroked his beard thoughtfully, removed his glasses to demist them on a corner of his shirt, then returned them to a perch on the end of his nose. "Then ze skull, which you did see - did it have fractures, malformations, any signs of trepanation?"

Julia was impatient with his erudite cross-examination, especially since she had never been fascinated by surgical details, nor conversant with the different torture methods of Fascist Spain.

"I'm not a doctor," she said curtly. Then, relenting, "I suppose, from the angle of it, maybe the neck was broken. But we never saw the entire skull, only the eye sockets, nose and cheek bones, - not even the jaws or teeth."

"Hmm. If ze neck was broken he could have been hung from a tree, or thrown off a cliff. I'm sure you know many were thrown zis way in Ronda, - yet ze youngsters there know nothing about it, their parents are too ashamed to tell. Well, near to Marte's the gorge is similar, just as steep. I've already been hunting for bones down zere."

Marte rolled her eyes at Julia as if to say yes, yes - I know he's crazy, but men do have these strange interests and these oh so weird ideas, and don't ask me where I found him or why I am with him because, well, we women too have strange tastes. Then, just to ensure that Julia understood the full bent of her eye language, and to remind her that her own taste in men was not impeccable, she said:

"Remind me to check your wound before I go."

"Ze trouble with war," Otto continued, "especially Civil War, is that when we take away ze normal barriers of what is morally acceptable, there are no barriers to human cruelty. With war, cruelty becomes a habit. So, each revenge killing is more brutal, until ze imagination competes for the most cruel tortures..."

"My mother once said we don't truly know someone until we know how cruel they're capable of being... Mind you, she was referring to my father, so thinking of emotional cruelty, not physical."

"Yah, yah, but zey are not so far apart. The stories I uncover are always of revenge or betrayal, zose emotions run deep in a Civil War. You would be surprised - people are often more brutal to friends who have become enemies than to total strangers. Yet we are told we dehumanize only strangers."

Otto looked to be settling in for several hours of discourse, so for Julia it was a relief when Alex, Lise and Marco returned from the Fuente. They seemed simultaneously elated and preoccupied. Otto, dimly aware that he had lost the interest of his adult audience, turned gratefully to Marco.

"So, how is young Marcus Aurelius Secundus?"

"Tertius," corrected Marco, "I prefer Tertius."

"OK, Tertius," Otto readily agreed, for any response was preferable to glazed silence. At home Marte had taken to reading Goethe throughout his monologues.

"Actually," said Marco, "I'd almost forgotten the skeleton. We've discovered something far, far more ancient still living in these hills."

"Aha! Let me guess. A caveman's drawings?"

Marco shook his head.

"A dinosaur's toenail?"

"Closer. How could a toenail be alive?"

"Ach so. True. A smilodon?"

Marco clicked his tongue in the style of Dolores. "Give up?"

"No. One more try...a protozoan?"

Marco smiled in victory, "A toad! - Well, two toads actually. Toads have been around since the time of the dinosaurs, they're four hundred million years old, according to my book! And they're now having babies."

"Well," said Otto, seeing the chance to share some of the points scored, "I'll allow you the victory, but with two provisos. One, ze toad species is perhaps that old, but your two specimens are much younger for sure. Two, you cannot believe what you read in a book. And I should know, for I am a writer." And he beamed in satisfaction.


Although Marco claimed he had almost forgotten the skeleton, he was not being entirely accurate. He had in fact taken precautionary measures in case, in what he now felt to be an unlikely scenario, it turned out to be authentically old. He had not even shared his secret with Alex, and that was unprecedented. What had happened was this: when the skull was first uncovered, while everyone was concentrating on the shock and its ill effects on Juanito, he had noticed a couple of stray teeth nestling between two rocks which formed the foundation line of the terrace wall, about a foot away from the skull. They were in a revolting state, green, grey and earthy, just the kind of vile condition which freaked out his dentist, but Marco immediately recognised them as

90

teeth because he kept seven of his own in a glass jar in his bedroom cupboard, and would quite often line them up for inspection.

He had made a pact with Julia which allowed him to keep them. She had told him some tomfool of a story that tooth fairies left pound coins under your pillow in exchange for clean milk teeth, but she had been clumsy and he had caught her red handed, in the act of placing the very first pound. So after that they continued with the fiction, but he had the double benefit of keeping both pound and tooth. Anyway, while Alex and Julia were engaged in reviving Juanito, and the foreman was busy phoning the police and convincing them his was not a hoax call, Marco pretended he was inspecting the wall for structural damage and scooped up the teeth in a single, deft movement. Then he secreted them in his jeans pocket. They were right now wrapped in a twist of cream tissue paper, cosily ensconced in the jam jar along with his seven milk teeth. But he was beginning to think he might have to find a more unlikely hiding place. He was unsure of his motive in snatching them, but he had a vague idea that, even if they failed to bring him fame or fortune, they might prove handy for the weekly Monday morning 'show and tell' session in his Primary School (if they ever went back to England), landing him lots of extra kudos from his classmates.


Alex meanwhile was playing canasta in his bedroom with Lise. The scores were comfortingly balanced but Alex felt this would not last, for try as he might neither his heart nor brain were fully engaged on the game. Instead, his mind kept replaying the vision of the gelatinous flow of toadspawn flowing, separating and coagulating, a silver clear jelly with milk white froth set against a dangerously green backdrop of dark murky water and sharp bright reeds. It was all so liquid, sticky and fecund that it made him squirm with embarrassment, and his mouth felt so unfamiliar he was not sure whether it was salivating or dry. The two toads had been surprisingly static, unlike the thrusting, pumping motions he had seen with dogs, so that he could not work out whether the voluminous effluent came from the male or female toad, nor imagine how either of them could have possibly contained so much liquid without being bloated to double or quadruple size beforehand. Perhaps it was a trompe d'oeil, for toads were linked to magic and witchcraft. Whatever it was, it would not leave him in peace, and he had a suspicion it had affected Lise in some disturbingly sexual way as well, judging by the way she was sitting.

After their visit finally ended Julia stretched out on the window seat exhausted. She felt sated by words. Marte and Otto had exacerbated her tiredness by a whole series of false leave takings, until she had wanted to scream. The first time they returned because Otto had forgotten his glasses, but Marte cleverly located them perched on his head; then it was because Lise had left an uncomfortable bracelet in Alex's room, next because Marte had suddenly felt she must warn them that toads had poison glands close to their eyes and should not be touched, and finally to leave Julia an unlabelled sample of Renacimiento 'just in case', at a time when Julia was too tired to refuse it.

"It needs a different name for younger peoples, so if one occurs to you zen let me know. I even will pay you royalties!" Marte giggled as she waved a cheery goodbye. For the fourth time.

Julia lay without moving a muscle, as if embalmed, watching the gentle play of sunlight and shadows on the stone wall as the leaves shivered in the faint breeze. The persian blinds reflected slatted shadows with occasional ripples of distortion, and Julia stared hypnotically, wondering what caused the distortions, the effect of heat on the pane of glass or the angle of the sun's rays. She slipped into a state of half-sleep. Eventually she noticed that the shadows had climbed higher up the wall, the air had an evening chill and the sounds of voices had relocated to the kitchen.

She had lost the wonderful hot climate habit of siestas, so instead of waking renewed and refreshed she felt drowsy and bewildered by the passage of an unknown time. She struggled to her feet and headed for the kitchen and Alex's bright laughter, hoping that a glass of cold water would shock her stupefied senses into proper functioning. In this slow-witted state she assumed that the two extra bodies seated at the kitchen table were Marte and Otto, returned for yet another bout of goodbyes, so she aimed a disapproving grunt at their backsides as she tottered towards the fridge.

"*Je-esus*, you are in a friendly state," Grant's voice was accusing.

"Sorry - I wasn't expecting more visitors."

"Evidently not," and he pointedly looked her up and down.

With consternation she took in the utter slobbishness of her appearance. Her hair was a tangled mess, slept on and unbrushed, her legs and feet were bare so she must have taken off her nether clothing at some moment before or during her siesta, and her old T-shirt, which she must have put on, although mercifully long enough to just cover her brief panties, was crumpled, lop-sided and not truly clean.

"Make yourselves at home," Julia told them, "I'll be right back."

More suitably clothed she returned to the kitchen where Veronika was profuse with compliments on the cute rusticity of her house.

92

"You have *such* a super view," Veronika cooed.

"Soon to be spoilt by our friend here."

"You expect exclusive rights to it?" demanded Grant tartly. "I seem to remember you fancied yourself a socialist once. Surely you aren't averse to sharing your good fortune with others, especially the old and infirm?"

"So it is intended for retirees then?" Julia wrinkled her nose, for many villagers still hoped it would breathe new life and stem the tide of depopulation to the coast. Retirees would only accelerate the escape of the younger generation.

"Well, it'll cater for their needs, but we do aim to attract a cross section. From all over Europe. Could call it Eurolandia - whaddoyou think?"

"I'm having trouble with thinking right now. It's called exhaustion. And stress."

"I understood that was how you saw my life, not yours. I'm the businessman caught up in the rat race on the concrete coast. Isn't this meant to be a country idyll?" Grant lent back, pleased that Veronika could experience his argumentative prowess and hoping she might challenge him more often.

"Perhaps news travels slowly," Julia found herself eyeing the clock, willing them to leave, "but out here we've had a taste of high-powered detective work. I assumed you'd have heard of it."

"Oh *that*," Grant sounded dismissive, but there was a discernible edge of anxiety in his next question, "It's not going to blow up into anything serious is it?"

"Depends what you consider serious."

Grant did not respond immediately. He stood up, fidgeting with the buttons of his mobile phone as if he had to answer a text message that nanosecond or a lucrative deal was lost, turning his back on them in case they were spying on his business portfolio details and about to make a hostile bid. After a half minute of deft button flicking he resumed the conversation.

"Serious for me would be if he'd had a health related death. Cholera - I know there were endemic outbreaks here up 'till the 1930s, for instance, - or worse still, leprosy. The sole remaining leper colony in Europe is still functioning, and with genuine cases of leprosy, only about a hundred K north of here."

"Oh God – you're kidding!" Veronika shrieked, instinctively inspecting her bare arms for signs of the dreaded pox.

"Far from kidding," Grant was working himself up into a lather, "only it's been a well kept secret. But now that fucking dumbarse Herr Otto is plotting an exposé. He loves the idea that the tourist playground of northern Europe, this land of health and sunshine, hides a dark corner where the most feared disease of Medievaldom still lingers on in living putrefaction."

"Then stop the article, honey. Phone Der Spiegel," Veronika was showing her mettle. "What Grant wants he gets," she confided to Julia, in case this truism had escaped her notice.

"Or..." Grant was off his chair again, "if he'd committed suicide. That'd leave a 'bad luck' stain. Or if the terrace wall fell in one of those minor earth tremors we get quite regularly round here. They're never serious, but old folks'll get jumpy about investing their life savings in an earthquake zone."

Grant by now was pacing up and down, as if the contemplation of potential disasters that spelt ruin to his latest enterprise was actually energising him.

"He could've been poisoned," Marco interjected.

Grant was enthusiastic. "Could be. Those campesinos sure go crazy with their poison - use enough against one rat or fox to zap a whole town!"

Marco shook his head, remembering the glossy, foamy spread of toadspawn. "I was thinking of poisoned water. From the well, or Fuente."

Julia noticed the glance Alex gave Marco, and wondered exactly what they had been up to with Lise. They had seemed strangely furtive after their visit to the Fuente. She also noted the look on Grant's face, and remembered the boys had spotted a bottle of 'Milagra' mineral water in his office.

But she took heart from the fact that he had obviously heard nothing of the rumours that the skeleton's death was recent, for if verified the Mayor would be one of the first to know, and Grant - as his new business partner - would be a close second.

# 11

The report at last came through from the forensic laboratory, and thus the game of guessing came to an end, or rather shifted from the 'when' into perilous alleyways leading more precisely to the who, why and how. The skeleton was proved by science to belong to a young man of twenty seven or eight years old, of slight build, medium height and European extraction. Time of death: approximately twenty five years ago. It could be that significant other details were also known but were being kept under wraps, for rumours emerged that the cause of death (which was, of course, not divulged) could equally be suspicious or accidental. Thus an inquest would be set in motion, although it would be handled not so very differently to a homicide investigation.

The news reverberated round the village. All dreams of classical antiquity were sorrowfully folded away and future fortunes based on them forgotten; instead of positive notoriety they now knew they were faced with a particularly unpleasant airing of dirty linen. All the recent brother and sisterhood dispersed as dramatically as it had formed. In place of smiles and solidarity came pallor, tension, stiff formal greetings and the revival of all those forgotten disputes and rancours from a quarter of a century ago. For the unpalatable truth was that anyone from a fairly long shortlist of potential suspects could be a murderer.

Dolores was elbow deep in flour when Julia called by, an unusual occurrence because all the yeast fermenting, kneading, plaiting, forming, proving and raising was normally done out of sight in the back room, lest any customer access and try to emulate her secret methods. But with all the murder mayhem going on she had lost track of the date, so that the special breads and cakes for Shrove Tuesday and Ash Wednesday had to be produced in a rush. She dusted off her forearms, smacked her thighs so the flour on her apron wafted into Julia's face, but was in too much of a hurry to notice.

"Your mother did the right thing to die before all this dead man hullabaloo," she said, coughing violently onto the back of her hand.

"I'm sure no-one would *prefer* to be dead," Julia replied warily, unsure of Dolores' drift.

So far she had not had the impression anyone thought Frances more culpable than others; however, they did not yet know about her attempts to halt, or at least delay the development. If anyone knew it would be the Mayor. Dolores no longer talked to him now, but she had then. Julia remembered her leaning heavily on him, sobbing, as they struggled down the cemetery path.

"Someone may prefer death to what's coming, is my guess," Dolores said darkly, then vanished into the back room with a cheerless 'Hasta luego'.

Julia carried her loaves gingerly. They were piping hot and Dolores had failed to wrap them in the usual twist of paper. She had left Alex and Marco in Bar del Bigot but was in no mood for the exuberant rantings of the cockatiel, who would doubtless have some new witticism up his sleeve. She tried to sidle through the door soundlessly whilst the bird was preoccupied preening its tail plumage.

"Psst, psst! Sssssh," it whistled, without even turning to see who had crept in. "Ssssssh!"

Eulogio and Celestino sat amidst a semicircle of the old men of the village, staring vacantly at the small fountain in the plaza. The jet of water repeated a cycle of two settings, high : low, half a minute each, so that their collective eyes moved in perfect unison up...down...up...down, as if they were programmed marionettes, or tennis enthusiasts watching a new vertical game. Today no-one was tempted by dominos. Instead they puffed on cigarettes and cigars while a murmured conversation passed between them, sometimes rippling round the semicircle like a game of Chinese whispers, sometimes jumping over the quieter ones to involve only the dominant. They were jogging their collective memories back to the year on everyone's minds, 1978, but there were disagreements on how best to anchor it; by reference to the harvests of almonds, grapes or olives; or by the strength and length of the autumn rains. The women, you could be sure, would be calculating it by village births and pregnancies.

Sra Bigot did not allow the latest breaking news to disturb her routine. She polished the glasses with her usual deftness, glancing, if anything, more quizzically at the convex reflection of her smiling face in the bowl of each glass, and sometimes thrusting her lips forward in an inviting kiss.

"To think you were only a teeny thing when that skeleton died," she leaned across to add an extra bonus of froth in Julia's coffee, "Didn't you hear it scream?"

Julia shook her head. "It worries me that he may have lain there for days, and if we'd only realised we could have saved his life. I'd prefer to learn he died instantly."

Sra Bigot kissed a reluctant farewell to her reflection and flicked a stray hair from her unfurrowed brow, "You've had such bad luck, dear. Two brushes with death in a few months…" and she clasped Julia's hands in an ardent squeeze.

Reggie and Colin had not even glanced at the crossword. The paper lay open but ignored, apart from Colin's surreptitious peering at the horoscope section, trying to decipher what bad news a haunted looking astrologer called Adele predicted for him. He could not rely on Reggie's brain to locate 1978 in his memory, at least not when it came to the matching up of local happenings, for Reggie only appeared in Milagra during 1999.

Colin was deeply apprehensive about his impending Guardia interview. He guessed most villagers would be questioned, some more punctiliously than others, so as to build up a full database and compare stories. Then gradually they would wittle away the irrelevancies, discard the inaccuracies, eliminate the obviously innocent, until they were left with a few stark facts and a suspect steeped in guilt. Yet knowing that others would have to go through the hell of interrogation in no way calmed him, in fact it made everything worse because obviously they might talk about him.


Did the people of the village like him? What might they say about him? Oh, If only he'd known that something like this was in the offing he'd have been far more friendly with the locals all along! He'd have improved his Spanish so he could have had regular friendly chats in the bars, played rummy in the Bar de las Pensionistas, shared their awful garish Roman Catholic ceremonies in that ghastly fake gold Christmas cake of a church, and been much, much more generous with his donation for the annual Fiesta.

The dead man was of course most likely the victim of a crime passionelle, and the local Latin temperament was surely the more prone to outbursts of unpremeditated violence. Nevertheless, he rather wished he'd seemed a more normal man in their eyes, pinched some plump bottoms, courted a few eligible young widows and danced the slow, smoochy numbers at Fiesta time. It was too late now to revamp his reputation. He had a shrewd suspicion they called him 'maricon' behind his back, and the delinquent group of young boys who played football in the vines beyond his garden had even imputed he'd done it with a goat last time he returned their errant football! His friendship with Reggie only made things worse, as had his previous well publicized antipathy towards Frances.

"What happened in the world at large that year, Reggie? All I need is some major event and I've something to steer my memory with."

"Give us a chance Colin, I'm not a mobile encyclopaedia. You've only given me two minutes to cast my mind back a great many years."

"Well, we're all supposed to remember what we were doing when Kennedy was shot …," Colin mused, "perhaps that other Kennedy, his brother Bob, got shot that year?"

"I think you're more than a decade out, Colin. And for your peace of mind, you should avoid death as your marker. Think of something cheerful."

Reggie looked up and was thankful to see Julia talking animatedly at the bar, for Colin's attacks of hypertension were beginning to grate on his nerves.

"Relax. Look at the situation rationally. They're hardly going to consider you a prime suspect. No-one in his right mind would think you capable of murder, so don't court suspicion by being so damn nervous."

Colin tried manfully to smile, but his hands twitched as they searched for the coffee spoon, and he could not even keep the beat as he tapped out his favourite foxtrot tune against the bouncing saucer.

"What I hate most is being questioned," he moaned. "If they know someone's done nothing wrong they shouldn't subject them to questioning. If I get the feeling they're looking at me suspiciously I'll go to pieces, I know I will. I'm the sort to confess to something I haven't done!"

Reggie was immediately assailed by a vision of Colin writhing prostrate on the floor, sobbing hysterically as he crawled before a line of police officers and kissed the metal toecaps on their boots. It made him wonder how on earth Colin had coped with the underlying viciousness of the army, - until he remembered that he had of course been discharged, possibly for failing to cope. He glanced at Colin who had at last mastered his rhythm, and noticed that a new raw-looking strawberry rash had broken out on his forehead.

It occurred to him that Colin might be reliving the moment of horror when he was discovered blind drunk and out of his wits in a baranca at seven o'clock in the morning, naked except for the bottom half of Frances' bikini that he reluctantly had to admit to having unpegged from her clothesline in the dead of night. His excuse was that Vicente had invited him to the wine pressing ceremony near Montejoven, where all manner of excesses are expected. The grapes are trampled barefoot, and the first deep ruby juices to seep through the slatted floorboards into oaken barrels below, called 'flor', are scooped up and poured over the head to trickle down the nose and into the mouth, on and on throughout the night, amidst much giggling, celebrating and stripping off of garments.

Basically Colin had soaked up too much flor and stripped off too many garments, so that when he was dropped naked just outside Milagra he had taken the wrong turn and headed uphill towards Frances' farmhouse, instead of downhill towards his own. Or so he said. He realised his mistake only on finding that his front door key was incompatible with her front door, and he must have borrowed the first nether garment he bumped into whilst traversing her garden on his way out, and sensibly, modestly, applied it to his person so as not to cause any offence should he meet anyone on his route home.

Reggie had to admit that this was precisely the type of antic that could cause problems, since innocent though it might be, it established a connection between himself, late nights, bizarre, uncontrolled behaviour, and the particular location where the skeleton had lain.

"Tell you what, Colin. If you honestly can't trust yourself not to confess to all manner of heinous crimes you've merely dreamt of committing, I suggest you hire a lawyer. That way they'll do the talking and you can relax. It's that simple."

Colin looked aghast. "You don't think I need a lawyer do you? The bastards cost a fortune...and they'll bloody think I'm guilty, otherwise why would I need one? Oh God, it's a hopeless, twisted, tangled knot!"

In the same way that Reggie knew Colin would be a soft target for the Guardia Civil, so did el Bigot fear for his brother, Manos Arriba. He was easier to protect, though, since he had wandering hands, not wandering feet. He was of course known to have groped a number of lissome young teenagers, but he always lurked in the narrow village streets at twilight or the dark recesses of the bar at other times, and had never knowingly strayed from Milagra on the hunt for succulent breasts to caress. Also, he might ogle the girls but he harboured no malice towards the men they preferred, in fact he was happiest when his attentions earned him a slap. So for him to suddenly throttle a man far up a mountain would be out of character. And he could certainly not be expected to understand or answer questions anyway.

Colin might not know it, but many in the village were, like him, casting their minds back and shifting uneasily, perturbed by some of the things they had said or done that would now be aired and could be misinterpreted.

1978 became a watershed. Those born in or after it could still swagger and laugh; those of an age expected to remember it had furrowed brows and long faces, for they would be obliged to talk. Juanito, born plum in the middle of '78, swaggered more than most, as was his habit.

But he did get enraged by the teasing. He had been reputedly the ugliest baby ever born in the village, with a huge, heavy head that he could not independently support until he was eleven months old, so his mother used to push him around in his pram, propping up his head with some padded wooden frame she otherwise used when ironing her husband's shirt sleeves. Those most annoyed by his current swagger, being just the wrong side of 1978, had re-adopted his old nickname of 'Medusa', which he took to be a woman's name and therefore offensive.

"Fascismo al diablo!" declared the cockatiel.

Alex took his eyes from the computer screen in the certainty that Otto had arrived, but was dealt a double blow of disappointment; not only was Lise not with him, but Marco cunningly took advantage of his inattention to beat him to the Sorcerer's Lair and capture the Sword of Power.


Otto nodded greetings to those in the bar who bothered to look up, and raised his hand to the cockatiel, now proven to be a bird totally after his own heart. While Marte hugged Julia like a longlost friend Otto exchanged pleasantries with Sra Bigot, who madly fancied his Castilian beard. For weeks she had been attempting to persuade her husband to swap the position of his facial hair from moustache (which interfered with their love making) to beard (which she sensed would not). She gave Otto's glass an extra special shine and filled it well above the measure, in gratitude for the sheer elegance of his beard and the competence of his spoken Spanish. By contrast she barely flicked Marte's glass with her tea towel, and made her camomile infusion from water that was merely hot, not boiling. Marte was used to the little slights she sometimes received at the hands of the ladies of the village, some of whom used to call her 'la bruja del norte' (the witch from the north) in whispered pillow talk to their husbands, whom they feared might have been smitten by her reputation for loose living. Now that she had so obviously settled down to a life of near respectability, with a man who could clearly read and write and wore proper clothes, and to judge by what should be the whites of his eyes drank alcohol but had no truck with drugs, they were far more accepting of her.


"I don't believe one word," Otto fumed as he invited himself to join Reggie and Colin. "It's an excuse to throw their weight around in ze village." He solicitously prepared chairs for Julia and Marte, "Next thing will be ze bones are German, you'll see."

Colin's blotchiness immediately increased, the redness deepening and the pallid contrasts fading to a blinding white. However well or badly he had protected the secrecy of his private life two aspects were well known in the village, one was his difficulties with Frances, the second his antipathy towards Germans. He inwardly quaked at this awful possibility.

"I sure hope not," Marte echoed his thoughts, "because of all the people who did crazy things in those days, the Germans were craziest. They were so used to rules zat anarchy sent them out of their skulls!"

Marte had also been reactivating her dormant memory, with great unwillingness because whenever she looked backwards she saw nothing clearly, merely a chaotic kaleidoscope of images fragmenting into warring particles of sexual greed and ecstasy, spiritual searching and loss, camp fires, naked babies, hairy dogs, long haired men and longer haired women drenched in Pachouli oil, sitars, Eastern philosophies, mysticism and African drums; all of it gyrating together and rendered indistinct by the smoke haze of marijuana, the fumes from chillums and the Alice in Wonderland effects of LSD and magic mushrooms taken in massive excess. If anyone had asked her a few weeks ago if she had to make only one wish, what would it be, she would have answered: *never* to relive that period in her life.

So far they had only found one skeleton. Well, considering how life had been, to have only one casualty was pretty remarkable. The numbers of men who must have left Frances' house in a state of confusion or despair, blind drunk or high as kites, if only the one fell off a terrace wall on his way down that too was a miracle. She wouldn't mind reminiscing about that era with a kindred spirit, but to say anything about it to the Guardia Civil would be courting arrest. She couldn't even begin to tell her parents yet, and they were mellowing with age. Or Otto, and he prided himself on his tolerance. So...well, she'd just have to lie.


Reggie felt almost guilty being spared the retrospective struggling of the others. Almost guilty, not actually guilty, for feeling bad about a stroke of personal good fortune would be plain stupid. Otto also could have celebrated his escape, having had no links to Milagra prior to Christmas, but he thought only of his bandolero. He felt cheated of his timely coup in being on the spot as the murdered corpse of a main character in his book was being unearthed. The intensity of his tunnel vision made him live for nothing but bandoleros and conspiracy theories, with just the occasional tickle of Marte's body in order to unwind before going to sleep.

"With the information you get from DNA these days we can be certain they know far more about the victim than they've let on. They'll know if he was Spanish, German or whatever, but they're cruel. They relish putting everyone under the microscope and making 'em squirm."

As he spoke Reggie tried to avoid eye contact with Colin, who indeed resembled a pink worm squirming on a fisherman's hook. He could have assuaged Colin's misery by pointing out that the greatest suspicion would surely fall on Frances, and by extension Julia was in the least enviable position. But of course he could hardly say that in Julia's hearing.

Julia was praying the dead man was not French. She had not forgotten her nightmare and, of all the men who wandered in and out Frances' life at that time, she still for some reason retained a vivid memory of him. Was it because the French were a rarity in Milagra? Certainly they had tended to stay within their own borders, proud in the certain knowledge that their country was the most beautiful, varied, genuinely republican and honestly egalitarian in western Europe, so why abandon it for somewhere inferior on every level?

The hippie exodus then had been mainly Germans seeking the sun and escaping conformity, Brits doing the same and fleeing the rain and greyness, Dutch through boredom of sub sea-level flatness and exhilaration with mountains, Swiss in retreat from their landlocked introversion and the exhorbitant cost of living, Scandinavians avoiding the long, dark, icy winters and the high cost of alcohol, and so on - apart from the French.

It could also be that she remembered him because he had an artistic face, or because his violin tore at the emotions, or because of his funny accent. There was even a vague memory she had of being his chosen future bride; hadn't he pointed to her whilst squabbling with Frances, recognising her as an ancient cohort of his? Cleopatra? (Had he been Caesar, or Mark Anthony?) Or Helen of Troy? Something she did remember clearly was that he couldn't say 'house'. He'd said to Frances "You have such a bootiful 'arse, how old is it?" and for ages afterwards, whenever Frances assessed her backside in the mirror, she would pat it, grinning and purring "*such* a bootiful 'arse."

Marco joined them. Even though he had beaten Alex to the Sword of Power he had ultimately squandered his superior weaponry and, after dying thrice, was out of the game. Forgetting his age he tried to squeeze in to sit on Julia's lap, for he sensed the tension in the air and, coupled with his own habitual defeat at the hands of Alex, felt in need of comfort. Otto smiled mournfully at him.

"Well, my friend, the Guardia have foiled us with their scientific plotting and their DNA trickery. You can no longer dream of your Roman gladiator and I have lost my best bandolero." He looked as if he might weep into his glass, so Marco thumped him affectionately on the back to eject the misery as if it were hiccoughs.

"I can still dream about my gladiator, but I'm sure that skeleton is what they say it is. You can't fake DNA."

"Aha, you are too young and too innocent to understand zese things. Grown ups are not to be trusted, least of all when wearing uniforms."

"And carrying guns."

Marco had gone deliberately close to the Guardia in order to identify the type of hand gun they carried, but it did not resemble any from his violent computer game that Julia would have banned had she known about. He turned suddenly to Colin.

"Weren't you in the army?"

Reggie saw that Colin was still trapped in his cage of anxiety and incapable of a response, so came to the rescue.

"Colin was the exception proving the rule. Colin *could* be trusted."

Marco eyed Reggie suspiciously, knowing that his whole statement was a load of chop-logic nonsense, but he left Colin in peace. Or, since peace and Colin were irreconcilable, he left Colin alone.


There was a sudden commotion at the other end of the bar. Julia had her back to it, so apart from the increased volume and tones of aggression the first she saw of the confrontation was Juanito muttering obscenities and storming out of the bar, slamming the door behind him with such violence that Sra Bigot's polished glasses trembled precariously and tinkled like a zylophone.

"Te has pasado," Emilio Fuster reproached Pedro the glass cutter, who was grinning triumphantly.

"Que va! He's been asking for it for ages." Pedro lifted both hands in a gesture declining personal animosity or responsibility for what he'd said.

"Puede ser," agreed Emilio "but you have your own axe to grind. We all know you fancy his sister."

"What happened?" asked Marte, always intrigued by quarrels.

She promptly left their table to sit with the younger men, who were sharing a steaming plate of albondigas and wafer thin slices of jamon serrano for their almuerzo. Lovers' fights were her favourite, kids' disputes the most predictable - and simplest to resolve, but macho collisions in bars, providing they took place in daytime, were highly diverting and pleasantly arousing due to the mild element of physical danger from a stray punch in the eye. When she came back she had mastered the story well enough to sum it up.

Pedro's theory was that Juanito was undoubtedly the murderer, and his motive jealousy. As a five month old foetus he had already developed enough self adoration and competitive spirit to know he wanted to be the best builder in the village, once he was born. Juanito's mother was a witch, the whole village accepted that, and together this witch and her big-headed foetus had telepathically conspired to collapse the wall on which the skeleton (himself an inspired builder and of course, gloriously handsome too) was innocently standing. The proof of this was that Juanito, held in the grip of his secret guilt, had driven his JCB like a guided missile straight into the buried skeleton which no-one else would ever, ever have found. Not only that, in a state of shock at the moment of discovery, he had swooned with remorse and called upon his co-conspirator in crime, for it was a well-known fact he had whimpered 'mama' before blubbing like a new born babe upon the earth.

"That is interesting for me," Otto stroked his beard in a way that turned Sra Bigot's legs to pedestals of jelly, "for zey are so very close to the emotions my bandolero had to contend with. Zese villages are hotbeds of superstition, jealousy and treachery. Is it not a line from your great Shakespeare's Romeo and Juliet - 'Civil War makes civil hands unclean'?"

Julia was wrenched from her reverie. "Hm, don't think so. Wasn't it 'civil hate'?"

"Shall we go to Scotty's?" Marte enquired. Like all disciples of Goethe she became agitated by the mere mention of Shakespeare. "We must meet Lise there, and Scotty will be sure to set our memories right. He keeps all his accounts and bills and IOUs from the beginning of time. He still reminds me I never paid for a chupachup Lise had when she was one year old, costing five pesetas!"

Julia caught sight of Alex's expression and said "Yes", albeit reluctantly.

Fortunately it was not the day for MISTERVISTA tours to visit, so bar El Molino Divino had few clients and a peaceful atmosphere. Scotty and Colin shared nervous dispositions, but Scotty coped far better because he was active, energetic and had to work for his living. The prospect of an imminent tax inspection or a visit from the Health and Safety officers would have made him sweat or shiver, but a homicide inquest didn't trouble him.

Everyone knew he was a pacifist, otherwise he would have smacked some of the men who had had it off with his wife, whereas all he did was add her drinks and other running costs onto their bills and that balanced it for him. He had not even flailed out at the Dutch dentist who eventually ran off with her, not even given him one little shove, so no-one could call him aggressive. In fact he seemed almost cheerful at the prospect of being interviewed, so that Marte suspected he had made a deal with the Guardia; forget the fine (which he had been paying in instalments since the unlicensed Degsy affair) in return for information.

"I'm Numero Uno on their interview list," he declared, proudly expanding his pigeon chest, "they know sure as hell booze talks. If a guy can take insults and cheatin' when he's tanked up and not get violent, he's a safe guy."

"Ah-ha, you've seen a lot of violence, not so?" Otto queried.

"Not what would interest you," Marte chipped in, "Scotty may be bald under his baseball cap, but he's no war veteran. He came to Milagra later than me."

"I came right at the beginning of the year in question, '78."

"Zat is indeed suspicious. No wonder zey see you first!"

"As a matter of fact," he swelled with importance, "I reckon they're after my version of Art the Stick," and he disappeared into the back kitchen to prepare his version of Canadian hotdogs, which he called 'wienies' (and the locals understood it as describing their pitiful size).

Art the Stick had gained his name from his crime. He had the ignominy of being the only foreigner known to have committed a crime of violence against a Spaniard in Milagra in the last thirty years, and yet he had somehow managed to draw such a veil of secrecy over it that it was not widely known. His real name was one of those Dutch tongue-twisters like Art Jungjantzen-Tuylens, and unlike the normal gruff but jovial Dutchmen who passed through Milagra he had a strain of cruelty that children sensed immediately, although adults were often fooled by his artistry with pen and ink into mistaking him for a sensitive soul. The 'Stick' was a heavy oak lintel that had been stuck in the corner of Scotty's passageway entrance until Scotty should find something useful for it to support, and Art in a moment of madness chose to use it as a weapon.

Late one night, at closing time, a stag party of a dozen men from neighbouring Montejoven arrived in an excited and drunken state for a final drink. Scotty, not one to refuse business or turn away revellers who were in no state to add up their bill, agreed to serve them on the outside tables. There was no problem, no-one urinated on the tables or vomited on the plants, but one poor man, perhaps unaware that Scotty had made a condition that they stay outside, walked through the doorway. He got no further, for Art was inexplicably incensed by his audacity and thwacked him on the back of the head with the lintel. Or perhaps it was not inexplicably, for Art was racist to the core.


Scotty did not see the attack, but he saw the aftermath. The man lay motionless on his front, blood spurting from his nose, mouth and ears from the sheer concussive force of the blow. It was only then that Art realised how insanely out of proportion his action had been, and he began to gibber in terror; if the man should die he faced life imprisonment, at best. Scotty, also conscious of the reputation of his bar and that it risked losing its Spanish clientele, ignored Art and phoned for an ambulance. Then he had to cope with the poor man's friends, who were hammering on the locked door and trying to break in to lynch Art. Without weighing the consequences he lent Art his car keys so that he could escape out the back, so that by the time the ambulance came Art was well away and his victim had to be rushed to hospital in Villahermosa. No-one came out of the situation smelling of roses, and those who knew the truth resented the fact that Art never fully paid the price. Somewhere, somehow, important money must have changed hands, but no-one ever put their finger on who paid what to whom.

Art was arrested three days later, found crouched and snivelling in his own broom cupboard, and somehow Scotty escaped a charge of being an accessory after the crime. Art himself disappeared for three years, but no-one was clear whether they had been spent in Spanish jail (which was grim) or Dutch jail (which was comparative luxury). The poor victim of the crime was the only one who suffered lasting effects and whose life was ruined; he remained in a coma for months and even when he returned home from hospital he had recurring headaches and permanent brain damage.

"I can't see why he feels honoured to be asked about Art the Stick," Marte growled in disgust. "He should be ashamed. He protected the rat. He should have let the poor victim's friends tear him to pieces."

"Kom, mine liebling, zat is not such a sweet, motherly attitude. It is like in the Bible 'An eye for an eye and a tooth for a tooth'."

Scotty, who was eavesdropping from the kitchen, reappeared like a jack-in-the-box, "I sure as hell didn't protect Art, I protected the man's friends from killing him and getting themselves done for murder. And, anyway, they wanna know about Goliath too."

Goliath was a huge German hippie whom Julia remembered, since he exactly resembled the drawing of the giant in her Ladybird version of Jack and the Beanstalk, including his apple red cheeks, leather sandals and worn leather jerkin. He always wore a broad smile and played thunderously deafening electric bass guitar which shook the mountains, but he had a nastier side when provoked because every so often his tiny shrimp of a wife would have to wear sunglasses to hide her black eyes. Rumour had it that he had been snapped up by the German equivalent of the SAS when he did his military service, and knew how to throttle people in five seconds with a coil of wire. Certainly a good few rabbits could have testified to the strength of his hands, for he could strangle and skin them in a two deft movements.

Apart from with his wife he only had one major quarrel, with an English drummer, a 'head' (slightly different to a hippie) who later became a disciple of a Tibetan guru called Norbu and lived alone on an atoll in the Pacific Ocean eating electric eels and stewed seaweed. Anyway, these two had a falling out over who lost the beat while someone else was playing an explosive guitar solo. Rocks were hurled but without careful aim so neither

106

were hurt, but a goat broke its leg when bolting in alarm and both their Mercedes trucks were battered beyond repair.

"Looks to me," Scotty continued, frowning as Otto helped himself to a top up as if he were a guest in a house, not a client in a bar, "putting two and two together, as if our skeleton died from a blow from a rock to the back of his head."

Otto narrowed his eyes, "So you assume our detectives have a method and are reviewing only lookalike acts of violence. You could be wrong. Zey might want you to think that while, meanwhile, they are studying...you, for instance."

Scotty skipped in fright. "Oh c'mon man, I'm a pussy cat, just a li''le guy. You can even beat me at arm wrestling."

Otto breathed satisfaction. "Ah, but until we know who ze skeleton is we cannot know what they're looking for. Maybe zey already know, maybe...it's your ex-wife's dentist-lover! Now *zat* would worry you, my friend!"

Julia had ceased to listen. For them it was a joke, a bartime diversion, and Otto was happy for anything that took his mind off the acute disappointment of his bandolerolessness. But for her the situation was far more serious, and maybe also for Marte.


She watched Alex and Lise chatting animatedly with a sense of disquiet, feeling the futility of that too. Death and secrets, both seemed to hem her in. It was not that she kept it secret from Alex who his father was, or that his father was dead. She had told him what she felt he had a right to know, which was in fact more than she had ever been told by Frances about hers.

Alex knew his father had been a renowned classical dancer already in his late thirties when Julia met him; also that he was Romanian and had to return to Romania, a strict Communist country at that time. He knew, too, that he had died soon after his return, from a stab wound to the chest. What he did *not* know, though, was that his father had been killed by his lover of many years, a younger man of twenty nine. Nor that jealousy was the motive; either of her, of her pregnancy, - or even of a new male lover (or female, for having broken the mould once it could surely be repeated). She did not want him to know that his father was gay, that his own tiny foetal beginnings might have ignited the jealous spark that killed him, and, worst of all, that if his father had lived he might have been aborted, because that possibility *had* existed. In a way he owed his life to his father's death, and viewed that starkly it all seemed terrible.

Julia wondered if she had not told Alex significant details for his sake, as she liked to believe, or for her sake, because she felt ashamed. And this dead man, who had lain so quietly there beneath the terrace wall for all those years, whose shame was he?

*Please, please may it not be murder. And please may it have nothing to do with Frances.*


On the way home she encountered a road block. A red and white barricade closed off the main square and a thick cordon of spectators jostled for the best view of whatever was happening somewhere beyond the fountain. The old fashioned Bar San Roque had spilled out onto the road with tables set for groups of eight, twelve and even twenty, but evidently their feasting had been curtailed just before the dessert course, for creme caramels and apple tarts lay untouched on delicate gold rimmed plates.

The school blackboard straddled the pavement, with numbered names from 1-20 chalked upon it. She recognised a handful of the names, five to be precise: Sangre de Toro, Eulogio, Fidel Castro, Primo de Rivera and Capitalista, - all pigeons corralled in Arturo's rear courtyard. The twenty names were matched to what could only be betting odds, and Sangre de Toro seemed to be the favourite at 7/4.


Suddenly the church clock struck three. Simultaneously from surrounding rooftops and balconies a flock of pigeons with different coloured plumage was released to flutter, circle and descend onto the square. Immediately the music wafting from Bar San Roque stopped, and the remaining diners from the inside tables (who had stayed to gobble their desserts) emerged. Julia and the boys stood on the Ayuntamiento steps to watch three smartly dressed men with official badges (the 'judges') fan out across the square, armed with binoculars, walkie-talkies and score sheets. They took up diagonally opposed positions to 'cover' the square, one squatting to report on pigeon movements beneath an old blue van.

The huddle of pigeons under the chassis promptly scurried out, hopped onto the lip of the fountain and squabbled for the best perches. Some in the crowd offered vocal encouragement:

"Go it Barbarossa!"

"Shaft her Innocencio!"

"Give her one for me!"

"Atta' boy!"

"Get yer pecker up!"

"Is it a *fucking* competition?" Marco asked, incredulous.

" 'fraid so," Julia said quietly. "It's all coming back to me now. That poor pigeon whose tail feathers have been plucked out is the only female. All the rest are male."

The judges would have undergone a stringent screening process. They had to be men, in full control of all their faculties, from outside Milagra, as honest as the day, without a criminal record, and with a minimum of fifteen years' intimate knowledge of pigeons. They also needed supremely sharp eyesight, for unlike footballers these birds did not wear named and numbered T-shirts but had to be distinguished by the colouring of their tail feathers.

Moreover the scoring system was notoriously complex. A male 'stud' gained one point for a 'contact' with the female - which could be as soft and fleeting as a light brush of feathers or a momentary clack of beaks, and five points for going 'all the way'. Some males were so busy narcissistically strutting and preening they never went near the female, and come the end of the competition achieved a humiliating zero score. Consequently they were not put back into cages and pampered for another year, but unceremoniously stunned, plucked, gutted and braised with finely chopped carrots and baby shallots beneath a layer of pastry.

Betting was a serious affair involving immense sums of euros. So anyone staging a hold-up in Bar San Roque right then could reasonably count on a handsome six figure haul!

There was a sudden fracas when someone threw pastry crumbs onto the tarmac (interference with the contestants was strictly forbidden). A clutch of four male birds made a run for the crumbs, but those with money on them hissed in fury, for hunger assuaged is desire diminished, even though the prey are different.

"If Velasquez eats I'm ruined!"

"Mine's not had a morsel since yesterday."

"What if those crumbs have Viagra?"

"Bon apetito!"

The church bell sounded its single note for the quarter hour and, perfectly on cue, the pigeons wheeled upwards, circled the bell tower and followed the lone and tail-less female in a dense cloud of testosterone, heading straight for the cemetery. Immediately the judges leapt like gangsters into waiting cars, and there was a raucous cacophany of car doors slamming, engines revving, motor bikes roaring and horns tooting as a cavalcade launched in pursuit. Sra Bigot leaned out of her bar doorway to jeer at the convoy.

There were very few occasions when she felt moved to make a stand, but here both her femininity and her allegiance to the cockatiel were under attack. Julia admired her pluckiness and noticed Muriel from Montejoven seizing the moment to step forward with a protest placard. STOP CRUELTY NOW! She had not even thought to translate these sentiments into Spanish, and the impact of her message was already weakened by her reputation as a complete nutcase who ran a stray cat sanctuary. She and her lifelong companion, Elspeth, ceaselessly toured the province collecting all the skinny, mangey alley cats who hung around the rubbish bins, then re-educating them to a life of indolent luxury reclining on sofas and camp beds in their three storey house in Montejoven. Being considered mad she was usually treated with respect, but this time someone did issue a mild challenge:

"Aren't cats cruel when they kill birds?"

But as it was in Spanish she merely smiled incomprehendingly.

# 12

The Guardia arrived next morning, not as Reggie had warned at five o'clock, but at the more civilised hour of nine.

Instead of driving their jeep all the way up they left it at the scene of the excavation, where they circled the earth mound, eyeing it with interest.

There were three; the Cabo from Milagra, a taller, stiffer man whose body language and stripes testified to his superior rank, but the third was an insignificant cog in the machinations of law enforcement, and he knew it and followed the two up the gravel drive as if he were a pageboy at their wedding. It was important she hit the right register; a respectful formality but without overdoing the ingratiating undertones, since they were a touchy breed whose collective consciousness had little in common with humanity at large.

Although Franco was long dead and Spain a modern democracy, the Guardia Civil were an outmoded hangover from times of dictatorship, essentially paramilitary officers who lived in army-style barracks. They were not intended to fraternise with local communities, and were deliberately posted to locations far from their homes so that personal relationships with locals would not influence them. Normal, human feelings were in any case systematically drilled out of them, and the profession naturally attracted power freaks, bullies, sadists, dimwits and weirdos of all types. Pen these into custom built barracks, stuff them into a uniform of black jack boots and ridiculously shaped hard hats, complete with baton and powerful handgun, and you have the perfect recipe for an irresponsible totalitarian police force. Julia quietly crossed her fingers, and kept her expression steady.

They seemed to take forever to reach the house. The superior officer stood like an imperious statue gazing contemptuously at her flowerbed of flustered looking pansies, presenting her with the view of his profile while the local Cabo clicked heels and rapped her door with his baton.

The third, hovering in the background, looked embarrassed. She sensed he was intimidated by her, but could see no advantage in that, when the other two were most certainly not.

It was the local Cabo who finally spoke.

"We've come in connection with the body. You will be interviewed in the Cuartel next Wednesday, at 10.30 in the morning." His pink tongue retrieved a droplet of spittle from his lower lip and Julia hoped it wasn't the prospect of the cross examination that made him salivate. "You should be aware it was found on *your* land. You are strongly advised to have a lawyer present."

Julia, unsure whether it was wise to say anything, nevertheless blurted out, "Was it *definitely* on my land? I understood the boundary to be ground level at the base of the wall."

This irritated the superior officer, and she immediately regretted her stupidity in splitting hairs. "A foolish objection," he snapped. "His position was the result of *your* wall falling on him, and after twenty five years the soil level has of course changed."

He stared through her as if she bore the transparency of a ghost. Then he clacked his tongue and the other two, obedient as collie dogs, strolled back to the jeep.

"We'll need your consent to DNA samples," he said once the others had gone, "from yourself and your eldest son. We'll have the forms ready at interview," and he turned on his heel and marched downhill, the gravel churning and scuffing his polished boots.


Alex and Marco watched their leave taking, also conscious, like Julia, that they had injected a supernatural chill to the atmosphere. It was as if their very presence made one shiver with the guilt of an unknown crime, although of course each had a genuine cause to feel guilt. Alex nursed the secret of where Jorgen's drug-filled juggling ball lay hidden, while Marco worried about the two dirt stained incisors so ineffectively disguised in his jar of pearl white milk teeth. Both felt a surge of panic that the house and garden would be searched, but neither dared tell the other of their fears.

Marco had a momentary wild idea of returning the teeth where he found them, until he realised with alarm that his finger prints would be all over them. Perhaps water, or something stronger like detergent or bleach would remove those finger prints, but without knowing he dare not try for a failed attempt would look guiltier than the present situation, which he thought he might just pull off as the innocent prank of an eight year old nutter.

Alex cursed the day he had sneaked off with Jorgen's powder keg - was it cocaine or heroin? How to tell the difference? And which was worse in terms of classification, A or B, under the Illegal Drugs Act? But then he realised that he was thinking of English law. Maybe in Spain there was no difference and both entailed longterm imprisonment. Would Julia ever forgive him? Or, worse still, would she be found guilty because she was the adult who ought to be responsible for him? Would Lise visit him in jail? She should, after all the heist was her idea in the first place, and he in a rash moment of bravura had fallen into the trap of courting her admiration by stupidly carrying it through. He hoped he could remember the exact spot where he had buried it. He flirted with the idea of digging it up and transporting it far away. But then dismissed it; tampering with the drugs now would leave a fresh, disturbed look in the garden which Julia - or the Guardia - might notice, and he could hardly travel far without Julia's knowledge and cooperation. He would have to sit tight, say and do nothing, and hope for the best.

Julia watched them leave. Their motions followed the exact same pattern as on arrival, but in reverse order. Arguably they eyed the earth mound with more familiarity and less respect, and certainly they kicked a few more loose stones out of their way as they prepared to climb aboard their jeep, as if to establish no obstacles could obstruct their path.

She went to wash up the breakfast dishes. To do something so symbolically housewifely struck her as odd, considering the bizarre enactment of masculine domination she had just witnessed, but the warm water and bubbles of soap suds had a genuinely calming effect. She had expected the visit, but the parting remark came as a shock. If they needed a DNA sample from her, not Frances (and Thank God they had not yet asked for that, since that was a horrifying prospect), then they must consider the dead man a relative of hers. Frances' side of the family was traceable. That left only the one dreaded assumption; they must suspect the dead man to be her father.

She made her way to her mother's studio where she could lie down and let the moment of nausea pass. Banking the cushions on the window seat she lay cocooned in an old cotton drape, staring blankly at the ceiling. It was as if she'd been administered a general anaesthetic and was counting down to loss of consciousness; she could actually trace the numbness as it spread from her core to her extremities. The paralysis was soon complete. She tried wiggling her little finger but it refused to respond, filled to bloating point with something tingly cold and chemical that had usurped the place of blood. Her brain gradually ceased to operate not only her reflex actions and her bodily functions but also her cognitive motions, and in this state of suspended animation time passed without her knowledge.

Alex and Marco peeped in from time to time, assuming for the first hour that she was exhausted and taking a nap. Then, as the hours ticked by and their twinges of hunger suggested lunchtime was approaching, they decided to intervene. They trod carelessly, banged the door, clattered the saucepans and turned the cold water tap full on so that it bounced off the sink and sprayed Marco in the face, but even his squawks failed to rouse her.

Then Alex grew alarmed. He lifted off the cushions in case they were overheating a fever or suffocating her, but she felt cool to his touch, almost unnaturally cool. Her eyes were closed but, when they held a mirror against

113

her nostrils, as they had seen detectives do with comatose bodies in movies, they were relieved to see a faint blue mist, so she must still be breathing. Marco claimed he could feel her pulse, but Alex overruled him for he was miles away from where any pulse would be, although it might be her heart.

"Actually I think she's pregnant," he told Alex. "There's something moving in her belly."

"She's probably digesting her breakfast," Alex said. The idea of indigestion seemed comfortingly plausible, so he sent Marco to find mint in the garden, forbidding him expressly to go near the Fuente for the sharper flavoured spearmint.


When they finally produced a steaming broth of mint stew, obnoxiously strong and a deeply unattractive brackish brown colour after the addition of several sticky spoonfuls of honey, they tiptoed close in trepidation and held it a hair's breadth from her nose so that the dense inhalations could revive her. And to their intense relief, and against all odds, her eyes did indeed flicker open and she began to register her surroundings. Her breathing grew regular and stronger, and the ghost of a smile showed that she had recognised them as her children.

"Wow, you had us worried there," Alex told her, steering a balance between being truthful but not alarming her. "Do you want the room lighter, or darker? This mint's for breathing not for drinking," and by way of illustration he clamped his hand over the glass, then slid it off, rapidly repeating the action so that puffs of steam rose like smoke signals. "You thirsty? Water or juice?"

"A glass of water would be good," she managed to answer, but her voice sounded unfamiliar to her ears, small and distant, with the quality of echo you might find in a squat underground tunnel quarried through damp clay.

When Alex brought the water the glass slithered through her fingers and shattered on the tiled floor, the water soaking the cushions and her clothing. This worried Alex almost more than her former state of inertia, so that when he had brought a second glass, and held it while she sipped, he made the decision Marte should be summoned. But Marte had not got used to the concept that mobile phones were a form of communication; hers was always kept on the mantelpiece like a trinket, face down, off and empty of charge. Even on the rare occasions when it was possible to leave it with a message, that message stayed in outer limbo, for Marte had no idea how to access it. Her terrestial phone had been disconnected over an unpaid bill, and her ring doves, that long ago she had used as carrier pigeons until too many of them defected to Vicente (who fed them superior corn) were only ever good for outgoing messages. The only way to summon Marte, therefore, was for one of them to walk there.

He could not let Marco go alone, because if obliged to cross a tract of countryside without human company he would be sure to amuse himself impersonating a wild animal. He would imitate a kangaroo and sprain an ankle, vanish lizardlike down some crevice, or, as had happened before, get stuck up a tree in the guise of a young and inexperienced racoon. Even though leaving him anywhere unsupervised was fraught with risks, at home under strict instructions to light no fires and attempt no cooking was safest.

Marco, once Alex had left, set about keeping Julia amused so she would not slip back into her strange, somnolent state. He was under orders to be peacefully quiet which severely restricted his style, thus he struck off with a short mime sketch that had gone down well with his classmates at an end of term talent show. He had double jointed elbows and could move his limbs with rubbery flexibility, making him physically ideal for the type of slapstick comedic mime popular in old silent movies. But unfortunately Julia's eyes stared vacantly in just the one direction, so his stage area was disappointingly limited and he had to curtail the final flurries of his repertoire. Even though his audience neither clapped nor smiled, he fancied he acquitted himself well.

He then asked if she would appreciate some music. She did not protest, and although he sensed she might be expecting a suitably soothing classical CD, he fetched his recorder which ought to appease her for she frequently urged him to practise more regularly. He made a complete hash of Greensleeves, then restored his reputation with an evocative Marie's Wedding, which he felt did penetrate Julia's incommunicado state for he caught the glimpse of a possible tear forming in the corner of one sightless eye.

He came closer to verify this, but grew alarmed because her eyes began to roll and show far too much of the less attractive white globular part, the livelier blue irises having rotated upwards to beneath her lids as if peering into the secrets of her inner brain. Muttering apologies and reprimanding himself for ignoring Alex's express commands for quiet, he sat in silent immobility for almost five minutes.

When he could endure this no longer he slunk away and returned with a book, and sitting cross legged he read her the chapter on reproduction from The Life of Toads. Finally he could no longer resist the allure of his hand held computer, but he tried to include her with the occasional commentary on his progress through the stages from novice nobody to ultimate superhero.

Marte and Alex arrived when he had reached a moderately heroic status, and he hurriedly packed away his game to prevent misconstructions of selfishness.

Marte was calm and efficient. She too consulted Julia's eyes, but read more into their opacity than he was capable of. Apparently she was not so much peering inwards as short of blood sugar, and Marte praised herself for her foresight in bringing so many of the right remedies. Julia was soon sitting up and obediently drinking a concentrated cocktail of fruits drenched in natural sugar, and the alabaster whiteness of her lips and skin slowly relented, allowing hints of colour to flow back. She had little strength in her arms, and still could not move her legs, but at least she could speak more clearly and move her head without dizziness, so Marte relieved Marco and Alex of their duties declaring she could cope alone.

"Right," said Marte, in a manner so redolent of Germanic efficiency she would have denied it her voice had it been recorded, "you are suffering from shock, severe shock . That, or it must be diabetes."

"I hope I never repeat that experience," Julia clung to her fruit concentrate as if it alone prevented her drowning. "I've never felt so helpless - I thought I'd had a stroke."

"Well, you must hope it's not diabetes. I'll keep an eye on you, just in case. So, the Guardia made a visit? Then they will come to me soon..." Marte's eyes drifted to the outside as she fretted over the damning impression her small mound of rotting vehicles would give them. They would associate her magnificent spot with a flyblown gypsy encampment, and ferret out a crime if they conceivably could. "Mein Gott," she cried, noticing as if for the first time the massive slice carved from the slopes below, and the newly tarmacked grid plan of streets that ran up it. "How this monster Holidaylandia has ruined your view. It's right in your face!"

"So many things have happened since," Julia answered, "that it's gone to the back of my mind." She looked searchingly at Marte and suddenly asked, "D'you know how old my father was?"

"Your *father*?" Marte looked concerned that her mind was less coherent than she had hoped.

"Yes. Was he older than Frances...or younger?"

In '78 Frances would have been thirty nine, while the skeleton was apparently twenty seven or eight at the time of his death, so considerably younger. If her father was older than her it would eliminate him... Marte screwed up her face with the effort of comparative calculations:

"I can't be sure, I didn't really know him - Frances kept him all to herself and then, when they split up, he never came again. So," she shrugged her shoulders, "they could have been about ze same age."

Inconclusive then.

Julia found that, just as the frozen immobility of her body gradually melted and returned to the soft, supple warmth of a living and breathing organism, so did the intractable wall of resistance that had blocked off her early memories gradually desolidify into fluid tributaries of sensitized experience. She had never known her father, but by pulling together throw away phrases from Frances, plus the few snippets of solid information Frances had allowed herself to reveal, a picture of the past gradually came into focus. Most of it due to Reggie's visit later that day, when he realised it was no longer possible to protect Frances' confidences.


They had met four years before Julia was born, and shortly after Frances first arrived in Milagra. Her father was out there combing the wild mountainous ranges above Milagra in search of rare butterflies, and one particular desperately rare species hovering on extinction, whose name Frances never could recall when she told Julia the story. She had taken Julia once to the place where they had camped out for five days in pursuit of this elusive butterfly (or was it a moth?), high on a windswept sierra where golden eagles circled overhead and the crumbling ruined walls of a Moorish Castle gave, if not a roof over their heads, at least some semblance of protection from the elements. They had slept, or more truthfully made passionate love and barely slept at all, in a little round borrie like construction that had once contained the castle's supply of olives and dried grain, and now provided the best shelter from the chilly north wind.

Frances' fingers and eyes, presented with what to anyone else was a chaotic muddle of shattered pottery fragments, could somehow, subliminally, recreate through a painstaking process the original pot. In a similar way Julia's father could somehow absorb the life forces of the butterfly (or was it a moth?) he was hunting. Frances described how he could sniff the air and tell exactly what flowers were in bloom and where, he could direct her to areas of moisture on a hillside, find hidden streams or different layers of soil, locate granite or quartz, slate or sandstone, limestone or chalk with unerring accuracy and no sense of pride in his strange gift. His instincts would lead him even in the dark to butterfly eggs, however artfully camouflaged in their place of hiding, and he could feel in his bones the slightest movement of caterpillars on the prowl, and recognise the chrysalis that wasn't a dead leaf in the midst of a whole forest of dead leaves.

He once joked that he must have been a butterfly (or was it a moth?) in a previous life, though what he had done wrong to be subsequently punished with a human incarnation he could not imagine! Perhaps he had betrayed his female counterpart, in just the same way he was currently betraying his wife back in England, but he did not lie to Frances and pretend to be free; she knew from the beginning that he was married.

Their relationship lasted three years. Or more accurately three successive winters through to the end of spring, those being the butterfly season and the time he could justifiably leave his wife in England and live with his lover in Spain, chasing love and hope and butterflies. He was a naturalist not a collector, so he didn't forage about in a panama hat waving a butterfly net at anything bright that flapped its wings, as Frances first feared might be the procedure. Nor did he catch and kill his prey, then display it in a walnut cabinet with Latin name, date and place of capture written in italic lettering. No, he researched the likely habitats, narrowing down to a realistic area that he could cover on foot through the diligent questioning of locals, which he managed in a fluent but very strangely accented Spanish. Thereafter he relied on his eyes, nose and uncanny instinct, and the success of his hunt was the heart stopping moment when his rare and beautiful prey was sighted, a moment he would record on celluloid with his old Leica camera and a telephoto lens. He also made field notes on the location and every conceivable related detail, even the atmospheric temperature and humidity level. Everything, in fact, except for the existence of his hunting companion, Frances.

She was not always there, though. She cherished the early period when butterfly stalking was an absorbing novelty and they craved each other's company so much that they could not be apart. But later she preferred resurrecting her pots and she had grown used to her own company, since by then she had spent more than two summers and autumns without him.

The time Reggie knew most about was the ultimate breakdown of their relationship, in late autumn of their fourth year. By then she had reached a point where she could no longer tolerate sharing him with another woman, a woman she never spoke with him about, never asked him about, and whom she knew absolutely nothing about; all because she did not want to feel either jealousy or guilt, both of which would eat away at their relationship and ultimately corrode their love.

So she gave him an ultimatum: he must leave his wife for ever to come and live exclusively with her in Spain, or their relationship must end and she would never see, hear or speak of him again. She had been fully expecting him to choose her, for the strength of his love for her, and hers for him, left no room for doubt in her mind. But she was wrong. For whatever reason - and she never knew because she would not let it be spoken about - he would not, or could not, leave his wife. He must have felt an immensely powerful sense of duty or loyalty or honour, - or maybe guilt. Whatever tie it was it defeated her. So she ended their relationship just as she had threatened, but with the final stroke of deliberately becoming pregnant with his child.

"I think it must have been torture for her," Reggie said, "knowing how proud she was, and how wholehearted about her feelings, to have to accept that the one man she truly loved voluntarily gave her up for another. But I never wanted to talk about it, and I promised her I wouldn't." He looked troubled, as if she might be listening and berate him later. Then he looked Julia straight in the eyes, "I especially don't want you to feel that she didn't love you for yourself, because I know that's not true. OK, the act of becoming pregnant was a weapon against him, a way of increasing his pain, and also a way of preserving his love in her life. But once you were born you were you, and everything else fell away."

Julia felt oddly grateful for her nervous collapse that morning. If she had not been through such a deadening experience she would not be so calm now, in the aftermath. Under normal circumstances she would have reacted emotionally, but as it was she simply accepted it, almost dispassionately, for what it was; a sad love story.

Frances kept her word. She adhered unwaveringly to the terms of her ultimatum. She blotted him out of her life by destroying all traces of him: photos, letters, papers, his sketches of butterflies, clothes and every tiny little gift he gave her. She even uprooted young saplings they had planted, and painted over the layers of whitewash he had applied to renew the freshness of the house each spring before they said goodbye.

She 'disappeared' him with such thoroughness that Julia's Spanish Birth Certificate confidently asserted 'Father : Unknown', and she remained obdurately silent on the subject, apart from the faint glimpse of their shared life that she inexplicably allowed Julia on the trip to the ruins of the Moorish Castle.

Julia's mind raced on, fearful, suspicious. What could have motivated that journey? Despite her attempts to relive the excursion as an older seven year old or a younger three year old, too many factors suggested that she must have been five. And logically, if one dared to continue that dangerous thread, the trip must have closely coincided with the man's death beneath the terrace wall.

Might it, then, have been an exorcism of guilt? Could it, could it possibly be that her father had returned to resurrect their love? Perhaps there was a jealous scene, Frances found sleeping with another man (at that time she invariably was sleeping with another man) and a fight ensued, resulting in his death... So, who might have dealt the death blow, Frances herself, or the lover?

Alternatively it might have been manslaughter, not murder... Perhaps an ugly scene got out of hand, and his death was not contrived but an unexpected, terrible, accidental outcome. Had they then panicked, lain his dead body at the foot of the wall, and then provoked its collapse in order to bury him where no-one would ever find him? Or, had he been running away in some kind of blind panic, missed the route in the dark, or tripped on a stone to accidently dislodge the upper section of the wall, so that it fell and smothered him? And then no-one even knew he was there...

Her worst fear was that it had been exactly as she had witnessed it in her nightmare; only she had mistakenly supplanted her father with the weird French violinist.

As at the time of Reggie's visit and his revelations, she now once again, wakeful in the small hours of the morning which are really more the very middle of the night, felt thankful that her attack of shock had left her so drained. For it enabled her to think thoughts and imagine scenes that normally would have affected her deeply, but with her present detachment carried virtually no emotional impact whatsoever.

# 13

Colin was extremely fastidious about the orderliness and strict cleanliness of his little house just on the outskirts of Milagra. But today he had been forced to embrace chaos and disorder, since the only way he could think of turning the key on the locked door of memories from '78 was to look through his accounts for that year. He had reluctantly climbed his shiny new loft ladder, braved the olfactory discomfort of dry dust (hopefully not the residue of joists chewed by woodworm) and the unpleasant sight of dead bluebottles who always died with their legs in the air, to hunt through his lines of neatly stacked box files, until he found three with the relevant date.

These were now upended, their contents strewn across his dining table and every other horizontal surface in his neat little living room.


Most of the bills and receipts were for everyday commodities or recurring items like petrol, bread, groceries, dry cleaning etc. with nothing unusual to provoke a specific memory. But he felt that if he laboriously trawled through every single crumpled slip eventually he would discover the one which stood out, the one which would set in motion a train of recall and unleash a whole chain of forgotten events.

Memory's like that, he told himself, shoving a handkerchief over his nose as he sneezed from the flying dustmites; throw a pebble into a still lake and the ripples radiate. Sra Mas Ivars, his twice-a-week cleaning lady for the last eighteen years, swept, mopped and polished around him, and he pretended to enjoy the way she fussed with the paper piles and slopped mop suds on his shoes, forever mindful of the friendly reputation he must stress and trebly stress before the ghastly round of interviews began.

There was no quick fix to his toiling. On and on, pile after pile. He missed elevenses with Reggie and persisted through a sandwich lunch and beyond, until his finger joints groaned at the repetitive motion of lifting, perusing and refiling. Some of the papers were so cheap and transparent it strained his eyes to read their fading print, while others had yellowed with age. It was boring, monotonous, depressing work, and it left him with the dismal conclusion that his life had been nothing more exciting than a perpetual absorption of tea, bread, beer and cornflakes.

At last, some seven minutes after he had partaken of his late afternoon beverage of Earl Grey tea diluted by precisely two drops of milk, along with two shortbread biscuits served doubledeckerwise on the saucer to the right of the cup, he was satisfyingly rewarded by a receipt that talked. It was from the ferreteria in Milagra, for a galvanised rubber torch and four batteries costing 450 pesetas (which on the prices of those days was quite some torch). He exuberantly celebrated with an unaccustomed second cup of Earl Grey, then put his feet up on the brocade sofa to indulge in a spot of reliving the past.

The only downside to this kindled memory was that it involved Germans, so before he went any further down the road of recall he made a silent wish that the skeleton would not prove to be German. This particular bunch of Germans his purchase of a torch brought back to mind were one of the weirdest he'd ever encountered. They travelled in and lived in a large black doubledecker bus, handpainted to depict the night sky with twinkling silver stars, a gold full moon and one or two ruby red meteors trailing tails of sickly lilac. The occupants of the bus were about twelve women, although the number was approximate because he never saw them lined up in a group so that he could properly count them, a hefty handful of children, and one revoltingly self-adulatory specimen of Teutonic manhood. This man, posing as some kind of King, God, Guru, or tribal chief, treated the women as vassals more than wives, and the whole carry on was enough to cause Colin palpitations and diarrhoea all over again, twenty five years later, just from thinking of it.

Inside the bus, which was afloat with purple silk curtains and red cushions and could only be compared to a cheap harem, the silly females had hung a lifesize portrait painted by the only wife with enough wits to squeeze out a tube of acrylic paint, and which depicted this abominable God-guru in a moment of divine contemplation, wearing a halo, or aura as they called it.

Every evening Colin would hear them chanting and worshipping this portrait, wailing and humming to the accompaniment of cymbals, bongos and triangles and chanting in what to Colin's practised colonial ear sounded suspiciously Hindustani. If he ever managed to fall asleep during this nightly caterwauling he would often wake with a start, shivering from a cold sweat, reliving the terrors of his babyhood in India when the excessive heat made the natives restless and dangerous. During daytime hours, which for them began disgracefully late in the morning owing to nightly activities he preferred not to think about, plus the consumption of quantities of stupefying drugs, the women would light fires and stir simmering vegetable stews and cook endless turreens of brown rice, as well as preening themselves and hugging each other to prove they had said 'no' to jealousy. Their grubby children crawled around digging in the earth, and since they had no toilet facilites and dug that into the earth as well, one could say their children played with their own faeces and not be exaggerating.

Colin had to endure them as neighbours because his garden bordered the vineyard of Diego Lopez Garcia, who had decided to rent them a narrow strip of land which did not interfere with his vines and normally made him no money. Colin, when he heard of the arrangement, had offered him twice the rent to keep the strip empty, but Diego disobligingly refused.

The man they worshipped was singularly unworthy. Colin was prepared to admit that he himself was no heart stopper; in fact confess in all honesty that with his ginger hair, freckles, pink skin and frequent rashes, not to mention dandruff, webbed toes and flattened buttocks he did not even manage to attract himself into practising onanism unless in an extremity of testosteronic frustration. But without risking the pot and kettle parallel he could truthfully deride this man as a nonentity. Some hippie males had style, Colin was not such a stodge as to deny that; they had long, clean, flowing hair, beautiful bronzed torsos and hiphugging faded blue jeans with all sorts of imaginative rainbow coloured accoutrements that just shouted aloud the glory of their triumphant masculinity, sexuality, creativity, originality and revolutionary spirit. But this one, well, it beggared belief what in God's name his female followers could possibly see in him. Most of them were perfectly acceptable looking, with bumps and curves in all the expected places. They could have had (more or less) their pick of men, yet they were prepared to live in squalor and queue up for their nightly turn of turning him on. He surely could not turn them on... not with his straggly, mousy hair, his sallow, expressionless face, his acned chin, protruding ribs, thin bandy legs and bulbous feet encased in broken sandals. And yet they would wash him with devotion, massage oil into his skin with reverence, and feed him like a baby, spooning the choicest grains of brown rice and the juiciest chunks of parsnip into his open, waiting mouth.

The only possible explanation, Colin concluded with a shudder of disgust, was that he must have a donger to die for.

Anyway, after several months of tolerating the daily stench of urinal and the nightly warblings of insanity, Colin decided he had had enough. He could have gone to the Guardia, because the kilos of drugs in their possession amounted to many prison sentences, but he had a strong aversion to truncheons and guns. Also the system of 'denuncia' meant that it would be common knowledge that he was the snitch, and in hippie society grassing to the pigs is an absolute no no, unless you want to court a most horrible revenge. So Colin went instead to Manolo the bee keeper, who had hated hippies ever since a troupe of Vegans had raided his hives for his best honeycomb honey, an act which apparently demonstrated their disapproval of humans who robbed bees by substituting honey for inferior candy. He agreed to lend Colin his pack of three fierce hunting dogs, with strict instructions on how to use them.

Colin spent the evening on tenterhooks, for his plan depended on the propitious interplay of uncertain contingencies. It was no fiendish murder plot, not like the old woman's dog training scheme in Maupassant's The Vendetta, but there were potential dangers to it nevertheless. Plus he wished to avoid harming either the women or children, or, naturally, himself.

He kept the three fierce dogs locked in his toolshed, appeasing them with expensive cuts of meat, whilst he eyed the clock nervously. Everything depended on strict adherence to habit. For some time now he had been closely monitoring their nightly schedule: after their communal evening meal and their subsequent musical jamboree of cult worship, the male god-insect habitually repaired to the driver's cab which had black tinted windows and doubled as the love nest. He took his first choice woman with him, and there they did whatever they did, and whether or not it produced sounds of ecstasy it was impossible to tell because the rest of them continued clashing their cymbals, tinkling their triangles, banging their bongos and wailing and ululating in high soprano voices. After first choice woman had finished her go, she was replaced by second choice woman, and so on and so forth.


Then came the interlude crucial to Colin's plan. After the visit of the sixth woman, so if Colin's total of twelve was accurate then halfway through his night's entertainment, the male specimen emerged alone from the cab and carried his enormously swollen penis over to the edge of Diego's vines to relieve himself during several minutes. There must have been something more potent than mere urine in the golden arc that sprayed the vines, for Colin had noticed with alarm that strange, strong and vibrant plants were newly flourishing around this spot, but now was not the time to puzzle over botanical conundrums. For this three to five minute interlude, which occurred nightly at any moment between 2.00am to 2.30am without fail, was the moment for the dogs to leap into action.


Although Colin was normally tucked up in bed by 11pm at the latest, he was so nervous there was no chance he would fall asleep by mistake. He tried to read but his eyes skated off the page, he tried the radio but the cheery voices jarred his nerves, so in the end he played game after game of solitaire, clenching his stomach at every tiny sound. At 2.00am he turned out the lights in the house, put on his alpaca coat and crept by the light of his 450 pesetas torch down the garden path to where he could hide behind the toolshed. The dogs growled menacingly at his approach, until they realised he was the giver of choice meats. He stood silently in the shadows, his hand trembling over the door latch, gritting his teeth at the unstoppable rondo from the female orchestra, waiting and waiting for the sexual organ to emerge.

He was not intending any disproportionate violence to ensue, for these were hunting dogs bred to chase rabbits or flush partridges out of thickets, they weren't biters or maulers like alsations, rottweilers or similar thugdogs. All he really wanted was for the organ to get a nasty scare and decide to move camp, so that he, Colin could regain a bit of peace and equanimity.

He watched the seconds tick by on his wristwatch, illumined by the low beam of the torch (it had two settings, accounting for its priciness), and trembled despite his alpaca, the wind from the interior being bitterly cold. At last the moment of truth presented itself; his ears were so alert that in spite of the music and the moaning of the wind he heard the click of the cab door opening. Then the tread of sandal on step, and finally the scuffling footsteps as the man steered his inflamed penis towards its outdoor latrine. The time had come. He lifted the toolshed latch and as he did so gave a low whistle to the dogs whose claws could be heard on the toolshed floor. In less than three seconds they had flung open the door and sprung into action, with all the pent up instinct of hunters bred for the chase. There was a moment of indecision as they collided with each other in their haste and had no clue as to their quarry, but only a moment, for then the lead dog heard the torrent of urine splashing among the vines and new, mysterious proliferation of plants, and he galloped headlong that way, followed by his pack of two all baying with the thrill of the hunt.

Confused noises followed, and Colin was in an agony of ignorance as to how to interpret them. The female choir warbled on through what must by then have been at least verse six hundred and eighty two, while from the vineyard came a perplexing mixture of yowling, yapping, pissing, thudding, thumping and whining, but it was impossible to distinguish which of the emissions were human and which canine. Colin was relieved there were no sounds of tearing flesh or gobbling of testicles, but he was also anxious that no harm came to the dogs, since Manolo was counting on their safe return. What could be happening? Had the organ brought about a lightning conversion and enlisted three new cult members? Would the dogs return to attack Colin? Was a vile act of bestiality taking place out there in the darkness? Had the dogs in their confusion turned on each other, letting the human escape unscathed?

Colin was growing desperate because he dare not remain alone in the dark, and he dare not return to the house without having locked the dogs safely back in the toolshed, and the sounds he now heard seemed more dribbling, slathering, slobbering noises. He tiptoed up the garden path in forlorn spirits, certain that his plan had horribly backfired, when the three dogs suddenly bounded up behind him, bouncing, frolicking and licking his hands. Ignoring his rule of no dogs in the house he ushered them in like honoured guests, and uttered not a word of complaint when they left a trail of paw marks on his powder blue carpet, or when his table lamp got knocked over by a wagging tail.

He never did learn exactly what had happened. The dogs seemed happier, bouncier and friendlier than before their sortie, but there was nothing to suggest that their frolicsome disposition came from engaging with an outsized penis. They licked his hands a great deal, but he had been told this was a dog's way of ensuring salt in the diet - either that or a mark of friendship, and he didn't have enough experience of dog saliva to know if the gooey stickiness was normal or a telltale sign that they'd recently supped on seminal fluid. He left the dogs to share the sofa and easy chairs while he went up to bed for what remained of the night, and although he put wax pellets in his ears to muffle the sounds he fancied that the singing and banging in the bus continued as usual until the early hours of the morning.

After breakfast he led the dogs to Manolo's casita. Manolo was delighted to find them in the peak of condition; their coats shone, their teeth gleamed and their gums were as fresh as raspberries.

"You must have given them solomillo de primera!" he said gratefully, rewarding Colin with a broad smile and a pathetically small jar of honey.

"Muchas gracias", Colin replied. He wanted to say he had fed them entrecote, not filet mignon, but he just could not master the advanced vocabulary.

By the time he returned home late in the afternoon, having lunched at Bar del Bigot and dawdled in the ferreteria, he was amazed to find the bus no longer there. The strip of ground was an utter mess with churning wheel marks, charred stones and ashes where their cooking fires had burned, mounds of faeces where their babies had crapped, and puddles here and there where the women had showered with saucepans of water, but it was wonderfully, gloriously empty at last.


Colin carefully placed the torch receipt back in its 1978 box file. What memories it had revived! How it had propelled him back! He chuckled to himself as he relived that night of bravery, when he and the trusty hounds had worked together to weave their magic and disappear that bus. How he was longing to tell Reggie the story, and how Reggie would laugh... Another pleasing aspect to the tale was that there was no violent ending to it, nothing that need perturb him in the run up to his interview with the Guardia. Apparently the man had been strong enough and whole enough to drive the bus northwards, for he had been spotted at the wheel wearing an expression of untroubled contentment as he negotiated the sharp elbow bends on the road between Milagra and Montejoven. The troupe eventually made it back to Germany, and according to Marte, who heard the news filtered through a number of supposedly reliable intermediaries, the man unceremoniously dumped his dozen wives and went to live in the Black Forest, where he leased kennels and bred prize winning Afghan hounds with whom he shared much more than was proper or decent.

It was only late that night, while Colin lay in his pyjamas and puzzled once more over what could possibly have been the man's attraction, that he realised the story could indeed potentially do him harm. If it was recounted by Manolo, and interpreted by the Guardia in the light of the skeleton's position, that is. Oh God! He would have to hope that Manolo had forgotten all about the loaning of the dogs and his hatred of hippies, and that the skeleton had no suspicious indents that could possibly have been dogs' teeth marks on any of his bones, especially not the cocyx, pelvis and ankles, all prime hunting dog targets. On second thoughts, better not tell Reggie anything about it...

Colin was of course not alone in his flashback researches, but it would have surprised him had he known that the Guardia themselves were having a hard time.

1978 was a long way back in police record terms, way predating computer technology for rural Cuartels. In those days the Milagra force had been under the command of an enormously fat Cabo who was almost as corrupt as he was overweight, and who rarely stirred abroad on patrol duty for two very sensible reasons. The first was that he could scarcely fit in the then patrol car, a little Renault 4, and even when he was squeezed in, a delicate, embarrassing and exhausting operation that involved three men and took more than twenty minutes, the car was so underpowered that it lacked the necessary revs to mount the steeper hills, and sometimes it got so exhausted it had to be towed back to Milagra by Juan's (father of Juanito) building truck. The second was that, should a sortie involve the pursuit of a serious criminal, meaning one who was armed, the Cabo presented such a broad target that even a hopeless marksmen, providing he pointed his gun in vaguely the right direction, could be confident of scoring a hit somewhere on his bloated body.

With so many good reasons not to go out he spent his time more profitably in the station counting fines, eating, drinking or questioning prostitutes. Otherwise he waddled over to the nearest bar to play on the fruit machine. About the only thing that did tempt him into the patrol car was the prospect of confiscating a high powered or prestigious make of foreign car, a Mercedes or a Jaguar, for in those pre-EU days cars with foreign registration plates had to be officially imported (at vast cost) after a period of six months of being in Spain. Those who flouted this rule risked their cars being confiscated, and although they were meant to be auctioned they invariably 'disappeared' into police hands. All in the vicinity of Milagra 'disappeared'.

At that time police records were typed on a squeaky 1943 typewriter with one top sheet and one carbon copy. Two carbon copies were the regulation, but the

Colonel flouted it because what he saved on paper he could spend on the fruit machine, and his weight was so ponderous that with the pressure from his thumb he could tilt the machine to make it deliver the jackpot. He had once been engrossed in a game while the Bank next door was being robbed by the habitual bankrobber of that era, called 'Easyrider' because he had the good sense to own a motorbike. Most of the village could remember the excitement of the chase; Easyrider zooming smoothly round the bends and up the hill with his swagbag held tauntingly aloft whilst the Guardia mounted a hopeless pursuit in their lurching Renault 4, lagging further and further behind with every second. Some spectators even dared to cheer!

A cross-eyed Sergeant was the Cuartel typist of that era, but he took so long with his single finger action that few people, faced with the prospect of spending six hours to make a simple statement or denuncia, bothered to involve the Guardia at all. Most just took justice into their own hands.

1978 came bang in the middle of the Colonel's reign, and records for that year were quite frankly disgraceful. Of the few that had survived their incarceration in the Cuartel cellar alongside the Colonel's vintage wines that had popped their corks one hot summer and flooded the place with fine Rioja, most had faded into abstract blue smudges, and the few that still resembled pages of words were so misspelt (the Sergeant had told no-one he was dyslexic) as to be incomprehensible.

Basically there were no records that could be used professionally, so the current homicide investigation would have to rely on present day interviews, and any missing person files Villahermosa might have kept.

Marte used different methods to Colin to take herself back. For her, paperwork was something you scrunched into balls and placed beneath the kindling in your open fireplace and struck a match to, so as to brighten up a cold winter's afternoon. She decided that aromatherapeutic meditation was the finest medium for transporting herself back in time, since it could double as cleansing agent and beautifier too. Twenty five years ago she might have used 'Yage', a potent South American vine that was no ordinary, run of the mill hallucenogen but could truly displace the mind, but these days she had grown too soft for such violent drugs. Also Yage induced vomiting, and Marte wished to enjoy her memories...

She set aside twenty four hours for the full procedure. Launching off with a clay and seaweed facial, she then sat on a footstool sipping an infusion of verbena to cleanse the digestive tract (colonic irrigation was no fun either), whilst listening to a Bach cello concerto to get up Otto's nose, for he reckoned it too highbrow for her. Then she heated canisters of sandalwood oil on every window sill and filled her hot tub to the brim, chucking in liberal spoonfuls of sea salt crystals and lavender for energised relaxation.

Because her memory might prove sluggish, forcing many hours of submersion, she preemptively massaged globs of comfrey butter all over her body, paying extra loving attention to her breasts, inner thighs and buttocks in case their natural love juices should be cruelly leeched out by osmosis. Then at last she lay back, arms folded over her heart like a medieval religious icon, and let her mind float free...


The first German from circa 1978 to manifest himself in her subconscious dreamplay rewind was arguably the most eccentric to have set foot in Milagra. He was unbelievably tall and thin, a Giacometti sculpture brought to life, always dressed in a loin cloth and invariably barefoot. In fact a Gandhi lookalike, yet twice as skinny and more than twice the height. He had escaped from East Germany in 1969, and although he would not talk about it (or any other subject, for that matter) rumours circulated that his legs were so long he simply strode the wall as if it were a flimsy athletics hurdle, and the machine gunner who should have shot him aimed in the dark at the height of a vital organ in any normal man, and therefore merely grazed his kneecap. He had lived like a hermit in his self-built tower on the coastward side of Montejoven, so Marte puzzled as to why her mind had regurgitated him in connection with a dead body in Milagra, but she knew better than to challenge the power of her subconscious with silly, common sense objections.

And even as that thought wandered through her brain the answer came to her; for he had been the unwitting honorary champion of a sub-sect of hippies who fervently believed in the supreme power of themselves.


They were disciples of Carlos Casteneda, treating his book 'Tales of Power' as a Holy Scripture. Their heroes were the two Mexican Indian magicians or shaman who could apparently harness their tremendous inner spirit powers in order to transplant themselves from one place to another (within limits, say, of forty kilometers) simply by focusing their willpower, - although they did need a hefty dose of peyote beans beforehand. He (the Gandhi man) had remained aloof from his younger acolytes, but they had formed a happy gang of desperados who gathered at midnight on mountain peaks and tried to project themselves through about five kilometres of air to land on the slopes the other side of the valley.

Alternatively they would perform another of Don Juan and Don Genaro's (the two Indians in Casteneda's book) capers, which was to run headlong down a mountain slope on a dark night, protected from harm purely by self-belief. Of course they suffered quite a few accidents, chiefly broken limbs, cuts, bruises and impalements on the vicious thorns that flourished in the wild terrain beyond the limits of agriculture, but that didn't stop them believing in the power of mind over body. They concluded that their failures were due either to the feebleness of their western-cultured minds, or to the lack of truly potent peyote. One of them had a friend of a friend who had a contact in Mexico, and a correspondence was set up and money sent, but the packet that eventually arrived had been tampered with. It contained a cheap poncho, a bead necklace, but not one peyote bean. Other hallucinogens were tried and tried in vain, - nutmeg, magic mushrooms, LSD and Lavender Floor Polish, but even though they often felt they were flying through the air or floating high above the world, and they saw sights of great beauty and underwent ecstatic spiritual transformations, disappointingly they always emerged from their collective highs on the same piece of turf where they had started.

Marte studied the rainbow beauty of the convex curve of a soap bubble as she emerged from her reverie to top up her bath, which was now slimy and tepid. The primary reason those Don Juaners had failed to displace themselves, she decided, was male arrogance. They'd maintained such a gender exclusivity to their silly little gang, convinced that because Dons Juan and Genaro were men, it categorically debarred women from the possession of magical powers. Well, bollocks to that. For if that were true, then why were European men so eager to burn witches throughout the centuries? And who did they often come snivelling and whimpering to, with their bruises and gashes and dislocations, just because they were too scared or too broke or too illegal to visit a Spanish clinic?

Still, setting aside her personal animosity, which she was quite prepared to do now that twenty five years had elapsed, she fell to wondering whether the skeleton could be a member of this Don Juan set. He might have tried a solo flight, or fallen during one of those crazed 'runs' down a mountain. The rest would simply have shrugged and thought to themselves "I wonder where old Helmut's got to? - Prob'ly flown out of his skull and landed back in Germany, but can't be bothered to let us know." And then forgotten all about him.

One would have expected parents to have expressed a modicum of concern at the vanishing of an offspring, but frankly in those days, to judge by the likes of her parents, many middle class, conservative minded fathers and mothers would have quietly breathed a sigh of relief that their hippie horror had gone off somewhere and was no longer embarrassing them in front of the neighbours, or asking for money to be sent here, there, and everywhere.

At this point Otto poked a bespectacled nose round the bathroom door to check that she had not passed out from the mixed cocktail of aromas, and to re-establish the fact that the bathroom was supposedly communal. Whilst he perched on the side of the tub and studied the ingredients of her bath emollient, she told him her newly forming theories of the Don Juaners. He was full of praise for her leap of imagination, and reassured her injured feminine pride by telling her Don Juan and Don Genaro were probably not men at all, but merely the fictitious inventions of Carlos Casteneda. He was a post graduate student of anthropology who bummed out in the Mexican desert, and the book was his thesis, tossed off in a tearing hurry when his University Department read him the riot act: write that forty thousand word thesis by Monday or forget your PHD. Otto knew about these things, being a Professor forced into issuing similar ultimatums himself. He magnanimously offered to pull out the bath plug and hand her a nice soft towel.

"You're wasting your time and hot water," he announced. "Ze skeleton is not a worry for you, you'll see. He's my bandolero. He was murdered in zis village, and stuffed into an alcove in the separating wall between two houses. Then zey plastered over him." He waggled his index finger at her, "I have it on good information."

"Tccch, so how come he was found on Julia's mountain? I suppose you're going to tell me he got bored and wanted a little walk?" Marte searched for her black eye patches, suspecting she might need to blot him out more effectively for her next foray into the past.

"No. He was carried there one night during the heavy rainstorm, just after they began bulldozing the Holidaylandia roads. Zey only needed to dig a little to bury him under the collapsed terrace wall, and because of the heavy rains it was easy to disguise the disturbed earth. By morning no-one could tell anything had happened; no footmarks, no nussing - just wet earth and water flowing everywhere."

He beamed with satisfaction at the watertightness of his story, and silently handed Marte the towel. She took it in silence, a little stunned by his plausible explanation. But there would be plenty of things that would fail to add up in his version of past events, she comforted herself, once she had had time and sharpened wits to debunk it. The water felt suddenly cold and her skin looked white and wrinkled, while her drooping breasts had sunk below her ribcage. She heaved herself out and sat wrapped in the towel, musing on her own personal past and realising that she was perhaps on the wrong track. Although she needed maximum information at her fingertips in order to answer any potentially awkward question, her main concern should be to utterly exonerate herself.

The Guardia might pay her a visit any minute now to fix a date for her interview. Her priority was therefore to sanitize her house in readiness, for they had eagle eyes for misdemeanors and eager hands for fines.

She became a fiery ball of energy. Neat labels proliferated as in a matter of moments her spices became colouring dyes, her herbs became spices and her jars of different strengths of marijuana became culinary herbs, although the strongest flowering heads, because their potent smell leaked from even the most hermetically sealed jar, were buried under a dense clump of periwinkles, for their starry flowers were anathema to sniffer dogs. All paperwork related to business dealings was swept under the carpet, and Otto was dispatched to erect a series of clotheslines around the rotting vehicles on the edge of her land, and then hang all the sheets and blankets necessary to provide a total screen.

She attacked the house like a whirlwind, sweeping, mopping, dusting, polishing and spraying, even ironing Otto's shirts with fervour, which was totally against her principles; but the all-important goal was to transform the place into a household of normality, not the dosshouse of a slob. Lise was ordered to change into a less revealing pair of shorts and work on the garden, digging, weeding, pruning, raking and hoeing as if the judges for The Tidiest Milagra Garden Competition were on their way.

There was no doubt her sixth sense must have been operating to perfection, for her lightning makeover was finished in the very nick of time. She had just achieved the level of effulgent shine on the walnut table that would surely have given her mother an orgasm when she heard the chugging engine of the Guardia jeep, and she prayed everything would pass muster. Casting a final eye over the living room she suddenly noticed her old fashioned and dearly beloved birch broom that was ideal for sweeping the outside patio of round river stones, and to prevent those ridiculous rumours of witchcraft that circulated of old returning to haunt her now she bit her lip to prevent a cry of misery and slung it on the fire.

# 14

Julia decided against going to the coast to seek out a lawyer on the following day. She felt better, but incapable of the concentration needed to drive a car, and uncertain what tack to adopt with a lawyer, or why she should accept she needed one just because the Guardia advised it.

Despite the fresh new growth of leaves and the bursting of early flowers the temperature had reverted to a bitter, mid-winter chill. The freezing air was so thin that the distant mountains were clearly visible, not darkly close as when rain is imminent, but bled of colour as if coated by hoar frost. The piercing wind was from the north, and it smelt and tasted of snow. The boys chose porridge for breakfast, Alex lit a fire in the grate, and they insisted on wearing mittens to protect their hands from the icy coldness of the spoons.

"D'you remember things from when you were five?" Julia asked Alex when they were seated round the table. She noticed that little clouds of breath accompanied each syllable.

"I can remember Marco being born, when I was only four," Alex grinned, "but that's because it was a shock. I can't remember normal, everyday things."

"I can remember being born," Marco was not to be outdone, "owing to the shock of seeing Alex and knowing he was my brother."

"Bullshit! Your eyes were shut and, as for knowing who was who, why suck my nose like a tit if you knew I wasn't your mum?"

She worried about the forthcoming DNA sample. Why did they need to involve Alex? How could a twelve year old be the offspring of someone who died twenty six years ago? Had they aberrated with their mathematical calculations? Or were they trying to prove Alex *wasn't* her son? Or might Grant be behind it, still persisting in his mistaken belief that Alex was *his* son? He had refused to imagine her capable of intimacies with another man less than two months after experiencing him. His arrogance insisted she should still have been swooning over his aftertaste, and he could not accept that all those thousands of energetic healthy sperm he injected had come to nothing.

As she puzzled over this she was struck by another of life's little ironies. For here she was, looking for signposts to lead her back to her five year old self, asking her own children how well their memories returned to that age, when there in front of her nose sat Marco, humming to himself as he ladled pools of honey onto his porridge so as to create two eyes, a nose and an upturned mouth. And this was exactly what she had done as a child! The memory flooded back...

"You're lucky to be able to do that," Frances told her, firmly screwing the lid on the honey jar so that some remained for another day. "I had to eat it like a Scot, simmered all night in the slow oven of the Aga, and flavoured with a pinch of salt - though it felt like a bloody handful."

"Salt - on *porridge*?" Julia was incredulous. But even at that age she had begun to realise parents had this tendency to favour stories illustrating how much more difficult their own childhoods had been.

"Salt on everything", Frances insisted, "even bleeding wounds," and Julia in spite of herself looked guiltily at the new sticking plaster neatly applied to her knee, and so did not repeat her request that they go out somewhere interesting for a change.

The place she particularly did not want to go to was the casita just outside Montejoven where a Swiss potter lived. At a period when eccentricity was often given a positive shine and called originality, he belonged in the outer reaches of the spectrum, way beyond originality, beyond eccentricity, even beyond oddness to the very furthest limits of sanity itself. The fact that he had a wife and child was in itself a miracle, for most people could not tolerate more than a few hours in his company without screaming. Frances would never of course have gone near the man (he was not attractive) had there not been a professional need; pots being their only shared passion.

He was a raku potter, enormously proud of his specialised Japanese techniques. He had absorbed many culinary customs from Japan too, and fanatically ate a solely soya diet; tofu for breakfast, soya beans for lunch and soya bread and miso (made from pure soya beans) for supper. He even looked remarkably like a soya bean: pale skin, pale hair, and cold, pale blue eyes set in a round, open beanlike face that had an expansive dicotyledonous forehead housing a veritable library of deadly boring stories that took hours in the telling. His wife was similar physically, although her darker shade of hair resembled more aduki bean than soya, and too many people fell for the all-too-obvious jibe that they were as alike as two beans in a pod.

Strangely enough they lived in a pod, but the space not vegetable variety; a perfectly round building that Horst (the man's name) had self-built from scratch. His raku kiln was similarly round but underground, built into the mountainside and covered over with squares of turf, and the only sign that distinguished it from the rest of the hillside was the little plume of smoke which rose from its tiny chimney when his clay objects were being fired. He was so strictly vegetarian that oral sex was utterly forbidden, and he would yell exactly five seconds prior to ejaculation so that his wife could hop off and avoid being contaminated with juices of animal origin. No-one knew how they had managed to conceive their beanlike son, Yakimoto, with these practices, unless it somehow occurred through the vegetable method of cross pollination.

The very first visit had not gone so badly. Julia had moderately enjoyed a game of hide and seek with Yakimoto the beanling, for their sloping garden, scattered with numberless raku 'objets' that Horst called sculptures but others by ruder names, was chockful of brilliant places to hide. Some of the raku sculptures were large and hollow enough to hide inside, especially for a slight five year old like Julia. She could then enjoy up to fifteen minutes of peace before the beano stuck his nose into the correct one. She was also charmed to hear that Horst was such a caring father that he rarely missed out on telling Yaki a bedtime story, which sounded like heaven to her, for although Frances meant to read regularly to her, invariably the ongoing pot would have reached a crucial stage come bedtime and the read would be postponed for the following day. Julia, who loved stories, had thus already been forced to teach herself to read.

However the charm evaporated when she experienced her first Horst story. She and Yaki had to sit in rapt silence, bolt upright, in lotus position and open mouthed while hours and hours ticked slowly by, during which time Horst droned on and on without any punctuation between sentences, and without using any vocabulary or grammar that she recognised. By the end Julia was as stiff as a garden raku gnome and Yaki's eyes were glazed with exhaustion, but neither had understood a word because Julia assumed the story was in Swiss-German, but Yaki insisted it had been translated into English for her benefit.

The visits came to an abrupt end when Yaki tried to inflate Julia into a balloon. While Frances was learning about a deadly poisonous bluegreen glaze that was horrendously expensive even for a Swiss person, and Horst's wife was fermenting soya been curds through an old pair of fine fishnet stockings, and showing a good deal of creamy white thighs in the process, Yaki led Julia off to the toolshed, a lean-to at the back of their livingpod.

"Would you like to fly through the air?" Yaki asked her.

He was nothing much to look at, apart from beanlike, but he was ten years old so due a certain respect for his superior knowledge of the world. At the time Julia was as naive as most five year olds, although looking back now, she decided she'd been a mite too gullible.

"I've always wanted to fly," she answered, emphasising the always so as to lend credence to the fiction of being closer to seven than five.

Yaki assured her she would have the flight of her life. She wouldd glide on the air currents, whistle with the wind, have total control of direction and speed, and even land safely exactly when and where she wanted, if only she did as he said. And what he said was:

"Pull down your knickers, bend over and stay really still while I pump up your arse with this bicycle pump."

At the time she did think it a rather curious way to get inflated. But it struck her as better than through the mouth, which would have smelt rubbery and might have hurt her wobbly tooth, and she knew they were the only two major wind passages of the body, so he must have got his science right. Nevertheless she bared her bottom with apprehension, wondering how he knew it would not hurt if he had never tried it himself, but only read the instructions in a book called The Trials and Tribulations of Human Flight.

He seemed to have inherited Horst's maddening slowness, for he studied her arsehole for what seemed almost as long as the first Chapter of one of his dad's epics, but at long last he claimed to have an accurate grasp of the measurements, so as to apply the right gauge of pump fitting. He applied some greasy stuff to make it comfortable for her, and easier for him to slip the pump in; and then with much huffing and puffing he began the frantic pumping action.

He had not got very far, in fact she sensed that she had only inflated just a tiny bit and it could take hours to get her airborne, when round the corner came Frances. Her reaction was so very far from what people used to call 'cool' in those days that even now Julia could not remember exactly what she said and did. An explosion of rage might adequately summarise it. Frances never needed to be physically violent; her verbal attacks were so terrifying that everyone cowered before them, especially if they were at close range and unable to escape the alarming sight of her flaming red hair and narrowed green eyes, her gesticulating bony fingers and her impressively tall stature. Yaki fled up the mountain with a yelp of terror, while Horst trembled so much he dropped his latest firing of a raku teaset.


In the end the nearest Julia got to flying was the fearful vertigo of the drive home, with Frances doing top speed in her Citroen 'Dos cavallos' which was mercifully old and extremely underpowered, but tilted round the bends with more degrees than an airplane entering a dive so that Julia had to hold a cushion to her head to avoid being concussed by the side panel.

It was the end of visits to Horst. And the end of Frances' experimentation with raku-style pottery.

Horst, though a similar age to the skeleton, was certainly not fated with the skeleton's death because Julia heard word of subsequent adventures. He very nearly did die, but later on, and at the hands of his own wife, about two years after the incident of the bicycle pump.

The rigidity of their macrobiotic outlook on the world had infected her consciousness to such an extent that she was no more than a set of scales, weighing and balancing everything in terms of yin and yang. She performed her domestic chores like an automaton, and one of Horst's absolute dictates was that the kiln door should be kept tightly shut during firing or glazing, for even the tiniest whiff of outside air (predominantly yang) would ruin the process. Sesame, as his wife was called, looked up from her bottling of homebrewed tamari to see that a spiral of smoke was issuing from the kiln chimney (which signified firing was in progress) and yet the kiln door was ajar (which spelt disaster for the pots). One of the distinctive qualities of raku firing is the intense and even heat required, which is why the kiln was perfectly rounded and why the door had been designed to fit so very snuggly. She therefore hurried down the garden path and shut the door firmly, making sure no harmful outside air could enter. Deaf to the desperate cries from within, and oblivious of the frantic hammering on the fastened door, she scurried back to her bottles.


What must have gone through Horst's mind during his oven roasting hell is difficult to imagine. He must have struggled in inner torment. On the one hand his belief system would have told him to accept his fate with tranquility, whereas his natural instincts would have urged him to fight tooth and nail to get out. As the temperature soared his hair frizzled, his clothing scorched and his skin wept and blistered, and he literally tore the nails from his hands with his frenzied clawing at the door. But fate was partly on his side. Fate may have married him to the wrong wife in the sense that she nearly made a fateful error, but she had balanced this by giving birth to the right son, for it was this particular Yaki whose sensitivity with smell, although it led him astray into an obsessive fascination with bottoms, at this moment told him that the smoke pouring from the chimney carried a new and unaccustomed tang that was different to the normal grey clay bake. Fate directed his running feet straight to the door which he flung open and, braving the wave of heat that seared his face, staggered in and as quickly out with his father's limp body in a matter of seconds. While Sesame continued unperturbed with her bottling, a process that should on no account be interrupted, Yaki ran to the nearest neighbour and an ambulance was summoned.


The hospital doctors saved his life by denying Sesame visiting rights. This was essential because she flatly refused permission for the use of any anaesthetic (too yin), for an intravenous drip (too yang) or any blood transfusion (the blood might have come from an omnivore), and objected to skin transplants because they was contrary to both nature and fate.

When Horst finally left hospital he went in the polar opposite direction to his house. He boarded a train bound for Switzerland and went home to live with his mother, changing his career to computer software expert and thereafter denying the existence of yin or yang. It seemed a bit hard on Yaki, Julia thought - and she was hardly an ardent supporter of his - but, as his mum no doubt told him, that's fate.


Julia emerged from her wanderings down memory lane with the conviction that this was absolutely not the sort of memory she could relate to a lawyer, but at least it was a start. She had thawed the ice, now it was merely a matter of channeling the flow in the right direction. And the right direction would ideally be a series of conventionally pleasant memories, depicting a Frances who did not get angry with a man, acquaintances who were not certifiably insane, and behaviour that was in no way deviant.

At least she now had a handle on herself as a five year old, and that was invaluable.


She fell to wondering where Marte fitted into the jigsaw of memories. Certainly Marte was around at the time, for she and Manfred had first bought their plot of land in early 1978. She could vaguely remember Marte, a much slighter, slimmer figure in those days, with smooth, flawless tanned skin from permanent exposure to the sun and piercing blue eyes that men found riveting, or perhaps inviting. Marte was only twenty four or five then, but having hurried to lose her virginity at fifteen seemed already worldly wise and cunning enough to be always one step ahead of her men.

Manfred was probably the only man she could not run rings around, for he was so consumed with self-love and so extraordinarily arrogant as to be blind to others' charms. That was why it was hard to understand what could have motivated him, in late 1978, to suddenly fall for the spiritual charms of a supremely cunning guru in Poona, a certain Bhagwan Sri Rajneesh. It was to Marte's credit that she resisted the fashionable rush to join the hippie exodus to Poona, for she was a true individualist and prepared to let go of Manfred rather than lose her own identity. Also she admitted to Julia later on that she hated the colour orange, which all Rajneeshies had to wear, because it set off weird vibrations in her ovaries and competed with her eyes for colour dominance.

Swami Dayan Yogi (alias Manfred) had all the right credentials of physical beauty and amorality to rise to dizzy heights in the Rajneesh organisation, which indeed he did, becoming no lesser a deity than Rajneesh's right hand man. However he retained enough perspicacity to recognise the organisation was going into a steep, irreversible decline in 1985, and fled back to Germany in the nick of time, just before the Federal Justices stepped in and Rajneesh himself made a bolt for it.

It seemed strange to Julia that Marte's path had again crossed with Manfred's in 1989, when she had returned to Germany to fiddle some unemployment benefit, and their passion was rekindled briefly, so that Marte returned to Milagra pregnant with Manfred's child, who turned out to be Lise. A cynical viewpoint would be that the unemployment benefit was proving tricky, and Marte discovered that KinderGeld was a far safer bet, - but the downside was you just couldn't wangle any without actually having a child.

Timing is sometimes uncanny. Marte had been in Julia's mind - and suddenly there she was, more fulsome of flesh these days and without the tan which is an enemy to older skin, banging her welcome on Julia's window.

> "Hi!" she cried and collapsed into a chair, seemingly exhausted by her mountain hike. She sniffed inquisitively under her arms, for the micro-flavours in the smell of sweat are an excellent barometer of general health, "Ze Guardia came yesterday."

> "You've survived better than me."

> "Yah, it is actually thanks to Otto. They get so easily impressed by silly things - to you and me. He flashed cards at them, his journalist ID, his stupid University Professor ID, even his Special Pass for the Bundesleague." She sighed deeply at the inanity of such false values. "By the end they were squirming with ze mere honour of meeting him, and now he is all puffed up with his cleverness, and says it is due to his fluent Castellano!"

> "He didn't mention his bandolero I take it", Julia could not help but smile.

> "What an arschlock!" Marte cried vehemently. But then she remembered Julia was young and single, and felt ashamed to present herself like an old married woman carping on about her partner's faults. "Come," she announced briskly, "I must look at your wound, and study your tongue."

Marte declared that Julia was not diabetic after a peremptory inspection of her tongue and eyes, but she spent longer studying her breast. Rather like a fastidious portrait photographer she circled and paced, examining each breast through narrowed eyes as if measuring, balancing and comparing. Then she perused in detail the asymmetry of the aureoli and the odd tilt of the nipple, finally massaging the bumpiness along the scar. Her hands were deft and pleasantly cool, yet Julia could not restrain a giggle.

"I've done well," she declared with gratification. "Ze infection is gone and it looks so much prettier. Mine hang low these days, but yours are firm and young and can still look good despite ze damage. If you have another child though, you cannot breastfeed from zis one," and she flicked it contemptuously.

"I wasn't planning on another child," Julia said, then realised how ridiculous she sounded, since neither of her previous pregnancies could be called in any sense planned.

Marte suggested a pot of herb tea and produced a floured fig and date slab which she had had the prescience to bring to fortify herself for the return journey. She then lay back on the old oak bench for a spell of deep breathing exercises, followed by flexing and unflexing the abdominal muscles which apparently are the very first to atrophy prior to the onset of menopause. Otto's success with the Guardia had nibbled away at her normally sturdy self-confidence, but Julia sensed that something else was also preying on her mind. Eventually the faint sounds of wind whistling through her nasal passages was replaced by short sharp snorts, whereupon she sat up abruptly.

"You must not think," she said slowly "zat we were bad people, or bad parents when we were your age. I know when I look back on zose days from the per - how do you say it?"

"Perspective."

"Yah, the perspecteeve of now, zen some things seem completely mad. But you have to understand ze world was different then. We were freeing ourselves from the terrible things of our parents' generation. Everything for them was grey and black, rigid rules and conformismus, and from zis type of serious attitude came world wars and nuclear bombs."

"My mother used to say much the same. Trouble is, your generation are in political power now, and where has all the love and peace gone? The world is as full of wars, corruption, aggression...as it ever was. Maybe worse."

"Yah, but zat is politics. Politicians were always ze straight guys or ze stupid ones, even then. But we inspired social changes which you take for granted. We fought for sexual liberation and we were idealists - don't laugh - we wanted to all love each other and share and not be jealous or possessive. We were against wars, greed and ze raping of ze planet. We experimented with another way of living - and we were not consumers," she declared, her voice muffled from munching another fig.

"Well, if I look back to when I was little I can remember all sorts of sneaky games people played, all kinds of competitiveness and jealousies."

Julia sighed. "Still, I guess Frances wasn't the ultimate model of a happy, self-fulfilled person. She was eaten up by something. But I never could decide if it was anger, jealousy or plain old disgust."

"Bitch! Whore! Fucking cunt!" Marte spat a half chewed glob of fig onto Julia's lap.

Julia leapt up in alarm more than anger, although her hand was tempted by the mug of hot herb tea and the target at such close range. Marte looked to be gearing up for more but struggling for suitable invective in English - until she caught Julia's eye and could not contain her laughter.

"Ha, you see!" she cackled, "You don't like it, but that's what *our* generation did for yours. Before us, to be an unmarried mother was a terrible sin, and that's what people thought of you. Now, zere are still some stigmas, agreed, but it's so much more accepted, believe me."

The fiery, belligerent glare in Julia's eyes faded and her hand no longer twitched to throw tea, for she had to acknowledge this truth. She had had her own firsthand experience of the problems Frances had faced as a single mother, living in a Roman Catholic country with a strong sense of family.

"Ze mistake we made," Marte continued, "was maybe to have no boundaries at all, not to keep anything private from children. Because our parents were so ashamed and secretive with their bodies, you understand; everything taboo, in ze dark and under ze sheets, and all ze nonsense of stalks bringing babies, we wanted to be open but did not know ze limits..."

Julia, in her mind's eye, returned once more to the morass of intermingled bodies surging and writhing in the aftermath of a typical heady fiesta of that era. The memory held a dark, menacing quality...but nothing was clear or specific. Was Marte now insinuating something more than just *seeing* what went on?

Julia did remember an American kid she met on the beach north of Villahermosa. They played in the fantastic glacial-green rock pools. He had run his tongue over the smooth wet rocks, sucking up the salt flakes, and then declared they tasted saltier than the goo from his dad's willie. This dad had fancied himself a rock star, and was continuously dropping names of American bands and famous guitarists he knew. He boasted how incredibly 'laid back' you had to be to handle the fame without flipping, and since he spent the whole day flat on his backside Julia foolishly understood it literally. Anyway his son, idiotically named Randy, proudly told Julia his dad was so sexually enlightened that he let Randy suck him off when he was in a really good mood. At the time she was surprised that what came out of dads was salty, but not by the sucking off. What did that suggest? Did it show that she accepted parent/child sex acts as normal?

It was only recently, when by chance she heard an American bass player named Randy on the radio, that it occurred to her it might be the one she met, and what he had said came back to her. She had wondered how he viewed it now; whether he had finally realised he was a victim of abuse and had sued for massive compensation, or whether he was still deluded he had an enlightened dad.

As for herself, apart from her underlying feeling of unease, she had no lucid memory of ever being abused. When rebirthing and hypnotism were all the rage she had once dallied with the idea of seeing if a professional could take her back to those dark areas of forgetfulness, the uneasy bad dream elements of her childhood where she might have suppressed unwanted secrets, but her natural distrust of psychobabble dissuaded her. Those kind of experiments had a way of producing the answer yes, the client had indeed been abused as a child, so what was the point? The point for the psychiatrist was clear enough; an abused client needed plenty of expensive sessions to work through their messed up psyche, so yes meant money.

She would not *be* thinking this way if the skeleton had not appeared and enforced this dredging up of the past. But for the skeleton, in fact, she would be back in England getting on with her life and her dancing, while the kids would be happily at school and amongst their own friends. Most probably her unease about her childhood had mainly been the lack of a father, and her awareness of the eternal sadness this engendered in Frances, and the way this sadness manifested itself in anger and contempt at the substitute men she kept sleeping with.

That plus her conviction she was a mistake, because Frances never was the maternal type, and was only ever really happy giving birth to pots.

# 15

Next morning came the news that someone had pinpointed the exact date on which Frances' terrace wall collapsed: October 17th, 1978.

At the end of September that year there was a torrential rainstorm, far worse than the usual 'gota fria' which signals the end of summer, in fact one of the worst in living memory. The owner of the bodega near Montejoven could still remember the time with painful clarity, because the grape harvest was disastrously lost when raging mountain torrents swamped the vineyards knee deep in mud.

The perfectly ripe grapes had to be abandoned and the campesinos became drunk with sorrow, for the air was tauntingly filled for days on end with the sickly sweet smell of grapes fermenting on the branch, and all the money hanging on the harvest was lost. Plagues of wasps swarmed like locusts, humming and buzzing as they lurched from grape to grape until they were too fat to fly. Then they sprawled in sticky pools, hiccoughing to death or waiting for their wings to dry before gorging themselves all over again.

The virtually dry riverbed which threaded through the gorge below Marte's had, by the second day of rain, swelled to a substantial river, audible from a distance as it thundered between rocky banks and clattered the rounded stones on its river bed, uprooting and dragging all the vegetation from its banks and carrying it like a torn fishermen's net in its wake. It raged through Milagra keeping the village awake at night, and at one point threatened to sweep away the finely arched eighteenth century bridge. When it finally subsided people strolled like sightseers, gawping in awe at the muddy tide marks and the height of the flotsam which measured just how close they had come to being submerged.

The Fuente above Frances became a leaping geyser, so great was the pressure from the subterranean stream; while the mountains around wept water in thousands of separate rivulets. All the terrace walls became mini-versions of the Victoria Falls, fine toothcomb splays of water pouring over the edge or filtering through the stones, flushing out the fine earth particles that acted like mortar and held them together.

Terrace walls are more likely to collapse during, or immediately after, a torrential rain, so this three week gap was puzzling. Everyone (apart from Otto and the Guardia Civil of course) hoped fervently that this news swung the balance in favour of a 'death by misadventure' verdict, but unfortunately it still left room for doubt. The wall would certainly have been weakened by the rain, so a person treading on a vulnerable spot could inadvertently trigger a landslide. But equally, a landslide could be more easily triggered intentionally, should someone have the motive to do it...

Julia remembered the rainstorm because it spelt the end for her wigwam. After three days of drenching, pummelling rain it was swept down the baranca and occasionally, later on, they found little swatches of its cheerful red and green material snagged on the rocks. It seemed strange she could remember the rain but not the wall collapsing three weeks later. Perhaps there was nothing remarkable about a falling wall for a five year old - unless they happen to know about a dead or dying body trapped beneath it, that is.

It did disturb her that they all - herself included - were so caught up with the concept of guilt and the desire to exculpate themselves from it that no-one seemed to spare a thought for the victim. The poor man had lain there, ignored for so long, and even now, after the discovery of his body twenty five years later, he was still of no personal interest to anyone. Of course she did realise all that would change if he was identified.

She thought back to when she used to run round the olive grove and wondered, not for the first time, if she had failed to hear his ever fainter cries for help. She tried not to dwell on why she had failed to notice the unusual, unpleasantly sickly smell of his flesh slowly putrefying beneath the rain sodden stones.

She was sitting on the beach in Villahermosa as she grappled with these thoughts, watching Alex and Marco replenish their collection of smoothd fragments of broken glass hidden in the pebbles. Their plans to make 'jewellery' had evaporated, but Alex had learnt the related skill of metal forging by helping Arturo el Ferrer weld balconies and rejas, while Marco plopped pieces of blue glass into wet plaster and called it a mosaic. She had stopped at the beach to take stock of her position before meeting the lawyer.

Dark lowering clouds skimmed the horizon out to sea, heavy with rain but teasingly taking it due north instead of delivering it inland. The threat of rain had discouraged sunlovers, so the beach was deserted.

Julia now regretted her visit to Scotty's bar on the way out of Milagra, brief though it was. She had absorbed some of his sadness, or more precisely the sad aspects of his life affected her because they had echoes of Frances' life, and her own.

But whereas Frances never ducked the issue of being abandoned by the man she loved, and was honest about being angry and hurt, poor Scotty died a thousand deaths every morning because his wife had left him, yet pretended he had got over it after a couple of bad days. Apparently he had restuffed his pillow with shredded photos of their honeymoon and early days of romance, so that in some bizarrely literal sense he still lay on top of her in bed. And the Dutch dentist had had to block calls from any of Scotty's numbers because he continuously phoned to make phoney appointments for fillings, root canal work and the like, or else shouted obscenities at the bewildered receptionist. Prior to this he never realised how much common ground existed in the vocabularies of dentistry and sex - but Scotty had sure shown him the way.

What a fool she had been to see Scotty! Needing strength, she had stupidly imbibed fear and worry, and back came all her paranoia about Frances and the dead man. Back, too, came the alternative scenario where Frances was not guilty, merely ignorant. The haunting images of her father returning unexpectedly after nearly six years of separation, hoping to see Frances and the daughter he never knew. As hard as she tried to close her eyes to it, she imagined him mounting the track, his forever unknown features indiscernible in the darkness. When he reached the almond grove he naturally cut righthanded along the top of the terrace wall, unaware that heavy rain had made it unstable. Suddenly the ground gave way and down he slithered with the avalanche, heavy stones crushing his fingers and fracturing his skull. After all movement ceased he lay scarcely conscious, buried beneath a tonne of earth and stones, hopelessly whispering Frances' name.

She could even picture Frances sitting alone in her studio as she often did, absorbed by her fragments of amphora. She would have glanced up momentarily, her precious concentration interrupted by the distant rumbling sound. Then returned to her work.

She tried desperately to dispel these fanciful scenes, to argue against them with all the immense weight of their improbability, but they returned with the same obstinacy as the waves on the pebbles. Even the cheery companionship of Alex and Marco failed to dispel them, on this dark day of impending rain. If only she knew her father's name she could combat these idiotic fancies by tracing and finding him, now fat and bloated and bald no doubt. Still nurturing an impressive collection of dead butterflies but otherwise forgetful of his youthful exploits.

It must be the DNA test that she was dreading, she realised, even more than the visit to the lawyer...

Grant had magnanimously offered to take Alex and Marco to the go-kart track while Julia met the lawyer. His villa held pride of place in the super-affluent sector beyond the bay of Villahermosa, where other palatial modern or neo-colonial styled villas climbed the headland in a competitive scramble for the best sea view. The current gardening fashion was no longer velvety, verdant lawns kept lush by a secret feeder pipe from the emergency reservoir, but acres of delicately shaded lilac or green crystalised gravel, out of which sprouted a wide variety of rarest cacti, amber coloured bougainvilla (absolutely not the common purply red stuff) and as many palm trees as would fit the plot.

They turned into the driveway where Grant's massive gates were forbiddingly closed, but the entry phone sensed their presence and obligingly lit up. Alex seemed to know the code, for after he punched in some numbers the gates obediently swung open, but she still had to phone Grant from her mobile because there was no code to pacify his snarling guard dogs, who surrounded her car with hackles raised and fangs bared.


Veronika came with a smile on her lips and a whistle between her teeth, which must have emitted a sound only audible to the dogs, for they suddenly slunk to their kennels.

"Do kom to the leounge," she invited, and they picked their way over the green crystals and around the cactus spikes, which looked artificial but were not.

Grant was pacing his 'leounge' like a caged panther, growling into his mobile with the same inflections as his dogs. It sounded as if things were not going well, and Julia hoped this did not mean the go-kart trip would be cancelled.

"Goddammit!" he exclaimed, zipping the mobile into his belt holster, "but who gives a......?"

"Bad news about Holidaylandia?" Julia enquired hopefully.

"Kinda' bad, nothing I can't cope with." Grant looked at Veronika, who in her heeled boots towered above him even though he was only a fraction under six foot. "Not those honey, they'll get trapped in the accelerator pedal and we'll lose to these guys."


As they drove off in convoy, Julia noticed with anxiety that Grant had awarded Alex the front seat, relegating Veronika to the back with Marco. This made no sense in a coupé owing to their disparate leg lengths, and showed he planned to show off his racing driving techniques well before they reached the go-kart piste. He did indeed leave a thick smear of shredded rubber on the ramp as they roared off with a dramatic skid-turn towards the theme parks and pleasure zones of tourist Villahermosa, while she headed in the opposite direction, to the Centro Ciudad and the law firm that handled the affairs of probate after Frances' death.

She knew them by reputation alone, since Reggie had dealt with them personally. It transpired she had been the legal co-owner of the property ever since she was eight, although of course Frances had never thought to tell her so. Nor had Frances bothered to make a will, and this casual attitude towards bureaucracy had done nothing - she could tell from the lawyer's tone in her only telephone conversation - to inspire respect.

The offices of Jose y Guillermo Gonzalez Hmns. were on the third floor of an old palacio building. Her footsteps echoed loudly in the cavernous stone stairwell which was dark after the sunlit street, and she had to climb the worn stairs because the prehistoric looking lift was labelled with a yellowing handwritten notice 'Fuera de Servicio' (Out of Order) that had clearly been there for ages. As soon as she entered the office via an almost three metre high double portal the strange, fusty atmosphere of forbidding legality hit her - even though she had anticipated it. She had carefully chosen her most suitably sedate clothes, but matched against the deep patina of polished hardwood furniture and the wall to wall décor of heavy, black, leatherbound legal tomes she felt she looked like a cheap tart on a working holiday. She meekly gave her name to the receptionist.

The woman did not even bother to check her appointments book. It took her the briefest of glances to assess Julia.

"You wish to see our divorce specialist?" she guessed with utmost confidence.

"No," Julia felt wearied by the predictability of it all. "I've an appointment with Senor Fernando Oliver Gomez, at 12.15."

No wonder she had dreaded coming. This place had all the charm of a nineteenth century prison and she had willingly walked into its time warp. Inside these walls Franco was still alive and well, Spain had little truck with the rest of Europe and the European Union remained a future dream. Otto would have sniffed around delightedly and doubtless found trails of blood on the stairs and the bones of Republican prisoners buttressing the walls. It smelt of leather and woodpolish, with a mild aftertaste of ammonia, and the morguelike chill made the warm, traffic-fumed air outside seem like a blast of fragrance. She waited forlornly in a squeaky leather chair.

When she was Alex' age she had visited the extraordinary monument where Franco is buried, called Valle de los Caidos, north of Madrid near Escorial. It was an enormous structure of cold marble, tunneled for hundreds of metres into the bowels of a mountain and designed to inspire fear and awe through sheer size. A gigantic cross, visible for twenty miles or more, was planted into this mountain.

It had been built as an expression of Franco's power by the slave labour of Republican prisoners, many of whom fell dead of disease, malnutrition or exhaustion on the job and were, it was whispered, simply disposed of in the most practical of ways - mixed in with the cement or plaster to add grist to the supporting substructure. Others were entombed in an immense section of the underground building, which resembled a church with long, corridorlike aisles.

Franco's body lay in state in a raised marble sepulchre beneath a vast dome in the central aisle. Julia wondered how he dared share his deathbed with so many of his lifetime enemies. What if their vengeful ghosts jumped out one night? They had the whole of eternity to take revenge!

"So sorry to keep you waiting. Do come in." A short man in a dark blue suit, pink shirt, greying sideburns and a deadly serious expression broke into her reverie with his immaculate Castellano.

He was clearly no firebrand. Some lawyers choose the profession because they have strong feelings for justice - and a corresponding urge to fight injustice. Others because it is a family tradition, well respected and well paid. He very evidently belonged to the latter category, yet his repetitive habit of twiddling a pen clockwise between thumb and forefinger suggested he might also have chosen it because it was neat, tidy and full of finicky rules. She felt certain he lacked any sense of humour - not that her situation was a bundle of laughs.

He had heard about the 'Esqueleto de Milagra' because it was headline news in the provincial papers. He evidently knew something of the investigation too, but kept quiet about the extent of his knowledge because he was naturally tight lipped and preferred to be the one asking questions.

At first he seemed more preoccupied about a possible damages claim from the victim's family, which had not even entered Julia's head.

"We'll need to show that the wall was in good repair before the rain, and that your mother had no cause to suspect it was unstable afterwards," he mused.

"Isn't rain damage an 'Act of God'?" Julia was impatient. The civil dimension was not her priority.

"Yes. But three weeks after the rain allows time to repair a dangerous wall."

"I'd rather focus on the inquest," she said tersely, an abruptness he immediately resented.

"So, why do *you* think they suggested you have a lawyer?" he snapped.

"I imagine because I was only five at the time, so questions related to that period have to be handled sensitively and correctly. Also," she cleared her throat, "because the death might be suspicious and it happened so close to my mother's house. And since she's dead, she can't answer for herself."

He was twiddling the pen faster, gripping it ever tighter. "You don't think you were advised to have a lawyer because you yourself are a suspect? Girls of five are quite capable of throwing stones that can fracture a skull."

# 16

Julia sat in a sidewalk cafe confronting a half nibbled croissant and the dregs of a cafe con leche. She did not remember ordering them, but they would not have appeared of their own volition. She felt moderately proud of the unflustered way she had extricated herself from Gonzalez Hmns. She had made not one offensive comment, just offered the wholly plausible explanation that she needed more personal rapport with any lawyer she hired. She felt calmer now. She still had two hours. Still needed a lawyer, granted, but there was no need for a whizzkid. Just someone who didn't rashly accuse her of murder.

Bereft of inspiration, she trawled through her handbag, and was reminded of a Samuel Beckett play she once saw. It featured five people stuck in quicksand and sinking deeper by the minute. Doomed to die, basically. Four were men, and they spent their final moments in intelligent, philosophical discussion; while the fifth, a woman, goes and wastes her last moments shuffling through her handbag! Julia smiled at her own similar idiocy, but gleaned satisfaction from weeding out the worst accumulated rubbish. Her wallet bulged with useless wodges of paper instead of money, mostly those business cards people like to give you that you forget to throw away. She discarded them methodically into the ashtray. Suddenly her eye lit on one: *Carmen Sanchez Ortola, Architecto*, with an address and telephone number from Sevilla.

At first she could not place where or when she had come across such as person, then - of course, on the flight from London in December, just after her mother's death. They had booked at the last minute so their seats were randomly scattered on the plane, until a man agreed to swap so she could sit next to Marco (five minutes of Marco's fidgeting and humming his favourite pop song convinced him).

Carmen had cheerfully stayed in her original seat on the other side of Marco. She had offered to change with Alex, but he preferred peace and quiet alongside a Canadian golfer. This was when Marco's hyperactivity could drive the most patient demented, so Carmen had special qualities indeed and fielded all his hundred and one questions with unwavering enthusiasm, asking him to correct her English grammar every time she made an error.

An architect was no lawyer, of course, but it was a professional degree nontheless; a lawyer even remotely like Carmen would be perfect. The only problem being that Sevilla was impractically far away.

Julia dialled the number. The warmth and immediacy of Carmen's voice flowed into her ear, with its quality of being instantly, genuinely friendly. Julia struggled to keep her voice steady, realizing in that moment how much she had missed relating to people her own age with whom she could share some affinity. Reggie and Marte were a generation older - and that was flattering Reggie. She spent so long on the phone that her right ear began to scorch with harmful radiation, but she was not idle meanwhile; she shouldered her much lighter handbag, paid at the bar and walked down the Avenida Mediterranea in the course of her conversation.

Carmen was efficient. She lost no time contacting a friend who was a lawyer in Sevilla, and who would surely know of a colleague from Julia's area. Within four minutes she called back with a recommendation - an erstwhile student friend of her Sevilla contact, whom she even knew personally herself. She insisted 'Es muy majo, muy simpatico', adjectives that do not translate properly into English. He was right now at the Palacio de Justicia, only five minutes away from where Julia was.

"He will understand your situation, believe me, he is not a judgmental type. His family is admittedly bourgeois like the last one, but he's relaxed - know what I mean?"


The Palacio de Justicia was an ultra modern building, a reflective wilderness of steel and glass, its interior so airless and sound quality so dead - not a hint of an echo - that she half expected the rules of gravity might also be suspended. It felt like someone clapped their hands over her ears as she entered, and instinctively she swallowed to relieve the discomforting pressure.

The courtrooms were accessed through identical doors ranged along the length of the building, each door padded (more soundproofing) in bright crimson leather, like a cheap sofa upended. The immense anteroom was filled with milling people. They wanted to talk to settle their nerves, but could not because of the unfriendly accoustics. Some sat resignedly, others paced fretfully. It was easy to identify the lawyers - they wore the same black flowing robes as in England; but it was impossible to distinguish the accused from their relatives, or who was a witness and who a victim's friend, because everyone wore the same expression of bored anxiety. The only ones halfway enjoying themselves were the uniformed Policia or Guardia Civil, because for them it was almost a day off work.

She looked at the list of that day's cases: two armed robberies, an aggravated assault, a vandalism, a homicide and a trespass. No-one was handcuffed to a prison officer, not even the armed robbers, so it was pointless trying to match each crime to the correct perpetrator despite the temptation to do so. Did *she* look the type to be accused of homicide, she wondered? The last lawyer seemed to think so...

She found his name. He was defending the vandal - or the case of vandalism. She *must* avoid the mindset of equating being accused with being guilty, because, like Colin, she noticed how susceptible to suggestion she was. The moment the lawyer had insinuated she could be the killer she had thought back to her nastier self...

She *might* have carelessly thrown a stone and unwittingly killed. She used to fire arrows at the trunks of olive trees, that summer when she wore her Hiawatha costume and pitched her wigwam in the almond grove. Eulogio caught her once when having his almuerzo early one morning. An arrow whizzed narrowly past his ear, and he charged down on her like an angry bull and snapped the bow in half across his thighs. She stammered her apologies and begged him not to tell Frances, because the arrows she had been bought had rubber suction pads instead of tips so as to make them harmless, and she had deliberately prised off the rubber and sharpened the arrow to a finely pointed tip. She later told Frances she trod on the bow by mistake and snapped it. So...she was not above lying to excuse herself.

A female usher emerged from a padded door to broadcast a series of names, and a huddle of people apprehensively lined up, a straggling queue of docile, humbled lambs to the slaughter. Julia went to ask her how to locate the lawyer, and she promptly added his name to her roll call. There was no immediate response however, so Julia stood awkwardly alone by the doorway for two long minutes.

She was about to give up and phone Carmen for an alternative rendezvous when a hand touched her shoulder.

"Hola, soy Andres Romero. You're waiting for me?"

She nodded, holding out her hand, "Si. I'm sorry to meet you here instead of making a proper appointment. But there wasn't time."

"No problem. Give me two minutes to sort something out, then we can talk." He turned on his heel and walked to the far wall of windows, where she could see him in animated discussion with a trio, two men and a woman, one of whom must be the suspected vandal.

True to his word he came back, and in one swift movement he shed the black barrister's cloak, pulling it over his head like a child stripping off a nightgown. Immediately he no longer looked like a legal crow or bird of prey, but a normal, much more attractive human being with hair that had been untidily ruffled by the speed of undress.

"Shall we go outside?" He deferred to her, but headed straight for the revolving doors without waiting for her reply.

The change in air pressure was again extraordinary. She noticed how people gulped like goldfish as they emerged, then reached hungrily for their cigarettes because the court had a no-smoking policy that was almost unheard of in Spain. A thick layer of butt ends encircled the building where hardened smokers had escaped for a quick puff, and Julia had already come across some rebels in the toilet who evidently knew its smoke alarm was merely decorative. Smoking is not normally frowned upon in Spain, but ranked as a necessary pleasure on a par with drinking, eating and sex.

"Depending how much time you have, we can either talk in my car," he shrugged, "unpleasant but private. Or we can find a bar," he smiled, "less private, but more pleasant."

She appreciated the easy way his legal mind interpreted the options. "It also depends how much time you can spare. The car's fine for me."

But inside the oppressively hot car she felt cramped and intruding on his privacy, with personal papers and possessions untidily slung onto the rear seat, and realised it was a mistake.

"I'm sorry, I don't think I can talk properly here. It'll crick my neck."

"No problem." He started the engine. "I know a quiet bar that's five minutes away."

As they drove in silence she wondered how much he already knew about her situation, probably just the bare bones (she smiled wryly at the terrible pun) because Carmen herself had only been given a sketchy outline. It was a novel sensation to be driven, to be in someone else's hands for a change. She glanced at his hands on the steering wheel, the tendons were pronounced and the nails nibbled at, but not as severely as hers which were gnawed to the quick. But she tried to avoid studying him too obviously in case he misread the signals, for he was attractive enough to be bigheaded in that way.

"Tell me, in whatever order comes to you, why you think you need a lawyer" he said once they were ensconced in an alcove where a small, shoulder height window gave a view of massive rocks artificially piled to form a kind of breakwater, and beyond it a thin strip of sea. "I know they say barristers only like listening to themselves –but I truthfully am a good listener."

And he did in fact listen with absorption, not attempting to speed her up or steer her in any particular direction, even though she sensed that some of what she told him must be irrelevant from the legal standpoint. She tried to be as succinct as possible, describing the discovery of the skeleton, its position, her mother's apparent attempts to stall the Holidaylandia development, and a brief sketch of her childhood circumstances and her mothers' lifestyle (sensitively abridged!) and the reasons behind the DNA sample. At least lawyers are exposed to wrongdoings on a daily basis, she thought, so they don't shock easily. Their antennae must be honed to pick up many signals, so they understand more than just the words.

When her pause was long enough to assume she had at least concluded a chapter, if not the whole narrative, he rested both hands on the table and his eyes on her face.

"The first thing I'd like to reassure you is that you can't be held legally responsible for anything that happened when you were only five years old. It's below the age of criminal responsibility." And in case she hadn't fully grasped this concept, "So you're innocent in the eyes of the law, whatever may have happened. OK?"

"Yes." She looked at the sea. The breakwater obscured what was close to shore, and the distant waves neither broke nor fell, but merely trembled. Carmen had evidently told him what the other lawyer said. "But there's my mother. I can think of many who'll immediately assume she had some involvement. Even if it was an accident – it'll be the result of her lifestyle. Indirectly her fault."

"That's why it's best to establish it was an unforseeable accident, due to the rain."


Julia watched him as he struggled to find the mobile in his left pocket. It had started ringing, if one could call the percussive opening bars of a rumba 'ringing', but he quickly flipped it off without glancing at the caller's number showing her that he did not want his concentration interrupted however urgent the call, which she appreciated. However, she noticed he had said 'it's best...' rather than 'we must establish...' So he had not yet committed himself.

"Tell me," he again looked at her steadily, "and this is not my assumption, but how a prosecutor would look at it. Why do you think your mother never had the wall repaired, for all of twenty five years?"

Julia met his eyes, which if not accusatory were certainly intense. "Don't think that hasn't occurred to me." She knew she sounded defiant, almost hostile. "But if you had any understanding of my mother's priorities and living conditions it wouldn't surprise you. It would strike you as typical."

She was aware that a spray of spittle accompanied the sudden concentration of explosive consonants, and prayed it hadn't spattered his face. His steady gaze showed no consternation, but then he didn't seem the type to overreact, or even react to such bodily embarrassments. He seemed more lawyer than human, she surmised. But then he'd been brought up bourgeois and relaxed, which was very different to alternative and hysterical. She had learnt to hide her feelings, whereas he looked comfortable with his - if he had them.

"The owner of the land below, onto which the wall fell, didn't he ever ask her to repair it?" he persisted.

She laughed, "He couldn't care less! It was Clemente, he barely worked it or bothered with it, because most of his land was vines between Milagra and Montejoven. He was rarely sober in any case - he worked in the bodega."

Clemente used to charm the tourists in the bodega with his little routine. He would sing snatches of love song and grab an unsuspecting and hopefully unattached lady from his tourist audience to dance two steps of a tango. Then he swooned in impassioned delight and reached for the leather wine pouch that he wanted to sell by the dozen, for the mark up on those was greater than for the wine. Squirting the cheapest red onto the centre of his forehead, he then squirmed and wriggled in what he imagined was a sexy fashion, directing the flow of wine so that it encircled his eyelid, traversed his nose, channelled the smile groove inside his cheek, was deflected to the corner of his mouth and dribbled comfortably home.

The only times he came to his terrace of olives with the broken wall were when he dropped his wife off to prune the trees - she could wield an axe better than any mediaeval executioner, so he never dared get too close to the female tourists. Or to prepare for the harvest by sculpting smooth, stone free circles beneath the trees where the olives would fall, and of course to pick them in late October. Since the stone and earth débris of the fallen wall only robbed him of a few square metres and did not interfere with his olive trees he was not bothered. In fact it gave him some nice shady nooks to hide a wine bottle in, for sustenance while his wife was not looking.


She was thinking so intently of Clemente and his antics that she neglected Andres, so he took the opportunity to check on his missed call. The clicking sound of his text messaging snapped her out of her reverie.

"I'm sorry, I'm taking up too much of your time. How shall we leave it? My Cuartel interview's on Wednesday..."

He was silent for a few seconds. "You don't really need a lawyer because, as I said, you can't be found legally culpable. Your mother," he smiled but with sensitivity, "has no problem either, because she is no longer here - no, please let me finish. I don't mean to be unfeeling – I'm simply presenting the legal picture. She can't be made to answer questions, can't be sent to jail - please, one more minute - she can only be left with a terrible stain on her character, a question mark as to her guilt..."

Julia jumped in, even though she knew he had not finished, "I know I came for a legal opinion, but I'm concerned with much more than the legal interpretation. Of course I realise a dead person can't serve time – I'm not *that* stupid! It's exactly that 'question mark' I don't want hanging over her; and I myself need to believe she didn't do it."

He met her angry eyes and said reproachfully, "If you don't let me finish how can we co-operate?" He then studied the distant strip of blue sea, which looked artificial itself because of the company it kept - the ridiculous squared off giant boulders piled like baby bricks, and she assumed he was deliberately stalling to punish her for her hastiness. "Can I finish - or do you want to put the right words in my mouth and talk for me?" he said drily.

"I'm sorry. I'll try to be more detached."

"How can *you* be detached? But it's something you should want a lawyer to be - otherwise his advice is useless."

She could detect a slight sarcasm. But she had to accept he was right. After all, she only approached him because he was a lawyer, and she was taking up his time and seeking his opinion for free, as things stood at the moment. He was neither a psychologist nor an old friend, so what right did she have to criticize? She studied her ugly chewed up fingernails with a feeling of disgust.

"Now I'll finish," he said, sounding wearied more than triumphant. "Although you don't need a lawyer for the reasons I've already explained, I think you should have legal representation at the Cuartel. This because they'll have to question you about what you remember as a five year old, and that's a delicate issue - perhaps they aren't even aware themselves of the demarcations. If you were five you'd have access to a child psychologist and there'd be all sorts of protections, you wouldn't have to face adult male detectives alone! My feeling is they don't even know themselves what can or cannot be asked, having doubtless never encountered this situation before. They want a lawyer present so there aren't complaints afterwards, for their protection as much as yours."

"I'm very grateful. Above all for having you present at the interview - if that's what you're offering to do. I know there'll be awkward questions and I'm afraid of blundering and incriminating my mother - or answering snappily and getting their backs up."

"I can imagine." She detected a gleam of amusement in his eyes. He consulted his watch and his eyebrows rose theatrically, "Dios Mio, I've no time now, but I need to go through things more thoroughly before Wednesday. Are you free this Sunday?"

She nodded, a shade doubtfully.

"Then I'll pay you a visit, if that's OK. I should see your house and the location to make sense in my own mind of what could have happened. Is that convenient - you don't have family commitments?"

She stared at him incredulously. "My mother's dead, so she won't be coming to Sunday lunch."

"You're very acid. I meant your husband and children, your living family."

"I'm not married. Some things do run in the family," she smiled.

"Contempt for men?" He returned the smile, but it was heavily barbed. "So, at three o'clock?"

"Perfect. I look forward to it. And I'm sorry I was...con tanta mala leche."

"No tienes que pensar. I'll drop you at your car."


She drove back to Grant's more spiritedly than she had driven into town. This made her question what Andres had intimated - did she actually get energised by a healthy bout of friction with a man? Maybe she did - although the opposite effect was true in her relationship with Marco's dad, and that was the only relationship to have stood some test of time. With that it was precisely the accumulation of fundamental disagreements and incompatibilities that had eventually sapped her energy.

She felt profoundly relieved to have a lawyer, and seemingly an intelligent one, on hand for the dreaded interview. The reason she drove fast, she decided, was not psychological but practical, for by now she was more than an hour late to pick up Alex and Marco and Grant would be resenting it.


Grant's coupé was sloppily parked inside the gates, which were inconveniently locked so that she had to use the entryphone.

"Let's test your memory" Grant's voice was teasing, "the code's the date we fucked - day, month and year : eight digits."

"You bastard!" Julia retorted, worrying how he had relayed the code information to Alex.

"If you've forgotten you don't deserve to come in," he exulted. "C'mon, year first – that can't be hard."

"Um, 199...1, I guess."

"Well done, not too much hesitation…now the month."

"You despicable....July."

"07 - very good. It was certainly hot, and so were you. Finally - the actual day."

"I haven't a clue so I'll go home. I know Alex and Marco'll be fine in your hands, which are surely more capable now than they were back then. See ya' next week, byeeee!" And she placed the entry phone firmly back on its hook.

As she had intended the gates swung open and no dogs came bounding over to intimidate her. Grant's chirpiness over the entryphone did not reflect the generally sombre mood that greeted her in the sitting room, and she realised all had not gone well at the go-kart track.

"Did you win?" she asked Alex, suspecting this the most likely cause of gloom amongst the other protagonists, excluding Veronika.

" 'Fraid so" he answered cheerfully. "But Marco lost, or let's say lost it bigtime."

The outing had begun promisingly, with double scoop cones of strawberry and pistachio Italian style icecream all round, and free T-shirts with the track logo on them because Grant had splashed out on a series of ten races multiplied by two in the most expensive, highest horsepower vehicles. Grant and Veronika had comfortably beaten Alex and Marco in the first doubles race, but once Alex got used to the circuit and handling the go-kart he was thereafter unbeatable, even after they changed teammates so that Grant drove Marco and Alex Veronika, just in case Grant's losing streak was due to the increased weight and Veronika's failure to lean courageously into corners and contribute positively to dynamics.

The subsequent solo sorties were when disaster struck for Marco. Grant had no idea he was only eight, and of course Marco was delighted to be taken for ten and allowed to drive the turbo-charged top range model. In a moment of wild and uncoordinated joy he attempted a rash overtake at a difficult chicane, collided with a barrier, skidded through 180 degrees and crunched head-on into another driver, ripping the wheels off both vehicles.

Go-kart organisers naturally expect accidents, they happen as a matter of course and the price of repair is factored in; but they were unpleasantly critical when they discovered Marco was underage for his vehicle, and gave Grant a stern talking to.

But this was not the cause of his depression - he actively enjoyed shitting on businesses that gave him a hard time. His chagrin was over Alex' series win in the solo races, where his lighter weight had - surely - to be the determining factor in his unexpected victory. By the time they left the circuit furious words had flown, the net result being that Marco was never welcome there again, and Grant would fucking well buy them out and fire the whole useless crew at 8.am the day he took over!

"They acted like I'd done a mass murder," Marco grumbled on the way home, "it was only a titchy accident. A coupla' broken wheels and a few dents."

"The other driver got whiplash," Alex reminded him. "How would you like a maniac kid hurtling into you head-on?" Alex had been forced to forgo a special prize for eight successive wins - the track record - owing to their vituperative departure.

"I don't want to hear about head-ons while I'm driving," Julia still had occasional flashes of her mother's accident. "Don't you think you should've said you were only eight, Marco?" Julia asked after an awkward silence.

"Um, I guess," he conceded reluctantly. "Would you have?"

"Probably not," she admitted with a smile.

But the admission perturbed her. Was anyone totally honest? Frances was always described as 'brutally honest' because she had no qualms about speaking her mind. She had the courage - or was it cruelty? - to tell people exactly what she thought of them, never hiding behind the niceties of conventional, polite behaviour. She had always *seemed* honest about herself too. But it easy enough to admit to self-evident truths, in fact foolish not to; real honesty meant admitting to things that were unlikely to meet the light of day, revealing what one would expect to get away with.

She herself had never told Frances half the things she had done as a teenager, although if asked a direct question she would possibly have given an honest answer. And she had not considered witholding information tantamount to lying. Supposing Frances had done the same. Suppose she knew about the death, but elected to say nothing? Until now Julia had only considered two possibilities; the death was a murder, or an accident that no-one knew about. It occurred to her now that it might be somewhere between the two. An accidental death that *was* known about – but for some reason was kept secret. And not necessarily by Frances - or by Frances alone.

Many people her mother knew at that time had personalised attitudes to life and death. They believed in individuality and their arch enemy was 'The State'. The State treated people as slaves, forced them to work their socks off all their lives like obedient lackeys, handing it their money to spend on its own corruption, wars, pollution - all evils they did not want, but were powerless to stop. This state machine was the enemy of human beings, and would eventually kill us off either through some nuclear war or incurable environmental disaster resulting in total meltdown. She remembered their message even though she had only been a child then. They were not all wacky hippies like Horst and Sesame and some still kept faith with their beliefs, and were forefront members of environmental action groups, or forceful members of the Green Party representing their countries in Brussels. Some were working right now to uncover the corruption at the heart of so-called democracies, finding the super-rich who hid behind 'The State' and really pulled the strings, owned the politicians and siphoned off the money.

These 'individualists' had deeply resented the artificial rules imposed by States, whereby one does not even own fundamental moments of one's own life, most specifically birth and death. Numbers, paperwork, money; that was the Government's view of birth and death. She could remember new young parents deploring the rule that births must be formally registered within so many days, and had to be presided over by a professional medic. Some had simply rebelled and gone their own way, given birth in a field or wood or on a hilltop, the father acting as midwife, cutting the cord and cooking the placenta as a healthy, protein rich fry up. Refusing to register the birth and give the child an official name. Marte actually had a German friend whose seventeen year old daughter went back to Germany to try for University and found she couldn't because she didn't exist! No name, no birth, no health record, no school record; therefore she was a mere figment of her imagination!

Presumably they had an equivalent attitude to death. Why should death require state intervention, a certificate, a coroner, an official burial or cremation, all costing exorbitant sums of money which most did not possess? She could visualise the scene only too clearly… A young man dies, perhaps from a fall or illness that he never entrusted to a doctor's care - why should he? He always stated a desire to be buried in a beautiful spot, high on a wild mountainside where he could return to nature, dust to dust etc. So his friends sympathetically treat him to a private interment in a beautiful spot just as he wished. Frances' tumbledown wall will do fine. No-one will ever find him there, he can rest in perfect peace for all eternity…

Julia even knew how they would do it. Tranquilly under the stars, accompanied by dirgelike singing and somebody strumming a soulful guitar, or maybe that crazed French violinist who was once a Pharoah playing lightning fast improvised arpeggios under a crescent moon.

Frances might have wished the same for her own final resting place…God, how she must hate to be slotted into the cemetery in her ill-fitting coffin, without any privacy!

Julia understood their philosophy. She could accept that in a way they were right; states *did* have too much power and consistently misused it, while democracies worked to benefit those in power – or the power brokers behind the politicians. Individual freedom was an ideal, never a reality.

However, even these idealists had their internal contradictions. Take Marte for instance. A staunch believer in individual freedom, alternative medicine, free love, absolutely no respect for the State and a grumbler at its pickiness and paperwork, yet substantially supported by generous helpings of State subsidy in the form of KinderGeld throughout! And so it was with many of them. She had met Australian single mums merrily globe trotting on their single parent benefit, and half of the wealth behind Rajneeshpuram in Oregan came from divorce settlements.

Perhaps she was beginning to sympathise with Frances' crabby attitude to her friends. Perhaps all of us are simply a disappointing blend of contradictory elements. Blatant hypocrites.


She was so immersed in her thoughts that she drove like an automaton, only becoming aware of her surroundings as she mounted the track because the recent changes came as a shock. The ugly new mushrooming growth of Holidaylandia and the gaping earth wound where the skeleton had lain filled her with dread.

She was unaware that Alex and Marco were wrestling with their own anxieties - also on the subject of honesty and suppression of truth. The problem of the two skeleton teeth gnawed away at Marco, inflamed by his troubles with the go-kart and compounded by a new soreness in his gums, signalling that another milk tooth was working lose and would soon come out, and have to be popped into that very jar.

Alex was disturbed by Grant's turncoat attitude to him at the circuit. Grant had always favouritised him and behaved like some buddy uncle up until now. But he had not coped with Alex being the better driver, and Alex wistfully sensed the rift between them would be permanent. His uneasiness with the continued possession of a ball of illicit drugs, which he had now dug up and reburied three times in all, was almost of secondary importance.

Oh God, Julia thought as she switched off the engine, that skeleton might not be the only one! There could be dozens buried in different areas of the garden or almond grove. Might that be why Frances was so anxious to combat Holidaylandia? Is this entire mountain flank the extended site of an alternative burial ground?

When will the Guardia suspect it, and come digging for more?

## 17

A lex remained brooding and distracted. The unclaimed go-kart prize irked him and he wanted other company than Marco's. Someone mature enough to accept blame when it sat so squarely on their shoulders.

He had hardly ever won a prize before, and the more he thought about it the larger it loomed in his estimation, so that by mid-morning Marco had robbed him of 500 euros and all the potential things he could have used it on. With that amount he could puncture the damn' juggling ball and ruin the contents, for Lise would still feel indebted to him if he gave her half - 250 euros - explaining that water had leaked in and contaminated the cocaine, leaving it worthless. Since he couldn't explain his feelings about Grant's withdrawal of affection to anyone, even to himself, the loss of the prize was a simpler, tangible grievance.

"I bet it was only a load of free tickets for their lousy go-karts. They wouldn't part with real money," Marco sniped.

"How d' you know? You can't even count your age. Or drive the right way. I saw it dumbo, it was in an envelope."

"Tickets fit in an envelope don't they? Why don't you phone them then? Julia'll drive you to get your precious money."

"What'll I do?" Julia overheard her name from another room.

"Oh, Alex thinks he was gonna' get a thousand euro prize. But because Grant's such a bad loser he missed out."

Alex snatched the milk from Marco. Since it was already tipped into pouring position it spurted right across the table and dribbled incontinently down the table legs onto the floor. "Don't dare blame Grant you ugly turd! He was trying to protect you, though he was a total arsehole to think you might be ten."

Alex stormed out slamming the door. When Julia reached the kitchen she saw only a mountain of cereal strewn across the table and a puddle of milk spreading over the floor, and finally Marco's protruding foot. She found him a soggy mess. He had been dabbing at the milk with an old motheaten floor sponge and simultaneously wiping his eyes with it to destroy any evidence of tears. Turning his face away he mumbled angrily, "I'm *not* crying over the spilt milk."

The three and a half months spent in Spain had so obviously benefitted Marco, but she was concerned about Alex. He would soon be thirteen, an age she associated with misery and frustration, when Frances momentarily lost hope and drank to oblivion. She knew Alex had his own frustrations - a hopeless infatuation for Lise, who behaved like a sophisticated woman of the world and very deliberately stung him with her sexuality, and a younger brother almost permanently in tow, from whom there was no escape or relief except for brief afternoons banging iron with Arturo el Ferrer.

In your teens is when you most need a dad and she had failed him, duplicating the same problems she had faced herself. The only difference being he knew who his father was, although that must be little consolation.

"How come you knew Grant's code?" she asked him when he eventually reappeared.

"My birthday, subtract eleven months" he answered.

At least Grant had not embarrassed her there; yet it underlined just how perilously close her pregnancy was to her brief time with him. But then all her relationships had been brief at that age; reckless, brief and ill advised. No doubt reflecting her negative feelings for Frances. Had she tried to emulate her mother? Or merely get her attention?


She had always believed her feelings for Gheorghe, Alex's dad, were different, unconnected with Frances. With him she had mainly been naïve and starstruck. He was the most astonishly perfect dancer she had ever seen, Romania's Nureyev - only incomparably better. His company had performed in Paris and London, and he stayed on, courtesy of some cultural Euro-funding to give a six week masterclass course in classical ballet to a handpicked dozen of the most promising students. And she felt so doubly and deeply honoured when, from that lucky dozen, he had 'handpicked' her!

It was difficult to genuinely re-enter the persona of her seventeen year old self. She could no longer recapture the emotions, the hopes and the lack of caution or fear she had then. She was naïve and headstrong certainly. But she could not deceive herself that she had been duped or misled by him because she never expected the relationship to have any future. It was a romantic dancing dream; the harsh, objective realities of the situation never entered her head.

In others' eyes she was a fool not to see she was being used, that it was a classic case of the older male predator with looks and fame entrapping a young innocent. Her slim, early adolescent body (it must've been its very androgenous quality that had attracted him, she supposed, for he'd said she was his first woman - but in retrospect was that likely?) meant her periods were always infrequent, so she considered herself virtually safe from pregnancy scares, and stupidly took no precautions. And since he habitually slept with men, he of course took no precautions either.

It was not until a month after his return to Bucharest that she feared she might be pregnant. The timing could not have been worse. The birth would come right in the middle of her A levels, and she had just been offered the plum role of Juliet in a modern ballet version of Romeo and Juliet to run from July until December - the perfect launch for her career.

Everyone advised an abortion. She herself, pale, bewildered and dishevelled from the sudden affliction of morning sickness, felt hopelessly torn. She knew it was her decision but all the same felt a duty to inform Gheoghe (just in case Frances had never told her father of his paternity, like she swore she had).


It might have been another infidelity that provoked his longterm lover's jealousy, but it was most likely aroused by the news of her pregnancy, she had to accept that. And, feeling therefore responsible for the loss of one life, Gheorghe's life, she could not deliberately cause the loss of a second. Imagining his poor lifeblood flowing out of the stab wounds, she wondered if her own blood might start to flow in sympathy, and she be relieved of having to make the terrible decision by miscarrying.

But despite the grieving, the guilt and the sickness, she did not miscarry. And against everyone's pleadings, Frances included, she refused to have the abortion.

Alex was born in June - just two days after she finished her final A level exam! On that count his timing was wonderfully fortuitous - except of course she never got to play Juliet, and her career was seriously stalled for some time and, according to many, permanently compromised.

She alone knew how precariously Alex's life had hung in the balance; how, had his father not died, he might never have been born. She had heard all the criticisms levelled at her only too often; how she could not handle the career pressure and had kids as a diversion; or she had only had kids to compensate for her lack of other family - no father, aunts, uncles, cousins or grandparents, and an alcoholic mother who never wanted her. But she knew simply that the alternative options were all closed, since for whatever debased motives she originally became a mother, she could now no longer imagine life without Alex and Marco.

"Let's go to Marte's," Alex had recovered from his ill humour, "I fancy a walk in the wind."

"OK," she said, in no mood to resist him in his perilous pre-teenage fatherless state that was all her responsibility.

Does free will exist at all, she wondered, or are we what our genes dictate? If the latter, then she was but the product of an ill-tempered, cold-hearted Scot with wonderfully deft hands and an English butterflyman wafted on the winds of chance, while Alex was all that plus a homosexual Romanian ballet dancer, and whatever ingredients his parents contributed. What freedom did he have to choose his life? Or Marco?

Out in the gusty, boisterous wind all introspection was blown away. It was nearing the end of March, but the old saying 'In like a lion, out like a lamb' (or vice versa) seemed likely to be disproved this year for it was ending as it had begun, leonine and bitterly cold. Signs of spring were nevertheless evident in the vegetation; wild flowers scattered the hillside and different bushes lit up and flamed with yellow flowers.

Small restless birds flitted ahead of them, anxious lest they tread on their nests hidden in the rock crevices, and jabbering incessantly to distract them.

As they neared Marte's the earth grew rusty and the rocks changed from pearl grey to a warmer cream, pink valerian flowers flourished in every hollow and different birds sang from the dark, hidden places in the pine wood. The path curved through the pines before emerging into Marte's clearing, and here pine needles smothered the ground so densely that virtually nothing could grow except a few viciously thorned plants and the occasional evil looking fungus. One short stretch of a dozen metres had a particularly malign atmosphere; cold, musty smelling and uncannily dark. Marco gripped Julia's hand as they traversed it - something he had not done for months.

Otto looked like an oculists' mannequin, with half a dozen pairs of reading glasses clinging to his body. Julia guessed it was to maximise time and motion, for he had complained about the hours lost hunting for misplaced spectacles, but possibly each had different strengths of lense to read the differing font sizes in his research documents. It was obvious he did research his subject, for his desk was littered with books and papers on the Civil War. The majority were Spanish, some English, but only two were German. A few sentences on each open page had been carefully underlined in pencil.

"Your book's not just focused on this bandolero then?"

"Mein Gott no! He is but a few chapters, vile it is a major study of ze Republican resistance to Franco. So, you take me for a dilettante?"

"He is showing off his hoch English vocabulary!" Marte cried as she entered the room fresh from the bathtub, one towel wrapped saronglike round her body, another turbanlike around her hair. "Major study..." she scoffed, "I'll tell you what's 'major' about it. It's a 'major' work of sophistry and plagiarism! Hah!" she crowed, pirouetting, "You see, I too have been at ze dictionary!"

Julia bent closer to the open pages and their neat underlinings, which she noticed had been numbered and given some indecipherable form of coding.

"So, you select sentences you like, translate them into German and hey presto: there's your book," she suggested, her tone mildly mocking.

Otto shifted his slouched position into something proud and ramrod straight, "There is nussing unusual in zis method, let me tell you. All research is based on previous research. Every writer does it. Knowledge is gebuilt zis way. I know, I am a Professor, after all." And finally, as if Sra Bigot had willed it from a distance, he stroked his beard.

"It is less plagiarism if you translate from English to German." Marte explained, "Or rather, it is less likely you get caught, for few Germans read English, and ze English never read German."

"You ladies may laugh, but us non-fiction writers can never win. Eizer we are blamed for inventing our facts - like you suspected me wiz my bandolero - or for not being creative, so for copying our facts."

"Ya, ya, ya!" Marte taunted. "Nobody blames you for copying facts you poor man. Zey are just worried that you copy ze exact words. Is it not a breach of copyright?"

Finally he decided to play the anger card. Slamming his hand onto the desk so that the papers flew up in a cloud of dust, resettling in a new and perhaps improved order he thundered, "Enough! I am not a cheat but a historian. Go back to your menopause and cures, which, I might add," he waggled a long and now bruised forefinger at her, "you are not the first to have invented."


With this mild catharsis over, life returned to normal and Marte happily wandered off to select her wardrobe and place a kettle on a flame. Lise lounged in a doorway and Alex gravitated there like a moth to light, while Marco curled up on a giant pouffe to cuddle the ginger cat. It was soon fast asleep from his rhythmic stroking, and due to its heavy night on the tiles. It was an unneutered male, always pooped out by nights of courting Milagran female cats and fighting rival Toms, quite apart from the efforts of hunting exploits and rummaging in rubbish bins - since Marte fed it an exclusively vegetarian diet to keep its proper hunting instincts alive. Marco soon joined it in sleep, equally drained by his emotional morning squabbling with Alex.

Julia noticed Marte's 'laboratory' was filled with bunches of valerian, the pink flowers she had spotted on the mountainside.

"What's valerian for?" she asked.

Marte stared at her in disbelief. "A woman, yet you don't know? It's *the* PMT miracle herb, ze best there is for relieving stress. It will be a twin to Renacimiento, - but I must find it a clever name and cunning label."

Once again she produced an A2 sheet of paper with overlapping scribbles and doodlings; nymphs reclining, dancing, skipping, leaping, preening, and one trapped inside a huge bath bubble.

"Sometimes I feel sympathy for Otto. Words are tricky - and I only need one."

"Why not Valerian?"

"It must be more original, Julia."

"Umm...Val-essence - Hang on a minute, give me a pen."

Julia, concentrating because spelling was not her strength, wrote down 'convalescence', then 'convalesce con val-essence' and then gave up.

"You're right. This'd only work for your Spanish market, and it's still pathetic. Does Valium have valerian in it?"

"Maybe so, but it is full of chemicals and harmful. Valerian is magic, it is zer gute for the immune system and makes you sleep like a baby. I give it to Otto to stop him snoring."

"Does it...induce abortion?"

"What a strange question... No. There are other herbs for zat."

"This may be a stranger one... Marte, when you used to help women have an abortion..."

"I never did!" Marte was indignant. "I only gave herbs. For me abortion means something different, some manipulation, interference."

"Well, when you gave your herbs...if the foetus was rejected, did you bury it back there...in the woods?"

Marte sat down on her work stool. It was immediately clear to her that Julia's mind was delving into past history in a way that would benefit no-one, given the current imminence of both their interviews at the Cuartel. Spain was a Roman Catholic country, and their feminine ideal, in the form of a million saintly effigies of Santa Maria La Virgen were about to be let loose for mass adoration onto the streets of every city, town and village in the Easter parades - and Julia had to start remembering abortions. The Spanish doctor who had had the courage and conviction to help women with unwanted pregnancies had been jailed for ten years for his pains, and Marte had had enough suspicious sniffing around long ago not to want it resuscitated.

"One skeleton is enough right now." She sounded schoolmarmly and distinctly cold. "Ze very last thing we should do, is try to prove our innocence by finding something to blame on someone else. Zat is a cowardly way."

"And not what I'm doing." Julia resented the slur. "I've a flood of memories. Some crystal clear, some blurred. I'm trying to pinpoint that period in my mind, that's all, and I've no mother to help me sequence events or distinguish between what really happened, and what's just my imagination. You're the only person I can ask. That should be obvious."

Marte knew a swipe at her intelligence when she heard it, but it was more usually a man's weapon. She could take insults about her age, shape, race, sex, and the odd knobbles on her toes that ill-fitting shoes had caused, but she deeply resented slights on her cleverness. She drew a sharp dividing line between intellectual and instinctive intelligence; the first she lacked but the second she had in surfeit. She could read emotional and sexual urges with the accuracy of a brain surgeons's scalpel, she felt the phases of the moon and could sense the whereabouts of an egg in a fallopian tube or the condition of ovaries. In fact she only needed to take a brief look at a woman to measure her menstrual cycle, whether she was hot and about to ovulate, or tetchy and about to menstruate.

She could also sense male arousal before the fools picked up on it themselves. When the sexual urges were out of kilter, and she included hunger and thirst for food and water (and alcohol) amongst the sexual urges, then a person was what traditional doctoring termed 'ill'. Here again she could identify the imbalance, and treat it. People like Otto and Julia could worship the mind for all she cared, for what really mattered was the body, and they were rank amateurs in its knowledge.

"OK," Marte said at last, "I'll tell you what I can. Yes, I did bury some little foetuses in the woods, when they were miscarried. Also there was one baby who was - how do you say it? - shtill born, that too was buried in the same area. I know of no other burials that were, how shall we call it? ... 'unofficial'."

"You don't think the skeleton might have been buried by friends? You know, if he'd died in an accident, or from a terminal illness, and they'd not wanted an official burial?"

Marte thought about it for several seconds, then exhaled slowly. "Not for sure. Zere was one American who was chronically ill with cancer. He walked off alone into the mountains and his friends kept quiet about it - it was his wish. As far as I know his body was never found, but he didn't walk past Frances' house – it was far away in the Sierra Caracoles, beyond Montejoven. Frances even buried her cats away from her own land!"

Suddenly Marte gripped Julia's arm, and there was an intent, faraway look in her eyes. "Ssh, we must stop zis talk right now! Someone is coming, I can feel it. English people. Zat pink wally, Colin. He must be zer ill to trust himself to my hands!"

Julia was genuinely impressed by Marte's seeming telepathy, for approximately three minutes later, certainly with sufficient time lapse for it to be impossible that Marte could have heard an approaching engine, Reggie's car struggled up the steep incline and Colin was indeed huddled in the passenger seat. They could not have phoned to make a prior appointment either, since Marte's phones were perpetually lifeless and Otto had none. Colin remained in the car, sinking ever further from view, while Reggie leapt out with alacrity. He was intercepted by Otto on his way to Marte's inner chamber, for Otto was delighted to be caught in the act of working and knew it did wonders for his street cred, Reggie only having ever seen him with a glass in his hand before now.

"I have now completed more zan one hundred thousand vords," they heard Otto's voice reverberate with pride.

"You keep an exact tally?" Reggie sounded incredulous. He never kept a tally of anything. It reminded him too much of his mother and her endless household accounts. "Why? Do they pay by the word?"

Otto's reply was muffled, but they caught the word 'commensurate' and Marte giggled and whispered, "Ze dictionary again!"

Reggie's head popped into view. "Aha," he said, "good to see you both. I'm afraid I've brought a sick patient. I don't think it's contagious but the victim is covered top to bottom in a rash and is going crazy with the desire to itch. He's tried bathing in ass's milk and honey, but it got no better. Shall I bring him in?"

"Yes do," Marte answered with little enthusiasm.


Colin did look truly terrible. An angry, red scabrous rash smothered every visible part of his body, and his eyes were wild and panic stricken, like an animal caught in a trap.

"I'm not stripping off in front of ladies," he insisted, shivering and twitching. "I think I'm going to die anyway," he added gloomily, "but I do rather fancy a pain killer to tide me over."

Marte looked at him witheringly, but Julia could detect an atom of sympathy in her expression as she studied the rash.

"No," she opined "You will not die, not of zis. It is only hives, but a bad attack."

"Hives?" Colin was so surprised he stopped shivering. "As in bees? I did put honey in the bath - nanny always said honey with apple cider cured mostly anything."

"Vot are you on about? Hives is a skin infection, and you are prone to it." She glanced at Julia, "As it happens, zis is one more thing that Valerian is perfect for. You will see."

"Valerian?" Colin was alarmed, "isn't that Latin for 'goodbye'?"

"A quick and painless death," Reggie cruelly pretended to read from a bottle label.

"That's valediction," Julia corrected him.

"Or Valkyrie or Valhalla, considering the northern European personnel engaged on the mercy killing task," Reggie pointed out.

"If all you two plan to do is jabber zen join Otto. I need to examine zis patient in some privacy," Marte announced imperiously.


Colin's eyes expressed an anguish bordering on terror at being left alone with Marte, but in the back of his mind he knew that baring himself to an older woman was preferable to nakedness in the presence of Julia, who could not help but compare him with younger, stronger, leaner bodies of her own age. Marte, monstrous, ogrous, witch doctor that she was, at least had experience of all physical shapes and sizes, plus a knowledge of the uglier diseases and imperfections that befell them. Also, she was familiar with Otto's gaunt and elderly frame, with which Colin felt he would not compare too unfavourably.

So his only real cause for alarm was her breasts. He had always been irresistibly drawn to ample bosoms, they filled him with fear, awe and a magnetic attraction. His usual countermove was to look fixedly elsewhere - for instance at a crossword puzzle, or to sit firmly on his hands so as to stifle their twitchiness. He could sympathise with 'Manos Arriba' although the man was fifty times worse than him, with virtually no control at all, because he understood how difficult it must be to live with the constant provocation of Sra Bigot's magnificent orbs thrust in his face at family dinner.

"Relax." Marte commanded. "If you lie on your hands how can you relax?"

"Will I hallucinate?"

"Not with Valerian, or Aloe Vera, that I must give you as well. They are herbal medicines, even the Romans used them."

"Phhh, the Romans got up to all sorts of hanky panky..."

"Is zat what you want?" Marte asked sternly. "To get high?"

She had no intention of telling Colin about her stashes of illegal substances, though privately she felt some cannabis cookies would do him a world of good. She must be circumspect in case he blabbed to the Guardia. And tight fisted; why waste good dope if he wasn't intending to pay?

"Right," she said in a peremptory way that excited him, "you cannot wear your usual clothes because they will irritate. Take this cotton djellaba, but wear nothing underneath. No undergarments - your skin must breathe properly to heal."

Colin obediently slipped it over his head. Had he missed being ordered around? Should he buy a parrot and teach it to bark orders at him? Oh dear, did he want to be whipped? No, no, of course not, if he was a genuine masochist he'd be enjoying the pain of a total body rash, not creeping to the enemy begging to be healed.

"How long," he asked "must I wear this Arab outfit?" How long am I confined at home, in other words.

"Until you are better," Marte replied.

He did not dare ask how he could recognise 'better', but for the first time in his life he experienced a longing to be better. She had a pleasant earthy smell that evoked beech nuts, bluebell woods and scurrying squirrels, he had breathed it in as she worked up and down his body spraying something cool onto his skin. But there had been no rubbing it in, no massage at all, because the skin had erupted in such a chronic way.

He looked so atypically at ease with himself and so little in pain when he emerged from Marte's back room in a cream and dusty grey djellaba that both Reggie and Julia assumed Marte must have allowed him a blast on her hookah. Marte exuded pride because such rapid improvement showed that her healing powers had strengthened a notch or two. Only Colin knew that his partial recovery was chiefly due to the intoxicating effect of her body odour.


Back home, Julia threw herself into a frenzy of cleaning and tidying, much as Marte had done prior to her visit from the Guardia. On approaching her front door she had tried to see her house as if for the first time, through the eyes of a stranger, and she was not impressed.

But even as she sprayed and wiped the window glass she debated her motives. On the one hand Andres' visit was a good excuse for a necessary clean, on the other it showed her up as ashamed of how she lived. And why should she be? She was not such a coward that she had to curry favour with a breed of conservative élitists, erstwhile Francoistas, a clique to which most of the legal profession in Spain belonged. She knew what their homes were like because Frances had occasionally been invited into classy houses, for reasons of cultural snobbery – being a ceramics expert. They always contained acres of polished marble flooring, huge collections of dark mahogany furniture with knotted legs, cluttered displays of silverware and endless family portraits in gilt frames, plus several huge and forbiddingly cold bathrooms from which one wrong turn got you hopelessly lost in a series of old fashioned upstairs bedrooms. They were as impersonal as hotels, with nothing out of place and no suggestion that anything happened there apart from polite conversing, eating, sleeping, and abluting.

Many in her mother's generation had rebelled against their tidy upbringing. As a child she'd entered hovels where windows were not transparent openings to an outside world, but impenetrable screens frosted over by years of accumulated grime. Every nook was a cobwebbed death trap for the insect species; moths, beetles, flies, bluebottles, wasps and small snails (who clung to anything wooden to suck at the resin). Tables, bespattered with food and other filth, were functional surfaces on which to load anything to eat, read, look at or mend, while floors were reservoirs for anything too heavy for the table, and whatever fell off it.

Bedrooms were storage for personal junk; a chaos of clothes, bedding, posters, pictures, half-eaten food (coated in ants), a music system, a mountain of cassettes, and always scores of chewed biros for rewinding tapes manually to save battery power. Bathrooms were depositories for all things jettisoned from elsewhere and, *if* they had plumbing, the taps would endlessly drip for they never had washers. The toilet was strictly for plants, since human business must be done outside, communing with nature and enriching the soil.

Those with the messiest, dirtiest living space were greatly admired; it was actually believed that only the truly enlightened lived in squalor. In fact ingrained dirt not only proved your enlightened state, but your artistic brilliance too. The fouler you smelt, the greater your genius. Occasionally you could tickle your teeth with a eucalyptus twig, or pour a lota over your bare bottom, but you absolutely mustn't wash or brush your hair. And curiously enough, although it looked like knotted strands of bladderwrack seaweed for the first few weeks, it did eventually learn to selfclean!

The system of course worked better for adults, because little kids were closer to the ground and easier for crawling insects to clamber onto, so they perpetually played hosts to the warring armies of ants, tics, nits, lice, fleas and flies, and consequently weren't much fun to cuddle.

Marte, even back then when filthiness was the trend, had allowed disorder but not dirt. Despite her contempt for rigorous Germanic domestic organisation her mother would have been proud of her shiny saucepans and limpid drinking glasses, and she always threw water over herself twice a day behind a living screen of Indian bamboo. Frances had a similar philosophy; she embraced untidiness and complete lack of maintenance but also drew the line on dirt. Even though there was no running water and hauling buckets from the well was an effort, they showered daily and the kitchen was close to being clean. The rest of the house, however, was given over to pots. Fragments in one room, pots in progress of being restored in another, completed pots ready for transporting to whatever museum in a third. These rooms could never be disturbed, so layers of dust soon settled on the pots like a silvery shroud, and Julia's earliest attempts at writing were with a finger in their dust.

All of Frances' mending instincts were exhausted by the pots, so anything else that got broken stayed that way. On the rare occasions that she had spare cash to splash around she might hire a carpenter (Emilio Fuster's dad in early days) or a builder (Juanito's dad, and he, unlike Juanito, could build) if the house seemed in real danger of falling down, but all the minor bric-à-brac of household breakages were ignored. Julia, when she was old enough to have steady hands and could read the instructions on an Araldite packet, took to mending anything that glue would bind, and by the time she was eight she could mix and apply plaster, and even render with a distinctly gritty mix of cement.


Suddenly, Julia felt a surge of hatred for the skeleton. He had trapped her. Literally and metaphorically. She couldn't return to England until it was discovered who he was and how he'd died, she couldn't make plans, couldn't look forward - was forced to keep on sifting over the past like an old woman with no future.

In this angry mood she became convinced he was a total idiot anyway who had died for some inane reason like refusing to use a path because it was too conventional and boring, so had tried a more 'original', 'artistic' route climbing up a weak wall that he should have foreseen would collapse. And the ripple effect of his dumb action was upsetting half the village; Dolores' bread had lost its taste, Eulogio had aged ten years, Celestino had Parkinsons disease, Scotty'd lost his customers though not being in the heart of the village, Colin was a nervous wreck, and Alex in an even stranger mood since visiting Lise just now.


And herself? She felt exactly like a child again, drowning in childhood memories, once again engulfed by the beauty and the bitterness that was her experience of Spain.

## 18

Andres arrived at three dressed for a hike in the mountains; jeans, chunky sweater and a tough pair of boots. His manner was more informal than his efficient, businesslike approach at the bar when he had only recently been in courtroom mode.

"What a beautiful place," he enthused, "and about to be ruined by those monstrosities."

He glared accusingly at the asphalted streets and concrete structures that were blotting out her view of Milagra. Already she had lost sight of the church tower and the tall plane trees in the plaza, and now the mottled rooftops of the upper houses were gradually being obscured.

"I'm trying not to see it that way. Instead of focusing on each new ugliness I try to look at the mountains and what beauty still remains. I remind myself how lucky I am, compared to people in this world who are genuinely - and brutally - dispossessed of their land. I tell myself to lose a view is nothing."

"Does it work?"

"Not always." Her smile was rueful, "I've just spent the entire morning reliving the past and cursing the skeleton for keeping me trapped here."

"They've taken your passport?" He sounded alarmed.

She shook her head. "No, but I can hardly leave now."

She let the boys show him the terrace wall and the area of excavation. She could not imagine what he was hoping to find, but he spent a long time there. Perhaps he expected the stones to divulge their guilty secrets. Odd snatches of their conversation drifted towards the house, and she overheard Marco's excited voice describing the moment of discovery.

"The skull was on its side, like this. Like when you read a book in bed, propping your head on your elbow. Juanito fainted!"

"And who is Juanito?"

By the time they returned he had been given a blow by blow account of the aftermath, including each detailed stage of the duelling between Marco and Otto over Roman Gladiator versus Civil War bandolero. Alex looked frustrated from barely getting a word in whereas Marco was semi-delirious, and Andres, although Spaniards are natural talkers and used to the noisy sociability of bars, looked shell-shocked from Marco's highspeed, nonstop chatter. Only Marco knew it was not so much attention seeking as distraction, due to panic about the two stolen, dirt stained teeth.

"Off you go now," Andres ordered, "I need time to digest your information. Any more now and I'll be sick."

"Don't rely on Marco for information," she warned. "He gets very carried away."

He laughed, "I rely on my own judgment, or I'd be fooled every time."

She felt the stirrings of resentment. Was he insinuating they had a reason to throw him off the scent, had something serious to hide? Perhaps he was no better than the first lawyer after all - merely better looking, and that gave him an arrogance which actually made him worse. Something warned her this visit might be a mistake. He had probably specialised in criminal law because it fed his innate sense of superiority, because he enjoyed analyzing and solving the devious workings of criminal minds.

As she left him to wander in the garden while she prepared a cold spread of food, she struggled against her tendency to overreact. She had been reliving her childhood self too concentratedly, she knew it, and it had only served to overstimulate her suspicious nature. Too many people had been afraid of Frances, back then, because she was beautiful and outspoken and too aloof in her world of pots. Not daring to tackle Frances directly, therefore, they got at her through Julia; either by hurting, isolating or ignoring her, or by deliberately befriending her to make Frances jealous.


After they had eaten Andres wanted to visit the Fuente with the boys, even though he confessed he belonged to the Eulogio school of non-believers in miracles, or miraculous visions of weeping Virgins. He drank the emerging water with eager relish, undetered by their warnings about toad's sexual exploits and the fizzy scum and jellied toadspawn still visible in the pool below. He was undecided about reincarnation, Alex learnt, but given the choice would choose almost anything in preference to a cold blooded reptile.

"I've a step-mother," he said darkly, "I know about cold blooded creatures."

"Gran was an ogre too," Marco confessed, despite knowing he was blurting out confidentialities to a stranger and being far too familiar, "but she did have her good side"

"And what was that?"

"She never made me feel bad about doing something wrong, or making a mistake."

As he told this blatant lie he looked accusingly at Alex, who was poised to kick him in the shin to shut him up before worse emerged. Worse being the extension to his original theory - which he'd discarded - that Gran had only metamorphosed into the toad because she really *had* murdered the skeleton and then, from remorse, gone to sit beside it, keeping it company in the damp and dark. Or she hadn't cared two hoots about its suffering, but only gone there to gloat.

"Don't tell my mother any of his crap," Alex pleaded.

"Never trust a lawyer," he replied with a deliberately wicked smile.

"So, how's your detective work progressing?" Julia asked when they returned, trying not to feel offended that he had ignored her so as to play buddy with the kids. She was not sure if his tactics were to make her feel superfluous, or to glean information from those who would least suspect it.

"Well enough. It's very evident they still don't know who the victim is. That means he's not on a missing persons' file in Europe, and he can't be Spanish."

"Just what I feared." Julia tussled with a knot in her hair, "A lot of foreigners cut themselves off from their families and backgrounds, same as my mother. Their parents wouldn't know - or care - if they were dead or alive, so they wouldn't have reported them missing. Can't DNA locate a person's geographical origins?"

"It can, yes. They may know if he's from…say France, Germany or England. But they still don't know *who* he is."

"Some in the village reckon the Guardia already know it was an accident, but are stringing us along for their amusement." She was hoping he'd corroborate this.

"Then they're fooling themselves. Village Guardia aren't the brightest, but they aren't running the investigation. It's in the hands of senior detectives, - that alone shows they believe it's a murder case."

Julia looked away towards the mountains, where the setting sun caught the rims of grey clouds with fine brushstrokes of crimson, like bleeding ribs on a grey torso.

"And my mother's suspect number one?"

He looked at her with an element of sympathy. "Not definitively. But it did happen close to her house."

"From a blow to the back of the head?" Julia resented the tremor in her voice.

He nodded. "Apparently so. There could have been a fight and he might have fallen - or been pushed off the wall - triggering its collapse. Or he might have already been killed elsewhere, and his body brought here and then the wall collapsed so's to bury it."

"*Why* couldn't it be an accident? Surely a serious head injury's likely if a wall collapses?"

"Sure. That's why there must be other injuries or other evidence to support the idea of a fight." He leant forward, "But remember what I told you; they can't find your mother guilty because she's not here to stand trial. And you have nothing to fear because you were only five."

"And I already told *you*," she tried looking him in the eye but found it hard to focus, "I'm not thinking only of legal consequences. Can't you imagine what it would be like to know your mother'd killed someone, even if it couldn't be proved?"

"I wouldn't be a criminal lawyer if I was only interested in law," he pointed out. "In your heart of hearts, what do *you* think?"

She laughed bitterly. "I wish I knew - I've gone through so many possibilities..." She stood up, then abruptly sat down again, "My worst nightmare is he's my father and she lied to me all along."

"You will know that soon enough," he said grimly.

"And the other nightmare," she said in a nervous rush, "is that it was me. I threw a stone or some such thing, and then I blanked it out of my consciousness and memory. I've even had mad visions of actually doing it - I shouldn't be telling you this I know, but I have to talk to someone."

"I'm only an unimaginative lawyer," he smiled, "but I'd guess that's hardly surprising. Children of five live in a different world, partly imaginative, partly real. It would probably be more strange if you hadn't imagined yourself killing him." He waited until he could see the reassurance relax her features, then continued, "You've mentioned almost every possibility except the most likely one. If there was a male fight resulting in a death, your mother wouldn't protect one of her casual sex partners, not if they'd killed your father. The only person she'd protect is..."

Julia nodded miserably. "My father..."

Marco was meticulously wiping every drop of blood from the bathroom sink, cursing himself for his utter stupidity in eating the turron Andres had brought. If he had not been so piggishly greedy his loose tooth might have lasted another week, he had been so careful up until now to chew slowly and avoid sticky sweets. Once all the tell-tale traces of blood were gone he pondered the prospects of glueing the tooth back in. It shouldn't be hard, it wasn't a tree with multiple roots, it had just one long spike that ought to fit neatly back - if it wasn't for all the blood welling out, obscuring the hole to plug it in. He needed more time to work out a brilliant solution for those vile black skeleton teeth, and he most certainly didn't want to cope with the rigmarole of the 'tooth fairy' today.

What if Julia wanted to look in the jar and count how many milk teeth he'd lost? Might she be that weird? It wasn't her style, but mothers get hung up on the strangest elements of data so he couldn't take the risk. It had occurred to him a million times that the sanest exit from his whole dilemma was to bin the skeleton's teeth and be rid of the problem. But having so successfully stolen them, and then so nervewrackingly looked after them, to now just dispose of them would be such a waste. He still had the vestige of a hope they'd prove useful, a wild leap of faith that they were Roman even if the bones weren't. *Could* such a thing be possible?

He studied his reflection in the mirror. It was just as he'd feared - the gap was glaringly visible. He would have to remain silent and unsmiling if no-one was to detect the loss of his tooth, and he had enough self-knowledge to realise silence from him would seem suspicious.

He wandered disconsolately off to review the state of his beach glass mosaic. He had used plaster of Paris for that, and some algae jelly stuff that Julia found, but neither of them looked mouthworthy. He sat staring at his work of art, and the longer he looked at it the uglier it seemed to be. Eventually his churning brain provided him with two possible solutions; he could either use thread to tie the lost tooth to its erstwhile companion teeth on either side, or he could attempt superglueing the tooth to its neighbours, having first blasted his mouth dry with a bicycle pump.

Alex was relieved Marco had retired to keep his own company. Perhaps he had at last realised he had said too much to a stranger, and would lie low. That would give Alex sufficient time to surreptitiously dig up the drugball yet again, and secrete it in the place he agreed yesterday with Lise, so that she could collect it when she had the earliest opportunity.

He didn't feel altogether easy about the arrangement, but as she'd reminded him, it did essentially belong to her - she had been the one to detect Jorgen's game in the first place, he'd merely dared to hide the ball where Jorgen couldn't find it.

Part of him was immensely relieved to be getting the stuff off the premises, especially since the police and now lawyers were prowling and sniffing about. Yet he worried over Lise's intentions. She'd been buzzing off on her moped to Montejoven with other Milagran teenagers most afternoons and staying away as long as she could, that he could understand, but also, money had crept into her conversations at every second word. Marte was admittedly tight: "Ven I was young we didn't believe in money, ze cleverest spent nothing and still looked cool," and she'd go on about how she made her own clothes, pressed her own paper, grew her own marijuana plants, had her own paddy field of brown rice, threshed her own lentils and plucked leaves off any old thorn bush and called it tea.

Lise was of course feisty enough to combat such arguments; she had pointed out that KinderGeld had 'Kinder' in it for a purpose, and that the desire to live primitive had lost its appeal aeons ago.

She had got her way to the extent of a fifthhand moped with an elliptical rear wheel and a weekly allowance scarcely enough to keep her in mascara ("Ve used to fabricate our own mascara too, and kohl is more natural"). She was razor sharp about the price of everything, and she had made shrewd guesses at the wealth inside that ball - a sum she would only know exactly once it was weighed. She said she was going to virtually give it away to a dealer friend of a friend, so as to be shot of the problem and have some extra spending money. But Alex did not believe her.

He wasn't so troubled if she sold it wholesale - though how she'd hide that amount of money from under Marte's nose and from everybody else in the area he had no idea - as about the risks of her selling it in small, expensive quantities. That prospect was alarming. If she sold it in grammes to the local dealers who operated from Scotty's bar on Fridays the process would drag on for months, and taking that kind of risk was madness. But what could he do? Lise was fifteen and a half; she didn't listen to anyone, not even her conscience, so she'd hardly accept advice from someone not quite thirteen.

He also prayed that if she *was* caught, she wouldn't drag him in. She'd always promised to say Jorgen buried it and left her the instructions where...

Just to be on the safe side (if there was a safe side) he had avoided touching the ball with bare hands. His eyes now darted in all directions, checking the coast was clear, and all through the operation of digging it up and reburying it in the prearranged place, his gloved hands trembled and his heart thumped like a caged fist against his ribs.

It had actually seemed funny in the beginning - just a prank to infuriate that arrogant Jorgen, and a delicious secret to share with Lise who had dared him to do it, and at the time he would have dared almost anything for her. Now, though, he knew it was serious. Part of him even wanted to tell Julia but he knew he couldn't; he'd promised Lise so many times and Julia had enough trouble of her own.

He dug up some wild garlic bulbs from the almond grove and replanted them in the soft soil covering the ball. That way, if a hungry wild boar came looking for garlic, which they sometimes did, it would hopefully chew up the ball along with the garlic. He watered the hopelessly drooping garlic plants and managed to put the hoe back in the shed just in the nick of time before Andres came out onto the patio.

"Louche tooth," Marco spluttered from behind a hand cupped across his mouth, to explain the chronically slow progress he was making with supper.

"Why didn't you tell me? I wouldn't have done spaghetti if I'd known."

"Sshawright."

"Sometimes it's best to pull them out quickly," Andres suggested, but Marco rolled his eyes in urgent dissent.

"He's got some weirdo thing about teeth," Alex explained, "he's always drooling over the ones in his jar."

Marco's eyes narrowed menacingly. This was highly dangerous ground, but his tongue was disastrously tied and unable to protect him. He had to find an alternative hiding place now, no question about it. And the stupidity was that, had he known it beforehand, he need never have attempted the madness of superglueing his teeth. Now he had surplus glue spread like a veneer all over his tongue, so he could taste nothing apart from the flavour of poisonous chemical, and for the moment say nothing - until he could manage to detach the tip of the tongue from his lower gums.

Superglue did still work in wet conditions, he had at least made that discovery.

Luckily Alex had recently bought a razor in the hope that shaving the down on his top lip would convince Lise he was really male, and with some deft manouvrings he should be able to neatly slice the tongue away from the gum. Trouble is, it was difficult to do delicate things from a mirror, the brain got confused by the image reversal.

Even after they had eaten Andres showed no sign of going.

"So how shall we leave it for Wednesday?" Julia tactfully broached the subject of departure.

"I'll be there," he said. "But we should talk things through before I go now. I've so far taken it at a relaxed pace because I thought that's what you wanted. But the lawyer inside of me feels underprepared." He stood up to glance out of the window at the darkening landscape. "I'd like to disabuse you about my own 'perfect childhood'. I know you resent my asking you personal questions and feel it's all one way."

"I shouldn't, I know that. I also do appreciate your help."

She had actually been wondering if he thought her self-obsessed, one of those people who attracted trouble to make themselves more interesting. Or if not exactly that, then someone who liked to talk endlessly about themselves, their childhood, difficult upbringing, and how everything that had ever happened to them, past present or future, was their bloody mother's fault.

"We don't have the time to waste on me, I only want you to know that my life hasn't fallen into place like clockwork, as I sense you imagine. My mother died when I was seven, since when I've had a stepmother - we've never got on."

"I'm sorry..." she said, aware she had indeed assumed him to be a typical Spanish mummy's boy, demanding and getting lashings of admiration every time he tied a shoelace right. 'Mirame mama!' - she used to hear it so often, and always shuddered.

"I don't want you to get the wrong impression of me either," she said impulsively. "I'm not this loving, dutiful daughter who's willingly dropped her life in England to come and mourn her mother's death and sort out her problems. I actively hated her from the age of thirteen, intensely at times. I left her on her own and rarely visited all through my twenties. Even when I knew she was almost crippled by arthritis I did nothing to help. When I heard she'd died I felt guilty..." She paused, breathless. "I did feel pain too - from the fact that she died violently, in a car crash. But at the same time I felt relieved a burden had gone..." She held his gaze. "Not very lovely, is it?"

"Who'm I to judge?" he looked at her, and she detected sadness in his eyes. "I respect your honesty, but - with respect - I'll have to steer you back to you as a five year old." He momentarily studied his hands. "There'll be questions about the men in her life, inevitably...and the provocations."

"Well, there was no shortage of either. She went through dozens of them, I hesitate to say hundreds, and there were always fights - verbal ones I mean. I don't know how many of the relationships were sexual but I'd guess most. I don't have to answer that do I?"

"It's exactly for that reason you need a lawyer. To field awkward or inappropriate questions."

"I don't want you to get the wrong idea about Frances," Julia's voice was quieter than before, "she wasn't an exhibitionist like some. She actually tried to be discreet about sex for my benefit."

"Did anyone ever take advantage of you?"

She had suspected he would make this assumption. In fact she felt he might have been working up to it all along. She tried to remain level headed and objective in her response.

"I don't think so. I do get uneasy feelings sometimes, but it's probably some kind of primordial, subconscious fear because I remember nothing specific. Most people were too scared of Frances. I knew some kids who were used sexually and it didn't shock me, so I guess I didn't see sex as a threat or as unnatural."

"If someone *had* touched you, what'd she have done?"

"She'd have killed....." The words tumbled out without her thinking, but as soon as she had uttered them her face drained of colour. "You bastard! You tricked me, you slimed your way into my confidence, just so you could idly slip it in - it's what you were after all along!"

His face blurred and she had a sensation of vertigo, similar to after the Guardia visit. 'When you feel you're going to faint', she could remember Marte saying, 'get your head down'. So she bent forward with her head in her hands, swooning like some delicate nineteenth century lady who'd mislaid her sal volatile, but staying conscious. She could feel a tingling sensation down the left side of her face as if she'd been slapped, and the darkness from her closed eyes pressured by her hands was disorientating. But fortunately the sharp smell of the onions she had recently chopped revived her. Her eyelids fluttered in an attempt to fragment the aggressive image of Frances' snarling face which might, or might not, be a genuine memory from the time of Yakimoto and the bicycle pump, and then she opened them.


But Andres was no longer there. For a fleeting second she imagined him driving off in triumph, her confessional words still ringing in his ears and of course securely recorded on a secret microphone, heading straight for the detectives. But then her senses returned. Her hearing had been muffled as if by the pressure change of an underwater dive, but suddenly she was overwhelmed by sound. Or more specifically, a shrill, bloodcurdling and prolonged screaming coming from the bathroom.

And in the same moment she saw Andres. He was applying his right shoulder to the bathroom door and charging like a rhinoceros.

The door was a heavy old oak carved antiquity from Toledo and would have probably resisted the charge of a real living, breathing rhino, but fortunately the bolt Marco had drawn across it was modern and one of the cheapest from the ferreteria in Milagra. It obligingly snapped and Andres catapaulted into the room, slamming hard into the far wall. Luckily Marco was not in his trajectory, and avoided getting more wounded than he already was.

The bathroom looked like an attempted suicide scene. Splatters of blood bespatterd the sink and Marco's dressing gown, while two bloodstained razor blades lay on the floor. However it was soon obvious that the blood dribbling through Marco's fingers - which were firmly clamped over his mouth - was coming not from his wrists but from his mouth. The expression in his eyes, although registering pain, was also redolent of guilt. Alex rushed into the bathroom hot on Andres' heels, and was the quicker of the two to assess the situation because he didn't ricochet off the tiled walls and have the distraction of a badly bruised shoulder. He also knew his brother only too well. He saw the razor blades immediately and popped them hurriedly back in their packet and into his pocket.

"Open your mouth you crazy loon," he towered over Marco, whose eyes were squeezed in pain, "it's a bit bloody late now to cut off your stupid blabbing tongue!"

Marco shook his head, tears welling from the corner of his eyes. "Jushabit" he struggled to say, swallowing and gulping blood. "Waa-er..." he pleaded.

Alex noticed from the corner of one eye that Andres was recovering. Being the owner of the razor blades he was anxious to play down the drama, which he sensed looked more serious than it was. He had bitten and burnt his tongue before, of course never been crazy enough to slice it with a sharp razor - but who apart from Marco would be? So he knew it was excruciatingly painful but had more muscle than blood, so Marco was not about to bleed to death. He led him, limp and pliant, down the steps to his bedroom and shone a torch into his mouth.

"You must know you're certifiable - don't answer, of course, or what's left of your tongue'll fall out. Jesus man - what were you thinking? Stay here."

He was back in less than a minute, having to an extent satisfied Andres' anxiety by what he prided himself was a plausible story. He had spun the idea that Marco had tried his suggestion (cunningly deflecting plenty of guilt Andres' way) of pulling the tooth out fast, using a winch and pulley system that he had bungled in the building of, so there was a bit more blood and injuries than there should have been. He had brought water and wads of cotton wool.

183

"OK, open up." Not only was there blood, but gleaming through it was a mysterious shiny substance like cling film covering parts of the tongue, gum and teeth. "Marco what *have* you been up to? People sniff glue but they don't bloody swallow it! What a mess!"

Marco said nothing. Along with blood, superglue and cut tongue he now had the addition of cotton wool padding and most of Alex' fist in his mouth, so speech was impossible. His major concern was to continue breathing. Believe it or not, he was beginning to feel better. He was over the worst, although he was undecided which had been worse: the asphyxiating petrol fumes from the superglue; the suffocating, gagging sensation of having ones tongue stuck down onto the lower gum, blocking the windpipe, and under that handicap having to eat spaghetti with feigned pleasure; or the sharp, swordlike pain from slicing off the tip of ones tongue. Now honestly *was* better because he had cut the tongue free from the gum, and the prevailing taste of blood was infinitely preferable to superglue. Also, Alex was in charge and could do all the talking, while his injuries were such that he had every excuse not to explain anything until tomorrow. And by tomorrow he would have thought of an inspired place to hide the skeleton's teeth, so his worries would be over.

Providing he survived the night, of course. *Could* you die from drinking too much of your own blood?

They heard Julia's approaching footsteps. "Let me talk," Alex hissed, as if there was any choice.

"How's Marco? Andres tells me he tried to pull it out with string..."

Alex nodded, "Messed it up, of course. Nearly got the wrong tooth - plus some tongue." He gave an irritatingly supercilious smile. "Don't worry, I've patched him up expertly and he's fine. Just wants to sleep, don't you Marco?"

Marco nodded obediently and smiled carefully, without revealing any teeth. Inspiration on where to hide the skeleton's teeth had suddenly struck him and he longed for the night to be over so he could act on it. Fortunately Julia took Alex at his word and did not explore his injuries; just gave him a brief kiss and cuddle and was gone.

For some unknown reason she looked even paler than him.

# 19

Well, that worked a dream, Julia thought ruefully. A masterclass in how to gain a lawyer's confidence.

He had been visibly warming to her mother for her appreciation of her traditional finca and the natural way of life it nurtured, had been gratified by her recognition of the wild beauty of the landscape - and even shown a kind of respect for her quixotic career. But all this positivity so vital for her case had been destroyed - by her. Wanting to seem this placid, rational person perfectly capable of managing her life, she had instead disastrously presented herself as ill-tempered, irrational, and, almost certainly, unbalanced.

She knew she had been verbally abusive too but could not properly remember the worst of what she said. Only Alex had emerged with some integrity intact. Well, he had shown the ability to take charge, to handle a tricky situation - even if he displayed a cruelly sadistic pleasure as he did so.

It was little wonder she had chosen to drive so far from home today…


The town they were heading for suddenly loomed above them, clinging to the only hill rising out of the coastal plain which stretched inland from Villahermosa. Its strategic position was immediately obvious. Any invaders approaching from the seaward direction would be as visible as black ants on a white tablecloth. The hill itself was crowned by this vast, and virtually intact, medieval walled castle, with the old town of Carocaballo wrapped around it like a sarong.

Just about every town and village that had ever, even briefly, been under Moorish occupation dusted off their costumes every year to celebrate the old rivalry in a 'Festival de los Moros y Cristianos', but the one in Carocaballo was easily the most spectacular.

As they climbed the cobbled streets towards the rampart walls the excitement in the air was tangible. The ground itself seemed to vibrate from the heavy pounding of horses' hooves, and the neighing and the trumpeting of a brass band mingled chaotically with the general hubbub from a huge crowd that was scaling the hill, heading for the castle forecourt where the main action would soon get started. They began to feel like fish out of water in their everyday clothes, for all around them swarmed 'Moors' in crimson, black or white silk robes, turbans, capes, heeled boots, jewelled slippers, and here and there the sun glinting ominously on the polished blade of a sharp curved sword.

The 'Christians' were heavily outnumbered because their outfit was boring by comparison - a plain cotton tunic under a dull grey sackcloth cape, the only splash of colour coming from a tiny blood red cross. Their cause, too, found little local sympathy for they had never actually managed to reconquer the town in any military sense at all. Its Moorish commander had of his own accord converted to Christianity after announcing he had seen a miraculous vision (not very dissimilar to Vicente's in Milagra; also involving angels, but with hellfire lapping at his feet instead of tears). Its timing was suspiciously propitious, for the Catholic reconquest was gaining momentum on all sides, and he was virtually surrounded. So he hastily publicised his vision, christianized his name and voilà; the Catholics could boast of a wonderful religious victory, while he and his supporters could carry on exactly as before in Carocaballo.

There was absolutely nothing precious about the medieval atmosphere though - this was definitely celebration time. Most of the 'Moors' wore designer sunglasses, had digital cameras dangling from their necks and mobiles in their hands; while the ladies, so demurely dressed in black burnouses and discreetly veiled, parted modern lips that gleamed with strawberry lipgloss and swigged their beer straight from the bottle. The cry "Llegan los Reyes!" (the Kings are coming!) rippled through the crowd, and everyone stared in anticipation at the massive stone entrance gate.

Suddenly a horseman galloped through it on a huge, dappled grey charger. His white silk robe danced in his turbulent slipstream, his crown sparkled and he looked every inch a genuine Moorish King. The Queen followed in the blink of an eye, mounted side-saddle but just as stunning in a long, turquoise silk robe, peacock plumes fluttering from a cap that flashed with jade and amethyst, and a smile that was regal and erotic in the same moment. On her heels came the Christian Royal Couple, trotting in unison as if training for a dressage competition, and much more soberly dressed in deep black velvet inlaid with mother-of-pearl. They lined up, Moors facing Christians, completely motionless in front of the now hushed crowd.

"Aren't they gonna' fight - or will they jssht share the cashtle?" Marco's swollen tongue didn't stop him disrupting the perfect silence of several thousand onlookers.

The spell broken, everyone went straight back to whatever they had been saying or drinking beforehand, and Julia breathed in the atmosphere with an intense joy. It was so Spanish, colourful and dramatic - and yet so light hearted, with no hint of trouble that the crowd might turn nasty, even though there would be no brakes on excessive drinking now that the horsedrawn carts laden with wine barrels were lumbering up the hill.

Free bars were quickly set up outside the church built on the site of the supposed miraculous vision. They sold wine, beer, soft drinks, mineral water, oranges, candy floss, lollipops, ice creams, flags, pennants and plenty of windmill-sticks with curved plastic sails that spun round with a sharp clacking sound in the stiff breeze.

Abruptly another horseman materialised from nowhere. Dismounting with a swirl of his black cape (embroidered with 'Allah' in Arabic script) he tossed the reins to a surprised Alex.

"Tomalo un momentin' por favor - vuelvo en seguida" (please hold him – I'll be back in a moment) and he vanished into the crowd.

They were not sure if this was spontaneous or part of the tapestry of the Fiesta, a minor episode repeated faithfully year after year. However no other boy seemed to be hanging about, eager to take over the reins from this rider with apparently urgent news for the ears of his King. Julia eyed the horse nervously. It was a huge chestnut stallion, seventeen hands at least, with an exaggeratedly arched neck and wild, flaring nostrils, and it was truly monumentally endowed. Marco stooped low to inspect its underbelly with obvious awe.

"For God's sake Marco, you can *see* it's a stallion. Don't go so close, it's got hooves like dinner plates!"

She then had to acknowledge that excessive consumption of alcohol, even if it did not induce lager loutish aggression, unfortunately *did* seem to arouse male lust. A gross, gum chewing Crusader leant right across her, almost brushing her with his chin and breathing heady fumes of wine straight into her face. He kept muttering obvious innuendos about the pleasures of riding, and of the difference between stallions and geldings, and was way too far gone to register her attempts to brush him off. He hung over her, drooling, while her only escape route was blocked by the seventeen hands of rampant male horseflesh. Silently she cursed the unknown rider, and worried how the Crusader might react to a slap, since his sword looked dangerously real.

Deciding the horse was the lesser evil, she grabbed the reins from Alex and led him (horse, not Alex) heart in mouth towards an arrow turret in the rampart wall, the crowd parting nervously before her in a neat swathe. The horse snorted impatiently and pawed the ground, its metal shoes ringing on the cobbles until sparks flew and showered their defenceless feet. She was searching desperately for a metal ring to tie him to - they must have needed to tie up their steeds in medieval times - when a familiar voice carried from somewhere in the crowd.

"That's some horse you have there."

Andres was not authentically dressed as a Moor, but his colours were chosen in sympathy. He wore mainly black - his T-shirt and jeans - with a crimson silk sash draped around his shoulders, Moroccan slippers on his feet and a single gold earring. He looked like a pirate crossed with a Moor, and wore a mischievous expression.

"A typical English tactic," he mocked. "Get aggro from a Crusader and you promptly take it out on Islam, stealing the Moors' best horse."

"If you'd only turned up earlier I could have dealt with that Crusader," she said, half shame-faced, half-indignant.

"*I* could have, you mean. You didn't seem all that capable."

"So you saw it and didn't come to help! It was no joke, Andres! This horse is terrifying - it must be descended from a battle charger."

"Well," he said, "I do have a good excuse. I've only one decent shoulder now so I'm not the horseman I should be. And I did come as soon as I could. I recognised young Marco's voice interrupting the holy silence."

The action around the castle seemed over, although both Kings and Queens remained inside the church, presumably praising God for fixing things so cleverly that Carocaballo never had to suffer a bloodbath and could switch sides so remarkably easily. Forty kilometres away to their east the sea glittered metallically in the afternoon sunlight, and inland stretched undulating hillocks of sparse grassland which looked ideal for sheep grazing, but which were actually the pastureland of these magnificent horses that were famous throughout Spain. Julia could not imagine how they grew to seventeen enormous hands on the sustenance of that spikey grass, but the solid evidence of it stood beside her.

She looked anxiously for the dark rider in the fast dwindling crowd, most of which had already spilled out through the narrow arched gateway towards the town, but he was nowhere to be seen.

"I'll wait for him," Alex said, "he trusted me with his horse, so... Tell me where you'll be and I'll join you later."

"He doesn't deserve such politeness," Andres answered harshly, "I know where they stable the horses during the Fiesta - we'll take it there. D'you want to ride?"

So they clopped and clattered down the cobbles, Alex grinning like a Cheshire cat from his vantage point in the saddle. In front of them the numbers of festeros were diminishing with every side street as people diverged into houses or bars, whilst behind them plodded a very old man with a capazo and shovel, hoping for fresh manure for his tomato plants should their horse decide to oblige. They waited by a bronze equestrian statue while Andres

188

delivered the horse to the temporary stabling in the forecourt of the municipal library, then went to an old inn where the rough stone walls were densely coated in chain mail, swords and shields alongside legs of jamon serano and strings of chorizo in all sizes and colours. The place was so full there was nowhere to sit or stand, so Andres headed upstairs to a small room with an empty window table overlooking the courtyard.

"You said nothing yesterday about coming to Carocaballo."

"I hadn't planned to come. But this morning I wanted to get away, and I suddenly remembered how spectacular this Fiesta is."

There was a squeak of alarm from Marco when the light in the room abruptly dimmed, and the window was filled with a giant's head leering in at them. Its face was garishly painted and devilishly wicked, a perfect caricature of the 'vicious and lascivious Moor' in every little detail. It promptly disappeared and was replaced by a saintly, blue-eyed Crusader who looked serious, yet stood cheek by jowl with a grinning African lady who appeared to wink at them, then just as suddenly sank from view.

They scrambled to their feet to look out from a better angle onto the courtyard below, and were just in time to see three humans, like little dwarves in comparison, scramble out from the skirts of each of these Fiesta giants, mopping their sweating brows from the efforts of parading the streets under such a weight of papier maché. The 'giants' were then carefully manouevred into horizontal position and carried feet first (except they were now without their 'feet'!) through a massive pair of iron portals into the crypt of the adjacent church.

"See the mixed metaphors we deal in," Andres said, "this town is Moorish, both in its sympathies and blood ties. Yet they don't mind a giant impersonating the stereotypical 'honourable' Crusader."

"He'd really of raped the woman and electrocuted the Moor'sh gooliesh." Marco had quickly recovered from his fright.

"That's *now*," Alex explained a touch impatiently "That's what they're doing in Iraq. But this festivals's about a war in Spain ages and ages ago, long before Columbus went to America."

"I see you boys know your history," Andres looked approving.


Julia was secretly relieved that Andres had to leave before dark, otherwise the pressure from Alex and Marco to stay on for the evening session of floodlit mock battles, and then the firework display afterwards, would have been overwhelming. Ever since her nightmare about her mother's accident she felt reluctant to drive at night. But as it was she got home by twilight, her consciousness delightfully awash with the colourful images from the day, and her spirits still glowing from an almost forgotten feeling of inner contentment.

The next day lowering clouds prolonged the darkness and settled low on the mountains. Her house floated on the cloudline. Above it even the nearby trees were engulfed, while below it the valley was fully visible and unnaturally dark, so that the empty buildings of Holidaylandia looked more ghostly than ever. It would be Easter in under a week yet the temperature, so blissfully benign yesterday, had plummeted once again. It made the Fiesta at Carocaballo seem all the more unreal, a wonderful sunlit atoll of fantasy perched on the rock above the sea plain, existing out of time and out of touch with the world of contemporary happenings.

The sound of a car engine dying and the slamming of a car door interrupted her thoughts. She looked out and saw it was Reggie, stepping jauntily up the drive carrying a couple of gross looking Easter eggs.

"Coffee?"

"Please."

He sat down without prompting. "So how was the lawyer? Word in the village was 'muy guapo y muy bien educado'."

"I didn't realise they'd seen him." But she should have guessed, for very little escapes village eyes - unless you want it not to. "He seems confident and competent enough," she answered, with a vagueness that was deliberate.

"So he won't paint you as the victim then?"

She frowned, "Victim? Of what?"

Reggie studied a tiny thorn in his index finger. "Oh, you know, only child, imprisoned far from others alone up a mountain, no phone or electricity, no father, no proper education, hand-me down clothes, bossed about and forced into slave labour by an alcoholic slut. Wild as a tiger. That kind of thing." He squeezed out the thorn and sighed in relief.

"Is that my village portrait?" She laughed, but it also offended her.

"Well," he said, "that's the broad gist and my translation and, as you know, I'm no linguist, a tabloid crossword stretches even my mother tongue knowledge. But seriously," he sucked in a bead of blood where he had extracted the thorn, "I don't want to feel he intends to vilify Frances. That wouldn't be fair."

She felt touched by his loyalty. "His approach is to say as little as possible. But he doesn't support your 'joking around' theory. He reckons they have enough to assume it was murder."

Reggie barely reacted, still preoccupied with his finger. "There's something else I should mention - should have mentioned before. I'm pretty certain there was another car on the road at the time of Frances' accident. Travelling the other way. I saw skid marks, as if it'd braked violently after coming round the bend."

"You mean it forced her off the road?" Julia shuddered.

"I honestly don't know. If I was certain I'd have spoken up, of course. There was no sign of any impact, just tyre marks. I pointed them out to the Guardia once the ambulance had collected her, but they insisted the marks were old."

"Why are you suddenly telling me now?" she asked sharply, although she equally meant 'why on earth didn't you tell me before?'

" 'Cause you've got a lawyer. If they want to play silly buggers and pretend she's a murderer now she's dead and can't protect herself, then they can damn' well face up to the fact they didn't look into her own death properly. They just assumed drunk driving - or deliberately covered up a piece of reckless driving by some other fat arse."

"Well, thanks for finally telling me," her sarcasm was unmistakeable.

"I'm sorry," he admitted grudgingly, "Maybe I've chosen to unburden myself by burdening you. That was the reason I'd kept quiet – so's to spare you."


She began to peel the metallic dayglo foil absent mindedly off one of the Easter eggs. She could remember Frances describing the processes of remodelling a shattered pot; it needed spacial awareness, patience, imagination, experience, guesswork and a knowledge of how earthernware breaks, but not logic. If you started assembling the pieces logically, especially if you thought you perceived a sequenced pattern in the glaze, you always seemed to get it wrong.

And that was how she felt about her mother's life and death; as soon as she thought she had sorted something comprehensible out of the chaos, up popped a new element to disorder it again.

"Are you religious, Reggie?"

"Good heavens no! Whatever gave you that idea?"

"Dunno. My mind's rambling."

"Well, speaking of rambling, Colin can't sing Marte's praises voluably enough, he reckons she's affected a miracle cure. He's given poor old Jaime doctor the bird."

Reggie was gratified when Julia laughed. "Even though she's German? Well - shows he at least is capable of laying the past to rest."


Colin was in fact lying in bed as they spoke, staring in wonder at the flight of beams on his bedroom ceiling and pondering the miracle of perspective. It was so bloody obvious really, why hadn't early man spotted it? How could he have doggedly drawn faces in profile and then slapped in an eye that looked full frontal on? And those horses, four legs drawn in a neat row, belying all visible evidence to the contrary. Was it affectation? Were they taking the piss? Did they actually know about perspective, but not draw it 'cos for some reason it was against their rules?

He sighed resignedly. He had cut himself off from so much because of rules. If he had a second chance to live his life again, would it be different? Trouble for him was, he was born in the wrong place, in the cradle of a dying Empire, then fed bottled cow's milk and too many allergies and taught all the manners of racism and conservatism. If only he was born five or six years later he might have had the courage to defy his upbringing and dared to grow his hair, a male version of Frances, red curls tumbling to the small of his back, and his back smooth and sexy. Like Frances. Oh God - better to forget Frances! Well, like Marte then, dark hair (OK, a few steaks of grey), nothing German about the woman at all, even she rejects the association - except perhaps the hard firmness of her hands as she runs them over your body with such efficency, like an iron smoothing the creases from a battered pair of trousers, hot and firm.

In place of all those years he suffered, itching in short sleeved button-down collared cotton shirts and flappy tartaned shorts, he could instead have swaggered around in cut-off Levis faded to hell and back, a chillum in the mouth and a joint up his nostril, he would have had more ladies in waiting than that ghastly guru with the black bus. When they talked Swami this and Swami that and how they drove the trail to India, bombed out on Nepalese temple balls and fed chapattis and dahl for free eight days a week, he could have said "Hey man, I was fuckin' born there!"


He puzzled over how Otto survived the prolonged ecstasy of weeklong close contact with Marte. How could he tap so prosaically on a laptop? Perhaps he only harped on about war, treachery, sadism, the band of brothers, mysogeny, mutilation, and masochism as a method of escape, and his whole image of intellectualism was actually fake. A defense mechanism. Just like his, Colin's, own ailments might be, or could he now dare to say *might have been.*

He caught sight of his bedside alarm clock. Nine thirty! He had never before, except when horrendously ill with a fever, and that time he was jetlagged even though he had returned from India on an ocean liner, showing it was really cultural adjustment fatigue, stayed in bed beyond eight fifteen on the dot. He peeped under the bed clothes; yes, it was not simply a rose tinted dream, it was reality. His hot, prickly, tantalizingly itchy rash had genuinely been subdued and his skin was calm as a baby's.

Marte had ordered him off all dairy products. Imagine! At first he was gobsmacked, "I'll starve to death!" She'd chided him so delightfully sternly, almost growing a moustache on her upper lip as the words thundered out, "Of course you won't. Eskimos survive on meat and blubber. You only have to cut out milk, butter, yoghurt and cheese, and all ze rest you can have."

Cutting the two drops of milk from his teatime Earl Grey came easiest, and marg was not so very inferior to butter. But his morning cuppa, not anaemic like Earl Grey but rich, dark and fulfilling, oh my God it was agony without milk! Luckily he had discovered Supermercado Tonica, at Scotty's end of the village, sold Soya milk. Yoghurt he always hated anyway, so cheese was the only other bereavement. Perhaps he would adjust to the loss over time, but right now in the fresh beginnings he dreamt of the taste of ripe and nutty Manchego curado.

Ah, at last - it was 10.05, late enough to get up and still be a rebel!

Marco, unlike Colin, had crept out of bed in the early hours of that morning to remove the skeleton's teeth from the jar and secrete them, temporarily, in his money box, which he locked, hiding the key in a sock in his top drawer. He slung on his dressing gown and slippers and crept outside, leaving a trail of footprints in the dewy grass beneath the almond trees. He had a pair of blunt papercutting scissors in his pocket, also carefully hidden because after Sunday Alex would moan about scissors even though this pair could barely cut through a tissue. He was looking for old, dried stalks of fennel.

Within five minutes he harvested more than enough and tiptoed quietly back to his bedroom. He then made another foray to the driveway, where he amassed a mugful of thin, spikey gravel. This took longer as the shape he was after was a rarity, but Alex must have grooved to his music until late last night because by the time Marco finished he still had not stirred, despite the rattling noise of sifting stones. Bending low over the gravel seemed to pour all his body liquids into his mouth and make his still sore tongue swell, so he had to sit upright in bed until the twittering birds and the whistle of the kettle for

Julia's morning tea told him the day had officially begun. After breakfast, he decided, he would get straight to work on his mural.

Sunday had been a catalogue of disasters. He should never have babbled so freely to Andres. It was his excessive talking that had loosened his already wobbly tooth, and his foolish loose tongue had been silenced with the punishment it deserved. Thank God, in retrospect, that Alex had prevented him launching into the story of Gran the murderer and Toad the comforter of dead bones. He must have been bonkers! It was partly Grant's fault of course, for if Grant hadn't been so dumb about the go-kart crash, hadn't purposefully laid into him and been so sucking up to Alex, he wouldn't have been so desperate to be admired by Andres. He'd of course lost all chance of that, but he had a feeling Andres didn't bear a grudge from the look they'd exchanged when Andres mentioned his injured shoulder at Carocaballo.

Anyway, today seemed like it might redress the balance. So far, so good. Alex was buried in a book and Reggie's early visit was a perfect piece of timing, for he'd buttonhole Julia for half an hour. Marco studied his mural through squinting eyes, plotting the next stages with uncharacteristic precision. Up 'till now he'd been completely spontaneous and - well, slapdash, the sort of thing that Marte would orgasm over. But now he must adapt it to something recognizably a landscape.

So far, thanks to his slapdash stage, he had a cluster of blue bottle chips that in future he would identify as 'sky'. There were already several patches of yeso (plaster) that he'd clumsily spilt over some of the blue glass; they could now be made to look intentional 'clouds'. He quickly drew a jagged line for the mountain peaks (they could be built up later with slithers of dark slate), and, working down towards the lower section of his 2m x 1m chipboard base, he sketched a speedy outline of two terrace walls with some lollipop trees between them. He rushed off for his mugful of spindly gravel, plus the dried fennel, returning again more cautiously, on tiptoe almost, for the clandestine molars from his money box. Then he mixed a tubfull of putty and became a silent, patient, ancient stonemason, building his miniature dry stone walls with such concentration that the two teeth embedded themselves amongst the gravel in such an amorphous way that even he could no longer distinguish them. The fennel stalks became tree trunks planted in rows on the terraces, and soon his smallscale world became so realistic he almost fancied he could hear birdsong from the branches he had yet to create!

Reggie was tapping his pockets, checking for lumps corresponding to reading glasses, house keys, car keys, wallets and the like, so Marco's timing, as with everything today, was impeccable.

"Wanna' come and shee my mural?"

"Yesh, shore do." Reggie evidently thought he was play acting.

As he led Reggie out, he noticed with a pang of loss that Julia appeared to have helped herself to his Easter egg. She must have decided to place a ban on sweets and chocolate, concluding that the ill effects of a sugar rush were the root cause of Sunday's mayhem. He felt aggrieved, but could hardly blame her.

"Wow," Reggie oohed and aahed over the quality of his mural, pacing right and left in a professional manner and luckily not resorting to his reading glasses for a magnified inspection. "You're a budding Michaelangelo!"

"Thanks, but I like Bottititti more," Marco informed him.

Reggie gave him a sly look "I'll bet – don't we all?" A strangely perplexing response - could Alex have possibly got the name wrong?

But no matter, for what was important was that to an average audience, and Reggie undoubtedly epitomised averageness, those two teeth blended with the gravel to perfection. They were as thoroughly hidden as if he'd thrown them down the well - and yet they were still around and available should they ever happen to be needed. He gave a sigh of profound satisfaction.

Julia was next. She represented a more discerning audience, and if not for the fact that she was over-preoccupied with lawyers, skeletons, murderous mothers, encroaching developments and the generally poor state of the world, not so very much could expect to escape her eagle eye. Thankfully, she stood back at a safe distance and was warmly complimentary.

"I'm impressed Marco. It's stunning."

Marco wriggled and glowed with embarrassment and pride, until the moment she stepped dangerously closer to inquire into his methods and use of raw materials. This was exactly what he didn't want.

"Hang on!"

He had raised his voice to a pitch which hurt his battered tongue and put pressure on the glued teeth, but relief came with the sight of a dirt cheap aerosol hairspray that Alex sometimes used to 'fix' his charcoal sketches so they didn't smudge. He snatched it and sprayed wildly in the direction of the vulnerable middle section of the mural, ensuring that plenty of misty chemicals wafted into Julia's eyes and up her nose. He did not relish the cruelty, but it was a dire necessity. Julia duly sneezed and turned on him with reproachful, watering eyes.

"You trying to blind me? Stop that or you'll asphyxiate us," and she prised the weapon firmly from his hands.

"Sorry," he mumbled, "but bits are delicate and can't be breathed on yet. Sorry mum," and he patted her comfortingly on the back, gloating and rueful in the same moment.

# 20

Wednesday morning dawned bright and cold, with ice blue sky to the east, and strangely dusty yellow clouds reminiscent of pipe tobacco smoke hugging the western horizon. Julia felt it could go either way, clear or cloud over; much the same as her Guardia interview prospects. Even her mood hung in the balance. Neither confident nor nervous, but oddly detached.

Lise arrived to babysit, although the term did seem ridiculous considering Alex's age. She was hoping Marte would come, but apparently she had just stabbed a cactus and had to urgently bleed it or its healing powers would drip wastefully away. It was impossible to delegate such a job, she relayed the message, being mortally dangerous and needing protective clothing and goggles - she would never forgive herself if Otto or Lise were struck permanently blind.

She slipped unwillingly into her suit, trying valiantly to disassociate it from the day of her mother's funeral, already feeling trapped by the way it restricted her freedom of movement. Then she hurried into the kitchen to say goodbye.

"You're coming back, aren't you?" Marco frowned, "They won't send you straight to jail?" - zapping what little was left of her confidence.

Andres was waiting as promised in Bar del Bigot, sipping a coffee and glancing at El Pais, which would brand him an intellectual amongst the Bigot clientele. Mercifully the cockatiel was so baffled by the staidness of her outfit that he forgot to welcome her with his gleeful 'Putamadre'! She ordered coffee and joined Andres, trying to blank out the background mini-drama of Juanito leering and nudging his companions at the corner table.

"I should apologize for Sunday. What I said was out of order - I'm very sorry. I know I ought to have brought it up in Carocaballo, but... that was a magical escape from normal life."

"Should apologize? Or *do* apologise?" he asked. With a twinge of guilt she noted that he winced with the pain of stirring his coffee and transfered the spoon to his left hand - but it might have been a humorous take.

"Both," she conceded, realising Bar del Bigot was a poor choice of rendezvous for Juanito was overexciteding himself, she knew the symptoms only too well. He had implanted two toothpicks, like a vampire, and was drooling all over Emilio Fuster's exposed neck. Fuster's irritated swatting merely further aroused him and he promptly lurched and burped his way across the room to draw up a chair chummily alongside Andres.

"D'you speak English?" he asked Andres in Valenciana, winking conspiratorially at Julia.

"I can make myself understood," Andres replied, and although he had always spoken Castellano with Julia he seemed comfortable in the local language, which was very unusual for someone from Sevilla.

Juanito immediately placed his bearlike paw on Andres' injured shoulder and laughed with the intimacy of a brother. "Ha, with this woman just two words are enough. Let's see if I can remember ..." he slapped his other paw to his forehead pretending intense concentration. "Aha, claro - they are 'effucke me'!" and he buckled over at his well-padded waist with the heartiness of his guffawing and the sheer brilliance of both his English and his wit.

"I'd love to," Andres whispered in mock intimacy, yet loud enough that the entire bar could hear without straining "but I fear your arse is way too big for my little prick."

Juanito listened with a perplexed grin, uncertain if this was a joke or not, and if it were, who might be the butt of it. He looked to others in the bar for a cue, but although there were smiles and one or two sniggers, those with greater self-control wore inscrutable expressions, especially El Bigot himself who had no wish to waste any more money replacing broken glassware. After half a minute of suspended time Juanito lumbered back to his table and Emilio Fuster coquettishly pulled down his shirt collar to expose more neck, muttering some nonsense under his breath.


It was either the best or worst possible preamble to a Guardia interrogation session, Julia reflected as they entered the three storey, khaki coloured concrete slab that was the Cuartel. Inside, the drabness of the décor was enough to dent the most upbeat of spirits; everything blended with the phlegm colour of their uniforms, so the officers were only distinguishable from their background due to the shiny blackness of their hats and boots, and the livelier colour in some of their complexions. They had to wait of course, and did so in silence because words produced multiple echoes as they bounced off the hard surfaces, and the fake marble chip tiles were so incredibly shiny and highly polished that Julia feared that from certain angles it was possible to see right up her skirt.

Certainly the younger Sergeant seemed transfixed by a section of the floor, but Julia's geometrical calculations were insufficinetly sophisticated to tell if this was the reflective danger spot. She stood ramrod straight, her legs tightly pressed together, hoping for the best. She also kept her lips clammed shut, for she was fighting off an irrepressible desire to giggle.

It must be nerves, she thought.

At last they were ushered down a long, dark corridor lined by closed doors. Were they cells? She caught a brief glimpse of the residential wing beyond the empty central courtyard, and its colour scheme was just as depressing as the working wing they were in, the colour of light mud, or coffee cream to give it a more flattering spin. The only splashes of brighter colour came from the washing lines suspended from balconies, and it was a relief to see that the wives and children were permitted to relax the khaki rules, but incongruous to see crimson bloomers, T-shirts with logos, and padded black and purple lacy bras bobbing and dancing in the breeze in such an otherwise austere, lugubrious environment.

They entered a rectangular room with an oval table and quantities of chairs – perhaps the room was used for seminars or group videos on how to improve police tactics. She and Andres were offered seats on one side. On the other four superior detectives stood in unison to receive them. Two local Guardia were also present, but in the role of observers rather than active participants, or so it would seem from the unobtrusive, almost coy way they sat huddled in different corners.

The manner of introductions all round set a formal tone, but Julia's brain could not retain a single name, and even her own sounded oddly unfamiliar. It struck her chiefly as insignificantly short, outsmarted by the pompous, long-winded yet magnificently imposing Spanish names, all with titles before and multiple surnames after - the pleasantly egalitarian custom being to attach the mother's surname after the father's, and sometimes a grandparent's too. Having had no recognised father, and a mother who could not be bothered with the complication of a second Christian name, she was just plain old 'Julia McIntyre', (pronounced like 'Giulia', not with the usual Spanish 'h' sound of a jota) whereas Andres emerged as being 'Doctor Andres Fernando Guillermo Rodriguez Catala Romero' no less. She took a deep breath to inflate her self-esteem.

At first it was a leisurely stroll through the preliminaries. The business of who she was in ID terms. No surprises there, no booby traps yet. She emerged as female in gender, thirty in age, of Spanish nationality (this had surprised Andres initially, even gratified him she suspected - except for the lack of extra legal protection it afforded her), place of birth: Villahermosa, birth mother, one Frances Catriona McIntyre, father unknown (ahem - but to be honest only one throat needed clearing), profession: baillerina (how odd it sounded, and how far away from her present day to day life, and how uselessly frivolous).

She must concentrate; this was her legal self under the microscope. How odd it all seemed, almost as if she had already lost her human existence and personal freedom to become a prisoner, allotted a number, and a cell to slot herself into.

Snap out of it you fool, she told herself, don't wilt just because you're the only creature here without a thousand names, a father, an ugly uniform and a penis between your legs. Get a grip girl!

With a sinking feeling deep in her intestines she signed her permission for a DNA sample to be taken, but miraculously there was no mention of one from Alex. Perhaps the maths had been done correctly, or Grant had backed off, but most likely it had just been an idle threat. It was, at least, a minor victory.

She twitched her lips in what might pass as a smile and concentrated on answering the questions.

"No, my mother retained her British nationality, but she became a Spanish resident." (Or did she? In truth Julia wasn't sure, but she should have done, so best to adopt that tack. Just typical of Spanish bureaucracy that we're dealing with a murder yet they get hung up on the minutiae of domiciliary tax issues).

"Yes, I've kept my Spanish nationality. I was born here and lived here uninterruptedly until I was fifteen. I consider myself Spanish." (Don't add redundant corollaries, you can see their flickerings of irritation. They don't warm to someone with your vacuous career usurping their national persona. They're impervious to you, just keep it simple). "No, my mother didn't only associate with foreigners. She had many Spanish friends."

"Yes, I guess the majority were."

"I suppose you could identify them as 'hippies'. But my mother worked hard all her life restoring classical amphora for very prestigious museums."

"I disagree. I would argue they were part of a social revolution that was common to the US and most European countries. Spain less so because it was more isolated under Franco's rule." (God almighty, if you want to say they were bandits and anarchists and swapped wives and lives and ate babies and killed their men in post coital delirium then just say it!).

"I assumed this was a police inquiry, and wasn't really expecting a discussion on philosophy." (Shut up Julia, he hates sarky cheek and you deliberately goad him - have you lost your marbles?)

Andres, his mind working on parallel lines, recognised the necessity to jump in before she inflicted more damage.

200

"It's important to bear in mind that La Sra Julia was so very young at the time, only five years old. We can't expect her to make objective judgments about the social mores of her mother's friends and associates. Children of five have respect for adults, and love and respect for their mother. It is only natural, and we should not seek to discourage it."

It gave her a vital breather, a moment to stand back and listen and remember some of the advice he had given her. She noticed his cunning use of 'we' to align himself with them and reduce the element of antagonism she had wilfully introduced, and she tried hard to reinhabit the kindlier soul of a five year old and help them to see her as a young innocent, not the dancer temptress they doubtless identified her as now. I bet they think I'm a lap dancer, she thought ruefully, recalling the time she carelessly forgot to cross her T in one of those timed coursework written reponses you have to do for Dance GCSE. It gave her a few sleepless nights prior to the results, but in the event it did not penalise her.

Why did she snap so easily? It had begun at an early age, a defence mechanism against Frances probably. Frances was so terrifying when she lost her temper that she (Julia) had needed a trusty weapon of counter attack, otherwise she would have been a cowering, blubbering sub-human. So, whenever she felt threatened, out would come her vicious, caustic tongue to cause maximum offence. It worked with Frances; she had gained a grudging respect, until of course in her teenage years when went way over the top and destroyed everything between them, a mad scorched earth policy. It had also caused her no end of trouble in the school playground, and later snapped friendships and soured relationships. Most people, she told herself, think before they speak and measure what they say. You do that most of the time, so why not when it's most important? "Scorpions sting with their tail" she remembered Frances saying "and snakes with their tongue." But she could no longer remember its subtext.

Wake up Julia! The nice man across the table with penetrative hawk eyes is asking you questions again... Listen, digest, breathe, think and only then, allow yourself to speak.

"No, that's correct. I didn't go to school until I was eight. My mother taught me at home."

"Well, I was only young so I didn't know about the law on truancy. I didn't even know I was a Spanish national, to be honest."

"Yes, for two years."

"I was - well - like any normal schoolkid, I imagine. Not an angel, but I had friends - and some enemies."

Don't answer that Julia. Don't say a word. You didn't beat anyone to death, it was just a few punches, a flurry of kicks. Now and again. Breathe in slowly....

"We must be aware of the context," Andres explained. "La Sra was the only child of a foreign mother in the school at that time, and the only blonde little girl." He leaned back in a relaxed, fireside chat manner before continuing. "I'm sure if we're honest we all remember getting into scraps at school, and wouldn't like to think our teacher's accounts carried any weight whatsoever." He smiled in a self deprecating manner, "I myself almost broke a boy's jaw for insulting me with the usual 'Maricon el ultimo'! Imagine the teasing and taunting she must have had..."

A slight change of key in the questioning, but you should be able to manage again, for a while. A pattern is beginning to emerge, rather like waves on the sea. A few introductory questions skirting the topic then, suddenly, a tricky one to catch you off balance. Should you only be looking at the one who's asked the question? Or attempt to make eye contact with all four of them? For sure you must ignore the fact it's being recorded. Or not ignore - whatever you say can never be unsaid.

"I was always treated well by my mother. Walking alone to the village and back was neither dangerous nor difficult. It was only one and a half kilometres and good healthy exercise. I enjoyed it."

"Well, all the village kids had grandparents to look after them as well as their parents. My mother was alone with all of the responsibility, she did her best."

"No, never."

"No, I don't remember the wall collapsing. Obviously I've tried very hard to pinpoint exactly when it happened", she shrugged in a way she hoped looked natural, uncontrived, "but I can't. I can't even picture it whole - I can only remember it as broken." (That's enough, you're labouring the point).

"I can't remember that very well either. I can vaguely recall some faces, but hardly any names."

"I might be able to."


This was a watershed moment. Andres had prepared her for the likelihood of an identity parade of sorts, in the guise of photos of missing persons whose physical proportions and genetic information approximately matched the skeleton's, and who were known to or otherwise likely to have passed through Milagra. 'Take your time looking at them', he had advised, 'they'll look unfamiliar in any case because they could be a few years out of date, no-one after all took a snapshot of the man on the day he fell, we have to presume.

Also your childhood eyes have changed; you'll be looking at a photo of someone your age now, whereas you originally saw them as a vast, ancient adult towering over you, a little five year old. I certainly don't need to remind you fashions have changed - so they'll look weird anyway!'

There's a video camera trained on you, Julia, so it's not merely a matter of guarding your tongue, you need perfect control of your facial muscles, your eye movements, and - something you've had problems with lately - your circulation. Don't blush, don't blanch, and don't dare faint...

It was like being a Russian Doll. When you knew that you were under the microscope and needed to appear relaxed and natural, yet naturally a little nervous (anyone would be), your inner feelings had to pass through many layers of careful filtering in order for the visible, surface expression of them to produce the desired effect. Imagine you're doing a dance performance on film, she told herself, be utterly professional, enter the role, be the character, flawlessly and completely, even in the close-up shots. Your role is innocence.

She focused on the first photo. It was the most incongruous image of a would-be hippie as you could dream up, almost descending into farce. It was a classic Graduation Day pic, a ten degrees off full-frontal view of a serious face trying not to gloat over the weighty parchment grasped in its plump fingers and clasped by a silken ribbon, a degree of perhaps lesser classification - but all the same a passport to better things. Certainly good things, judging by the broad cat-got-the-cream smile and the unfurrowed forehead of above average brain, brown hair touching the collar and a Beatles' fringe topped by a jaunty mortar board. Its comfortably fed, slightly pudgy body was encased in a black gown with a tract of claret silk (would that be History? Economics?), and if one was to transport the features and demeanour to anyone she had ever known or seen, the closest candidate (and that wasn't remotely close) would be Reggie! Might Reggie have had a brother? Could he, oh my God, could he be looking for his missing brother, a little belatedly...? But she dismissed this fantasy immediately, for Reggie's lack of interest in the skeleton was patently genuine, not pretence.

One should not be leaping to conclusions. Many a graduate whose conventional middle class parents crowed over pictures such as this were, two years later on, fretting and tearing their hair out, bemoaning the diasastrous influences young Teddy had got himself into since moving to a drug infested flat in Fulham filled with layabouts and commies. Saturated by marijuana fumes and daily knocked sideways by fresh orange juice laced with LSD for breakfast, within six months he could easily have lost six or sixteen kilos, grown his hair down to his nipples and taken up electric guitar. A year on and he could have shacked up with a Patchouli girl who had a VW camper, and they could be headed for Morocco or Nepal where the cool mountain air might clear their brains, only somehow Spain got in the way.

Why did she assume this face was British? Was there some quintessential spirit to it, or was it simply the particular pinkness in the skin and blueness in the eye?

"No," she said eventually. "I'm sure I've never seen this person."

But it gave her an odd feeling to realise that nor had anyone else, as he must have been missing for twenty five years now. Tragic - unless they added in some control photos amongst the genuinely missing ones, like placebos in the trial of a new drug, and this man was now happily married with two kids around her age; a retired accountant in Kidderminster.

The next photo wore a very different expression. Yet this was more likely due to the time and place of its taking rather than the personality of the subject. It was almost certainly one of those cheap photo machine shots taken for ID purposes at a booth in a metro station, because she recognised the haunted expression that she wore under such circumstances. It was a black and white photo, and the man appeared to have light hair, slightly thin and straggly, wavy, shoulder length and tapering at the ends. He had brushed it behind his ears, perhaps to detract attention from its length, and the shadows under his eyes suggested he all too frequently burnt his candle at both ends. Whereas the previous man seemed to have savoured the cream, this man had had none in ages. His cheeks were hollow, his cheek bones and chin angular and well pronounced, as if food played a minor role in his life.

"I saw many people like this, but there's nothing that stands out as being individually recognisable I'm afraid."

The next one she knew almost before it was placed on the table, the compelling eyes boring a hole through the photographic paper so as to stare arrogantly out in both directions. It was the one she had anticipated, expected, and dreaded. The glowing black hair had been carefully brushed and tossed and buffed with a soft linen duster and the lighting cunningly arranged to pick out its burnished, deep chestnut highlights, the symmetrical face was flawlessly beautiful and the eyes showed a proud satisfaction in that conviction, compounded by the knowledge of aeons of worship as God, Moses, the best of the Pharoahs, Jesus, Napoleon and Vilayat Khan. She could almost hear the seductive French accented "You have a bootiful 'arse" slipping from between the faint curl of self-satisfied lips, lips that were born and reborn so auspiciously to mouth orders at inferiors and to kiss and above all be kissed, and to curl at the emotive power and beauty of those improvised violin flourishes. Very few women were equal to his physical and mental splendour, although he had grudgingly admitted Frances to be nearly on a par appearancewise, though naturally much younger and altogether inferior in the spiritual dimension - for she had only experienced four thousand years of reincarnations, whereas he was nudging the twenty five thousand threshold, after which you departed the treadmill of earth for some higher plane altogether.

Fancy going missing during your very final reincarnation! Such bad luck! - Might it be like sliding down a long snake on a Snakes and Ladders board, forcing you to work your way back up again? Keep up this feeling of humorous contempt, Julia. Don't let yourself be enthralled by the intensity of those self-loving eyes and the awful horrors of your earlier nightmarish vision. Above all, don't show any sign of emotion. Steady your face and ensure that your hands neither clench nor sweat nor tremble.

"This man I do remember. I think he was French and that he was a musician, maybe a composer, but I didn't know him well enough to know his name."

"No, I don't remember how old I was at the time. I do remember he had a dog, a huskie dog with an Eskimo name, which went with him everywhere. If he'd had an accident - like falling under a wall - then this dog would not have stopped howling."

"He might have changed his name. To God, probably. He certainly believed he was immortal."

She was conscious of her mouth emulating the same supercilious curl as in the photo, while her hands remained obediently calm and cool. I am a dissembler, she thought, just like he was. Her heart was in her throat, but she swallowed it down without any outward sign of discomfort.

There were three more photos after that, only one of which kindled inklings of faint and possible recognition. He was blond and Teutonic; most likely a Swede, German, American or Australian. He had an almost hairless bare torso, was tanned and seemingly happy-go-lucky, judging by the twinkling blue eyes and broad, genial grin, - unless he had just been sucking the water pipe dry and was stoned out of his mind. Perhaps Marte would have a better chance of recognising this individual, for he was of a similar physical type to Manfred, although larger proportioned and with a heavier, squarer jaw. He could easily have belonged to the band of nutters who tried to fly and move mountains, the ones who lived in the open air and said houses were for suckers.

Or the American who was on a mission to humble himself, and swapped living quarters with his goats, giving them the run of his house and trotting around on all fours with his wife in the goathouse, bleating and rutting at all hours of the day. She remembered helping him plant alfalfa seeds. They arrived from an Eco centre somewhere in the mountains of Colorado all prepared for planting so any witless fool could do it properly. The seeds where stuck in jello tape at exactly the correct planting distance, so all you had to do was dig a long, shallow furrow, unwind the jello roll, stick it in and cover it with earth. He grew mung beans and borage and purple sprouting broccoli, slaughtered his own rabbits, made sickly apple wine and a very fine goats' cheese. He never did get properly humble though; (a) because he was an American and (b) because he had to swap back with his goats, for after three weeks in the house they stopped producing milk due to an imbalanced diet of far too much wooden furniture and fluffy cotton bedding.

"There *is* something familiar about his face, but I can't be sure about it," she said after studying the photo closely. "The person it most resembles is apparently now a Republican Senator, so it can't be him. Unless the Senator's stolen his identity." (Don't get facetious from the sheer relief of getting through the ordeal. Remember this is but stage one that you've survived).

Walking back down the corridor was curiously as challenging as the previous way, for her head felt light and vacuous yet she must not wear an idiot smile and appear elated, while her legs were flaccid and jellified and her feet leaden and impossible to steer. Emerging from the cold, echoey silence of the morguelike Cuartel into the lively streetlife of Milagra was similarly strange, like pinching yourself back to reality after watching an engrossing film in a cinema. Imagine what prisoners confined for twenty years must feel as they step outside, she thought. But the closest she got in her own experience was the state of mind you have after sitting through a vital exam, or a dance audition to land a role you have been longing for, or surviving the potential disasters of your mother's funeral.

"I'll say goodbye," Andres told her "for the sake of protocol. It'll undermine my usefulness if I don't." He smiled, "Someone will notice my car driving off towards Villahermosa, and just about everyone would know if it didn't."

"You're right," she said, wondering if she was capable of driving herself with her feet of clay. She had not thought beyond this point, and it had suddenly snuck up on her unawares. She felt bereft of words.

"I'll phone you. Cheer up Julia, it went fine."

She nodded and tried to smile, but the elasticity had gone from her face. She could only manage a mumbled, "Hasta pronto", before they turned their backs on each other to go their separate ways. It was strangely anticlimactic.

Alex kept half an eye on the passing time, partly because he had some conception of what might be happening in the Cuartel, and partly because he wanted to broach his concerns with Lise - but not until near the end of her visit so as not to sour things prematurely. He waited until Marco was thoroughly engrossed in his collage or whatever you called it - which was surprisingly good compared to his previous horrors with paint or plasticine.

"Arturo says there are moles - informers - in Scotty's bar. And some dealers are happy to break people's legs if they try to horn in on business. *Please* get rid of it safely Lise."

" 'Course I will. D'you take me for a fool?"

"I've a right to be worried," Alex pointed out, "seeing as I looked after it for so long."

"But not any more." Lise grinned at him. "Don't worry, you're *way* too serious about this stuff. I told you I'm not into risks. I'll take it to Montejoven to be rid of it. I'm not even getting much money out of it."

"Then it's not worth the risk." Alex grumbled, irritated.

"What's gotten into you? You're hardly my father! Are you pissed off at not getting something out of it yourself?"

"Fuck off!" he grew even more irritated, "You know I didn't look after it for money. I did it out of friendship."

"Don't dare tell me 'fuck off'!" Lise snapped. "Look at the size of you! Jorgen was bloody right..."

"Jorgen? You mean the dumb arse juggler we took the stuff off in the first place? How could *that* turd be right?"

Lise shook her head tauntingly. "You're just so stupidly wrong. Look, Jorgen asked me to get you to hide the stuff in the first place. He didn't want too much on him when he went South, and you kept it nice and safe for him. So don't get thinking *he's* the one with no brains."

Alex was momentarily too stunned to speak. He understood that he had been used and made a fool of, but the intricacies of Jorgen's plotting still had not fully dawned.

"Why not just bury it himself then? Why risk us both knowing about it? It doesn't make sense..."

"Well that's age and experience for you, I guess," Lise said acidly. "It's actually very clever. He didn't bury it because he didn't know the terrain and might never find it again - or it might be discovered if Julia decided to plant vegetables. It was much smarter to get you to bury it."

Alex was beginning to grasp the detail now, in a way that pounded uncomfortably inside his skull. "So," he stared at her, "*you* were in on his plan then. You've lied to me all along."

She shrugged offhandedly, "If that's how you want to see it. I never actually told a lie - just implied it was my idea, not his. You wouldn't have done it otherwise," she finished, a touch more humbly.

"You lied," he stared at her with Frances' eyes, "You're a fucking lying bitch."

Lise looked startled, alarmed by the sudden venom in his voice. She sniffed and muttered plaintively, "It's not been easy for me, y'know. I can't help it that I fancy him. I didn't want to get you to bury it, but he told me you would, because you fancy me, I guess." She looked at him with pleading eyes, willing him to sympathise with her tortured plight, and to remember how slavishly he fancied her.

"Well," his glittering eyes glanced off her to fix on a small bird twittering on a gnarled tree branch, "just don't go baring your tits to him because he'll only bite 'em off. At least that's what he tried to do to Julia."

His smile was a blend of vindictive triumph and rueful sadness as he dealt this trump card.

# 21

Marte's hands ached from holding her bottle at exactly the correct angle to catch the slow but regular drip, drip from the cactus wound. She had tried unsuccessfully to rig some way of aiming its juice into the container without her needing to be there - it was extraordinary how exhausting sitting still and doing nothing apart from holding a glass aloft could be. She would have to admire Otto. He had the stamina to not only hold onto a glass for hours, but also to keep refilling it, tipping it and emptying it down his throat. But of course it was the variety of action that relieved the exhaustion of monotony, that was the secret. How could she be so silly - no need to admire him at all! Except for sitting at a laptop and eternally plopping on keys. That did require persistence.

Drip, drip, drip. It was exhausting, beautiful and depressing. Beautiful because the droplet formed miraculously slowly, oozing then billowing out into a teardrop reflecting the world, in the foreground of which was the bluegreen cactus stem and Marte's own philosophical face peering farsightedly into the meaning of life. Amazing what the flattering convexity did for wrinkles, better than a face lift, better even than Botox or collagen implants.

Yet depressing because the steady drip, drip was like the slow ticking of a time bomb, the gradual, inexorable loss of life blood, the death of cells, the passage of a finite number of female eggs discarded once a month until menopause, the preordained life cycle of every living creature, including herself. You might delay it with the illusion of extended youth, with the aid of Renaissance and whatever she would call this cactus juice for the face, but you never defeated it. The sadness with which the very old regarded the very young was not simply regret or yearning, but the weight of knowing that they had it all to go through, generation after generation, an endless journey to nowhere. Oof, she thought, this bleary outlook is not like me, positive Marte. Perhaps this cactus has some superstrong negative vibes, which must be purged away. Right now I need a cup of tea.

While Marte watched the blue lick of gas flames encircling the blackened base of her kettle, softening her skin meanwhile with steam from the spout, Julia climbed the hillside towards her, feeling on top of the world. Her burst of energy and high spirits was remarkable considering how dead she had felt immediately after the interview, but relief evidently had a delayed reaction. She had not realised just how dark a shadow had been cast over her by the skeleton's discovery until this moment of release. But it was only temporary release, she knew that. Frances was not off the hook yet, and nor for that matter was she. There was still the burning issue of the missing immortal Frenchman. Andres knew nothing of him, beyond what she revealed in the Cuartel, but now she would have to tell him. Or would she?

She waited on the highest point of the hill, watching the clouds scudding towards her, constantly changing shape as they extended and withdrew their vaporous tentacles like performing acrobats.

The day was typical of spring, fast moving, pulsating with energy. That morning she had set off for Milagra with her tail between her legs, leaving Alex, Marco and Lise in what she took to be a harmonious mood. But now it was she who embodied the carefree child, striding ahead, waiting for the slogging progress of two weary parents plodding behind her.

Alex had not even come. He preferred a work session with Arturo, but without enthusiasm - more as if it were an obligation he had undertaken for forty years, and the only spark to keep him going was the hope he would one day retire. Marco was engrossed by his mural and wanted to stay home. He had some harebrained scheme of imitating the action of the sea by stirring a broken wine bottle in a bucket of wet gravel. This because apparently all beach glass was blue, never green.

"Why's it blue when the bottles are mostly green?" he kept asking. But no-one knew.

He was reluctant to accept that, after his little escapade with tooth and tongue, he would not be allowed to stay alone and stir glass unsupervised.

Lise was inexplicably glum. She made deliberately slow progress up the hill, lagging further behind Marco, sulking and sniffling. Julia had tried to probe but was rebuffed by a tearful, frosty stare and hostile silence.

So Julia strode ahead, keeping her happiness tactfully out of their way. She did not trust Lise to go home alone, for she was in the kind of unpredictable mood that if she happened to stub a toe on the wrong rock she might throw herself off a precipice simply to spite the world. Julia remembered fifteen; realising from her own lack of sympathy now how much she must have irked Frances. Especially since Frances was fifty and prematurely arthritic. Why is it that we understand everything too late? But such thoughts were fleeting, for the wild wind blew away her troubles.

The gap between Marco and Julia had closed considerably by the time they reached the wood, but there was still an interval of separation between all three. Julia had purposefully not waited for Marco to catch up, sensing that this way he would keep an eye on Lise, and thus she would be brought safely home as if towed by an invisible thread.

Marte's door was warped from the wet winter, so it could neither be locked nor closed, thus it was customary to warn her of your approach with a whistle or shout. Julia, however, felt reluctant to interrupt the stealthy silence of her walk, so only the nudging, shuddering sound of the door scraping over the heavily scarred tiles warned Marte she had a visitor.

"Wiert," said Marte, peeking from under a bath towel, busy clearing her sinuses, "I sense when many peoples are coming, but not you. Zat means you are either very subtle - or very sly. How is it you say - a dark pig?"

"Horse," Julia corrected, not flattered by the insinuation.

"What's with Lise?" Marte inquired, noting the dejected slump of her shoulders as she slunk round the back to her room, while Marco headed straight for the swings with the cat slung like a stole around his neck.

Julia shrugged. "She was fine when I left, miserable when I returned. She won't talk to me."

"Perhaps Alex no longer worships ze ground she treads on," Marte mumbled, distracted by the need to burst a white head which the kettle steam had softened.

"That'd be good."

"For who?" Marte asked sharply. "Him, her, - or you?"

Julia frowned, "For him of course."

"Sometimes the fresh beauty of fifteen is difficult for us all. Alex gets to an age when he no longer worships you. So, you maybe have reason to be jealous." Marte pursed her lips into her mirror, having wiped away the puss.

"Bullshit! The first real day of spring and everyone but me seems bitter."

"Zat's because you have a sexy lawyer, and your interview behind you. Mine is still to come." Marte folded away her tartness and wore a sweeter smile, "Lend him to me, Julia, please."

Julia was taken by surprise. "You can't be serious! There's a conflict of interest, obviously. We're both - in a sense - suspects. There could come a point when," she blushed faintly, "our memories conflict. You might say something to incriminate Frances, or me, - or I might somehow incriminate you."

"I'm glad you've said it," Marte's voice was sharp, "best to get it in the open." She frowned with the concentration of pouring three cups of tea, "I will of course pretend you were a little angel," she cursed as the strainer tipped and tea leaves spattered her thighs, "zat is bad luck...yah, unless I have no ozer choice."

Julia decided to ignore the warning, assuming it primarily blackmail to gain the services of Andres. It reminded her that blatant happiness irritates others unless they can share it, and it showed her Marte preferred her to be in pain or suffering so she could take pride in 'curing' her, and, more crucially, that Marte's testimony could potentially do her most harm. She spotted Otto tucked in a corner. He was wholly encased in a bubble of plastic sheeting. The intensity of his cerebral activities and their translation into keyboard fingerwork had created a strange, blue miasma formed from breath and beads of fine sweat inside the plastic, so that he appeared as a shimmering, unreal figure. Messianic or Satanic, one could not be sure.

Marte pranced over to knock on a plastic flap.

"Te, mein Herr Professor," she announced with mock reverence.

He blinked through misted spectacles. "Vot? Ah, I komm directly."

Julia watched as he struggled to his feet and flipped aside the doorflap to climb out of his capsule. The distortion of the thick plastic curtain had made him a giant, but he shrunk to human size as he emerged.

"Welcome to ze real world," Marte said. "We too have conspiracies, Julia and me..."

He took his tea cup with a trembling hand. Perhaps the capsule distorted time as well as space, so that he was tragically galloping through his life at twice normal speed; that, or overwork and a constant overdose of screen and too much local wine at night, must be the root causes. He was a chameleon; sometimes he looked dead on his feet like a scaly old dragon wasting away. At other times he appeared the upright, serious professor, boastfully proud of the length of his thesis; and very occasionally he looked almost sprightly, like a man with a definite purpose.

"You look tired," Julia said. It was the politest way to phrase it.

"He takes ze troubles of ze world to heart," Marte said, pummeling him gently to restore basic circulation, "and he has zis mission to tell the truth. He is sure to look awful."

Otto sipped his tea. "We live in an evil world," he declared. "vere politics is ze art of mass deception. And because I am German, hmmn - therefore of course responsible for Hitler and all his craziness, I cannot now point my finger of blame in ze right direction." He sighed, then looked nervously over both shoulders in case some secret service personnel were hiding behind Marte's billowing curtains.

212

"You know Julia, we now have a missile aimed at my hut. When he says too much - or if his next book, the one after the bandolero, gets published- zapp, kaput, we are finished!"

"Except," Otto smiled despite his world weariness, "for Unamuno's saying. Remember it? 'If you want to keep a secret, put it in a book'."

"Yah, yah. He meant Spain, a Spanish book. Yours will be in German - some Germans do still read. My grandmother..."

Otto looked at Julia. "German books are nussing. To be properly read it must be translated into the great English Language, but in zat language publication is of course controlled by ze enemies of truth." He gave a weighty sigh and sloppily poured more tea.

"Ach so," Marte patted his knee, "zen I am not so stupid. You pursue ze truth and get nowhere - except suffering for knowing the injustices of the world and ze black lies of politicians. I do my silly women's things and make people happy, whereas you spread ze misery."

"But nothing matters more than truth - or we bury our heads and lead selfish lives." Julia was acutely aware how pompous she sounded, and how she was tempting fate regarding the skeleton. "We've got children Marte, that's why we try to be optimistic - for their sake."

Otto suddenly slumped submissively onto Marte's lap and looked up appealingly, "Mein liebling, du musst massage the weight of ze world from off my shoulders."


Julia left them clucking, stroking, giggling and renewing their vows of affection on the padded straw mat. She wanted to reassure herself that Marco had thought to disengage the cat, in particular its claws, from his shoulders before mounting the swing. She was relieved to find him swinging alone and relaxedly, whilst the cat watched imperiously from a branch. Swinging appears so effortlessly natural, she thought, and yet it isn't. You have to learn the technique. Instead of moving with the swing little kids first do the opposite, kicking their feet straight forward then bent back out of time, not falling in with the rhythm, losing momentum. She remembered getting so frustrated one time when teaching some snotty nosed little monster; pushing the swing far too high so that he sailed out and fell - fortunately into a harmlessly soft tangle of bracken. He was not hurt, but the high pitched scream of terror that rent the air and sounded too spine-chilling to have come from his young lips brought the violent wrath of his parents down on her.


She had always felt she had a raw deal with justice. Frances was so free in many ways (well, sexual ones) but she did draw lines as a parent; there were rules of engagement, forms of behaviour and regular bedtime hours to be observed - whereas most hippie parents allowed anything. They followed the dictates of freedom so blindly that their kids could do exactly as they pleased and never ever seemed to be in the wrong. They could stay up past midnight, torture the cat, poison plants, burn trees, eat whole jars of peanut butter without any bread, crap wherever, pee in the sink, hit their parents and it was all fine, just fine - because they were simply 'expressing themselves' and 'mustn't be imprisoned by rules'. Yet whenever she disliked what they did she was a boring old disciplinarian hung up on convention. If they kicked her their parents would say "Oh, he's just being honest with his anger, true to himself. We can't stop him." But if she got angry and lashed out that same rationale didn't apply. Instead she was evil and scheming - and jealous of little whoever's free spirit!

Frances had attracted jealousy just as she attracted men, but it was safest to make Julia take the brunt of it. Occasionally her mother would wade in to protect her, but more likely she would be absorbed in the reassemblage of her latest pot.


Julia knew she should not be sitting like this in the shade chewing over the past, reliving negative moments when she had sulked on her own beneath the shade of similar pine trees. But Marte's comment about her non-angelic nature hurt. It revived so many childish incidents when she suffered injustice, and someone else's spite got rewarded. Thank God it was Frances who found Yaki red-handed with the bicycle pump! Left to his parents, Yaki would have been acclaimed an inventive genius on a par with Leonardo da Vinci, while she would have clumsily, wilfully distorted the pump valve (perfectly yang) by excessively squeezing it between the cheeks of her plump and young - but outrageously yin - bottom!

Not all had been little monsters, of course. Some were amusing and loyal friends and one or two she had loved to distraction. But whereas they had travelled on, she had remained becalmed and alone in Milagra.

Most vanished around the time of the skeleton's demise, as a matter of fact, joining the mass migratory exodus to Poona. This could have been mere coincidence but perhaps for one person - or two or three - it happened to be a wonderfully fortuitous timing. In fact their Sanyasin philosophy might even have permitted the act of murder now and again, for the right reasons. So he, or she, or they, had been spared the inconvenience of guilt. If those hippie parents who had berated her for trying to control their kids' nastier instincts had been in charge of morality out there, then for sure murder would be seen as free expression in its purest form (provided of course the victim was somebody they didn't like). It was bizarre how easily brainwashed we are, she thought, how easily deceived. And not just by politicians, minority cults or mass religions, where it should be more obvious to us because of who stands to gain and who loses.

What did her generation believe in? Anything? She studied the pine needles intently as if they might provide her with an answer. They were plentiful enough that they ought to have a voice. They would assuredly complain about environmental damage, how they were being systematically decimated by acid rain. Her generation were essentially fatalistic, she decided. Or maybe they could not be blamed because they stood no chance against the overwhelming forces of globalisation. If man failed to ruin the planet with his environmental myopia then he surely would some other way. So much for that new mood of optimism she experienced as she climbed towards Marte's - where was it now?

She watched Marco swing casually to and fro, a blissfully dreamy expression irradiating his face. Would he look back on a happy or a chequered childhood? As if on cue he leapt from the swing at the apex of its arc and landed neatly on both feet, whereupon the cat promptly scurried down to rub its fur against his legs in self-stroke ecstasy. He laughed at the tickling sensation and wandered over to join her.

"Where's Lise?"

"In her room."

"No point my going there then," he decided. "She an' Alex had a flamin' row."

"What about?" she asked, knowing that she shouldn't pry.

"Jorgen, I think", but he sounded doubtful.

"*Jorgen*? - The juggler?"

Marco nodded, but Julia was none the wiser. How could Jorgen place a wedge between Alex and Lise?

The sharp snap of twigs warned her of Marte's approach, which was otherwise cushioned by the flexible carpet of thickpile pine leaves. Marte sat down, placing a hand on Julia's shoulder to support the manouevre and as a gesture of renewed friendliness. Marco and the cat retreated to a nearby hollow to construct a woodcutters' hut.

"Thanks God he sleeps now." She cradled her head between her hands "War, war and more war - and such conspiracy and treachery. My mind goes crazy!"

"Has he given up on his bandolero?"

"No. He awaits developments - whatever zat means. Julia," her voice was suddenly tremulous, atypically timid, "my interview's tomorrow. I dread it."

"But you've no cause to. They'll just want to know if you remember anything unusual, that's all."

"Yah, I know I should be more bold. I've done nussing wrong - but I don't have much trust in justice. OK, some in the village do like me, but many don't, and have mistrusted me since years. Ze Guardia don't like me neither, they think my junky old Mercedes cars which cost so little in Germany are too luxury for me, so I must be into shady stuff."

"Don't worry, the Guardia aren't involved. The inquiry's being led by a homicide detective squad."

"Oof, that sounds more scary - but fairer all the same. What must I do?"

"Just answer questions and try to identify photos."

"Photos? Of murders - yuck, I am...how do you say?...squirmish?"

"Squeamish," Julia smiled. "I was ordered not to talk about it, sub judice - but..." She darted glances right and left as if expecting spies behind each pine and lowered her voice to a whisper, "I recognised one. D'you remember the mad Frenchman, Moses we called him? He'd been just about everyone famous or powerful since life on earth began. Played the violin and was Vilayat Khan in his last reincarnation?"

Marte's face returned to life and normality - the enjoyment of life. "Yah, yah - how could one forget? Well, he must have left ze 'golden wheel' or whatsoever he called zis life business and entered a higher plane. Probably he left his skeleton behind as a little joke to get up Frances' nose! Ha! She got so angry because she was a nobody of four thousand years, but I," Marte puffed with pride, "was almost twelve thousand!"

Julia had omitted to mention the one who resembled Manfred. It was somehow instinctive - she did not want to give Marte too great an advantage, for the 'angel' remark still rankled.


Alex returned home in high spirits, fired by the heat, sparks and melting of metal under naked flames. Even as a baby he had a fascination with fire, and would watch eagerly for the miraculous moment of conflagration when paper burst into flames or kindling ignited, rejoicing with a gleeful 'ffffff' when it occurred. He would stare mesmerized by the patterns of the flames, gesticulating ecstatically at the rare vapours of electric blue. Medieval priests must have had problems with people like him, whose natural bent was to favour the chemistry of hell.

Arturo was thankfully a man of few unnecessary words and plenty of patience, so their arrangement worked smoothly. Today, especially, it had purged him of whatever had soured his relationship with Lise and a weight seemed lifted from his shoulders.

Colin had still not returned the djellaba. The arrangement was for it to be handed back as soon as his rash had gone, but he figured that the very definition of a rash was surely its suddeness, its unpredictability. He anxiously checked on his body every five minutes, and mostly the rash was not there, but sometimes there were hints that it might return - slight variations in skin tone and sensitivity that indicated, just as a fleeting shadow indicates a haze cloud passing across the sun, that it might be returning.

Mind power was his new weapon. Will power more precisely; self-help, positive thinking, 'bye-bye to self pity and cold shoulder to fear. A hundred percent pure cotton attire and a dairy-free diet were also contributory factors, he was prepared to admit. And exercise. Every day he did twenty minutes of strenuous bicycle riding motions, the blood pumping round his body and his calf muscles flexing beautifully, whilst lying back on his bed. Also the recitations of Shakespeare, confined of course to the quotes with 'rash' in them. There were a surprising number of these, but far and away his favourite was Juliet's caution to Romeo, "I have no joy in thy love tonight, it is too rash, too sudden, too like the lightning..." He would mouth it in all sorts of unlikely bodily positions and from all manner of unusual nooks and crannies inside his house, sometimes moaning it sotto voce and sometimes singing it with the powerful roar of a classical tenor.

He wanted to take his new emboldened persona out into the world, or at the very least the environs of Milagra, but yesterday he had made an embarrassing preamble. He went for a jog at twilight round his local patch, just a couple of circuits of the vineyards beyond his garden, clad only the djellaba. It was a suitable garment for a long-striding walk, he discovered, but flapped at the lower legs in most irritating fashion as soon as one broke into a lope. He countered this by hoisting it up so his legs could canter freely, so imagine the embarassment of rounding the final bend at full tilt and running almost smack into Diego himself, who had come to admire the first vine shoots of Spring and had to cling in shock to his pruning shears. It took time for him to recognise that it was indeed Colin, his old neighbour, for neither the garment nor the exposed area of tackle were the accoutrements of Colin he had ever seen before. Still, it was testimony to Colin's newfound health and steadiness that, despite the excruciating awkwardness of this encounter, he managed to mumble his way out and retreat home for a salutory splash of cold water and still remain rashless.


It was not so much his new, improved physique that he wished to parade abroad for the adulations of the village, whatever Diego might be bawdily telling them in the bars, but rather his new mental toughness. The army brass who recommended his discharge would be eating humble pie should they see him now. They had thought him witless and whimpering, an hysterical hypochondriac (although the official reason given was chronic allergy syndrome, so as not to impute any blame on the original brass who signed him up without recognizing his unsuitability).

He particularly enjoyed imagining them crawling like lizards before him, wallowing in the desert dirt whilst he strode at them in his billowing djellaba bearing the unmistakable look of leadership and the awesome charisma of a new, twenty first century Lawrence of Arabia.

Somewhere a cautionary note dinned in his ears. What was Marte's warning? 'Don't let ze pendulum swing too far the other way, too many peoples I knew tripped up zat way'. He knew what she meant. He was in danger of rebounding so far from his previous life cowering in fear that he might gorge himself on self-love and over compensate, becoming just another ego-fanatic. And how right she was...already he could sense himself slipping into self worship, patting himself too violently on the back, self-adulating, feasting on his reflection in his attic mirror where he had had to place a slop bucket to catch the floss (or was it flor?) of his ejaculation after he jacked himself off. Which he did regularly now, to celebrate his renunciation of fear. He would undoubtedly beat that old hippie guru of the black bus to a sperm contest, or who could wank longer or spew further or attract more dogs, if they were to compete in single sexual combat these days. Aaargh, wasn't that exactly the danger trap lurking ahead? Don't Colin, don't! Don't boast, don't brag! Be modest, be humble, *try* to be yourself...

Really what he needed was a model to emulate, an icon for his new identity. Otto was too old, studious and tunnel visioned; Reggie too sardonic, dry and sexless; Manos Arriba skillfully got his hands in the interesting places but was doolally in every other sense; El Bigot was too silent, secretive, inscrutable - except... Well, for want of anything better, for lack of the real thing, which was closer to Lawrence of Arabia but without the insanity and self-obsession, El Bigot would do.

# 22

"**A**ndres, it's Julia. I'm phoning to thank you. 'Pouring oil on troubled waters' is how I'd describe in English the effect you had. I dread to think what disasters could have happened if you'd not been there."

"They might have treated you more courteously, who knows? A lawyer *can* be counterproductive."

"Well I'm very grateful - even if you don't want to give yourself the credit."

"It was my pleasure. Julia...?"

"Um?"

"There're still things we should discuss - before any second interview."

"I know. I'm not saying goodbye. Just thank you."

"I'll come over. It's better we meet at your place."

"Well, how about next Sunday? I'm sure they won't see me again," she cleared her throat, "before the DNA results are through."

There was a long pause. "Why not now - while it's fresh in my mind?"

She was aware before she made the phone call that he might interpret it as a green light, but knew she had an absolute obligation to thank him. The abrupt way they had parted after the interview had given her no chance to express her gratitude then, plus she had felt too drained to speak another word.

She immediately noted the different tone to his voice. Or was it register? Prior to now it had been faultlessly formal, thoughtful and unfailingly precise. Yet his sharp quip to silence Juanito and the Andres of Carocaballo should have informed her there was an earthier, sparkier side to him. She did not want to lose the more aloof Andres she was used to, nor feel that at night he automatically shed his other qualities to become simply a male who operated typically when it sniffed the chance of sex. Was that why he had agreed to help but refused to discuss payment? Had he all along been expecting to be paid in kind? Suddenly it struck her as sickeningly predictable, and she felt a fool for not having had the intelligence to anticipate it.

"Are you still there, Julia?"

"Yes... Andres. Listen, I'm very grateful for your help, but I don't want us to have misunderstandings. Please don't be offended, but if you come it's only to talk, OK? So if you can't make it by nine at the latest, let's leave it for another day."

"Don't worry, I'll be there long before nine."

She tried to pretend nothing had occurred, that it was just an evening like any other. Yet a myriad of contradictory thoughts jostled together, interlocking and colliding.

She had become used to her solitary, ascetic life, even though it had been fraught with troubles, and she at last felt disconnected from her old life. On the positive side, relieved to be free of the unrewarding relationship with Marco's dad, but on the negative, bereft of the anchoring strength she derived from her dancing career, and concerned that it might be harder to resuscitate it the longer she stayed away - even though for the moment she had no choice.

She next tried not to think but to compose herself through mundane, practical actions like cleaning her teeth, having a shower, brushing her hair. But this only prompted an annoying inner voice that needled her at every turn; "You're just cleaning your teeth so your breath tastes kissing sweet! You're just brushing your hair 'cos you want it stroked! You're only swilling out down there 'cos you want it licked!" It was infuriating! And untrue. Because her desire to keep a distance was stronger than any underlying desires (although she could admit she did have underlying desires). Also, after Jorgen she harboured all the more reticence; once bitten, she thought, looking down at her mangled nipple and grimacing more from the terrible double entendre than the pain it revived, twice shy.

Now it was Andres she appeared to have misread.

After Alex and Marco went to watch TV she became fascinated by the clock. Magnetized, she watched it move slowly, inexorably past nine, and finally to nine thirty. Only then did she allow herself to feel relief, confident that he would not be coming. Perhaps he, too, had come to his senses. He must have been off guard when she phoned and reacted without thinking, then his common sense had prevailed. After all, in a macho culture you're not a real man if you let slip such an opportunity - as when the woman makes the running by phoning first. Then presumably you remember the taboos; for surely lawyers, like doctors and teachers, must have a professional code of conduct to dissuade them from sex with clients.

I'll dance, she decided. It's the best way to relax and silence thoughts. I've always preferred dancing to thinking.

She went through her usual warm-up routine, feeling all the more urgency towards floor exercises now that her first interview was over, because there was a glimmer of hope she might soon return to London and leave the forgotten winter (in career terms) behind her.

She studied her reflection critically in the mirrored wall. She seemed to have lost weight and muscle strength. A problem athletically and aesthetically. Not only would she lack the necessary stamina to survive long performances, she looked too frail for a leading role - too vulnerable, waiflike. This unpalatable image persuaded her to ignore the mirror, even though it was vital for monitoring the technical perfection of movements, so as to dance freely and far more strenuously.

She originally began dancing to amuse herself while Frances took a break from ancient amphora and used her pottery wheel to throw pots. She used to spin like a top to the whirring sound of the wheel. This whirlwind of dangling limbs, which threatened to sweep off the newly thrown pots that were patiently drying on their shelves, both maddened and distracted Frances as she laboured away. Also the water from the clay spun out in a fine red spray, spattering Julia's clothes and hair so that within minutes she looked like a liver spotted dalmation puppy. It forced Frances to wash them, and in those days before the electricity came she washed by hand and in cold water too, because the gas water heater was temperamental in ways Paco el Fontanero could not fathom.

But, to Frances' credit, her annoyance never got the better of her. Since no pots ever did get broken she realised Julia must be exceptionately coordinated, and she eventually agreed to pay for dancing lessons with a strange woman, haunted by an unknown sorrow, who once danced professionally but now waxed legs and bikini lines with a mournful dedication in the only beauty salon in Montejoven.

Julia danced until her energy drained, then consulted the mirror for any beneficial changes to her physique. *Could* her body have miraculously plumped and curvaceously matured? She stared at it, wondering if it were mainly the skin-tight black leotard and cut off black tights that exaggerated her slimness. Then, purely for amusement, she strutted some classic 'babe' postures of the playmate kind, pouting exaggeratedly at her reflection. Finally she peeled the leotard down below her waist and squeezed her breasts together to achieve a deep cleavage, then, jutting the cheeks of her bottom virtually into the mirror, she wagged them in a blatantly erotic way.

But her fantasy moment of humorous sexual preening was suddenly, brutally interrupted by energetic knocking on the door.

She stood for a few seconds in frozen immobility - until she had the sense to wrench up her leotard and slip on her overcoat to present a more respectable front. Might it be the Guardia? She retreated for a nervous glance at the kitchen clock: 10.40. Outrageously late for them to call. Yet it was exactly the kind of psychological ploy they favoured.

However it was not the Guardia, but Andres. She recognised him through the distorting fish-eye peephole when she returned to the door, and whether it was her imagination or the weird lense distortion, he appeared to look infuriatingly self-satisfied.

"It's 10.40 Andres! *Not* what we agreed...Why come this late?" She was almost shouting, and she made no move to open the door.

"I've actually been here some time. But you were dancing and had turned the music up so I couldn't attract your attention."

"You mean you've been watching - like a voyeur." It made her all the more angry that he must have spied her stupid sexual posturing at the end.

"Not at all - what's got into you?" He sounded extremely irritated, then tried to temper it with a milder, "Julia, let me in."


If she complied his tactics would have succeeded and he would be all the more self-congratulatory. But if she locked him out and her suspicions were wrong, then she would be acting shamefully and unreasonably, considering the apparently altruistic help he had given her up until now. Should she not be applying the legal presumption which, after all, she wished applied to herself and Frances; innocent until proven guilty? But *why* did he have to come so late and land her in this quandary?

Slowly, reluctantly, she opened the door, but her expression was far from welcoming.

"It's not fair to come this late. Especially after what I said, and meant."

But far from being smug he seemed exasperated and looked dishevelled. He flung his jacket irritably on a chair as he strode in. "I can't understand why the time's suddenly so important to you. I got delayed by a client who, frankly, has a far more serious problem than yours, and then, from recklessly speeding to make up for lost time, and not daring to waste two minutes because of your bizarre deadline," he paused for breath, "I didn't stop for petrol when I should have and, of course, ran out just outside Milagra. Why the hell else have I come on foot?"

She was impressed by his ill-temper, in that it seemed genuine enough. She also noticed that his shoes were damp, tallying with the probability that he had cut through her almond grove in the final approach, and certainly there was no sign of his car as she glanced deliberately down at the driveway. However that was not definite proof. It was easy enough to leave the car out of sight where the steep embankment near the broken terrace wall obscured the track. His whole story could be a cunning ploy to ensure that he stayed the night, since the nearest petrol station was midway between Milagra and Montejoven, ten kilometers away. Moreover it shut at eleven, and the pernickety attendant would refuse to sell petrol in anything but a proper, customized container which doubtless neither of them possessed.

Andres was a fluent reader of her suspicious mind. "You can suck petrol from your car if you need to be rid of me that badly," he grumbled. "I can't - I'm allergic."

She did not look at him, but suspected that his lips bore the ghost of a smile. She could have accepted the situation with good grace but petulantly chose not to.

"Stay then. You've contrived the trap so I'm stuck with it."

"Up 'till now I've had nothing but admiration for you, d'you realise that?" he replied stormily. "But tonight you've tried your hardest to make me feel despicable. It's the typical tactic of a racist. The very thing I felt you weren't ."

It was not the comment she expected. She had anticipated 'sexist'. "How *can* you think me a racist?" she sounded stunned, her anger momentarily subdued.

"Simple enough. You see me as a typical Spaniard, another Juanito only a bit classier by virtue of a degree and more respectable profession. But basically the same - tongue hanging out for a piece of precious white northern flesh."

"Why is that *racist*? What about that image, exactly has to do with race? Come on, you're a lawyer; definitions and terminology are your forté."

She was conscious that their anger was mounting of its own momentum and without any real, deep seated cause, and sensed that she should be soft pedalling as opposed to goading him or it could, potentially, turn aggressive. This kind of taunting could earn you a slap in the face - not that that had ever deterred her before.

"I'll ask *you* a question, then." Andres was trying to appear reasonable, "What prior experience have you had of Spanish men to make you this antagonistic?"

"I left Spain when I was fifteen, Andres," she replied witheringly. "What do you take me for - a child nympho?"

"No, a racist. You may have a Spanish passport and be a fluent speaker but you think, feel and behave like an Englishwoman. Suspicious and contemptuous of foreigners; cold or hot - but always in the wrong context." He turned away as if finally bored by their stereotypical conflict. "To be honest I'm completely exhausted. I had to be up very early this morning and I - unlike you - do have to operate to a timetable. Just point me out which inch of floor you'll allow me to sleep on and I'll leave first thing in the morning. The only act of human kindness required of you is a lift to the gas station."

"No problem," she said tartly, secretly relieved that she need not continue hostilities since she was not convinced that justice was unequivocally on her side. She found a pair of faded single sheets and an old duvet and slung them unceremoniously on the window couch in her mother's studio. "Buenas noches," she muttered, as without a backward glance she climbed the stairs to her bedroom.

Sleep, though, did not come easily. She fought off invading images of Guardia guns and green uniforms and green walled rooms, in one of which the long haired French violinist was crouched, cooking slippery pancakes over a woodfire which burned too brightly, so that the dancing flames caught his long dark hair alight until someone - whom she could not see - had to douse him with a bucket of water. She ought really to tell Andres about this violinist, since they had shown her his photo at the Cuartel, but perhaps it was all too late now.


It was not exactly a dream because she was not fully asleep, but lying, semi-conscious, in a ball in the darkness and fully submerged under the bedding. Perhaps she made a noise, perhaps that was what alerted Andres. Whatever it was, in her strange somnolent state curled up like a naked foetus, she felt his body worm into the bed alongside her, and an electric current ran through her as his skin touched hers. Was that what she had been wanting all along? She might have murmured a brief protest, a faint "No, Andres", but she could not be entirely sure she even did that, for in truth she felt no resistance towards him at all. His body was comfortingly warm and his skin blended immediately with hers, smooth, relatively hairless and with a natural, alluring human smell unsoured by the acrid stench of stale sweat that clings to many men. He had an almost feminine texture to his skin in fact, but his shape, proportions and muscular strength were totally male. He lay close for a little while without doing anything more, to reassure her - or perhaps, artfully, to make her realise that she wanted more.

Then, once he did begin to touch her with his hands and lips she no longer tried to resist - her mind maybe momentarily flickered into life to feebly question the wisdom of what was happening - then was extinguished as her body took over and responded. Already that night her strenuous dancing had energized and exhilarated her, so that her body was especially alive, and there were many months of tension to be released. She could hardly pretend that she did not enjoy it, for once she had overcome her initial caution and relaxed she became increasingly ecstatic, flushed and overwhelmed. Ultimately she no longer seemed attached to the earth and no longer aware of her surroundings, her room, her bed, or even her physical body or which way up or round it was. It had melted into another kind of being, perhaps a bird or fish, even an amoeba, so that afterwards she understood the sexual symbolism of surrealism a little more. He was a very selfless lover, very giving, and she could not say the same about herself for she had dissolved into a receptacle of pleasure but was incapable of taking initiatives.

'All she needed was a good fuck', that same insidious little voice warned her might be Andres' concluding thought, but she emphatically shut it out. Already the first tinges of dawn were blanching the night sky as they finally fell asleep, lying intertwined and exhausted. And only when the excessive noises of Marco and Alex condemned to making their own breakfast filtered through did she surface from sleep into a half wakefulness, opening reluctant eyes to confront Andres lying beside her, watching her thoughtfully. Immediately their eyes met he put his hand on her forehead.

"Don't think about it, please. You'll put a wrong interpretation on it, I know you will. Don't think - just accept it was perfectly natural, very beautiful, and what happens."

She lay on her back immobile, straining not to think, but various thoughts seeped in nonetheless. Just as once a baby has been born, has squeezed its perilous way down the vagina and burst into the world, there is no possible way it can retract and turn back to the dark comfort of the womb; so once you have had a full sexual experience with a man you cannot pretend it has not happened, and relate in the same way as you did before. It must be like the letting of blood or some primitive sacrament, the pooling of juices must set off a chemical change. Why should it be that way? She had no answer, but she knew it to be the case. It somehow transformed a friendship; even the hippies and all the subsequent adherents to casual sex and threesomes and foursomes and roastings and whatever had not managed to totally banish emotional complications like possessiveness and jealousy from their sexual affairs. So what now? They had spawned a new problem, and would both have cope with it. Almost as if on cue he leaned over and kissed her scarred breast.

"What happened?" he asked, then with the ghost of a sigh as he realised the ramifications of his new feelings about her body, and at the same time the immense gulf that ignorance about each other's lives placed between them, "or would you prefer not to tell me."

She smiled wanly, "It was bitten - by a sadist." She propped herself up on one elbow, "Ironically enough he was last person I slept with before you. It was soon after coming here for my mother's funeral. You could say it was my fault," she looked him meaningfully and gave an ironic smile, "for sleeping with someone I knew nothing about."

The remark hit home immediately. She could see it in his eyes, and his body instinctively stiffened although he continued to stroke the nipple tenderly.

"I'm sorry," he said, a remark which could have many meanings. "I hope it doesn't still hurt," and he kissed it gently.

But she could read his thoughts. He too was equally aware what had been unleashed, and struggled with the thoughts of her previous lovers, and with his feelings towards this one in particular who had left his cruel signature for ever carved into her body, which he, Andres, must avoid all instinctive urges to regard as his. It occurred to her also that he was inevitably married, partly because he was such a considerate lover, and partly because it was difficult to imagine that he would not be. She wondered what excuse he had given his wife for his absence. Consulting with a client, most likely - the best deceptions are closest to the truth. She also wondered how much of his current discomfort was guilt towards his wife, and whether they had the kind of relationship in which he would tell her in full and graphic detail about his infidelities. Some marriages get more firmly cemented that way.

"He wasn't Spanish, don't worry. He was a German," she continued with tangible irony, "and since us English are habitually the *most* racist towards Germans your theory somehow holds."

"I was offended last night, Julia. Please don't throw everything back in my face." He attempted to smile "We're all meant to be happy Europeans now."

There was a loud crash, something else that was fragile impacting against something resistant, followed by curses, mutterings and squawks. She guessed Marco had probably dropped a bowl on the tiled floor. Sure enough his anxious voice floated upwards.

"Julia!"

"Coming!"

"Oh Marco, you *are* a jackass! We could've dealt with it. She's not alone," she heard Alex's accusatory tones.

She got up and wrapped herself in her dressing gown. Then she looked down at Andres with slight mockery.

"Feel free to enjoy my bed for as long as you want. I take it, since it's already late, you must have planned to take a day off work?"

"I'm afraid I did," he agreed, a little sheepishly.

She was gratified that at least he had the honesty to admit he had pre-planned his sleepover, but felt the more regretful she had rolled over so very easily.

Meanwhile the hours ticked inexorably on for Colin. He had spent a fitful night gripped in the spell of the particular crunching tick of his bedside alarm, which in the end he stuck deep down into the toe region of a tartan bedroom slipper to muffle it. Eventually he gave up on the prospects of sleep, went downstairs and sat bolt upright ('to attention' in army terms) at his kitchen table, persuading himself to swallow a brackish liquid afloat with twigs which looked as if it had oozed from an Irish peat bog, but which Marte had proclaimed was 'Mu tea'. It apparently cleansed the digestive tract, balanced wayward hormones, settled fidgety nerves and fortified resolve, and he was rather counting on it to deliver.

He absentmindedly tipped oatflakes all over his pictorial placemat (a print of Constable's 'Flatford Mill'), because cornflakes were now forbidden since all traces of wheat and gluten and God knows what else were enemy territory until he'd rearranged his blood supply, which evidently took from two to four weeks. Flush, cleanse, eliminate; flush, cleanse, eliminate; relax, meditate, empower; relax, meditate, empower. He wished someone would come and admire him, congratulate him and who knows, even love him for all the stalwart efforts he was putting into this curative mantra. Marte would surely relax her frown and pat him encouragingly, but whatever action served best to open up the armpit zone and release the priceless panacea would enrapture him. However he was not meant to visit her before another two weeks of dietary restrictive torment. No it was not torment, no no: renewal, rebirth, reawakening, revival, renunciation and rejuvenation! Positive thinking Colin, you can and you will!


Today was crunch day. A tester to see if the new improved and empowered Colin could cope.

And coping he was, so far - apart from the slip up with the oats and no bowl to catch them. And then the soya milk, slurping all over and splatting against his privates so that a second shower seemed necessary - until he ingeniously applied the waste-not-want-not principles and licked himself clean. He was amazed to find he was so dexterously double-jointed as to able to apply his tongue to his own tinkiewinkie, and tried not to regret that he hadn't made this remarkable discovery much, much earlier on in life.

But just as well Reggie hadn't chosen to come a spot early and catch him at it, red tongued as it were. For Reggie had agreed to be his crutch, accompanying him in moral support to the Cuartel, for the day of his interview had finally arrived. Fleeting thoughts suggested to him that the whole sorry passage of his life so far had been inexorably leading up to this moment, this prodigious hour. Eleven. He licked his lips around the sound of it. Tasting of soya and spunkie-wunkie. Yes, it was the hour of truth, the hour of reckoning, D-hour, and he would not wilt.

Reggie knocked on Colin's door with a sinking feeling of trepidation. At least the man had got rid of his ghastly battery operated pushbutton thing that played the first two bars of 'Bluebells from Scotland', and finally installed a solid, masculine door knocker to alert him of visitors. He knew Colin had been busy reinventing himself as a man no longer of conservative cowardice, but of newborn courage and conviction, yet he had no faith the conversion would survive the rigours of an encounter with the detective squad. In fact he was half expecting to find Colin had shrunk overnight to a pixie, and would open the door smothered head to foot in his old purple rash, and then have to flunk the interview until he could be resuscitated by Marte.

He was therefore pleasantly surprised by the determined wrench with which Colin asserted himself against a truculent door (it needed planing, but Fuster had scorned the job despite the offer of a crazy callout charge), and by the rashfree qualities of the forearm that performed the wrenching. Colin's face looked unfurrowed and admirably confident too, although the lips were somewhat flecked with milky saliva and could do with a judicious pat from a napkin. It all looked more promising than Reggie had feared. The only mild puzzler was Colin's indecision at the electric junction box behind the front door prior to their exiting. He flicked it off, on again, then off once more with a whisper of a sigh.

"Leave it so Old Bill Burglar bloody stubs his toe or bleeding bumps his head, eh old chap?" he said, grinning strangely.

"I think you'll find 'Old Bill's' where we're headed Colin, on the right side of the law," Reggie said drily, for he wasn't overfond of being hailed 'old chap'.

They drove in silence towards the Cuartel, each inhabiting their private world of anxiety driven contemplation. Reggie was heartened by Colin's choice of country suit and very English tie, which had lucky horse shoes and the odd hunting whip embroidered on an emerald silk background, and would establish his credentials as the archetypal old-fashioned English buffoon. He also approved of Colin's overzealous approach to corroborating his ID; he had brought a battered heirloom of a briefcase bulging with paperwork, including all passports to date (four, by the looks of it), two albums of family photos (from Delhi and Surbiton), military records, discharge papers, driving licence, tank license, Health Card, E111 papers, National Insurance Card, Birth Certificates (Indian and British), Copia Simple and his Escritura (Deed) for his house.

He had long ago decided that the best way to present Colin was as an eccentric English loony, and this plethora of papers fed the image to perfection. The only aberration was the inclusion of Colin's current day comfort blanket, the djellaba, which had grown grubbier by the day and was gripped like a lucky mascot in his non-briefcase bearing hand.

"Best to leave it in the car," Reggie said coaxingly as he parked near the Cuartel, but not so near that some idle Guardia might be tempted to measure the lack of tread on his bald rear wheels.

"No no," said Colin with sudden fervour, and to Reggie's horror he slipped it over his head. He even pulled up the hood, so that with his single visible lock of red hair and his wild piercing blue eyes he suddenly resembled Peter O'Toole having his first stab at donning the mantel of Lawrence of Arabia.


They waited in uneasy silence for their turn, and Reggie tried to ignore a nervous tick that looked as if someone had planted an extra pulse the shape of golf ball in Colin's temple, praying it was merely the cogs whirring in his brain. His hands looked steady as he signed his name in the 'In' column, and his voice was a register lower than usual when he enquired the time, so as to enter the 'Time In' column correctly, but Reggie had been thrust off balance by his strange remark:

"You've been a real stalwart as a friend Reggie, don't ever think you haven't."

"I'll never think I haven't," Reggie reassured him, but without being reassured himself. He had a hunch that Colin was up to something, had a plan up his sleeve, but worryingly there was such a wealth of hiding place in the copious sleeve of a djellaba.


Steps resounded in the corridor; one set clacked with authority but the other sounded dull, flat footed, almost lifeless in defeat. It was these last feet that turned out to belong to Marte, who emerged from the corridor into the reception area looking, quite literally, as if she had seen a ghost. Reggie was amazed at the transformation. Last time he set eyes on her she was perky enough, her eyes shining with health and fecundity - the final throes of enhanced fertility women get just prior to menopause, and her mind whirring up tempo, doubtless adding and subtracting, wondering what to fiddle and who to diddle. Or was that unfair? Anyway, here she was now looking the spitting image of his own grandmother, not as she was now (or wasn't, in truth, not any more) but as she had been the last time he set eyes on the old bag twenty odd years ago. Her face was pale as a nettle root, new grey strands had sprouted in her hair, and her muscles seemed to have atrophied for she could only drag her feet, barely lift her hand to sign out, and not even raise the shadow of a smile or show the remotest sign of recognition as she steered her lumpen body towards the door. It was as if she and Colin were the opposite canisters in an hour glass; the life, soul and strength had drifted out of her and passed through the narrow connecting neck flowing straight into Colin.

Still, Reggie decided, whatever horrors had corroded the last vestiges of her youth back there in the interrogation room they were not so catastrophic as to put her in irons; she had at least struggled out to freedom - and without paying bail. What was more concerning was the effect it had on Colin. He did not so much look at her as breathe her in. Reggie noted the heaving chest, the flaring nostrils and the frantically bobbing Adam's apple, like the float on a fishing line when a whopping great fish has been hooked. He feared an epileptic fit or asthma attack to begin with, but once the gasps gave way to regular deep breathing and the measured rise and fall of the rib cage, Reggie relaxed once more; perhaps it was part of the therapy and the teacher-pupil encounter had subliminally brought it on.

What he did not know was that Colin had caught the whiff of serious alarm; all the comforting scents of rich musky earth, decaying beech nuts, moist leaves and delicate primroses that Colin normally inhaled from Marte were drowned by the sharp acidic stench of sweat and fear. Reggie only saw him clenching and unclenching his fists like a pumping piston, and before he could wonder if this was a sign of courage or cowardice they were summoned to the room of doom from whence Marte had just emerged.


The initial stages were swift. Colin had the contents of an office to prove his identity and the local Guardia broke silence to confirm their longstanding knowledge of him. Mercifully his voice was firm, though his English accent was so pronounced that even when speaking Spanish it sounded like English. Reggie had come not only for moral support but also greater linguistic proficiency, but in the event one of the detectives was fluent enough in English - although Reggie prided himself he would still manage to outmanoeuvre him in a crossword competition or a round of scrabble.

Reggie's mind began to wander. He idly perused those architectural aberrations of the building that were visible through the window, together with the vileness of the interior colours of the room, plus the risible, ridiculous outmoded uniform of a Guardia Civil (who could have come up with the shape of those hats? And more mysterious still, who the hell could have actually approved the design?). Only when he heard the danger word 'Alleman' (German) did he suddenly refocus.


But all conversation stopped as out came the photos, and Reggie brightened up by several shades. A fairly classical hippie line-up, though one or two looked pretty 'straight', if Reggie remembered the terminology correctly. Especially that bozo cuddling his degree.

Then, out of the blue, with the speed and shock of an American Tomahawk missile and with just as devastingly destructive impact, he saw Colin's rock steady finger pointing at the blond bombshell one, and he uttered insane words:

"That one I'd have liked to have killed, since he was all over the woman I loved, Marte. But the one I did kill was a more pathetic, paler, punier version of this. Another German, of course. Kicked him in the goolies, punched him in the pusshole and knocked two teeth to smithereens, then flung him off the terrace and caused a right old earthquake. It buried him in a pile of rubble I can tell you. The tike got just what he deserved. Ugly punk!"

"Colin," Reggie gasped, "what are you saying?" But all his eloquence had deserted him, and Colin in any case was in no mood to hear his words however humdrum.

"Not to worry Reggie," he mouthed with tightening lips. "This is something I have to do. It'll do me a world of good."

There was instant commotion in the room. A local Guardia sprung to guard - or rather block - the doorway, his hand stroking his gun, and the detectives consulted rapidly in lowered voices. One made an urgent phonecall, presumably to their Superiors, while the English proficient one stepped into the questioning breach, leaning forward and tersely informing Colin that he had the right to remain silent until such time as his lawyer could be summoned. He had permission to make a single phone call.

Colin turned to Reggie, "No need to phone you old chap, since you're right here already." He patted Reggie on the knee, "I can trust you to find me a legal eagle can't I?"


Reggie nodded wordlessly and rose to leave. Colin gave him a sheepish grin as he reached the doorway and the guarding Guardia stepped nimbly aside, and Reggie's final impression of Colin was of being almost impaled by the strange mad stare from those blue eyes framed by an unwashed greying djellaba hood.

# 23

Reggie swore irritably as he grazed his elbow trying to stuff Colin's overflowing briefcase into the rusting boot of his car, an action made more awkward because some thoughtless, witless Brit, a newcomer *of course,* had parked his ostentatiously new 4x4 far too close. Unfairly blaming it for shaving yet more precious tread from his illegal rear tyres, he gave it a vicious kick in its flashy front fender.

His first priority was to find Colin a lawyer. Julia had rubbished the only outfit he knew of on the coast, for anything trickier than probate work that is, so he planned to ask about her new lawyer; either steal him away if she had finished with his services, or try someone he could recommend. As he drove past Bar del Bigot he stifled a low moan of regret at the passing of his uneventful, banal life; by rights he should now be enjoying a comforting coffee across the table from Colin, chewing over the simple puzzles of a mindless crossword and lackadaisically exchanging a quip or two.

He decided that the delicacy of the present situation outweighed its urgency, so he would rather visit Julia than phone. Colin could be held in custody at the Cuartel for up to two days, so there was no frantic hurry. Jesus, he thought as his rear wheels slithered on the new tarmac approach to Holidaylandia, if Colin had not managed to stomach life in the army, how could he possibly imagine he would cope in a high security jail? At least in the army the bullies are notionally on your side, but in jail you're in enemy territory round the clock!

Julia could read Reggie's mood the moment she saw his face in the doorway.

"What's up?"

"Colin," was his economical reply. "I need a stiff one, I'm afraid."

He helped himself to a chair and, gradually becoming more attuned to his surroundings, realised that the shape in Alex's dressing gown was assuredly not Alex.

"Sorry for intruding," he apologised to Julia, then glancing down at the bare male legs and bare feet, "hope I'm not interrupting anything." Finally, as an afterthought, he addressed Andres directly, "Hablas Ingles?"

"I understand it," Andres explained, keeping to Castellano, "but can't speak it very well."

"Good man," Reggie drank thirstily from the brandy Julia handed him, "most of us are sadly the other way around."

It took him more than twenty minutes to convey the twists and turns of Colin's meandering progress from the depths of recent nervous despair and head to toe rashiness, to the unnatural steeliness and iron resolve of that morning. He included Colin's much earlier premonition that he was the sort to confess to crimes he had not done simply by dint of the remotest suspicion that he might have, and that Colin had presumably been ejected from the army because he was the type who 'wouldn't hurt a fly', and broke out in a plague of boils plus heat rash every time they reminded him he had signed up to a killing machine.

Having laboured long over this portrait of innocence, nervous hysteria and multiple allergies, added to his previous unblemished history without (apparently) any further skeletons to suggest other possible victims, he then changed tack – but not before he swallowed a second fortifying brandy. This time he launched into a vitriolic attack on Marte, blaming her for Colin's recent personality change, for luring him into a hopeless, unrequited passion for her body and - he hinted darkly - setting him up to this preposterous confession in order to let her and her compatriots off the hook. He even suggested that Colin's personality switch had been brought about by the cocktail of drugs she was administering, and that her ham acting of the part of old crone who had just seen the spectre of her own death down at the Cuartel was intentional, and the final catalyst for Colin. Julia had never seen Reggie so eloquent or so aroused.

"I think you've gotten carried away by Marte's laughable reputation as a witch. You know damn' well she isn't, Reggie."

"Not in the black cat, cloak and broomstick sense of it, no. But she's a canny, self-serving, manipulative bitch if that's what she has to be. Don't think I'm just an old fool, Julia. Remember I had a close relationship with your mother, so I have more on Marte than you know. Oh, she's a good healer, I don't take that away from her…"

Julia felt a sudden apprehension. There was much she wished to ask but Reggie was already ploughing on:

"Colin needs a lawyer who'll understand the kind of crazy character he is - but not find him so damn' crazy he'll be thrust straight into an asylum."

"Are you asking *me*?" Andres spoke English for the first time, very carefully, "because I am…what is the word?...already compromised." He glanced meaningfully at Julia, who Reggie noticed returned the look with little warmth.

"Someone like you," Reggie conceded. "You don't have a colleague?"

Andres slipped away to make an exploratory call, then returned to say he had arranged for an English speaking lawyer from Puente Real, inland from Montejoven, to see Colin at six that evening. He would like to meet with Reggie fifteen minutes beforehand.

"Is there any chance of bail?"

"No, very little chance - unless the injuries are not the same as he say he...er..."

"Inflicted," Julia prompted.

"Yes. And they will check the army records. Perhaps he was in an Especial Force, trained to kill - how is it you say it? - hand to hand." Andres frowned, "Not good for bail. - And why he got his...le dieron de alta." Andres looked to Julia, frustrated by his limitations and Julia translated "discharge" for Reggie's benefit.

Julia felt gratified that he had to struggle in English and could not rely on his normal communicative prowess, for his remark about her being racist kept resurfacing. Even though she knew it to be mean, she was enjoying his experience of inadequacy.


Reggie's ears were more finely attuned to sounds than theirs despite the brandies, owing to having slept soundly the previous night. He detected the same shuffling, dejected footsteps he had despised at the Cuartel, only they had perked up a little from that lowest ebb, regaining the vestiges of a spring.

"I'll be off then - but I'll keep in touch. Thanks for firewater and both your help."

He left with such speed that he almost crashed head-on into Marte. Their hackles instantly rose as they edged distastefully past each other, but he did not strike out until he found she had almost blocked him in with her gangster Mercedes. Even then it was a feebler kick than he had delivered that morning, because he suddenly felt a mild affinity on noticing her rear tyres were even balder than his.

Marte flopped onto Reggie's chair despite the unwelcome warmth that warned her it had hosted his behind. She fanned her face with an old magazine and closed her eyes.

"Oof, I have been to hell und back - you cannot imagine!" She drained Reggie's untouched glass of water in a single gulp. Then, remembering the malign effects of a slumped posture she reared upright, swept back the hair that had drifted over her face like a misshapen curtain and, suddenly startled, noticed an unknown young man only three feet away. "Do you not introduce me, Julia?"

"You know it's Andres. This is Marte, my neighbour."

"And friend, surely not? For many many years."

Finally Julia smiled, because Marte had begun so blatantly to smooth her rib cage and admire the rounded volume of her overhanging breasts, surreptitiously eyeing Andres to see whether he were fully aware just how wholeheartedly they put Julia's small crab apples in the shade. Until she abruptly remembered this was no time for preening.

"Mein Gott!" she cried, "zey have zis photo of Manfred in his prime! You must surely have seen it Julia - he is on ze list of missing persons. I cannot understand it…when we fucked in Germany and Lise was conceived, already zen he was officially missing for some years."

"The blond? I thought I'd seen him somewhere before."

"Not recognise Manfred?! Julia! - But then you were so little, not yet interested in men …" Her eyes swivelled to Andres, and her smile was full of charm, "Julia tells me you will only help her in this matter of ze skeleton. But I so badly need just a little advice."

"Can we speak in Castellano - my English is too poor."

"Claro. Well my problem is zis. Zey want my husband's name and last known address and Social Security zis and zat, and date of birth and…oof, I don't know any of it! I never knew it and I haven't seen him since twenty years! But zey were nasty and threatening. Zey don't believe me."

"You don't know his *name*?"

"Ah, zat I do, but only zat. Tomas Schlock. Unforgettable because ze jokers called him Tom Arschlock! We were married for two months only. It was not a serious thing."

"Then you don't have a problem. Just tell them his name."

"Yah, yah, natürlich. I already did. But zey want proof on paper. It is zeir nasty attitude that troubles me. Zey have no respect." She sighed so deeply that her entire body heaved. "Can I lie on your divan, Julia? I think I am in shock."

"Of course."

Once Marte was ensconced in a darkened room Julia wandered out into the garden. Although climatically spring had been disappointing, with few sunny days and frequent showers, the vegetation had flourished like a tropical jungle. As her eyes scanned the greenness of the mountain range she could imagine herself in the mountainous interior of a Caribbean island. Even her mother's garden, which was frankly a hodgepodge of often competing, incompatible plants that stubbornly refused to flower, was unusually ablaze with purple irises. And what Frances optimistically referred to as 'the lawn' for the first time nearly resembled one, although if Julia had mown it, which would decapitate all the cheerful yellow dandelion flowers, disappointment might lurk beneath.

Today the sun shone on her tired eyes, and she shaded them in time to glimpse a pair of hoopoes, African birds with buff coloured bodies, black and white striped tail plumage and neat little bristling crests of black, white and pale arctic blue. Their flirting was so utterly full blooded and unashamed; the male with his bristling crest simultaneously strutting, bowing, cooing and circling the female who continuously thrust her upturned bottom in his face and then retreated as if she had not meant to, that it both amused and depressed her.

The depression was two-pronged. One, she only had to look down at the fast encroaching city of concrete, with its criss-crossing streets that now lit up at night with an artificial glow, to realise that wilderness birds like hoopoes would not be returning to nest next year. All the wildlife would desert her. Reminding her that - far from being in the Caribbean or the Pyrenees or any other wild green mountainous natural area - she was in fact firmly in the hub of modern coastal Spain, where developments could spring up anywhere unannounced, providing the local Mayor was pliant and corruptible and prepared to ignore the planning rules, and that some unscrupulous, greedy developer like Grant could produce the funds. The only certainty was that the buildings would be ugly, foreign owned, and probably overwhelming filled by the crudest possible kind of ex-pat Brits.

The second source of depression was last night. It struck her that the hoopoes were enacting an innocent parody of herself and Andres, and her tiredness made the taste more bitter. Why, when she had recognised the utter stupidity of sleeping with your lawyer, had she then succumbed? Well, even 'succumbed' was inaccurate, 'begged for it' would be the way he might describe it to himself no doubt, or laughingly to his mates, if that was his way. And he would not be far wrong. Ever since their first meeting she had been crystal clear that the boundaries of their relationship should remain firmly professional. How could she then lose her head, again?

Occasional cheery shouts wafted from the almond grove where Alex and Marco were playing football. Once the Holidaylandia golf course was turfed over and the surplus building sand scraped up and stuffed into bunkers it might no longer even be a safe place for their football 'pitch', for she could imagine the fusillade of hard golf balls whizzing in to crack unwitting skulls. She shivered involuntarily.

On the plus side Marco would enjoy collecting errant balls; maybe he could even sell them back at half price!

She strolled down to watch them do their usual unnerving penalty shootout, which involved Marco trying to appear a size and force to be reckoned with, while Alex mercilessly drove shots the speed and force of a cannonball at his head. She assumed Andres was still in the kitchen, or being artfully seduced by Marte, so was surprised to find him in goal. He still wore the ill-fitting dressing gown, and was leaping and diving at saves with total disregard for personal safety or decorum. If he did not dislocate his shoulder as opposed to the mere bruising on his previous visit it would not be from want of trying.

He probably has kids of his own, she thought, along with being married - that's why he relates so easily. I can feel a taste of sadness, of jealousy, infecting my mouth. The ripple effect I so clearly foresaw and tried to avoid. How can he play football so thoughtlessly when he's caused such a problem?

I don't want to wonder or worry about his life, I don't want to feel jealous. I liked you as a friend Andres. *Why* did you change it?

Even though she was at home she felt she had nowhere to go. She wanted to be alone, but Marte had closed the shutters of the living room to create a dark, womblike retreat and seemed to occupy the entire house with her post traumatic siesta-ing, while outside the sounds of happiness forced Andres on her mind, and her mind needed private solace.

She climbed to the Fuente, where the dampness had nourished a mountain oasis so startlingly green it was mesmerising. She sat among the bamboo fronds and listened to the regular dripping of the water which slid through the rock fissure, and wondered if even a single baby toad had wriggled alive from the scummy lake of toadspawn that had recently covered the pool's surface. For certain species the odds against reproduction, and thereafter survival, are stacked so high that life is truly a matter of chance, a miracle. Why couldn't she see *her* life as a miracle? How many times must Frances have soaked in sperm in their thousand, and yet only one had fused with an egg to form her.

It could only be bad to stay so long in a place where her emotions were forever stuck in the immaturity of a five year old's.

"Julia?"

"Um?"

"Oof, such a schlecht sleep! What a nightmare…ze skeleton's finger bone was like a cloud in the sky, pointing accusingly at zis valley. Horrible."

"Well it *is*." Julia pulled up the blinds, startling two gheckoes who were enjoying a quiet tête-à-tête and now fled. "Aren't you aware what Colin's done? He's gone and confessed to the murder!"

"What?!" Marte jack-knifed into sitting position, "Mein Gott!"

"Reggie's not best pleased. He thinks you effected a personality change, and dosed him with a guilt-inducing mushroom."

"Then he's a fool, a bitter, twisted fool. I don't *care* what he thinks. Colin was a whimpering mouse, he only got stronger, that's all."

"Well, he'll need his newfound strength. He's locked in a cell in the Cuartel right now, waiting for a lawyer."

"D'you ...d'you think he could have...?

"I don't know what to think. I know he used to hide and watch Frances sometimes, but she always thought he was harmless - apart from stealing her knickers off the line."

"Oof, we humans are so strange..."

Marte was soon upright and mobile, bouncing back to life with an alacrity that suggested she found the news about Colin more invigorating than her siesta. Reggie would not have recognised the confidence in her footsteps as she rejoined her car, oblivious to the new dent in the rear wheel arch because its bodywork was already more randonly pitted than the surface of the moon. Julia watched with faint amusement as she trotted nimbly over to the footballers, who now lay panting on the grass exhausted, but seemingly forced by the deadlocked score into the further rigours of extra time.

Marte was demonstratively warm to Alex and Marco, ebulliently spinning Marco round and round in a whirl, so that Julia suspected the close hugging action was vicariously intended for Andres. Once disentangled from Marco she could be seen talking animatedly with Andres, gesticulating helpfully in the direction of her hut. Girlish cries of 'Bye bye' and 'Hasta luego' continued to escape from the open driver's window as she descended the first section of the track, until the sounds of her leave taking were finally absorbed into the brooding shadows cast by the brutish structures of Holidaylandia.

"Is Colin *really* a murderer?" Marco asked mid-mouthful during their late lunch, his eyes widening with wonder.

"I don't think so. He never struck me as violent - but on the other hand you never fully know what goes on in someone else's mind. Even you, innocent though you look," she teased "must keep secrets."

She was too busy watching Andres out of the corner of an eye to notice Marco's wriggle of embarrassment, which he attempted to disguise by deflection. "And Alex," he added hastily.

"My secret's a thing of the past," Alex declared enigmatically.


"You don't have a job, or life, to go back to?" Julia asked when they were on their own once more.

"You're very bitter," he looked defensive. "Of course I can go, if that's what you want. I'm not proud of what happened. It's not how I meant it to happen."

"So you admit you had it planned?"

This time she ignited a spark of anger. "It's not a crime Julia. I didn't rape you, though that's what you seem to want to believe. You've denigrated it now, but at the time, well - I shan't say what I think. Yes, if you want to know, I 'planned' it, or hoped for it, after the first time I met you. In some ways I think I showed remarkable restraint."

"Restraint! So it's standard practise for lawyers to fuck their clients? Oh I know I'm not being entirely fair, having enjoyed it - perhaps even more than you. But what angers me is that I did try to stop it. I knew it would hopelessly complicate everything."

"And so did I. It is completely unethical for a lawyer to sleep with a client, especially when she is in a difficult, vulnerable situation like you are. You can make a formal complaint against me if you wish."

"Don't be a fool! But, to probe the complications we're in - I guess you're married?"

A shadow crossed his face and he looked slightly chastened. "I'm separated."

"What - since yesterday?"

He sighed, acknowledging the classic triteness of his own position. "For several months. I wouldn't be here otherwise, Julia."

"I'm not trying to take a moral high ground, please understand that, or even be nosey. Disregarding what my body wanted, my head foresaw clearly that we shouldn't have a relationship. Early on you even recognised it was unfair that you knew so much about me and could ask all the questions. So, to compensate, what d'you do? You go and tell me you have a stepmother! For God's sake! What kind of an intimate revelation is that - unless you're sleeping with her too."

Andres frowned. "You've totally distorted the context. We were talking childhoods, not sexual experiences, at the time."

"Huh - legal niceties! Lawyers can argue their way out of a paper bag..."

He looked mystified.

"Oh, it's an English metaphor. And I think I've got it wrong."

She gave an ironic smile and touched him lightly on the hand in a gesture suggesting some faint kind of truce.

"I'm going outside. It's so rarely sunny and I feel claustrophobic indoors."

"I must get dressed - I feel a fool in this dressing gown."

"Now there you're right," she said with a genuine smile.

Evening was approaching and the sun had dipped low in the sky, giving a mellow warmth, with light, feathery, good weather clouds hovering to the west. She would need to accustom herself to a different aspect. Until now it was natural to look downhill. Both house and garden were orientated that way. But now that Holidaylandia had sprung up to blight that view she would have to look north east, towards the Fuente and the grey limestone cliffs rearing to the mountain summit. It felt as unnatural as sitting backwards in a train. And it made her queasy, like lying in whole body traction with her feet raised high above her head.

Her days of solitude on the mountain were almost gone. Soon the new inhabitants would flock in; silence and birdsong would be replaced by the strains of TV and radio, DIY drilling, raucous conversations, revving cars, ringing phones and rows on the golf course about whose ball was in the rough. Enjoy it now, she told herself, suddenly noticing a new whining vibration from the recently erected electric cabling on the shimmering new pylons (Frances had paid more for bringing it underground, to preserve the landscape). She also noticed a new guard dog compound enclosed by high wire fencing to discourage vandalism. She had heard from Alex via Arturo, who had been installing rejas in the development, that a graffiti artist had sprawled "Vete Yanqui! Fuera de Espana! Fuera de Iraq!" all over the walls of the new clinic.

The noise of an approaching vehicle could be heard; it was Grant. Might he, she wondered with a flicker of consternation, be coming to blame *her* for the graffiti?

He roared up the final incline, almost crunching into her car. The loud rasping of the gravel as he applied his brakes set her teeth on edge. Could he, the grim thought suddenly struck her, possibly have been the other driver on that fateful night - the one who forced her mother off the road and didn't bother to stop?

She remembered, sickeningly, the smear of shredded rubber on the ramped gateway when he accelerated towards the go-kart piste, and the way he always used to throw his car like a rally driver into the mountain bends. He had always hated Frances. Did he know she was trying to mount a challenge to his Holidaylandia development, and happen to recognise her, a nervous woman driver on a steep, dark, lonely road? She felt her flesh crawl... Stop it Julia – you're paranoid because you don't know whom to trust. And that's because of Andres. And Colin. Grant, despite his obvious and manifold faults, would certainly have a troubled conscience over killing someone. Be patient, of course keep your eyes open, but don't go leaping to wild conclusions.

Grant appeared to have made the journey on the spur of the moment and in a hurry, judging by the way Veronika was still preparing herself to leave the house. She sat plucking eyebrows, applying lipstick, and brushing her hair all at the same time in the special swivel passenger seat.

"I hear an old English looney's admitted to the murder - what the hell's happening?"

"Colin's made a confession, yes, but like everyone else around here, he may - or may not - be telling the truth."

"He's the freaky gingerhead, am I right? He always looked a nutcase to me. Has he finally flipped completely?"

"I'm not qualified to judge sanity. Why does it bother you?"

"Why d'you think? Use your head Julia - this outfit's meant to be a retirement village, a safe bloody haven for old dodderers like him. How can they sleep easy with the knowledge there's a murderous crackpot on their doorstep?"

"But he won't be. Maybe not in the States, but here you still get jailed for murder. Unless it's made to look like a road accident, of course."

At that moment Andres emerged from the bathroom in his own clothes at last, his hair dripping wet from a lengthy shower. Grant's mind whirred visibly, whilst Veronika smiled with relief. It made Julia wonder whether she always accompanied Grant because she couldn't bear to miss out on his company, or because she didn't trust him.

"Hi there," Grant was determined to establish seniority. "I'm a good friend of Julia's from way back." He smiled affably, proud of his ease in speaking Castellano, "You are...?"

"Her lawyer."

"Pleased to meet you, man." His smile persisted, "Here's my card, we must have a chat some time."

He waited expectantly for Andres to return the compliment, but of course Andres had no cards, not having come equipped for that sort of business. He patted his empty pockets and raised his eyebrows in mock dismay, then offered Grant his hand.

"Andres Romero. My office is in Calle Ribero, quite close to yours."

Grant's eyes sparkled. This time he spoke gleefully in English, "Undress ha? Meaning, 'Get naked'? Well, I guess I don't need to tell you - Julia always was...only too ready for that!"

Julia could see Andres intuitively sensed mockery, but struggled for a moment over the exact meaning. Sufficient understanding presumably dawned, for his retaliation had appropriateness.

"Grant ha?" He then wisely switched to his own language, "Meaning 'subsidy' or 'handout'? Well, I guess I don't need to tell you - European funding's got tricky these days after all the corruption." He gave an intentionally idiotic smile and shrugged, "We Spanish are too greedy. We should learn your fine American sense of fairness and restraint."


Grant grunted. The Spaniards were too damn' cocky, just because they had conned so much money out of stupid foreigners and played the Euro gravy train so well. Perhaps this young punk was behind the wave of graffiti springing up not just here but on Villahermosa developments too. Lawyer my eye! If he *was* a lawyer he would have come by car, and there was none here apart from Julia's. Doubtless he had been showering off the tell-tale marks of his black graffiti paint!

# 24

Colin was feeling peckish by late afternoon. For lunch he had been served an insipid puchero with no meat that he could readily identify, a mere couple of chick peas hiding guiltily beneath the greasy surface of the vegetable broth, and one leaf that might or might not have been the dreaded 'penca'.

His neighbour Inocencio revered this plant as Lord of the vegetable patch. In fact all Spanish campesinos held it in high esteem, in those golden, olden days when they cared about the land before modern villas and money came to disconnect them from it. It had a pretty, silvery green colour and spikey leaves, looked like an artichoke leaf and probably was an artichoke leaf, but was no end of trouble to prepare. You had to thrash it, press it, and beat the living daylights out of it (this to get its evil juices flowing) then leave it overnight, or as long as two or three days under a fistful of salt, which did its best to absorb some of its caustic bitterness. Finally you cooked it, if you could stand the fumes of paint stripper that filled your kitchen, and ate it, if your mouth and tongue were doughty enough to survive its searing, corrosive acids. Anyway, Colin had always hated it as much if not more than okra, and even being in the same cell with it threatened to bring back his rash. He and the untouched bowl of puchero went into opposing corners of the cell like a couple of lightweight boxers between rounds, which as the cell on a generous estimate measured two by two and a half metres, was not far enough apart.

He pined for mu tea and oaten biscuits, which had taken over the half-past four refreshment slot from Twinings Earl Grey and a couple of custard creams, owing to his new Marte diet. He hoped he was not weakening so very soon. How long had he been locked up? Three hours, four maximum. Probably the first ones were the worst, as with most things. We are such creatures of habit we fall in with almost anything, given time. He had a vague idea man could survive for thirty days without food or drink, and much longer if he refused the food but kept on drinking. For him it was the food that posed the problem; if he ate standard prison fare his allergies would return with a vengeance. So if he refused to eat, would they force feed him or let him die? Would they demand the British Government intervene? Would they transfer him to a British jail, even, where the food might be many times worse?

Oh God! Shepherds' pie, baked beans, bangers and mash, frozen pizzas, wobbly custard, sickly trifle…

Colin groaned aloud and the officer on guard came swift of foot to check that he had not slit his throat or wrists with the cheap plastic knife from the Milagra Ferreteria.

After a time of inactivity Colin decided to explore the length and breadth - and height - of his cell. It had puke green walls and a lime green ceiling, with a grey flecked linoleum floor instead of the pretend marble cement tiles elsewhere in the building, presumably to deaden the noise should a rowdy prisoner decide to stamp in protest at his incarceration. It was normally inhabited by single nighters locked away for being drunk and disorderly, Colin presumed, hence the precaution of the puke greenness of the paint and the underlying stench of bleach that wafted up from the floor. He had to keep breathing in sustaining wafts from his crumpled djellaba, which retained a homely, slightly oily smell that was both warm and comforting, and brought to mind thoughts of Marte mingled with herds of wiry Moroccan sheep, which was odd since the thing was pure cotton and not even blended with wool. He dreaded to think how he would keep a handle on sanity once he was separated from the djellaba and togged out in prison garb, which he knew would happen once they transferred him to prison proper.

His cell had neither chair nor table, nothing but a narrow bed with a metal frame and a metal mesh base which sagged like a hammock, ensuring that prisoners became even more spineless due to slipped discs and lower back traumas. The sheets were grubby grey and the single coarse blanket dark charcoal with a thin maroon stripe reminiscent of his old school tie. There was one narrow window with bars, and even though the view would have been unutterably ugly anyway, it was blotted out by the kind of bubbly, swirly glass he associated with public toilets.

Lastly the ceiling, lime green to reflect biliously upon the prisoner. This boasted no cornicing, no artistic flourishes of plasterwork, just a dull, flat surface lit by a bare, dangling bulb. But, as he studied the charm of this bulb, as perfectly pear shaped as he felt Marte's torso and nether regions must surely be, he noticed the tiniest gleam of tinfoil protruding from its plastic disc.

Being considerably taller than the average drunk Spaniard he could just about reach the ceiling, if he stood on tiptoes plus the thrice folded thin foam pillow from the bed. Yes! He successfully grasped the tin foil and contents, and plucked them from their hidihole!

He hid them up his sleeve for a while, in case he was being subjected to CCTV footage and the viewer happened to have missed the moment of capture, only to have their interest aroused by a too blatant inspection of the prize. Its smell he recognised immediately, having breathed it in so often at Scotty's bar in the evenings, and recently sniffed it on Marte's clothing. It could only be hashish (or was it more hip to call it cannabis?). He waited a minute for the possible video camera to lose interest, then began to study it. It was a hard, dark brown nugget about the size of his thumb nail, and held against his nostril it smelt wanton and enticing. He had no doubt sampled its odour from his pram as a baby, if nursey ever left him parked somewhere too near the servants quarters, but that would have been superior Nepalese, he surmised, while this was doubtless low quality Moroccan.

What to do with it? Finders keepers and all that, he guessed it had been stashed there by some drunk who was too legless to be searched on the way in, and who had sobered up enough to realise he would therefore be searched on the way out, so had to offload it into the only cavity available. Then he dimly remembered a story circulating Scotty's years ago that some English painter had been locked up overnight for trying to mow down a policeman in his death trap of a car, but then they found the car had defective steering, so freed the man and impounded the car. Maybe this hash was his.

And if it were it must be dynamite stuff, for rumour had it the man had suffered artist's 'block' ever since, pining from the lack of its inspiration. Colin wondered if, like wine, it matured with age or, like basil, lost potency. If they ran art classes in Spanish jails, as they apparently did in England or Holland, he might enrol on one.

As a temporary measure he stashed it in the hem of his djellaba, where a missing stitch left an inviting gap. He knew it would have to be transferred to a bodily orifice before he went to jail and was dispossessed of his personals, but did not relish sitting on it and trying to keep a straight face while he talked to his lawyer.

Now he had it he was determined not to lose it. It was like a secret toy, a seed of rebellion. Moreover he hoped it might boost his cred with the other jailbirds, and failing that he could always eat it if the prison nosh was as dire as here. They might body search him on the way into jail, of course, but he had a hunch they would refrain if his rash returned, and if he ate his puchero it surely would!

His parents would die of shame of they could see him now he thought, suddenly morose again, so just as well that they were dead already.


Reggie waited in an inconspicuous spot where he could see the entrance to the Cuartel but would not be associated with it. Not because he felt humiliated on Colin's or his own behalf; it was purely a pragmatic desire to keep his distance from policemen. They were a nosey bunch, and could always find something illegal to pin on you. His car would fail its MOT on more counts than he had fingers, he knew that, and he was not officially resident anywhere on the globe and paid no taxes, so they might wonder about his little peach business cards and his NIF number and his lack of official input to the Spanish economy. He could say he was an artist if they asked, as they were expected to be bums. Or a writer like Otto. He probably looked more of a writer.

This lawyer was bound to be late. Six could easily mean seven. Reggie worried that he would recommend an insanity plea once he saw Colin, and quite frankly it was difficult to argue against it - since what sane person (apart from a hired assassin) would admit to a murder they hadn't done? .

Reggie knew Colin better than anyone, and even he was stymied by his confession. *Was* it actually possible his eccentric, oddball persona had been purposefully cultivated for twenty five years as a cover up? This struck him as hugely far fetched; more so even than bewitchment by Marte, which he so strongly espoused at Julia's at the height of his emotion but now seemed thoroughly implausible, especially when he imagined justifying it to a lawyer.


What would the lawyer be like? Julia's one, he suspected, might have been chosen more for appearance than sharp legal brain. Frances had cheerfully admitted choosing men for their bodies first and foremost, and yet she had a very decent brain inside that beautiful head of hers. It was only when she had lost her looks - or most of them - that she went for brain rather than body, which was where his own appeal resided he didn't mind admitting. What was it she had said? Ah yes, she had parodied the Dalai Lama's remark about his taste for women: "I like my women like my tea, hot and sweet," with "I like my men like my soup, hot and thick!"

Reggie suddenly composed his face to a suitable gravity and walked slowly across the road. The lawyer had come.


They held a brief pow-wow in the bar closest to the Cuartel, so that Reggie could give the man some background on Colin. It was not easy. Youngsters of thirty odd brought up in relaxed, modern Spain could scarcely be expected to comprehend the unsettling ingredients of Colonial parents with Victorian mores, ayahs, English public school, military training, Northern Ireland and then a kind of voluntary exile on the periphery of a hedonistic colony of hippies shedding their hang-ups in the midst of Franco's Spain!

Reggie hoped he painted a sympathetic picture of a gentle man battling bravely with inferiority complexes, of both neurological and emotional origin; a courteous nineteenth century man trapped in a mad twenty first century universe. But, as he waited anxiously alone while the lawyer saw Colin, he condemned his portrait as hopelessly deficient. He would have done better to allow the man to reach his own conclusions. He had most likely suggested not a deluded innocent but a classic psychopath.

It took nearly two hours for the lawyer to get to the bottom of Colin's story. Not the preamble that Reggie had tried, but the interlude of the murder itself. There were digressions, confusing scenes of Germanic sexual supremacy involving black buses and twelve vestal virgins that the lawyer found hard to fathom, occasioning him to question whether his knowledge of English was as good as he previously thought. But the night of the murder was a starkly straightforward tale…according to Colin.

He had hidden in Frances' garden, behind a lemon tree that had since died, where he had an unimpeded view of goings on inside. He often went there, as a matter of fact. That night there was a party, with festive supplies of drugs and raucous live music. The usual couple of German males hogged the bongos, banging out the same incessant beat for hours and drowning anything musical that might have emerged from another instrument. Anyway, this relentless bonging ate into Colin's skull, so that when he saw these two self-same Germans clamping Marte in a flagrantly sexual manoeuvre, he became enraged.

Eventually one of them came out to take a pee on the roots of the lemon tree (which subsequently died). His army training automatically surfaced, the old wartime refrain from his regimental anthem 'Never let a Boche piss on you' dinned in his ears, goading him on. As if robotically programmed, he emerged from behind the lemon tree whilst the man's hands were still buttoning up his flies (hippie types were against zips because metal sends depressant vibes to the organ area), and powered a closed fist like a canonball at the man's mouth. His two front teeth shot out, along with a quantity of severed lip and much blood, and the victim crumpled unconscious onto Colin's feet. Still enraged by the insensitive drumming, not to mention the overt sexuality and discourteous urination, Colin picked up his inert body and carried it to the lower terrace.

After a couple of calm minutes it began to groan, then started slowly struggling to its feet. But Colin had been well trained in hand to hand combat. Strike while the iron is hot, or in combat terms while your opponent remains disadvantaged. Before the man properly regained his bearings, when he had risen to his feet but still had his back to Colin and his trembling hands were gingerly exploring his battered mouth, Colin struck him with a powerful rabbit chop to the back of his neck and he fell like a stone. Half a minute later Colin threw the body contemptuously off the terrace wall, and had to step nimbly backwards to avoid being trapped in the avalanche of mud and stones that thundered after it. The party revellers did not even hear a thing, because the surviving German was still beating hell out of his drum and some Argentinian was now competing on the castanets.

"Do you believe him?" Reggie asked, stunned by the cold blooded violence that bore no resemblance to the Colin he knew. The Colin who trembled, itched, and was only ever competitive over crossword solutions.

"Not really. Well - I am not too sure. He tells it in realistic detail, also it corresponds exactly with the forensic evidence. He might have seen it happen, but not done it himself."

Reggie's eyebrows rose, "You mean, he's shielding someone?"

"Could be so." The lawyer sounded unconvinced, "But I think much more likely it's a kind of wish fulfilment, that he is identifying with 'the stronger man'."

"So what now?"

"There's no possibility of bail, I'm afraid. He will be sent to Alcantarilla prison until the trial. I'm sorry to say these things take time in my country. It could be in one - or as long as two - years time."


Reggie drove past Bar del Bigot for the second time that day and felt again an emotional wrench in the pit of his stomach. This time, however, he did not resist the lure of normality and the fact that it was after eight o'clock and well past the cusp of his drinking graph. When he entered the deafening silence from the cockatiel confirmed, as if further confirmation were needed, that something truly strange was afoot that day. The clientele, normally predominantly male, was at this hour of the evening exclusively so - apart, of course, from the indomitable Sra Bigot.

The surprise customer was Otto, for he had been mysteriously reclusive in the last few weeks owing to the dangerously seditious nature of his researches into the evil undercurrents controlling the world. Apparently he was now being stalked by secret service operatives, and unknown numbers of their most ruthless terminators had been sent to Spain to seek and destroy him. All because he had created an audacious website under an assumed female name, via which they sent him frequent rude and menacing messages (also under assumed names, *of course*, but he was not fooled by that). Perhaps he had chosen Bar del Bigot for his first public reappearance because any would-be assassins would have to contend first with the cockatiel - who was trained to spot spies, then Sra Bigot, who would defend his beard with her very life.


Otto seemed lost in reverie, until with a start he recognised Reggie, who would normally have poked him in the ribs in friendly fashion to announce his presence but was anxious to avoid being mistaken for an assassin.

"How's it going?" Reggie tried to seem cheerful.

"I come here because it is hell at home. Ze whole hut is upside down and inside out - you have no idea!" Otto grumbled. "Marte hunts for her marriage certificate, which is filed somewhere, but has not been seen in years. She is...possessed. It is a madhouse."

He drained his glass and held it out for Sra Bigot to replenish, and she did so with the girliest of giggles.

"Never knew she was married. Who was the lucky man?" Reggie tried to soft pedal the heavy sarcasm.

"Ach, some potter, I think. It was more a joke to annoy his parents than a serious alliance, she tells me. So, your friend has confessed?"

Reggie shrugged, "The world is mad. Even I, a confirmed cynic, can still be amazed. He's doing it for effect, I'm sure of that. Your partner Marte, didn't put him up to it did she?"

"Why should she do that? He was paying for his medicine, far as I know."

"Just a hunch." And one I'm loath to abandon so soon, Reggie thought to himself.


Despite the fact that he averaged two hours a day in Bar del Bigot, Reggie was a mid-morning customer and found the atmosphere now, at eight thirty in the evening, strangely unfamiliar. It was a time for the older men of the village to drink and while away the hour before dinner, and for the younger generation to subsidize Scotty's, or other similar haunts with modern music and an up-beat feel.  Youngsters like Emilio Fuster, Arturo el Ferrer and Juanito would not be seen dead in Bar del Bigot at this hour. Reggie looked balefully at the lined, wrinkled faces, the bald heads and berets, and computed the average age to be over sixty five. In fact it was more or less the entire displaced crowd from Bar de las Pensionistas. It made Sra Bigot seem positively young and skittish - as well she knew.


He studied Otto's profile. The man had evidently been spending too much time gazing at a computer screen, judging by the stronger lenses in the glasses that hung on chains at his neck, and the protruding dome of his forehead that bulged with brains - or was already the breeding ground of a malignant tumour. Reggie was growing concerned about his own sanity, if the truth be told. For, instead of looking at people and imagining them in utterly different settings (such as transposing El Bigot into a seventeenth century buccaneer), which he was previously inclined to do with men; or imagining them naked, which he was prone to do with the younger women, he had lately begun to picture them as skeletons. It made him aware how similar all humans were in that most basic state. He knew experts *pretended* to reconstruct faces onto skulls because he had seen it done on TV, but there was no proof their reconstructions were accurate. His new game was distinctly morbid, he knew, and he ardently wished he could shrug off the whole perverse preoccupation with death.

Otto's thoughts had wandered into similar territory, if indeed they ever centred on life more than death, for he suddenly leaned over and hoarsely whispered in Reggie's ear.

"Ve are ruled by ze Skull and Bones fraternity, did you know?"

"Wasn't aware, I'm afraid. How d'you get your internet access with Marte's phone bill arrears still unpaid?" (Reggie had been cut off three months' back.)

"Ach, so simple. I said I recently bought ze house and they wrote off the old debt. Ze only trouble is I had to give my real name as subscriber."

"Your real name's a problem?"

"Of course. I write under a pseudonym, or it's too dangerous. You must surely know what General Douglas McArthur once said: 'In war, news you suppress, all ze rest is propaganda'. Ha! Remember I am a History Professor, so I have studied lies closely all my life. We are perhaps now being fed more lies than ever before."

"Oh I'm utterly in agreement there. D'you know I..." but he got no further, for Otto suddenly gripped his arm with iron pincerlike force and this time breathed more quietly even than a whisper into his ear. "If you want your credulity stretched on one score, my friend, meet me tonight at 10.30 outside ze Carniceria Muntaneta. And tell no-one, OK?"

"OK," agreed Reggie, with a frisson of alarm, but an even more compelling surge of curiosity.


However, when he stood conspicuously in the dappled moonlight at 10.30, leaning as nonchalantly as was possible against the stone wall on the opposite side of the road, facing the Carniceria doorway, he felt stupidly conspicuous - like a naïve teenager tricked into a fake date, or a prostitute touting for business in the wrong street, instead of a co-conspirator of Otto's. It was extraordinary how jumpy one became in the darkness of night and under the mysterious shadowplay of moon and flitting clouds, because this street was as mundane as could be in daylight. Then it was filled with the sickly smell of freshly slaughtered flesh from the Carniceria, toned down by bunches of dried herbs hanging off the ceiling: rosemary, thyme, sage and tarragon, which if you bought more than two kilos of meat were freely gifted. He consulted his watch dispiritedly. Already it was fifteen minutes past the allotted time. He decided to wait for five more, then wander despondently home.

Someone was coming his way; he could hear footsteps ascending the street at right angles to his. But they didn't sound like Otto's. He began to walk towards them, for it would be normal enough to be encountered taking an evening stroll, but questionable to be found hanging about, waiting at a prearranged spot.

Just before they drew level the man stopped in his stride and spoke quietly. "Ven comigo hombre."

Reggie recognised the voice but could not put a name to it; the man was a friend of Eulogio and Celestino, but whether he was party to some crazy prank of Otto's, or engaged in some unrelated form of chicanery that was coincidentally taking place on the same night, Reggie could not decide. He wracked his brains as he obediently followed the man; was today perhaps the Fiesta de Las Bromas? Or could it be a rehearsal for the Fiesta de los Moros y Cristianos, which took place every June, and he was unwittingly being auditioned for the role of traitor? Or was there perchance a dimwit who fell as easily as an innocent babe into enemy hands? Did he, under torture, reveal the secrets of the town's defences, or admit there weren't any so it could be taken ever so simply by riding into the plaza on a piebald mare with a barrel of wine strapped to the saddle, and hoisting a flag onto the church tower? (That's what occurred every Fiesta).

Suddenly the man disappeared into an open doorway. Reggie, heart in mouth, followed suit. The downstairs hallway was dimly lit and empty of furniture as far as he could see, although the polished sheen of the tiled floor reflected milkily what little light there was, and Reggie caught sight of an umbrella stand and a vase of artificial flowers at the base of the staircase. A conversation in low voices floated down from above, either from the first or top floor which was a single attic room in the peak of the roof; Reggie knew the layout of these houses perfectly because he lived in one himself.

They climbed the stairs, Reggie behind but automatically falling into step with his guide so that their legs moved in perfect synchronisation. It was more than uncanny.

At the crest of the staircase his guide turned into the back room, which overlooked the small courtyard garden at the rear. A pleasant smell of some flowering shrub breezed in through an open window, but otherwise the room was dusty and smelt of fresh plaster and wet cement, so was obviously undergoing renovation of sorts. Reggie tried to silence his mind and simply be a passenger on this weird journey, for he was not by nature bold or reckless. On the contrary he was singularly adept at leading a placid, uneventful life without ever getting bored.

He had to judge the room mainly by smell because here again the light was dim, its source a small camping gaslight on the mantelpiece above the bricked in fireplace which gave off a bluish light and a mournful hissing sound. The electricity had been turned off due to the renovation work, Reggie assumed. A huddle of men stood near the bricked in fireplace, and instantly recognisable towering a head taller than the rest was Otto.  Florentino and Eulogio were also there, and three others whom Reggie knew by sight but not by name, although he thought the only youngster was Diego (del Yeso).

Otto looked up as the newcomers came in, raising his arm in a mock salute.

"So, you made it here my friend. I'm glad. Perhaps now you will no longer take me for a liar."

Reggie nodded in greeting, not in response to his words; as yet he had seen nothing to corroborate or disprove any of Otto's stories. He waited patiently for more revelations. Otto steered him to the left of the defunct fireplace, the flat of his hand pressed against Reggie's back, and gestured up at an alcove alongside the chimney breast which had recently hosted a large glass cabinet. This now rested against the far wall. Reggie peered into the shadowy recess. At first he saw nothing but the pitted surface of plasterwork that someone had been busily demolishing. Then, gradually, his eyes adjusted to the meagre light, and he startled at a shrunken body draped in bedraggled clothes, rather like the strange mummified corpses he had once seen when a tourist in the catacombs of a Sicilian monastery. They made a profound impression on him at the time, because so many were incongruously dressed in cloth caps and striped pyjamas because their relatives were too stingy to donate suits.

"Cal vivo (quicklime)," Otto announced, "zat is what they used to preserve ze body so it didn't decay and smell. Amazing, no?"

"Absolutely. But who are we looking at? A medieval man?"

Reggie shivered at the thought of life and death in those days, imagining the man had maybe died from starvation whilst hiding from the Inquisition, or perhaps from the plague whose germs would be sterilised by the causticity of the lime. Or had the poor guy been thrown into quicklime whilst still alive as punishment for some heinous crime?

"Zis is – or voz – we think, Eulogio's eldest brother, Sebastian. Three of the brothers went missing in '37, but Eulgio thinks this is Sebastian because in the pocket of his trousers we found the key to zeir house. Sebastian was always the reliable one who kept ze key!"

Reggie experienced a desire to sit down, but as there was no chair he merely swayed a little, then took a firmer grip on himself. Eulogio appeared

252

extraordinarily composed, Reggie felt. His face was emotionless, as if this were an everyday occurrence, although he did clutch the old house key as though it gave unique access to a mighty treasure previously lost to mankind. Reggie felt he should say something, so he patted him lightly on the shoulder and muttered in his best formal Spanish,

"Please accept my condolences."

Eulogio slapped his thighs and guffawed, but not so loudly as to attract unwelcome attention from the neighbouring houses. "Cojones!" he said, and a few other choice expletives, which Reggie took to mean that formality was the wrong register, quite apart from it being a bit too late for condolences. The grieving and the bitterness had been gone through sixty seven years ago.

"Vamos. We'll bury him now in the proper place." Eulogio let Reggie know he was now included in their little band by laying a large, commanding paw on his shoulder.


And so it was that roughly ten minutes later a strange procession wandered quietly - but feigning casualness should there be a chance observer - up the steep path beyond the church, towards the cemetery gates. The moon was bright enough to obviate the need for a torch, but the moving shadows they cast as they climbed were distinctly spooky. No-one spoke, and Reggie wondered once or twice what would happen if the Guardia should arrive. He was particularly jumpy over the difficult stage of scaling the iron gates of the cemetery, which were always locked at night. He assumed someone would invent a plausible story to explain the venture, and surely no outsider would ever expect that the hessian sack slung over Eulogio's shoulder contained his dead brother's body. Even if they did insist on inspecting the sack, Reggie comforted himself, they would not know what to make of it. It did not look human; more like a large glove puppet, even a dead rabbit if the inspection was cursory, or perhaps a scarecrow that Eulogio had decided to stake in the ground of the cemetery, to ward off the crows.


Once his nervousness about the Guardia subsided he began to puzzle over exactly where they were heading. Eulogio was renowned for his anti-religious beliefs and all his brothers were Communists, so why were they wandering through a Roman Catholic cemetery as if it were home from home? The place was bristling with religious symbols, everywhere you turned you brushed against a statue of the Virgin Mary or ripped your shirt on a crown of thorns. How could Eulogio tolerate it as an ultimate sanctuary? And yet, Reggie had to admit, where else in Spain was the place for the dead? Maybe major cities had facilities for other religions, or for atheists, but not here in this mountain village.

Even in the murky moonlight he recognised their whereabouts. They were uncomfortably close to Frances' tomb, and with each stride closer. He counted the men, although he knew perfectly well there were six. Reggie, non-religious and unbelieving, silently prayed he would not have to take them on if they decided to stuff Sebastian alongside Frances. Her tomb would, after all, be easiest to access being the most recent (the cement would barely have hardened in the wet winter months). Also, likewise a non-believer, she would be considered a suitable companion. Reggie fervently vowed he would protect her in her solitude, despite his slim chances of overcoming such superior forces. He was immensely relieved when the procession continued past her tomb, Eulogio merely branching off the path momentarily to retrieve the pick-axe.

Two blocks further on and they finally came to a halt. Eulogio smashed through a section of the brick façade of a large, imposing tomb four storeys high, which must belong to his family because its carvings were overtly pagan. Olive branches entwined with barley sheaves, and all around them bunches of grapes and flocks of turtle doves were carved in relief on the stone lintel capping the structure, but Reggie only glanced briefly at them because mostly he kept a nervous watch on their rear. He feared the horrendous noise of Eulogio's banging, which echoed alarmingly in the quiet of the night, might summon hordes of watchmen.

At last there was a sufficient gap to slide the pathetically small remains of Sebastian unceremoniously through, and apart from this thin slit nothing betrayed what they had done, so even if the villagers came now they could pretend perfect innocence. Claim they were hunting for snails, setting traps for marauding rabbits, or even paying tribute to Frances at the exact hour of her death, which it probably was if you took into account the change from winter to summer time.

Some crossed themselves, even Eulogio dipped his head and performed the ghost of a genuflection towards the tomb. Then, as silently as they had come, they descended the path with the moon behind them, trampling on their own shadows.

"Al bar" grunted Eulogio.

# 25

Marte sat on her living room floor, encircled, like the central pivot of a clock, by twelve gigantic piles of papers which were all that remained of the hoardings of her life. It was actually just as well she had burnt so much each winter, otherwise she would have too much to trawl through.

Her father had been so organised, so meticulous. He even had a cut-out replica shape of his moustache reproduced onto a stiff sheet of transparent plastic, and would hold this to his face to trim away stray hairs that fell outside the rigid contours of the cut-out. She had despised his fastidiousness then, yet now she longed for the orderliness of his neatly arranged bureau, with all life's vital documents folded into different drawers, the cataloguing instructions printed and mounted in a nearby picture frame.

She knew the marriage certificate had travelled to Spain originally. She had even set eyes on it in the last four years, because she remembered deeply admiring the flourish to her signature of that long ago era, and had spent half an hour reproducing it perfectly in her current sketch pad. She still had the page, and planned to sign her new healing product range with the same calligraphic artistry. How was it that Otto, with all his chaotic thoughts, multiple researches and illogical ideas, managed to find immediate printed proof of whatever crazy fact he wanted to impress her with from inside his mad upside-down work cubicle? It was grossly unfair...

As was her current position vis-à-vis the detective squad. On one hand it was flattering they assumed the two men in her life, Manfred and Tomas, had been bitter love rivals. But on the other, it was embarrassing to be known to have had a silly, sham marriage, and then to have run to Manfred simply because Tomas could not repair his van.

She thought back to the day that sealed their 'divorce' (not a real divorce, on paper, because she still seemed to be legally married to him, despite the fact that that particular paper was the missing one!) In the context of those days her behaviour was not outrageous. It was only *now*, and especially in the eyes of State Police, that it appeared cruel and immoral. Yes, she had left poor Tomas sweating under the chassis, struggling with a heavy wrench and spanner, tools his emaciated vegan physique was unfit for, to walk to the nearest village in hope of finding a real mechanic, and even, with luck, an actual garage with a tow-truck. But what was unfair about that?

The bar was *always* the best source of such information, so naturally - not selfishly as some later claimed - she headed for the bar. Once there her fate was sealed; she had mulled it over many times in order to arm herself against a charge of unkindness, but really she had no choice. Captivated as soon as she saw the bronzed back and long blond locks of Manfred, the more enraptured when he turned and smiled. She was as helpless in the grip of fate as any heroine in a Greek tragedy. She forgot all about poor Tomas and his wrenches, never asked about a garage and least of all a mechanic, because vans and journeys to Morocco suddenly lost all appeal. Her life became focused exclusively and intensely on one man, one spot, and one brief moment in time.

She tried hard to remember Tomas, her husband. At the time he had faded quickly from her thoughts, but she now realised that at some point on that fateful day he must have understood she would not be coming back, with or without help. There followed a gap of several days, perhaps a week, in which she rode deliriously on the wave of her infatuation with Manfred and was otherwise oblivious. Then they returned to normal social circulation and descended to buy bread and vegetables in the village, remembering their bodies needed food as well as sex. On one such foray they bumped into Tomas who had got his van working again, although only with the most dismal, tell-tale clanging sounds - like the tolling of a funeral bell - coming from its rear axle. He greeted her with a wan smile and a friendly pat, even giving Manfred a brotherly strike of the hand as if they were old college mates. That was the custom in those days; no clinging, no possessiveness, everyone trying their damnedest to live fully in the here and now. Optimism and positive mantras. It was difficult for anyone not immersed in that culture to understand.

Thus Tomas appeared to have put their relationship, journey plans and brief marriage sensibly behind him. They had only got married to confound his parents, who objected to Marte when she moved in with him encouraged him to give up both meat and thinking like them (narrowly). Tomas had definitely stayed around Milagra for a while, because she had overheard the dull knocking sounds echoing round the mountains as his van struggled up hills, and sometimes run into him at social events, like parties, paellas, musical happenings, hot tub conventions and what would now be called all night raves. He had never looked cheerful even at the best of times, and his anaemic, prematurely lined face looked no more miserable after she left him than when they were together. So why did people assume she treated him unpardonably cruelly?

She had done no more than many others did at that time; swap partners, move on. Frances did that more than anyone, Gott in Himmel!

One day, however, she woke up to the realisation that he must have gone, since she no longer heard the discomfort of his van or saw his peaky face. Either he had carried out their original plan and headed for Morocco, or had returned to Germany. The latter was more likely, since he lacked the resolve to try new horizons on his own and had anyway told Horst, the raku potter, that he was feeling homesick.

Now, however, she was confused, even deeply perturbed. Those detectives had not spelt things out precisely or added up the figures they threw at her, but behind their steady questioning she could glimpse at a possible, terrible truth. She would not accept it yet, so she simply pondered the known specifics - if she had understood them right with her not-so-perfect Spanish. The known facts were: Tomas her husband had been in Milagra for a time during 1978, as had her lover Manfred. Also in 1978 (or was it 1979?) Manfred Schneider had been reported missing by his parents. The last official trace of him was when he collected the money they sent him to a named bank in Villahermosa. This money was sent to fund his return journey, but in fact spent on the strip of land she was now sitting on, as *she* knew (though *they* did not). There had been no subsequent trace of him; his passport had lapsed, his empty bank account had lain dormant, and no-one had used his National Insurance number or ID since that time. Thus his name and details entered the missing persons file, and had remained there ever since.

However *she* knew he was with her (fully and passionately) for six months after collecting that money, during which time they cobbled together phase one of her mountain hut (now rather pompously called the salon, where she was now sitting). They had lived in soporific bliss until he suddenly and somewhat inexplicably became caught up in the cult fever and abruptly declared he was off to Poona with all the other lightning converts. Although she agreed she might follow, she dithered for months before emerging from her period of infatuation with the realisation she despised the false religious movement and hated the colour orange too heartily to do so.

He sent two postcards from Poona proudly announcing his new name: Swami Dayan Yogi. She had to write it down for the detectives, one of whom spluttered - so maybe this new lead would enable them to trace him. She knew he had travelled to the States and then eventually returned to Germany, and that he was definitely still alive in 1988, for she could swear the man she slept with in Germany so that Lise was born nine months later was the same man she fell in love with. The man she knew as Manfred Schneider. Or *could* she? He was the same, yet *not* the same, for no way was he as Godlike or as beautiful. Mein Gott, what a horrible possibility...!

Tomas, on the other hand, *had* disappeared from sight and from Milagra during 1978, yet he was never reported missing, either then or subsequently! She would have imagined that with his parents, so ultra conservative and so very correct, his absence would have been noticed, and the police informed. Since he was never declared missing, surely she could safely assume that he had indeed returned to the bosom of his family and been forgiven for marrying - against their wishes - a lower middle class slut whose Deutsch was not sufficiently 'Hoch'?

What had disturbed her was the eager way the detectives lent forward when she wrote down Tomas' name, as if they were bursting to check him out. And their ill-controlled anger when she could not remember the spelling (due to the silly jokes) and how they threatened her with something - a subpoena was it? - meaning she *had* to produce her marriage certificate within two days or else... She resented their contempt, their chauvinism - purely because of a frivolous marriage to a husband she walked out on then lost, and whose name she could not spell properly. They then had the impertinance to demand if he was rich! Idiots! - If she married him for his money, why would she have left him so quickly, and without any alimony?

Marte looked up from her ruminations and to see the sun already hugging the horizon. The entire day had ebbed away. She would have taken comfort from Otto's presence, but today of all days he had finally gone out. What had he said? Some nonsense about his bandolero, and the right day for burying him. Such nonsense.

She shivered. She did not want to spend the evening alone. Lise had gone to Montejoven as usual so there was no-one to distract her from her nagging fears. From the beginning, when she first heard the news, she remembered praying that the skeleton was not a German. Now she prayed with a more intense fervour. And after praying she made the decision not to stay alone. She had to talk with that lawyer of Julia's, however sniffy he pretended to be, and however exclusive Julia attempted to keep him.

To her consternation she found the place deserted. Julia's car had gone and the house was locked. Luckily she had more than a passing knowledge of that house, for Frances may have been fierce and formidable but at least she had some hippie principles, and always left a key hidden in a gnarled cleft of the carob tree for visitors who came while she was out. She was possessive only about that silly, sacred relationship with Julia's father, but not about her property. Marthe was delighted to find the key still there, although she had to bang it on a stone to remove the lumpy crustaceons of rust before it would let her in.

There was something about other people's possessions, particularly houses and household paraphernalia, that brought out the communist in Marthe. She had always enjoyed mocking those who believed their belongings were private property, especially the parents of boyfriends who clung to this capitalist creed. They made ridiculous attempts to control her access to their property by means of formal invitations, times it was deemed impolite to phone, and rooms they egotistically considered their own personal domain: larders, fridges, food cupboards and their bedroom, their bathroom. The English were super-possessive; 'My house is my castle' was their modus operandi.

Marte's spirits rose at the prospect of inspecting and sampling Julia's toiletries. She was no snoop, papers and documentary secrets had no lure at all, she simply enjoyed trawling through what others ate and did to their bodies, a sort of sweeping sensual probe. Not being pressingly hungry she bypassed the kitchen and went straight to the bathroom. However she had barely sat on the bidet and begun applying moisturiser when she heard the danger sound of a car engine, and had to replace all the bottles and tubes in a frantic, scrabbling hurry. She sensibly locked the bathroom door, then ran the tap and flushed the toilet to create a diversionary noise.

Perfect timing. When voices and footsteps entered the house she emerged from the bathroom feeling well refreshed. Her body was saturated in creams, a confusing kaleidoscope of perfume oils had been dabbed behind her ears, and a bikini line wax kit was hidden in her handbag for later experimentation (a fair exchange since she had gifted Julia plenty of medicines). She was curious to see how indignant Julia might be, and whether she had anything of a sharing nature.

In the event Julia registered no surprise; it had quite slipped Marte's mind that her old Mercedes was parked in the driveway.

"Where's your lawyer?" Marte's disappointment was audible.

"Coming with Alex, *if* they can start his car."

"Thanks God," she said.

"More trouble?" Julia did not sound especially sympathetic.

"Yah. It got worse from thinking. I did not articulate it well when I told him it before."

A coughing, spluttering engine struggled into the driveway, reminding Marte uncomfortably of the complaints cars made in Tomas' hands. But it was not Tomas' ghost, nor caused by the irregular flow of petrol as Julia suspected, but by Alex at the wheel having mastered the steering but not the skill of changing to a lower gear. When Andres was within earshot Marte loudly inquired,

"Do you still mind, Julia, if I explain my problems to Andres?"

"It's not up to me - ask him yourself."

Her tone reminded Marte of the delightful interactive tensions of threesomes. She had not experimented in a long while, but remembered they could be surprisingly fulfilling.

"So" she said, "vot happens if I cannot find zis certificate?"

"You can be charged with 'Failure to provide a document', - a minor offence, or Obstruction of Justice, which is much more serious."

"But how am I being obstructive?" she wailed, "I'm trying my best to find it!"

Andres shrugged, "That's how it is. The law isn't based on kindness."

"Madre mia! And all zis time *you* were the little worrier, Julia. 'Zis skeleton is on my doorstep', 'Oh dearie me, zey vill be blaming Frances', 'I must have my own lawyer all to myself'… She gave Julia an accusatory look.

"Right now Colin's in the worst position," Julia felt irritated by Marte's deliberate belittlement of her fears. "And it's not over yet, for any of us," and she left to make Alex and Marco something to eat.

Marte studied Andres appraisingly. He was certainly attractive; for her part she knew she disturbed him but not why. Age, experience, cunning, power, - it could be all or any of them.

Silence, she concluded, would be her best tactic. Especially since her Spanish was so inferior to Julia's. If they sat in silence, he would be the one who had to break it.

"Julia said you were an old friend of her mother's," he eventually remarked, and Marte considered he placed undue emphasis on 'old'.

She snorted, "You think she had friends?! Huh, she hated everyone! Men more than women. If Julia were Frances, you would be gone already." She lowered her voice in case Julia was listening from the kitchen, "The more men turned her on, the quicker they got thrown out!"

He did not flinch. "At least she had the good sense *not* to get married."

Ach so, he was sly as well as pretty, but she quickly recovered from the rebuff. There was virtually nothing relative to a person's body that she did not notice, and her hawk eyes picked out the faintest change in gradation of skin colour on his ring finger which indicated that, until recently, a wedding ring had nestled there.

She stared at it as she replied, "I see I'm not alone in making zat mistake."

260

She studied him acutely, and sure enough noticed a faint shadow flit across his face. Momentarily she revelled in the extra kudos of outwitting a lawyer.

"Tell me," she continued, "zis Colin, who has confessed to ze murder, how long must he wait for his trial?"

"One to two years. But," this time she felt his eyes probing her face, "other evidence may yet disprove his account. They have new leads to follow now."

"Tomas and Swam…Manfred, you mean?" She gasped in spite of herself.

He nodded. "If you spelt their names halfway correctly, I imagine they'll have traced them by now…*if* they're alive."

She bit her lip, unable to retain her upperhand. "Gott, I hope they are."

Andres said nothing, but she knew what he was thinking.


Julia immersed herself in the domestic trivia of preparing supper, aware that Andres had still not gone, even though Marte's noisy departure ought to have prompted him. Maybe he was simply waiting for her ill-tempered, ungrateful truculence to pass, so they could part on affable terms and his conscience remain serene. And that would be a fair resolution, she did admit.

Watching him from the kitchen, Marco happily squirming onto his lap, witnessing his tactile closeness to her children, gave her a strange physical feeling. The problem is me, she thought, not him. He is perfectly natural. I'm the one whose reactions are strange and contradictory, who wants and doesn't want, who is afraid because of past experiences and preconceptions, who doesn't want a relationship for fear of its addictive qualities that suck me in.

After supper Alex and Marco easily persuaded Andres, whose reluctance was patently pretence, into watching an English comedy. She could hear their laughter bursting in unison from the upstairs gallery, and it isolated her all the more in her withdrawn and private pain. As she sat alone, watching the oncoming darkness, she felt tears flow down her cheeks. Damn you Andres, she thought. I don't want to be emotional, I'm sick of feeling emotional. There was no need to meddle, I was fine as I was. I wanted to bury my mother and go back to England to get on with my life. You should never have interfered.

"Julia!" Marco shrieked. "Come on! It's getting to your favourite bit!"

"OK. I'm coming," her voice was unsteady.

She splashed cold water on her face before joining them, and recovered enough to laugh on cue when the moment came, so that a lighter atmosphere reigned until the boys went to bed.

When she emerged from the boys' bedrooms Andres was in her mother's studio, fingering the ancient pottery fragments that had sat gathering dust for years.

"They're just the surplus pieces, left over after she'd completed an amphora. She was meant to send them back."

"Such an unusual thing to spend your life on - but someone has to do it, or ancient cultures are forgotten." He smiled wistfully "It's happening here. The past is a dirty word - except for a minority of aficionados."

"Is it greed or stupidity? It was one of the reasons my mother hated Grant, the one who came this afternoon. He despises the past; 'Invest in the Future'. - That's why Holidaylandia looks like Florida, not Spain."

"You slept with him, didn't you?"

She sighed. "Yes. Long ago. But it's none of your business - you notice I'm not asking about your past?"

"I know. Please don't be tense, Julia. It could be simple, only you won't let it be."

"Maybe it *should* be simple, but for me it isn't. After watching my mother suffering and withering away underneath all her bravado, am I ever likely to find emotional attachments simple?"


She had been intentionally keeping her distance, out of his reach, but in a moment of unpreparedness as they were looking out at the blaze of cheap street lights demarcating the grid pattern of Holidaylandia, she felt his hand caress her hair and she froze. Was she a cat, to purr at his mere touch?

"I *am* going to go," he said, "in a minute or two. I know you don't want me to stay. Will you be all right on your own?"

She frowned, "What a strange question. I've been more or less 'all right' on my own my entire life. Why should I suddenly go to pieces now?"

"You deliberately misunderstand me. D'you want me on my knees to beg forgiveness?"

She smiled, faintly, "I don't blame you for last night. It went far rather fast, that's all. We hadn't had any physical contact whatsoever before, and...well I responded strongly, I'll admit that. It's thrown me off balance, along with feeling very tired."

"I did mean to get here before nine," he said gently. "I wish I had."


They walked together down the driveway towards his car. In the past this spot, shaded by a tall mountain ash that was just coming into leaf, had felt peaceful under the soft moonlight but not any more; she found she had to shield her eyes from the blue neon glare of the arc lights on the perimeter of Holidaylandia. Perhaps they had been mounted to discourage the grafitti artist. Andres opened the driver's door and switched on the engine, which spluttered and choked uncomfortably, then eased into a steady throbbing. He promptly switched it off, whereupon the Holidaylandia guard dogs set up a furious volley of barking, gnashing their teeth and rattling their chains.

"Thought I should check I wasn't stranded again," he smiled. Then he held her against him so she felt the rise and fall of his chest and the steady beating of his heart, and smelt the warmth of his neck and hair. "I'll phone you," he said.

Then suddenly he had gone, in barely the blink of an eye. She watched his crimson tail-lights descending the track, and heard the barking rise to a crescendo of aggression as he accelerated past the dogs' compound.

# 26

Julia slept fitfully. She had been expecting her physical exhaustion to gift her a deep and dreamless sleep, but her thoughts tossed and turned.

They replayed images of Andres: with a piratical earring at Carocaballo; in his legal gown in the Palacio de Justicia; at the Cuartel, subtly controlling the questioning; diving - a mad goalie in a child's dressing gown; and finally naked in her bed. But it was incomplete. What of the Andres she did not know? His private life in Villahermosa, the married Andres with a wife lurking in the shadows of an impermanent separation, the lawyer in a perfect position to get to know all the intimate details of clients' lives without revealing any of his own.

She realised he had held up a oneway mirror, one that reflected her childhood in Milagra and her relationship with Frances, yet nothing of himself. And, from the recent twists in the investigation, it now seemed she could have sidestepped her way adequately through the legal hoops without a lawyer, now that the finger of suspicion was less directed at Frances. Perhaps she had unburdened her soul for no reason.

And had she been too passionate? Her body might be strong in a tensile sense, but it was also weak. She was a parasitic plant, a convulvulus or creeper. She would cling to the warmth of another's body and feel bereft without it. She missed his physical presence. Was that why Frances got herself angry enough to immediately throw men out, before the insidious filaments of connection began to fuse? Was she crazy enough to preserve her one original love by cutting adrift any subsequent threads that threatened to attach her?

It was a mistake trying to sleep in the bed they had shared without first changing the sheets. If she had replaced them it would be *her* bed once more. Instead, she was conscious of lying on 'his' side, aware of a slight depression in the pillow where his head had lain. Almost angrily, she pluffed it up so that his imprint vanished.

It seemed ironic that Andres - prior to yesterday - had given her such a comforting sense of security. He had been her protection against potential abuse of her legal rights, and had seemed so steady and reliable. Now he could not *be* her lawyer, not any more. If, for instance, despite the interventions of Colin and the mystery of Manfred being 'missing', her DNA sample positively identified the skeleton as her father, he could no longer represent her because he was compromised.

What could have prompted him to come so late? Had the Cuartel interview excited him? Four detectives against her, was that it? Or had he really wanted his wife, but per their separation agreement she was not always available at his beck and call?

Another voice derided her for attributing the motivating desire to him. Oh she knew exactly what interpretation Marco's dad would have. In his version *she* was the manipulator. She would have intrigued him with her stories and her confidences, thus setting the trap. The well-placed bait would be the strategically timed phone call to thank him, as good as an invitation. Then of course she had danced and flaunted her body in front of his nose (knowing he was waiting outside), and then spiced it further with a show of rage. 'You know how hot you get after a quarrel, Julia,' she could hear his voice in her ear, 'a good row really turns you on.' Flouncing off to bed was just an excuse to waggle her bottom in his face, the ultimate invitation to join her upstairs. Andres had merely fallen into her trap, and in such a dumb way he had left himself open to her favourite strategy - the guilt trip afterwards!

She fell asleep eventually and did not wake until the sun was already high above the mountain ridge. On her way downstairs the phone rang. She ran towards it, then stopped; shouldn't she just let it ring? It must be Andres... Taking a deep breath she reluctantly picked it up.

"It's Reggie. Sorry to bother you yet again Julia, but...I need to talk to someone."

"Well, I feel more 'anyone' than 'someone' - but you can talk to me."

Reggie laughed. "Is now OK? You're not...er...tied up are you?"

"No, no. Talk away."

"It isn't something I want to commit to the phone."

She presumed it related to Colin. A favour no doubt; feeding a marmalade cat or watering pansies. She would willingly do a favour for Reggie, but she hoped it would not involve too close a contact with Colin's house since she had never found him physically savoury. She knew it was an unchivalrous attitude but it originated from her childhood and his kleptomania over her mother's knickers. She wondered idly if he still had any stashed away in a box in his attic. She knew he had a cleaning lady; surely he couldn't be crazy enough to still keep them under his bed!

However Reggie's tale was of the night's adventures laying Sebastian to rest. She, like Reggie, had consigned Otto's bandolero anecdotes to the realms of fantasy, even though she knew he conducted careful research into the historical aspects of the Civil War. He must surely have had a tip-off for advance knowledge of the body's whereabouts could only come from a personal source. The only thing Otto got wrong previously was exactly which wall his bandolero was buried in, she realised that now.

Sebastian must have been suspected of double dealing, and murdered by his own brothers. She shivered. Had Eulogio hid the secret all his life? What must it be like to live through a Civil War, where everything is a matter of life and death? In a sense we are living in a situation not so unlike Civil War now, she thought, owing to the notion that opposition to the party in power is treachery; 'You're either with us or against us.' What a totalitarian premise!


She was right about Reggie requesting a favour. It was not caring for Colin's domestic world, however, but something much grimmer: he wanted her to go to Alcantarilla prison. Colin was being transfered there 'as we speak.'

"I know it's a big ask," he said sheepishly, "but I'm an awful coward when it comes to entering prison gates. Your company would ease the pain immensely. It's a high security jail, with the most vicious and violent, and they'll make mincemeat of Colin if they suspect he's gay. If I turn up alone that'll be the assumption. But a glimpse of you might save his bacon."

She grimaced. "It's the last thing in the world I want to do, and for anyone else I'd certainly say no. However, I owe you, just let me arrange something for Alex and Marco... Oh God, you're not planning to pass them off as Colin's kids?"

"Not a bad idea," he considered, "we'll keep it in reserve for later."

"Reggie I'll go tomorrow. But not a second time."

"OK, OK." He looked wistfully out the window, "Perhaps he'll come to his senses and retract that stupid confession. Or other evidence will emerge so there'll be no second time - even for me."


The day passed, somehow or other. Thoughts of Andres hung in the air, but she knew that whatever had been between them was so fleeting that the tinge of sadness she felt now would quickly fade. It was highly unlikely he would ever phone, unless to pass on the DNA results. 'I'll phone you' was usually code for 'Don't you be the one to contact me.'

Two weeks ago she would have felt blessed to be in her current position - the first interview over and Frances no longer the prime suspect. But instead of celebrating her sense of release she felt a new sense of dread - of the grimness of prison. She had a hunch Reggie had mainly asked her because her car, which she had bought secondhand from the money Frances left in their joint account, was a little more roadworthy than his.


She consulted Alex about the following day.

"I don't want Lise here," he said firmly, "nor to go to Marte's. She'll only rope us into hunting for her certificate."

"Her deadline expires tomorrow anyway," Julia assured him, wondering at his vehemence about Lise. But since Alex had always denied any special feelings for Lise she could not probe.

"How about Andres, or Grant again?" Marco suggested.

"Grant!" Alex was derisive. "You mad? After the humiliation he had at that go-kart track he'll never want us again!"

"Well, Andres then," Marco said defensively.

"No," Julia was firm, "You'll have to forget Andres too. I can't ask him a favour like that."

"Is it *that* awful to be with us?" Marco asked.

"No," she laughed, "that's not what I meant - and you know damn well it isn't. He has his life, that's all."

"I think he quite liked me," Marco sounded doubtful, "though I could be wrong. Usually they reckon the sun only shines out of Alex's bum."

"Arse," Alex grinned, "at least get it right."


Marte had not simply lost her marriage certificate, she had lost everything. That was her conclusion as she sat on the cold, dusty tiles in the empty living room, staring balefully at the high peak of the ceiling where carefree spiders span webs and trapped flies beyond the reach of her extendable cobweb brush.

This room symbolised her life. Now that she had emptied it of all the pretty little trinkets and objects she had lovingly collected over the years, or that people had given her in gratitude or love, what was left? An empty shell.

Outdoors the rampant spring growth of succulent grass, bright green fennel and wild mountain flowers had been flattened by sprawling heaps of worm-chewed furniture, clothes, bedding, bottles, papers and such an assortment of nonsense she had no name for it.

Before she engaged in this monumental clear out her house had looked homogenous and pretty; now it looked old and disasterstruck. And, in spite of all the hours of heaping like things on like things, so that each pile had its category, she had STILL not found the stupid certificate!

Her despair had been exacerbated by the contrasting triumph of Otto. He had blundered home in a delirium late last night, crowing dementedly about victory snatched from the jaws of defeat. Even the sickening crash as he lowered himself onto a bed that was no longer there, because she had moved it to a poetic spot beneath the whispering pines, barely seemed to dent his celebratory mood. She applied arnica to the worst and bluest of the bruises, and then had to listen in horror as he boasted of his glorious successes in and out of bars via attics and eerie cemeteries, and every boast had an unspoken 'I told you so' mocking her. She then had to lie listening to his contented snores through what little remained of the night, and fret at the stickiness that dripped down in an invisible drizzle, and must be some discharge of resin from the pine needles. By morning the bedclothes felt like bread spread thickly with honey, her hair had a layer of lacquer that stiffly rejected her hairbrush, and the only dismal prospect for her day was more fruitless searching for a certificate she was now nearly certain had irrefutably vanished.

She tried to picture the different balls of paper she had shoved beneath the kindling on cold winter evenings. Could she have been dopey enough to miss the difference between stiff cream parchmenty official stuff and the thinner, flimsier texture of parental letters censoring her lifestyle, till receipts, freebee newspapers and the occasional splash out on a Frankfurt Allgemeine Zeitung? The question was of course futile; she had habitually lit the fire with any old papery thing that happened to be within reach.

Just how stupid were bureaucrats to store important information on *paper* of all substances? What, when you think of it, could be more fragile, lightweight, and insignificant? It blew in the wind, dissolved in water, tore in a quarrel and was instantly consumed by fire. At least the Romans got their priorities right. The more valuable the coin, the richer the substance, from copper to gold. Yet what do stupid moderns do? Substitute gold money for paper money! Why, she had a friend who went almost crazy whilst her washing machine slooshed and schlossed its way through her 500 euro note, which she had inadvertently left in a trouser pocket. And the bank obstinately refused to accept that the little niblet of sodden paper she brought them, proudly pointing out its 'water mark', had ever been money at all!

Marte decided to make morning tea. Her kitchen had been transported to the patio beyond the curtain of live Indian cane, where she had set up a camping stove run on canisters of butane gas, and nailed a shelf unit for basic ingredients into the drooping branch of a rowan tree. This was like old times. So much so that when she peered through the canes to Lise's 'new' bedroom location, which she had shown her by torchlight when she returned at midnight, she was shocked to find not a tiny little burbling baby tucked into a cot, but a fully grown teenager with splendid curves and bulges, sprawling nearly naked on a bed of powder blue sheets. Very tenderly, very gently she pulled the top sheet over the more sensationally exposed areas, deciding Lise's stature, complexion and pubic hair were pure Manfred, whilst the rest was her at that age. It was, in fact, the very age she lost *her* virginity.

Sipping her tea from the relative comfort of a mossy stone she finally accepted she would never find the certificate.


Julia and Reggie headed relentlessly south. The first two hours had been pleasantly relaxed, even jovial, but then an edginess crept in because Reggie, after consulting the map, could find no correlation between where they were and where they ought to be.

"Maybe this stretch of motorway's new," Julia suggested, "and they haven't put the signs up yet."

"Could be," he sounded doubtful. "Or they've forgotten to leave an exit for Alcantarilla, or not done one on purpose, so's to embarrass friends and family of prisoners into having to ask the way."

He was worrying he had failed to notice the exit about half an hour ago, on top of which the petrol gauge's unwavering position on 'empty' unnerved him. Julia claimed she had learned to calculate the petrol since the gauge broke, but he feared she had never gone this distance before. Running out on a motorway was no fun and fiendishly expensive, and he would naturally have to foot the bill.

"It's not as if our area's short on criminals," he grumbled, "why don't they distribute the prisons more evenly round the country? It's damned inconvenient of Colin..."

"Maybe the high security ones are few and far between."

"Why are you the sensible one? That's my role."

"You've not been a parent and coped with kids, that's why you get so easily narked."

"I've had to father Colin," he muttered peevishly.


But once they had found and taken the exit, they headed inland through a strange landscape of rock and earth of all different hues within the red spectrum: purple, crimson, orange and ochre (it reminded Julia of an experiment she made as a child involving a glass tank, layers of soil, and a dozen earthworms). Finally, after entering the cruelly spiked gates of the prison, they realised the nervousness of being lost on a motorway was a mere rehearsal for the horror of prisons and imprisonment.

Architecturally it was modelled on a fairytale representation of a wicked ogre's castle, only modern, rectangular, and without turrets. Barbed wire and sharp shards of broken glass ran along the top of a high, black metal perimeter fence, to deter any would-be escapee should he actually manage to elude the armed perimeter guards, plus all the search lights and sirens that Julia imagined would switch into action the moment anyone stepped out of line.

There were no trees or plants, not even a grass blade to alleviate the dark grey concrete sweep which covered all surfaces, vertical and horizontal, so that a spirit of gloom and guilt immediately descended. Julia even felt guilty as she identified herself as 'friend' on signing in, whereas for Reggie that at least was the truth. The corridor beyond was cordoned into two sections, men divided from women, for a briefcase/handbag and outline body search to ensue. Julia considered that her female 'searcher' was unnecessarily assiduous in the way she scraped her hands hard down the inside of her thighs. They sat in silence in a chilly corridor for whatever further processes had to happen before Colin could be prised from his cell and brought to the visitors' cubicles, and it seemed to take an eternity.

Eventually they were led right, left, right, left and on until they arrived in a kind of cavern with cubicles. There was no privacy; the electronic eyes of video surveillance cameras blinked pinprick red lights, a plate glass screen separated visitor from prisoner, and a guard watched every move from the prisoner side.

Colin, when he finally arrived, looked surprisingly well adjusted to a life of imprisonment. In fact he looked no more ill at ease than he sometimes did in Bar del Bigot, when frustrated by a crossword clue. They had to wear headphones to communicate across the screen.

"I brought you some marmalade and oatcakes. I guess you'll be given them at some stage - unless they consider them bribes and gobble them themselves."

Reggie looked apprehensively at the impassive face of the guard and Julia was tempted to giggle. She wondered whether his uneasiness came from embarrassment at being such an old nanny bleating about marmalade, or from terror that the man could overhear despite no headphones, understood English, and might shoot him on the spot for his slanderous suggestion.

"So kind of you to come." Colin blushed immediately. Even he saw the incongruity of this clichéd welcome of polite host at a cocktail party, while his hands, likewise on autopilot, explored the thin shelf his side of the screen, as if searching for dishes of tasty tapas to offer them.

"Watch out when you're in the shower - that's Otto's advice. To attack from behind while a man's distracted by icy cold water is a well-known strategy. Don't want to alarm you, but it's best to be forewarned."

Reggie's hand instinctively rose to reassure Colin with a friendly pat, and there was a hard clonk as it hit the glass screen, and the guard lurched to attention.

"Funny thing is," Colin wriggled on his seat, "I'm actually held in high esteem here, even by the hardnuts. Don't deserve it, but...well, story's spread that I'm a man of reinforced steel. Killed my girl's lover with my bare hands, buried him beneath a wall I felled with a single blow from my left toe. Then carried on living in the same ol' spot for twenty five years without a wisp of remorse. They give me quite a widish berth you know. Most extraordinary."

Reggie looked sharply at Colin, "What's extraordinary? That's pretty much the story as you told it. You wouldn't be here if you'd just nicked a spanner from a ferreteria."

"Oh please - don't bring that one up again. I'm deeply ashamed, dunno what came over me." He studied his hands with a troubled expression, as if their antisocial behaviour was beyond his control. Then he smiled brightly at Julia, "How're the boys?"

It was Julia's turn to register surprise, for Colin had never before seemed to notice their existence. "They're fine. They're with Arturo, spraying black paint on rejas and doubtless making a mess," and then she inwardly gasped at her tactlessness, talking of iron grilles to a man forced to remain behind bars.


Awkwardness settled on them, a lull in their attempts at conversation. Julia looked to Reggie to break the deadlock, for Colin was his friend and she just an accessory. It was not conducive to easy conversation, hearing the faint whir of a video camera, being watched by a guard and being cut through the middle by a grubby sheet of plate glass which seemed to be misting over, particularly on Colin's side. His breath must be hotter than ours, she thought, or else there's a temperature difference either side of the glass.

"For God's sake call your lawyer if you have second thoughts about any of it," Reggie's voice had a new urgency. "And do take care." He stood up, suddenly. "We'll be off now, marathon journey and all that. Julia drove us here like a dream," Reggie smiled at her, and she could see the effort he was making to part on a cheerful note.

Colin whispered hoarsely, "I'll never drive again," and a haunted look clouded his eyes.

The prison effect lasted for the first ten minutes of the drive back, although the worst of the tension evaporated as soon as they left the grounds and turned onto a real road, back into real life existence. The treeless landscape of hot coloured earth looked less vivid in the reverse direction; perhaps due to the changed eyes of the beholder, or perhaps to the light change now the day was waning. It no longer resembled Africa, but looked like a pastel rendering of an imaginary landscape painted by a timid artist who had shyly muted the colours with plenty of chalk white. They had only spent a few minutes with Colin, but the whole prison procedure had taken more than two long hours.

"I'm weak with hunger, along with the weakness of my cowardice," Reggie announced. "How about we stop for a bite?"

"Fine. Your talk of marmalade and oatcakes whet my appetite."

"Stark raving bonkers, I'm afraid. I'll get onto the lawyer, who seems good, though not as classy as yours." He gave her a shrewd sideways glance.

"Please" Julia shuddered faintly, "I don't want to talk about him. I'm too confused."


With a wrench that sent Reggie nearly sprawling onto her lap she turned off the road into a lay-by, raising a storm of dust.

"You must see the old water wheel," she told Reggie, who was tenderly exploring the articulation of his neck for whiplash damage. "It's an amazing feat of engineering - Frances brought me here when I was little. I have to admit the thought of seeing it again was one of the reasons I agreed to come."

The enormous wheel was a miracle of engineering, spinning ceaselessly on its massive hub for hundreds of years - perhaps even a thousand. It circled with low, rumbling murmurs from its wooden pinions, and the lighter, merrier sounds of eddying, frothing, and splashing water being lifted upwards a staggering thirty to forty feet on the delicately curved blades of the wheel. These blades scooped the water from a slow moving canal in a culvert below the road, deftly pouring it out into a narrow, gurgling channel on the embankment high above.

Of all the manifest riches the Moorish presence brought to Spain, of music and maths, science and medicine, craftsmanship and architecture, this gift of water, especially how to use it for irrigation in agriculture and relaxation in a garden, was arguably the most precious.

Julia could remember that the fine spray thrown off the blades as they circled had formed a rainbow in the sunlight, but she could not now recapture that vision. Maybe they had stopped too late in the day and the angle of the sun was wrong. A few other sightseers stared in wonder at the wheel, but as a tourist attraction it was extremely low key. A small rutted carpark, a notice giving a few bald facts and figures, and a prefabricated hut selling cold drinks and stale crisps.

They stayed for no more than ten minutes, but it refreshingly washed away the taste of prison.


Not many kilometres further on they stopped at an old hostal with thick stone walls and immense poplar trees shading the courtyard. The interior was cool and, although the tall shivering poplars were the only trees visible in the landscape, it managed to contrive the atmosphere (or maybe simply the décor) of a forest hunting lodge, with hunting rifles and stuffed stag's heads mounted on the rough interior walls. Their table was directly beneath the head of a wild boar with bristling whiskers, curved white tusks and bright pink gums, and he looked so intensely alive that Julia instinctively repositioned her plate fearing he might dribble onto her food. They ordered the Menu del Dia, and Reggie happily drank her allocation of wine as well as his own. With each glass the spell of prison gloom faded, and he had to eat her dessert along with his in order to soak up the excess alcohol. He was unusually generous with his tip.

"Just as well you're driving and I paid, otherwise I'd feel more irresponsible and more of a pig than I do anyway. I'm sorry I made you come, Julia."

"Don't worry, it's been a salutory lesson, and I badly needed a break from home."

"I wish Frances could have seen you as you are now..."

She knew he was looking at her, but kept her eyes on the road ahead, aware from the vibrations that she was travelling at speed, but not from the speedometre because it worked no better than the petrol gauge. He mopped one eye with a handkerchief. She had not seen him in an emotional state before, but then she had not watched him down an entire bottle of wine before either. After a few more minutes she noticed that the handkerchief lay idle in his hands, and stealing a sideways glance she found to her relief that he was sleeping like a baby.


The boys were waiting eagerly outside Arturo's almacen, but Arturo was the more eager. He took her lateness with such good grace it showed her starkly the positive side of a Spaniard's nature - in utter contrast to the arrogant brutality of the prison guards. The qualities of humanity, patience and philosophical acceptance; qualities even Frances had derived calmness from.

Before they climbed in the car she spread sheets of old newspaper across the back seat to prevent the black paint seeping from Marco's clothes and hands onto the upholstery.

"He did fine," Alex was reassuring. "*Some* black paint went on the ironwork. I already cleaned his face."

Halfway up her camino she noticed headlights in her rearview mirror. A car was following them. Its jerky, swinging lights suggested aggressive driving, and the gap between them was rapidly narrowing. She felt a surge of alarm, but concentrated on the bends ahead rather than the distraction of the following lights, which were almost tailgating her. She turned into her entrance, deciding it would be safest to stay in the car with the doors locked rather than trying to leg it to the house before being overtaken, and overpowered.

She heard a car door slam behind her. Good, she thought grimly, at least there's only one. Alex and I should manage to deal with him - unless he has a weapon.

"Don't move," she whispered, "until we see who it is."

Instinctively she flinched as a hand knocked on the driver's window, and her heart was in her mouth as a head bent to look inside.

"It's only Andres!" Marco's voice was loud and cheerful.

She laughed in relief at her unfounded terror and sprung open the central locking. Alex was out first, being the most embarrassed to be caught cowering in the safety of his own driveway.

"We mistook you for an assassin," he explained. "At least Julia did."

Andres gave him an affectionate brotherly hug, and was about to greet Marco in similar fashion but backed off when he saw the wet stickiness of the paint.

"Ah! I see you wisely blacked yourself out to fool the assassin," and he clapped Marco on the only bit of shoulder free from paint.

He waited for Julia to struggle free of the car and all its restraining safety belts, for her legs and back were stiff from so many hours behind the wheel. He said nothing, just held her close so she could feel his heart was beating almost as fast as hers, but presumably from aggressive driving not an immediate fear of being hunted down and killed.

"I'm not completely mad - you did say you'd phone." It was more reminder than reproach - to explain her fear at the wheel.

"And I did," he said, "many times. You didn't even answer your mobile."

"Oh. I forgot to take it with me!"

Marco nipped ahead and fetched her mobile. He summoned the voicemail messages in a few deft movements, and Andres' disembodied voice echoed strangely through the room. Andres strode forward with alacrity,

"That's enough! I don't want them replayed. I need my dignity." He grabbed the phone from Marco and positioned his finger to delete them. "D'you mind?" he asked Julia, "I was a bit crazy with worry by the end, after a whole day not getting through," he smiled, "rather like you in the car."


Andres followed Julia into the kitchen. "You said you were nearly always at home. That's why I worried. I thought...I don't know why, but that you'd maybe suddenly gone to England."

"I've been to prison, believe or not!" He looked startled, so she explained, "Reggie, the older guy, remember? The friend of Colin's, wanted me to go with him to visit Colin in Alcantarilla."

"I'll bet he did!" Andres declared hotly.

"Oh for God's sake!" she half-laughed. "He had a two year relationship with my mother, up until her death. Imagine, no-one else got more than two days in a row, apart from my father that is, so that shows how strong their bond was. I owe Reggie a favour, after all the loyalty he showed my mother. He's like a step-father."

Andres winced, "In the circumstances, that's none too reassuring."

She looked up sharply, but decided not to pursue it. Instead she stroked his arm affectionately. She felt unaccountably moved by his presence and his emotional state, so markedly different to the cooler mood in which he had left two days previously. His eyes looked darker brown, and troubled.

"I went through hell Julia. It's not been easy these last two days. I've tried so hard to leave you alone and to stay away. I knew I ought to, but...in the end I couldn't manage longer than two days." He gave a wry smile, "kind of the reverse of your mother."

## 27

Julia's reservations about Andres faded, but a hard kernel of worry persisted, to do with his private life, and the obvious and inevitable stupidity on her part of becoming too deeply involved with him. At home in London she had other friends, the dance company, even the distraction of the kids' lively social life in and out of school. But here there was no-one her age she knew well, and although she tried not to dwell on it, with her mother dead she felt very alone.

It was only in the last moments before sleep that she felt uneasy. Worried by the temptation to cling to him. Worried by the sensation of belonging. At Alex's age she had been haunted by the story of male Siamese twins who lived in the States in the last century, having read about them in her encyclopaedia. They lived, joined together, successfully enough (whatever that meant!) until into their forties. Then one began to drink heavily, and would not give up despite the sober one's entreaties. Eventually the alcholic one's liver failed and the long suffering healthy twin had to lie patiently beside his dying, then dead twin's body, waiting for his own inevitable death. She read about it at much the same time as she obsessed about her mother dying of cyhrrosis, so it must have been during her heaviest period of drinking. It had hung like a shadow over her life for days on end.

She burrowed closer to Andres. He was deeply asleep and she yearned to climb inside him, share his blood flow, his breathing, the comfort of his vitality and the currents of his emotions. She should obviously have been born a marsupial. That way she could have enjoyed the sensation she longed for, crouched in a pouch, able to feel the heart beat and warmth - except of course it was always the mother who carried their young in their pouch, not a male lover! Her mother never had been the cuddly, maternal type. So was she now using Andres, childishly seeking to return to the warmth and security of the womb?

Andres was watching her intently when she finally woke up.

"You've a nasty bruise on the inside of your thigh." There was an element of suspicion in his voice.

She inspected it. "Must be the prison guard. She acted like I had weapons and drugs in the most intimate places."

His eyes flickered angrily. "Son animales - I hope you're not thinking of going back there again."

She shook her head sleepily, "I already said I wouldn't." Then she sat up abruptly, "D'you know how you sound? As if my thighs belong to you and you don't want them 'blemished', and where I go is up to you to choose. I wouldn't dream of trying to restrict you in that way."

He stared at her in disbelief. "It was an innocent comment Julia. You always suspect the worst of me. First I'm after a trophy fuck, having lied to - and lied about - my wife. Then I'm insanely possessive, and intent on controlling you!" He pulled her gently but firmly down onto his chest. "OK, I feel a little possessive and I hate the thought of prison bitches daring to hurt you, but isn't that natural?"

"I'm like that because...I'm possessive myself."

He stroked her hair, "You have nothing to fear."


But he had made meticulous preparations to stay, despite the impression he had given yesterday of driving wildy on the spur of the moment to find out what had happened to her. This time he was so well prepared he had brought a change of clothes and his work. She raised a quizzical eyebrow when, after breakfast, he fetched a legal file and his laptop and set up a kind of mini-office at one end of the long table, with Alex and Marco doing their 'lessons' on either side. Then he returned with a large sketch pad and a box of assorted charcoal, graphite and lead pencils.

"I didn't bring oils," he said "because of the drying time. I couldn't risk smudging my work - if forced to leave in a hurry."

Was he teasing her? He opened up the sketch pad and sat lost in thought, then reached for a stick of charcoal and began with swift, confident strokes to portray something or other; she had no idea what because he seemed utterly absorbed in his own world and she decided her only recourse - if she were not to resent this calm self-sufficiency - was to retreat into her own.


She put on her current favourite, an evocative composition of classical infused with Flamenco, and retired to the wooden floored area of the room to run through increasingly strenuous and contortive exercises, initially in a self-conscious manner, but gradually freer and more relaxed as she found she could genuinely forget his presence. After half an hour or more she stopped, and noticed Marco dreamily sucking his thumb, a sign that he had reached a mathematical impasse.

"How come a minus number multiplied by another minus number makes a plus? Isn't that nonsensical?"

Alex shrugged. He had his own problems with absolute monarchy. "Just one of those things, Marco. No point questioning it. Two negatives make a positive too."

"OK," Marco sung the two syllables, picked up his pencil and filled in all the answers with a flourish of speed. Then he consulted his watch. "Breaktime for sure. Fancy a kick around?" he asked Andres, nudging him when he did not appear to have heard.

"Uh?" Andres looked up, evidently far away in his thoughts. "Football? Sure, is Alex coming?"

They were almost out the door when Julia noticed he had left his mobile on the table. "What if it rings?" she asked Andres, suddenly anxious. What she most dreaded was an emotional wife. But a client or step-mother would be equally unappealing.

"Leave it or answer it, whichever you want," he said, casual in the extreme.


A trap? Tempting her to look through his call history to see if he had genuinely called her mobile many times? Or who else he had called, and how many women were listed in his address book, and which might be his wife? Perhaps he knew full well his wife would call that morning and he actively wanted her to field the call. What a simple way for them to find out about each other, without him having to explain. One that would boost his ego, not theirs.


She chose instead to look at his sketch pad. It would tell her *something*. She half-expected a mess of doodling, thinking he might have teasingly decided to pose as an artist to poke fun at her dancing pretensions, or at Frances' pottery, or the whole pseudo-hippie-craft subculture. It gave her quite a shock, therefore, when she saw he drew well, with freedom and confidence, an acute eye and a distinctive style. Moreover her assumption that the pad was new was wrong, the morning's drawings were already halfway through it, and his earlier work was much better. It was doubly mortifying, to have arrogantly misjudged him, and then not even inspired him!


Perfectly cued for their return, his mobile rang. He kicked off his shoes and crossed the room to answer it, wandering out into the garden through the side door for privacy. So, it had to be a personal call, otherwise he would have needed the relevant paperwork. Her ears pricked to overhear, and a nervousness gripped the pit of her stomach, and it annoyed her that she cared at all.

Suddenly he reappeared in the doorway, holding the phone towards her. "She wants to speak to you," he said without any trace of emotion, almost smiling.

She shook her head, whispering urgently, "But I don't want to speak to her! Are you crazy?"

He frowned. "How can you react like that, when you don't even know who it is?"

So she took the phone, inwardly quaking. "Holà." She hoped it didn't sound too strangled.

"Julia!" answered a warm voice she immediately recognised as Carmen's, and she rightly felt a fool.

Carmen was merely checking she was all right, because Andres had phoned her late on the previous day in case she knew Julia's whereabouts, Carmen being their only common contact. They chatted happily for a while, but Julia was careful to say little about Andres, not knowing how much Carmen knew, or whether she might not be a close friend of his wife's. Or even...*could* she even be his wife?


Over lunch Marco steered the conversation to Colin. His fascination in the skeleton had been excitingly reborn.

"Did he look *more guilty* in prison?"

"I don't know Marco. When Reggie first said he'd confessed I didn't believe him remotely capable of killing anyone. But yesterday he did seem, well...strange."

Marco shifted his interrogation to Andres. "Can *you* tell when someone's guilty?"

"Yes, I've got good antennae for that. I don't often get fooled by false protestations of innocence."

"So, what about Colin?"

"I haven't seen him Marco. If I saw him I might know." He looked steadily at Marco, "I can tell *you* have a guilty secret!"

Julia was not sure whether Andres was being intuitive, or joking, or whether he said it merely to divert the conversation away from Colin because he sensed her discomfort, but the effect was dramatic. Marco looked stung. He remained motionless for a few seconds, then thrust his fork to impale his half-eaten lamb chop with a vengeful force, and ran from the room. Julia sat staring at the vibrating fork in amazement.

"D'*you* know what's up?" she asked Alex.

He shook his head. "Give him a minute or two. Then I'll go talk to him."

"He's a remarkable kid." Andres declared warmly.

"Marco?" There was incredulity and genuine pleasure in her voice.

He laughed, "No, not Marco! Alex. He's extraordinarily sensitive and intelligent, Marco's bloody lucky to have him for an older brother."

"Oh, not you too," she sighed, deflated. "Everyone admires Alex, it makes me feel so sorry for Marco. He likes you - and that's rare. He usually picks up on adult disapproval."

"I know you feel protective, Julia. Don't misunderstand me - Marco's a great character and I love him dearly. But he's still young and cute." He looked away from her, "You shouldn't undervalue Alex or take him for granted."

She resented the criticism on principle, but it was the more unfair from someone who knew nothing of their past. Of her undoubted closeness to Alex, and the reasons behind her protectiveness of Marco, over-compensating for his dad's indifference. She felt sufficiently aroused to at last take the bull by the horns.

"You have sons, I assume, with your wife or ex-wife? I take it you're speaking from personal experience?"

He searched for her hand and held it in an almost painful grip. "Don't get so riled. I've had the experience of being an older boy with a younger brother, or half-brother. I know just what it's like."

She noticed he had not answered the comment about children.

But at that moment Alex returned, with Marco trailing several paces behind him.

"He has something to tell you," he announced, sitting back in anticipation.

Marco hobbled at a snail's pace to his chair, slowly prised the fork free from the lamb chop and let it clatter onto his plate, then closed his eyes to tell his tale. He began mechanically, almost inaudibly, but, perhaps gathering strength from the lack of interruptions and the safety of his dark, private world, he upped the volume and described in detail finding the skeleton's teeth, his reasoning at the time of their capture, their lengthy sojourn in the glass jar with his own milk teeth, his panic at the Guardia visit and greater panic when Andres' turron loosened his own tooth and discovery seemed imminent. Then he explained the superglue and the slicing of his own tongue to free it, and finally hiding the teeth in the midst of his collage. He sighed as he reached the end of his tale, but his eyes remained tightly closed.

Andres was first to speak. "I'd like to see them."

So Marco finally opened his eyes and led him off to the studio.

"Thanks Alex," Julia said quietly, once they'd gone.

Alex gave her a brief, pained smile. 'You wouldn't thank me if you knew' he thought, but could not possibly voice it. He was desperately wondering how to get hold of Lise, or rather how to get information out of Lise, having realised that the disovery of the teeth and their position at the base of the wall might still not clear Colin. Lise was the only person who knew how to contact her dad, and Alex now understood (after eavesdropping on Marte's talk with Andres) that he - Manfred - was somehow a vital missing piece in the jigsaw. But he knew firstly Lise would fiercely protect that information, secondly she was not speaking to him anymore. She had deliberately turned her back the one time he set eyes on her since their 'row'.

Andres returned with the two grey teeth held gingerly in a clear plastic bag. He went outside with his mobile but still clutching the teeth, Julia noticed, as if he were actually afraid someone might steal them!

"They want them in Villahermosa," he said on returning, "so forensic can check them immediately. Two of the original team will come here," he told Marco "so you can show them *exactly* where you found them. OK?"

"OK." Marco looked uneasy, "What'll...?"

Andres chuckled, "I've had no problem convincing them you're mad as a March hare - you won't get in trouble."

"Will it get Colin out of jail?"

"That I don't know. If it disproves any part of his story it'll certainly help."

He drove off with the teeth sitting incongruously on the passenger seat, as if he planned on conversing with them to while away the journey. He told her he would try to come back that evening, but it might not be possible; the very sort of vagueness that compounded her unease. He had not taken the sketch pad, but he had packed his legal files despite the hurried departure. She guessed, therefore, that he was not really planning to return that night. In any other situation she would have had no qualms about being direct, but the curse of him being married made it so difficult. 'Separation', after all, held many shades of meaning. If she had ever questioned Frances' self-defeating inflexibility in laying down the law: stay with me all the time or I never ever see you again, she was beginning to understand it now. Being the waiting one, the passive one, living in the place where you met and made love - but only and always at the other's convenience, when they had space and time to fit you in. That was no life. It was living in limbo, what a haunting religious concept. Andres must surely be a Roman Catholic, - they have such a strong allegiance to family and marriage, she thought, that it's more or less unbreakable. So if he does have little kids as well as a wife, regardless of any separation, they'll always come first.

Suddenly she resolved to take her life into her own hands again. Five months. Five entire months since her mother died and she left everything on hold to hurry to Spain on the first available flight. She had then become entangled by events beyond her control. At first the aftermath of death; the funeral, personal possessions, papers, emptying the rented village house. Then she had been hypnotised by the Holidaylandia Development, the horror of seeing it rear up in her face, concrete poured across the earth and grass and trees she had loved to look at ever since she was a child, and on a practical level making it surely impossible for her to sell the farmhouse now that it was hemmed in. Then the skeleton had trapped her. And finally, Andres...

She had drifted long enough - unless she went now she might lose the chance.

Propelled by an urgent impulse she dialled the old familiar number. For once her timing was propitious, the summer programme was only five weeks away and auditions for the two shows that would run through the season were scheduled to start next week.

"I'll audition on Tuesday then," she proposed, and so it was agreed.

She need not commit herself yet, in fact could not assume she would audition successfully, but at least she had the opportunity to regain lost momentum. At thirty you cannot afford to drop out for long, before you know it your body has lost its peak of athleticism and suppleness. Not yet atrophying, of course, but very, very slowly stiffening, therefore more prone to injuries that spell the end. She booked a return flight. Her trip would only last two days. Reggie would agree to look after Alex and Marco for that short a time, if she left meals already prepared. If she landed a prominent role they would move back to London. And if not, well, she would take it as a sign she needed to rethink her career.

Having settled on a course of action she felt elated, and wandered exultantly out into the garden which grew visibly, almost noisily, after the spring showers. At last she had the space and peace to admire the entangled knots of morning glory, the agonisingly beautiful blue of the jacaranda flowers, and the patter of drying, falling algorroba leaves that as an evergreen had their own autumnal cycle in sharp contrast to others' spring.

It was only when she saw the delicate, fluttering wings of a dead butterfly impaled on an inchlong thorn of the prickly pear cactus that a lump came into her throat. In Spain they have a saying: wherever you live when you're seven is where you leave your heart.


Andres returned, entirely contrary to her expectations, in the golden light of late evening. His car resembled the English army in Macbeth, - a host of moving trees, as when Birnham Wood 'comes' to Dunsinane Hill. He had the sunroof open, and the slender tops of at least two dozen young cypress trees shivered in the wind of motion as he drove the camino, slowly this time. He looked inordinately pleased with himself.

"After a year, once they've had a chance to grow, they'll blot out the obscenity of Holidaylandia for you," he said. And he began energetically unloading them.

He was so busy with the task that he did not see her look of remorse. For she now knew she was unlikely to be there to water them through the summer to settle them in, and she had always had a mind to sell the house anyway. By the time he did glance her way she had reasoned with herself to look on the bright side; take it in good spirit, she told herself, it's a brilliant way to blot out the buildings and it'll be a wind break from the strong westerlies, for whoever owns this house. You never can foretell the future.

Alex, Marco and Andres did most of the strenuous work of digging holes and planting, she merely had to wander effeminately to and fro with a watering can.


Later on though, her conscience demanded that she tell him her immediate future plans. She lay against him, watching the moonlight strike the bedroom beams already slatted by the Venetian blinds, so that the play of light and shadow was slashed in two different directions, like a battleground - yet beautiful.

"Andres, I'm going to England next week for a couple of days. I have an audition."

He took a slow, deep breath. "I expected it, somehow. It was my main fear yesterday, apart from the irrational terror that you'd all come to some harm. If you remember - I said I thought you might have gone."

She wormed closer to him. "I may not get the part. In fact it's most unlikely I will. But I have to take my chances, dance is something that doesn't last. I already lost the best years, being pregnant or having babies." She shrugged, "Of course that was my choice."

He turned to face her. "You're too beautiful, Julia. Every movement you make is a form of dance - even just brushing your hair. So…I can't bear the thought of you dancing, not with a male partner, not in public - it's *my* intimacy." He covered his eyes with his hand as if already forced to spectate. "I'll have to get used to it. Somehow or other."

She felt a wave of shame for provoking, even enjoying making him suffer this abstract jealousy, which she knew to be a kind of spiteful payback for his own freedom to come and go, his reticence about his private life, and her own feelings of insecurity. Of course she was justified doing what she had done, the prime motivation made absolute sense, but nevertheless there was a hurtful thread of malice in it that she found abhorrent.

There was a subtle shift in their sex that followed. Guilt made her less rapacious of her own enjoyment and more conscious of his, while he must have been competing with strong and finely tuned male dancers and fighting off physically perfect rivals in an exhausting, spiralling, menacing dance, for his love making was far more aggressive than it had been before. Afterwards they lay drenched in sweat.

"Teach me to dance, Julia. Then it'll be easier for me."

"But it takes years and years! *And* you have to start really young."

"I'm still young. I'll learn quickly."

She laughed at his naïvety, at his ridiculous ideas. It was the very first time he had made any mention of the future, or shown that he didn't see his life as permanently confined to a law office in Villahermosa.

# 28

R eggie noted how very differently the other drivers on the motorway
behaved.

Two days ago, when he made the journey with Julia at the wheel, he had
observed some appalling examples of bad motorway driving. It was only by
keeping her wits constantly about her that she had avoided at least five fatal
collisions, and doubtless more because he had slept through most of the return
leg. Some wove in and out of the fast lane without signalling, pushy ones
passed on the inside lane, far too many yacked away on their mobiles
oblivious to other traffic, others closed their eyes to groove better to their
music systems on top bloody volume, and a few were clearly so tanked up
they took it as a challenge to the death if you dared overtake them. The fact
that she was a woman and a looker, instead of being a calmative seemed to go
to their heads.

But today, sitting silently in the back of a marked police car, he noticed how
butter could not have melted more tellingly in the other drivers' mouths. Ones
ahead who were so obviously speeding cunningly reduced speed without
touching their brakes so no telltale rear lights could give them away, the hogs
of the fast lane subserviently gave them precedence, and instead of tailgating,
correct distances were meticulously observed, so that altogether the journey
miles were eaten up in perfect peace.

He was not au fait with the reasons behind this chauffeur driven second outing
to Alcantarilla. Apparently it was to do with essential paperwork, his signature
was required. The two taciturn police drivers had waved some paper with the
prison seal on it, but he had not bothered to read it. Eight o'clock in the
morning he considered a brutally early start, giving him no time for tea, toast
and marmalade, but apart from hunger pangs he could not fault the comfort of
the journey. Without the responsibility of map reading, and better still (given
his finances) of paying for petrol or motorway tolls, he could sit back and
admire the landscape.

Spain, even on a mere two and a half hour drive, was a country of contrasts. In
England you would never travel far or variedly in that time, perhaps across
London in the rush hour, or halfway to the sea in an August traffic jam, but on
a Spanish autopista you fairly floated along. They began amongst greenery,

steep mountains and curving roads. Then the first stretch of coastal plain near Villahermosa had been picturesque enough, the wall to wall villa developments of ten years ago now bordered by palm trees, bougainvillea and other brightly ostentatious flowers. It was only when they had forged south of Villahermosa that the overall aspect turned hideously ugly. Houses tumbled frenetically and aggressively over one other to get the better view, high rises muscled in, and every stretch of road was clogged with clumsy concrete mixers or lumbering lorries ferrying building materials. And every inch of skyline was cross-hatched with idle or jerkily rotating orange cranes.

As he glided past on the steeply embanked autopista he wondered if it would all merge into one enormous Babylonian city in twenty years' time.

Further on, however, the buildings abruptly fizzled out, the sparse orchards vanished, and even the casual musterings of weeds lost heart as they entered a desolate area of baked mud and dust. Here the rocks were a uniform bleached grey colour, visibly disintegrating in the bone dry, salty air. It looked as if you could simply shovel up the landscape, crush it, pour it into a paper sack and call it cement. Maybe the rural economy actually *was* that. It resembled the surface of Mars, or how Reggie imagined ancient Carthage must have been after the Romans vindictively sowed it with salt. The mere sight of such dry dustiness made him scratch at his scalp, and experience surprise when it was not encrusted in dandruff.

Not even those Northerners who only come for sun and cheap booze and never mind the view would be tempted to live in this dust bowl, he decided.

At last they drove through an imperceptible frontier back to a land steeped in colour, although still there was no greenery - just the mineral colours of earth in all its varied hues. Then gradually the gentle contours swelled into rolling hills and vegetation did reassert itself; olive orchards shivered their silvery leaves and tall poplars lined the entrances to villages, or grew lustily on the banks of parched rivers. They were finally closing in on Alcantarilla.

Reggie eased himself out of his stupor. He felt brave enough to face even a fiersome prison Commandante but he regretted not being comfortably at home. As they drove through the iron entrance gates he therefore cursed Colin for the stupid, unnecessary farce he had sucked him into.

Even though he was headed directly to the Commandante and under police escort, so unlikely to be loaded with weapons, drugs or semtex, he was still made to pass through the usual hoops and barriers. ID clearance, cursory body search, signing in, and a maze of corridors to march through.

His first shock was the sight of Colin's clothes. Not the prison ones, but the ones he had arrived in, neatly folded on a chair in the Governor's Office. The Governor stood up to shake his hand.

"I am very sorry" he said gravely, speaking a careful English.

Reggie did not bother to tell him no-one had thought to inform him, such petty objections seemed pointless now that he understood the stark truth. On one level he needed no time to adjust, since the fear had been in the back of his mind all along that Colin would never manage to cope with prison. The surprising thing was more the idiotic complacency he had experienced on the journey; why on earth, now that he had been brought brutally to his senses, would he get chauffeur-driven for a mere bit of pen pushing? And in Spain of all countries, where officials just love making people run around like blue arsed flies over paperwork... What a fool he was not to have anticipated this; his only excuse was the lack of breakfast and the dose of caffeine to sharpen his wits.

"How did it happen?" Reggie asked.

"Last night. I'm afraid you will have to formally identify the body, it is not so nice - he swallowed bleach, a very strong type of bleach, you understand."

"I see." Reggie detected the Governor's slight uneasiness. "How did he manage to get hold of it?"

"It was locked in the cleaners' cupboard in the lavatory. He broke in."

Reggie nodded. Privately he had his suspicions that someone had been negligent, but there seemed little point now in making an issue of it. Colin must have been very determined to have chosen such a painful method, and even prisons that take the utmost precautions to minimize risks have prisoners who manage to hang themselves with a forgotten shoelace.

"Let's get it over with," was all he said.

The medical wing with its small mortuary meant negotiating yet another kilometre of gloomy corridors.

The position in which Colin's body lay testified to the agony of such a death, but at least it proved no-one had tampered with his body afterwards, to straighten his limbs or rehumanise his face so as to soften the impact for any viewer. It must sizzle through everything except bone on immediate contact - but Reggie tried hard not to think through the process. He did force himself to look fleetingly at Colin's face but could not manage for long; he could identify Colin from the back of his head in any case, from his unusually ginger hair and cluster of freckles on the nape of his neck. He had seen him from that angle so many times, when he arrived 'late' at Bar del Bigot by

Colin's standards of punctuality - still influenced by military training despite thirty five years of exposure to a more casual approach. Colin would be sitting upright and expectant, a cafe con leche in the grasp of his right hand, pencil at the ready, crossword unfurled, in his chair at their table at exactly eleven thirty every morning. Reggie tried hard not to think about that either. The body was expressive of such a profound pain, but after they left it a numbing sense of fatality settled on him, and all emotion drained away.

In this dulled state he accepted everything they handed him. Colin's clothes were packed into a carrier bag, he was treated as Colin's 'next of kin' because that was how Colin had entered him on a form and he lacked the will to argue. He had to sign his name here, there and everywhere, and in the back of his head was the faint worry that, now that he had co-operated with all these signatures he would be of no further use to them, and he might be expected to struggle homewards for several days on a series of local buses. However, once he signed his agreement to take charge of the body it became clear he would be chauffered back - not in a hearse, for the body still had to undergo an autopsy for prison records, and would follow two days later - but in the same car he had arrived in.

On the journey back his eyes stared fixedly through the window but he registered nothing of the landscape. For him the saddest thing in the carrier bag was the sight of the djellaba. He had to push it down so it was no longer visible; strange, it was not even Colin's, but of all his possessions it typified his unusual qualities and spoke of the optimistic new start he had tried so hard to embark on.

When he got home he was too tired for anything. He could contemplate neither food nor alcohol, despite being vaguely aware he had eaten and drunk nothing all day. Dimly, through the fog of his exhaustion, he recalled that Colin had told him the whereabouts of all his important documents along with other trivia about the house and its functionings (water mains switch, electricity 'interruptor' and the like). He did so in such a casual, drip-feed way that Reggie had thought it just another example of Colin getting his knickers in a twist about housekeeping fluff. Only now did it occur that Colin might well have been operating to a plan. Unfortunately - in more ways than one - he had not paid the slightest attention at the time. He was too tired to accuse himself of short sightedness or wallow in self-recrimination, however, and simply lay back on his sofa fast asleep.

Alex had been feverishly plotting. His quest for a means to track down Manfred, Lise's dad, had assumed a Holy Grail-like importance that held him in its grip. What he had to do was blindingly simple really; get hold of Lise's mobile and find Manfred's number on her list. He knew it was there - she had shown him it, that day Jorgen was busy showing off his juggling skills, but of course back then he had not seen how it could ever have relevance for him.

Although he was still only twelve (but at last within sight of thirteen - only two months to go!) he had managed to grow nearly two centimetres all of a sudden, and he fancied his face had matured. Thirteen was nothing though. Fourteen was *the* crucial age in Spain, the Rubicon. At fourteen you could ride a 50cc bike (and many rode 150cc ones masquerading as 50cc) and you switched from kids' school to sophisticated colegio; if you were a boy you started regular shaving and pretended not to be a virgin, if a girl you slapped on the make-up and longed to lose your virginity. The one cast iron rule, however, was that no-one over fourteen could associate with a mere twelve year old. It was too humiliating. Lise, now that she had decided to 'fit in', therefore found their former friendship a serious embarrassment. So she not only avoided him because she hated him for his comment about Jorgen, she *had* to avoid him for reasons of peer pressure and the right image.


The groundwork he had already done was gain an invitation to a fifteen year old birthday party. The birthday girl was Begonia, Arturo el Ferrer's kid sister, who belonged to the Montejoven colegio set that Lise hung around with. He had persuaded Arturo to keep quiet about his true age, and over the past weeks, so actually before he harboured any ulterior motives, he became quite friendly with Begonia. Fortunately she was only five foot one so discernibly shorter than him, and without telling an outright lie he had given her the impression he was fifteen. The reason he had no motorbike, he pretended, was because he might imminently return to England and could hardly smuggle it onto the plane.


He spent the day in nervous anticipation perfecting his plan. Julia had agreed he could go to the party, which began at 9pm, and that he need not be dropped off like a baby but could walk there by himself. They crossed swords over the 'afterwards', however. He originally tried for midnight and walking home, but in the end they compromised: he must leave on the dot of eleven and she would wait in the car outside Dolores' Panaderia.

He ironed his jeans and a long sleeved shirt - he couldn't risk showing his arms because they surely ought to be hairier at fifteen. He had bought a couple of condoms from the vending machine in the Farmacia on the day they spent with Arturo - a terrifying experience because the shop was filled with old ladies buying cough syrup and elastic stockings for their varicose veins. He did not (well, truthfully could not) plan to use them; they were just there on principle, at fifteen you took them to parties and that was that.

There was actually so much to worry about that he stopped worrying. It was counterproductive - unless he felt confident he would never succeed in getting the number.

Instead he counted his strengths. He could handle a bit of alcohol without going wobbly or throwing up, he knew how to French kiss and had an almost double-jointed tongue - he had discovered that in the first year of secondary school when they played 'spin the bottle'. And though he might be inept at the slow, touchy-feely dancing, at least he could hold his own against anyone at break dancing. He had learnt the basics from Julia, then developed a wicked repertoire with an amazing kid from school, Dwayne, who was so loose he was surely made of rubber. Plus dancing was in his blood anyway.

The only unplanned step was how to actually gain possession of the phone. He would have to improvise. Once the party got going he must watch for - and snatch - his chance. He had this highly optimistic daydream of wowing Lise with his spectacular break dancing, then cosying up in dimmed lighting, he expertly stroking her buttocks and hey presto (she always kept her mobile in her jeans back pocket) the phone was his! But…what if she wore a dress? If she didn't like dancing? If she carried on avoiding him? He knew the answers really, and that was why he had half an alternative plan in place. Julia's mobile was almost identical to Lise's. She had agreed to lend it for the party so she had a means to contact him if, for any reason, he failed to show up at the panaderia. There ought to be a chance to swap them…


One thing did bother him however. His motive. He preferred to see himself a noble seeker after truth and justice, the sort of person Andres probably admired. He knew Manfred (or Yogi, *if* they were the same person) was in some way ignominiously involved in the skeleton mystery, and since had skulked under the Yogi pseudonym (again, *if* previously Manfred). Anyway Lise's father (whichever one he was) had never returned to Spain, and had ordered Lise not to tell Marte how to contact him. Why should *he* escape when others had to go through interview hell, and Colin even break down and confess when he was so obviously not responsible? Why did Colin have to be in jail when this guy, who was acting guilty whether he was or not, kept safely out of trouble? Moreover Lise was protecting that rat Jorgen, so by also protecting her father that as good as proved he was a rat too. That, anyway, was his honourable motive.

His other was ostensibly revenge. Even so he hotly argued *some* merit for himself. After all Lise and he had sworn to keep mutual secrets, a bond of honour. Well, he had kept his side of the bargain, had looked after those drugs, told no-one. But all along she was laughing at him, toying with his feelings for her and sharing the twisted joke with Jorgen. So *she'd* broken their pact, not him. Even now, knowing that she knew her father's

290

whereabouts, he could decide to be a real shit and tell Andres who would inform the Guardia. That way, faced with the threat of a drugs charge, she would be so scared she would willingly trade the information on her dad's whereabouts in return for softer treatment over her involvement in Jorgen's cocaine dealing. That's what he would do if he was a real bastard...

Legally I'm a bastard anyway, he comforted himself, so it's lucky for Lise my method, although admittedly it does give me *some* pay-back, is actually less bastardly than it could be.


The time for thinking was over. At last he was on his way down the camino, halfway to the party already. Marco had looked crestfallen at being left behind, but he had got so much better at coming to terms with being four years younger. He found the condoms (of course!), but had not made a big deal out of it, not told Julia, not even tried them on, blown them up like a balloon, or any of the things you could swear he would do six months ago.


Inside the village his nerves resurfaced. Too many of the older generation knew his age perfectly, who was he trying to fool? The party was in one of the disco bars called Bar Alhambra, and although it dug into their profits the bar staff liked to offer you mixed shots or give you an extra strong measure, just to test your mettle. He must be on his guard. Not only to avoid getting leglessly drunk but also to refuse any other substances without seeming a pathetic wimp. And he could not even handle a cigarette without coughing his guts out, judging by the one time he tried the tiniest puff.


Bar Alhambra was squeezed into a small square beyond the church, and his heart sank when he saw the array of gleaming motorbikes parked in their tubular slots. All the guys had driven there - even from just around the corner, fifty yards away - except for him. They would guess his age the moment he set foot in the bar, why had he set himself up for this humiliation? He shrugged his small, narrow, young boy's shoulders that had not even begun to broaden towards manhood and stumbled miserably up the steps to the bar, his eyes riveted by his stunted, pre-teenage feet that still fitted into the cheaper boys' size trainers. Maybe he was so damn' small they wouldn't notice him. He could grab the mobile in his chubby baby fingers and escape before they knew he'd arrived!

Inside the music was so loud it made talking impossible. Well, at least that meant no-one could hear that his voice was not remotely in the process of breaking. Once he adjusted to the fluttering activity inside his ears he looked around and was surprised to find the scene not like a party at all - in fact no different to the one and only time he came here with Arturo. The guys with their freshly gelled hair were bunched together near the bar or playing the machines in the arcade area; while the girls were grouped unromantically close to the toilets, admiring each other's clothes, bodies, and hair, all giggling conspiratorially. A few moved suggestively to the rhythm but stopped short of actually dancing. Everyone was so busy being cool and self-contained, whilst surreptitiously measuring the competition and eyeing the prey, that he could blend in without any trouble whatsoever.

Although his worries about being rumbled as a mere twelve year old evaporated, an unforeseen worry took their place - Lise was not there! Nine thirty became ten, then ten thirty, relaxation turned beyond anxiety to near desperation at the thought that he would fail due to the one and only mishap he had not even considered, for he knew from Begonia she had had every intention of coming. Had she gone to Montejoven? Had someone stolen her mobile before he could? Was Jorgen still around, and they having it off in an almond grove? Or - worst of all - had she just been arrested for dealing drugs?

At twenty to eleven, with time fast running out, he decided to phone her. She might recognise Julia's mobile number and avoid the call, or answer and hang up when she realised it was him, but he had to take the risk. She answered on the third ring.

"Hi," he said, trying to steady his voice. "Why aren't you at the party?"

"Alex?" She sounded breathless. " 'Cause my stupid moped's broken down, that's why."

"Where are you?"

"Pushing it from Montejoven. I'm nearly dead. I'm just getting to Scotty's."

"I'm coming!" he yelled, and ran out the bar without a word of thanks to Begonia.

Running at speed had a beneficial effect on his brain, for the albeit modest amount of drinking he had done made his eyes swim and elongated the houses by narrowing the streets to begin with, but by the time he saw her distant figure sagging with the uphill weight of her moped his eyes regained accurate focus. It was not drink that made him barely recognise her. Instead of being cool and aloof she was exhausted, her party dress flecked with oil and layered with dust, her blond hair not in its usual sleek and meticulously brushed state but lank, colourless and flat against her skull. She lent against the roadside wall when he reached her.

"I'm totalled," she said, "I can't go another step. It weighs a ton."

He took the handlebars from her and wheeled it forward, listening for sounds of friction because he knew mopeds were not that heavy. He crouched down to inspect for obstructions.

"Lise," he said reproachfully, "the chain's catching, that's all. How come you didn't notice?"

"Because I know nothing about mopeds," she snapped irritably. "I can't go to the party now. I look a wreck."

He could scarcely disagree so he bent over the chain, then had to straighten gingerly before the beer he had drunk defied the downward pressure of gravity. He guessed it must be after eleven, so his allotted time was over. Just as he had imagined, at the last minute he had no plan to follow. He could only improvise.

"I'll borrow a tool off Scotty. Can you lend me your mobile - I've got to phone Julia 'cos I'm late already where she's picking me up."

"Why not use yours? You phoned *me* on it."

"Battery's too low."

He thrust Julia's mobile into her hands, hoping this would make her more trusting, praying she would not bother to check its level of charge. Luckily there was no nearby street lamp, and she did not even glance at it. She merely hunted through her bag and reluctantly handed him hers.

"Don't go phoning London. My mother doesn't pay my bills," was all she said.


He rushed through Scotty's bar towards the toilet, praying it was not the night the dealers took over the anteroom with its washbasin for their business. He felt more like throwing up than hunting for Manfred's number, but having come this far it seemed insanity not to proceed. He looked wildly at the 'occupado' sign on the door, rattling it energetically so the occupant got the message. Eventually he heard the toilet flush and some huge, pot bellied man struggled out and he rushed inside, his fingers shaking as if he were committing a heinous crime.

Having practised on Julia's phone he knew the internal layout perfectly and soon located her address book section, but - there were so many numbers to choose from! Did she call him 'Manfred'? Or - what was his full religious name? Swami something? Or was Swami only the prefix, like Mr? He began to panic...he was so close but so stupid to be stalled by this. Why hadn't he asked someone the German for dad? He had a vague memory she sometimes called Marte 'Mutti' when she wanted a favour, 'Mutter' was the proper word, as was 'Vater', surely...it surely couldn't be 'Vati' could it? Nerves formed an obstruction like a ball of fur in his throat, and he promptly vomited into the lavatory.

Fortunately it cleared his brain and calmed him, so that he recognised what he had been shown so long ago, soon after they had first arrived in Spain. *Papi*, that was her name for him. In a frenzied hurry, since he must have been gone for ten minutes by now, he found the pencil stub and scrap of paper he had so carefully stashed in his jeans pocket, and scribbled down the number. Then he went oh-so-casually to the bar and asked Scotty if he could lend him a spanner.

"It's for Julia," he lied, knowing Scotty's weakness for her. "I'll return it in a minute."

As he ran back he could hear Julia's mobile ringing. It sounded like a shrill alarm reverberating round the hills and he yelled to Lise from thirty yards away that she should answer it. By now Julia would be worried. She must be phoning from a call box and if it went unanswered he would be too late to return the call, because she would never hang around in an empty booth.

"Hello," Lise's voice sounded sullen and reluctant.

"No. It's Lise. Alex is just coming right now."

"Yah. I've been busy. 'Bye."

She threw the phone into his hands as if it were Julia herself and equally as hateful, and he had to drop the spanner in order to catch it.

"I know, I'm sorry mum, I really am. It was kind of an emergency."

"I can be there in under ten minutes. Or, we're outside Scotty's, d'you want to pick me up here?"

But Lise was frantically signalling 'No!' so he became confused, and hoped he had persuaded Julia to wait where she was.

"You *said* you'd phone her." She looked at him accusingly, "You must be bloody pissed – don't you even remember why you borrowed my phone?"

"I threw up," he said as if that explained everything. "Also, I did leave a fun party in full swing to come and help you."

Lise sighed over the vast complications of her life, and watched him fix the chain and test that the rear wheel moved unimpededly once more.

"I'd have thought you'd have bought a new moped by now," Alex looked up at her, "after your big business deal." Having got what he wanted he could risk almost anything, though oddly enough her washed out look robbed him of the desire to be excessively cruel.

"Fuck off! I didn't do it for money did I? But I still got bloody cheated of course."

Then she took the handlebars from him and abruptly flicked on the engine. It purred into life. She lent over, faintly brushed his cheek with a hurried kiss, mounted her bike and rode off shouting 'thanks' over her shoulder almost as an afterthought before disappearing left at the first junction. Alex stood holding the spanner in one hand and Julia's phone in the other, blankly surveying the road, then blinking as Julia's oncoming lights dazzled him.

"Put the spanner down," was all she said when he had climbed into the car, "it makes me nervous."

"I'm sorry," he said. He waited for his brain to adjust to the movement of the car. "I don't want to talk about tonight right now. I'll explain later."

She nodded. She could see he looked pale and shaken, while his eyes loomed large and intensely dark. She fervently hoped the flakiness was from drinking as opposed to drugs, because on that account she had noticed a rapid change for the worse in Lise - although perhaps, due to Lise's evident grudge against her, she was ill-equipped to make an objective judgment. She then wondered whether the 'party' had simply been a fabrication so that he could meet Lise at night. Oh God, she thought, I knew there'd come a point when Alex would adolesce and be a source of worry, but I never thought it would be this soon.


Alex felt utterly drained. He would have expected to feel elation at his success in obtaining Manfred's number in the face of such seemingly insurmountable odds, and to have managed it so simply in the end, but instead he felt wretched. How could he have guessed that Lise after being first his golden goddess, then a vicious traitor, would turn up tonight a grumpy, crumpled dishrag and he would end up feeling sorry for her? It was not just the changed physical feeling he had for her, it was also the knowledge - which he shared - of what it was like to live without a father. Seeing the word 'Papi' was a knife through his heart, because even though she barely knew her dad it suggested a special bond. For all he knew, his own father might have been a similar shit to Manfred, since you normally get killed for a reason. What would happen to Lise now, if her father truly did have a sinister reason to have stayed away?

He no longer knew what to do with the evidence burning in his pocket. Should he go ahead and tell Andres as he had planned? Or tear it up and keep the secret?

## 29

Julia eyed the letter suspiciously. *'For Reggie and Julia'* was written on the envelope in spidery writing, just the sort of script one would associate with Colin. Neat, precise - but nervous. She felt shaken from the tragic news of his death, and now the idea that he had addressed any of his dying thoughts to her deeply disturbed her, the more so because the sadness of death mingled uneasily with the aversion she had always felt towards him. Reggie, who had read the letter already, looked haggard and kept insisting they wait for Andres to arrive. He had phoned Andres on his own intitiative earlier in the day.

> "You'd no right to interfere, Reggie. Andres was in court and shouldn't have been disturbed. He has his own life, and I don't want him to come here except of his own volition. I'm not a baby. I can read a letter without someone holding my hand."

But Reggie guarded it like an old mother goose incubating the last egg she would ever lay. Only when he heard Andres' tyres on the gravel did he stand up, hand her the envelope and leave.

She pulled the letter out with unsteady hands. It was several pages long.

*Dear Reggie (but also for Julia),*

*I'm sorry to put you through this, and this letter is me trying to explain why.*

*I don't think of myself as a thoroughly bad person, but aside from not doing very much with my life, basically wasting it, I've also done some things that I'm ashamed of. I don't quite know what to offer in my defence, except in some ways it all started to go pear shaped from the word go. That part you'll appreciate more readily, you know the basics; born in the wrong place at the wrong time, weedy mother, bigoted father (oh yes, I can see that now, clear as daylight), fed all the wrong values and stuffed with food I was allergic to. Not exactly Mr. Popular at school and then daft enough to go into the army. I'm not going to moan away about the army either, for that's all ancient history now and nothing to do with the rest, I'm just resumeying (sp?), I'll say summarising in case you can't fathom what I'm on about, so I'm, you know, summarising the early bit as a preamble to my life in Milagra.*

*I came to Milagra in '69. Stunningly beautiful place it was then, absolutely unspoilt and roads barely tarmacked, more suitable for mules and carts than* cars back then, and the locals could only afford those little boxy Seats in any case. I could lose myself here, I thought, so idyllically peaceful and still quite primitive for somewhere in Europe not that far from the Mediterranean. It had golden eagles, wild boar, rabbits everywhere and foxes galore. Anyway, not wanting to ramble on about the nature of the place, it all changed quite abruptly. First Frances arrived. She needs little introduction to you Reggie, except to say you didn't know her how she was then, thirty years old and the most dramatically striking woman I've ever seen. A wild Celtic redhead, green eyes, danger personified, and so it proved. Perhaps if she'd been born in a different era her life would have followed a different path too, or if she'd been just that little bit less headstrong, or had sisters not brothers - who knows? She wasn't, she was bang in the generation of hippies and women's lib, and she had plenty of axes to grind against men, and more as time went on.


Anyway, first comes Frances and buys her ruin and stirs up a hornet's nest amongst the men of the village who go besotted and wank behind trees and whatnot, and all the women tut but can't compete. But not to worry because she's not temptingly alone for long. Whether she's the magnet or whether it would have happened anyway we can't guess, but in a month or two hippies are arriving in their twos or threes, and later dozens, and the whole social fabric is thrown into sixes and sevens (or is it sixes and nines?). Bloody mayhem. Villagers are a tolerant lot, more tolerant than me, as it goes. I guess the locals profited from renting out their ruined crumbling casitas without a single mod-con and with gaping holes in their rooves, but apart from a bit of extra trade in the food shops and ferreterias there was little benefit to them. 'Course the hippies didn't compete for jobs or anything like that so they weren't a threat, they lived off next to nothing; fresh air, sunshine, bowls of brown rice with soya sauce, and got handouts from countries of origin or selling homemade crap goods in the markets.

But I digress. So, Frances falls in love with her butterfly man and they scamper the hills and she's out of harm's way for as long as it lasts. Butterflies are the most beautiful things - but die so soon. She should have been warned, shouldn't she? Once it's over she must have uttered a curse covering all men. How can I tell you this? I guess I...got myself obsessed with her. You know Reggie, she had a magnetic power, even old and scraggly how you knew her, well imagine how mesmeric she was in her prime. Got me to the state that I couldn't sleep at night, didn't dare to daydream even, for she popped into my mind every bloody minute. I know it was mad but I couldn't resist. She fucked just about everyone else, but she refused me. I had to resort to underhand means, even now I blush at the thought of it; I'd creep up in the small hours and unpeg her underwear off the line, I'd sleep with them under *my pillow, I'd use then as hankies - I can't tell you it all, even now. I can't tell you the half of it.*

*But on we go. Eventually life took its toll, she got old and I got old, and I no longer needed her underwear off the line. I admit there was still a residual longing, for I felt a great deal of pain when in you breezed with no extravagant masculine charms (sorry Reggie, don't take that amiss) and unaccountably struck a chord with her, on more levels than I cared to consider. I got to know your mental attraction for I guess you're the closest to a friend I've ever had, but I breathed shattered glass every time I contemplated the idea of your knowing her body, or my body as I saw it. So I don't think it got much easier, even towards the very end. And I should get to the end, although that's the very difficult bit... Please don't hate me, Reggie.*

*Remember my car? I tried to forget it I can tell you, and nearly succeeded, very nearly. I told you it failed its MOT didn't I, just like yours would if you dared to put it in for the test? A lie I'm afraid, a black, blacker than black lie.*

*My hands are beginning to shake now as I try to tell you what happened, but I have to overcome the terrors and proceed.*

*You will hate me, I sense it, but there's really no escape from that, and since I won't see you again I've got to get it out in the open before it's too late. I don't want to die with this thing weighing on my chest, and I don't want to live with it either, hence the self-imposed trap I've sprung for myself. I must get to the point. I sense I'm stalling.*

*You were right, Reggie, although I made a good pretence at hale and hearty laughter at the time, or some such ham acting when really I was in agony. You were right about there being another car on the road, when Frances was killed. I've almost as good as said it now, but I'll spell it out for you, I don't want to chicken out of the details.*

*I was driving the other way, with my headlights on because it was dark, it gets dark early on in December. I was coming a little fast on the winding bit above Milagra, but not out of control, although I can only guess now that I probably was a little over the centre of the road. I don't think that was her problem, though, possibly she would have managed to round the corner even with my poor positioning if it hadn't been for my lights. Oh God Reggie, I forgot to dip my lights! How could that happen? I've asked myself that ever since, in every hour of every day.*

*The answer remains the same though, the unalterable fact is that I kept them on main beam and dazzled her, I know it because I saw her face lit by all that too powerful wattage, stricken, terrified but trying frantically to react and save herself. I keep seeing that face.*

*She was blinded by the lights and couldn't remember the exact curve of the road, which she'd seen in the glare of her own headlights before mine confronted her. I could sense her trying to make the bend from memory, but she just misjudged it, and in my rearview mirror I watched her two red tail lights vanish over the embankment. I stopped and I could hear it all, the sounds of scraping metal and breaking glass and snapping branches and slithering and thumping, it was like the earth groaning in pain. And what did I do, you will ask? Did I leap down the steep slope with no thoughts of personal safety and try to rescue her, call an ambulance, react to the emergency? Did I hell! No, I stood there shaking like a leaf, tears of fright streaming down my face, inwardly shouting 'Oh no!' a thousand times, praying that the car would not burst into flames as the situation suggested it surely would. That prayer, at least, was answered, but not the other ones. Not the futile one 'Please God may it not be France' when I already knew it was, or the other one 'Please, don't let her die'.*

*You know, but I don't, the extent of her injuries; and whether my cowardice at this point had any bearing on her death. Perhaps she died instantly, I'd prefer to believe that and I won't now ever know any different. It goes without saying that I did a despicable thing in not phoning for an ambulance and the police immediately, in retrospect I could have done that and still not had to have faced even the remotest suspicion of being complicit. It was dark, drizzling, I could have been driving as safely and sensibly as I normally did and simply been a witness to her going off the road. But I didn't think that way. I got into a panic and I drove right through Milagra, and phoned from the public call box near Scotty's so the call couldn't be traced. I even put on a fake German accent, I'm ashamed to admit.*

*Well they found her quite quickly I presume, and then contacted you. I was aware how much of a brave face you put on it, almost as if you didn't care that much, so we were both keeping up an act. But your motives were honourable, not mine. Reggie you needn't have bothered because the whole village knew about you and Frances, and there was no reputation to protect. I'm not knocking what you did, because you must have had your reasons to not grieve openly, and you so obviously prefer laughter to tears. I would have preferred tears though; your relentless brave smile and forced jokes made me want to scream. But who the hell am I to say a word let alone a preference?*

*I'm slowly running out of steam now Reggie, so I'll try to cap it off as briefly as I can. I drove my horrible loathsome car to Villahermosa and left it in a second hand car lot. By an almost fiendish coincidence the thing gets sold a month or two later, and guess who offers me a lift home that day? Yes, Julia of course, she might remember it, I nearly died and lied that I'd left it in a garage. You can't imagine how awful I felt as she drove me home and I had to watch her forearms on the steering wheel, so beautiful and graceful and so like Frances'. I think I knew then that I couldn't let myself get away with it, that I'd need to punish myself one way or another.*

*Then of course the skeleton comes along. I didn't see my way out straight away, but slowly the plan formed in my mind. It wasn't that difficult to play scared, I'd been doing it most of my life after all, and you took on a protective role to perfection. You mustn't feel conned Reggie, because believe me I was scared, totally scared of every step in the path I'd chosen. I needed your reassurance, just like I needed the strength I got from Marte's massage and medicines, some of which she gave without even knowing what they were.*

*I'm nearly finished now. My plan wasn't fully complete you know until yesterday, strange that. Up until then I had this idea I might just punish myself with two years or so of imprisonment, the sort of sentence I might well have received for manslaughter by negligent driving, if I'd faced up to what I'd done from the very beginning. I knew that I'd never get convicted of killing the skeleton once it came to trial, although the risk was I'd be sectioned as insane, but if not, I thought I was being rather clever to punish myself appropriately but still keep the real reason a secret. It was you and Julia that I wanted to keep it a secret from, I just couldn't face you with the truth. No, I think it was myself, I couldn't face myself with the truth that I'd killed Frances, after all those years of loving her so painfully and unrequitedly.*

*What finally made up my mind to kill myself was the unexpected treatment here. Not from the guards, they're just exactly the nasty pieces of work I'd expected, no, from the prisoners. How was I to have guessed they'd give me respect like I was some hero? I couldn't tell them 'Look, lay off a minute, I didn't kill that man I said I did, I actually killed a defenceless woman in a car accident, something like a hit and run'. Or maybe I could have, maybe I even could have persuaded them to kill me, so I could have avoided the more painful method I've chosen to go by at my own hands. But it's pain I'm after. The only way to expiate the terrible thing I've done is by enduring pain. I keep seeing the fear and pain in her face, over and over again, and I want to see the same expression on my own face the last time I look myself in the mirror before I go. You might even glimpse it on my features Reggie, if you have to identify my body. If so forgive me, I pray it doesn't haunt you like Frances haunted me.*

*I hope I can go through with it properly, and don't cock it up. I hope somehow you'll find it in your heart to forgive, and that Julia can too. I've hardly dared to look her in the eye, you know, all these months - and seeing her in the prison was a stab right through the heart, as well as the final trigger to make me do it - but of course you weren't to know. I'd like you to give her this letter so she has a chance to understand - why I said forgive just now was a bit bloody presumptuous, I meant understand. I want her to know, too, how sorry I am I watched her as a child.*

*That's all I have to say. On the practical side you'll find my Will amongst my private papers, but I don't feel practical now. I'm very sorry, very very sorry.*

*love Colin*

She stayed sitting in the chair without moving a muscle. It was almost peaceful because thoughts fluttered somewhere nearby but never properly formed into coherent structures, and her feelings were equally quiet and restrained. Fragments of old memories trickled past like the paltry flow of water from the Fuente in the summer heat; moments featuring Colin, or Frances, or herself, but they were only fleeting glimpses, little cameos, they carried no specific meaning. She was relieved that no-one came to see her to find out how she was, because they would have expected her to speak and silence was her comfort. She could not have told them in any case whether she felt sad, angry, bitter, or relieved, or any one particular emotion, because she felt simultaneously many things and nothing. In some ways Colin's responsibility for her mother's death was not a bolt from the blue because her own nightmare had suggested it, and Reggie always thought there was another car on the road. What hurt her was her own meanness, her all-to-ready assumption that her mother's driving had been at fault, due either to carelessness or drink. Apart from her moments of suspecting Grant's duplicity it had never realistically occurred to her that her mother was totally blameless.

Eventually Andres did bring her a glass of water, silently questioning her with troubled eyes. He sat down beside her and then, after a while, a sentence did form.

"What a life," she sighed, but her voice had vanished and she needed to sip the water. "What a terrible, lonely life."

But whether she refered to Frances or Colin Andres had no way of knowing. He continued to sit beside her, without saying a word. He had the sense not to reach out to her at all, understanding that she needed the inviolability of her own cocoon. Eventually her eyes fell back on the letter.

"Read it," she said. "I would like you to."

He took his time, not skimming but working through every sentence with infinite care and sometimes rereading, for both the language and the form of the handwriting were unfamiliar. When he had finished he brushed his hand across his eyes as if their focus needed readjustment.

"I don't understand why people say suicide is cowardly," she said. "How can it be? It must take such courage."

"I suppose it depends," he paused "on what you have to lose. While I was reading, I was wondering what I would have done had I been him, with the life he had. But can *you* feel sorry for him?"

She nodded feebly. "But I feel more sorry for my mother. She always said 'Don't worry, he's harmless, just a lonely old lost soul'." She paused, "I wonder whether she knew it was him in the car..." and then the tears did begin to stream down her cheeks and she tried feebly to wipe them away. "I was such a blind, self-centred child. I hadn't a clue…about anyone but me."

Then he moved closer to hold her. "How could you possibly know? They were both deceiving themselves, in their different ways..." Then he asked, "What did he mean 'I watched her as a child'?"

It was difficult to speak through her tears. "He used to hang around in the trees somewhere and watch, imagining I hadn't seen him. He never came close. It wasn't scary really - just weird. Sometimes he'd be there for hours and hours, but not every day." She cleared her throat, "I got used to it, after a time. Frances always said it was just loneliness, but of course it was sexual too, though not towards me. I think he was only interested in me because I'd come out of Frances, and maybe jealousy of my father was part of it as well." She looked at Andres, "I don't blame myself for *then*, it's recently I'm thinking of. I despised Colin and closed myself to his being a human being, with any thoughts or feelings - he was almost an object of ridicule. And I saw my mother so hatefully - as an embittered old woman - that I was only too willing to accept it was drunk driving. That's the selfishness."

He licked the tears from her face. "She wasn't an easy mother, and you have Alex and Marco to care for. You can't mother everyone."

"But I could have been so much more understanding."

"So could we all." He stood up, gently pulling her to her feet. "Come upstairs Julia."

"Now? Isn't it..." she searched in vain for the right word, "…callous?"

"Not at all. It's a...reaffirmation of life." He smiled, "I'm sure your mother would approve."

But even with Andres she had made the wrong assumption. By the time they reached the bedroom it was crystal clear that he had wanted her upstairs only to be certain Alex and Marco did not follow and could not overhear.

"The DNA results came in. He wasn't your father, Julia, and now it's confirmed. Thank God you didn't have another shock to cope with."

She nodded. Words would not come for some reason, or not in Castellano. For the first time she was aware of thinking in English and being disconnected from her other tongue. This means, she told herself, I don't have the responsibility of worrying where to bury the skeleton, whether he should go next to my mother in her tomb, or on his own. She had not realised until now how worried she had been about misinterpreting Frances' wishes over this. – She's *dead* Julia, she can't *be* angry with you anymore, get that into your skull.

"And the other thing relates to the skeleton too. Sit down Julia, please - you need to - believe me. Alex has given me Lise's father's phone number. He got hold of it last night, rather cunningly as it happens, but he feels he played a dirty trick so he won't want congratulating. It was Colin's death that prompted him to tell me; it made him realise that sooner or later everyone should face up to what they've done."

"So you feel convinced it was...Manfred?"

Andres nodded. "It's all too neat to be mere coincidence. A man who loses his old identity, goes missing, joins an organisation that absorbs individuals and conveniently gives him a new name, then stays out of Europe for five years... That man's got something to hide, don't you think?"

Julia could feel the creepings of guilt that had circulated through her system for so long - ever since the skeleton's death had been dated and her mother placed under suspicion - beginning to escape her body. But of course the guilt would now simply go elsewhere...

"I would hate to be Lise," she said. Then, almost as an afterthought, "Or Marte."

Andres snorted. "You can be sure Marte knows. Deep down she must do. She lived with the man for six months afterwards, I can't believe there weren't some intimations, for someone who claims to be so sharply intuitive. She'll be desperately hoping Manfred can't be traced..."


In the event it did not take the German police long to pick up Manfred, or Swami Dayan Yogi as he viewed himself, and still liked to be called in certain more spiritual or environmentally conscious circles. Or Tomas, as he appeared officially, on bank accounts, bills, and electoral roles. Nor did it take long for the information to travel back to Milagra, where it instantly became the latest hottest news. It did not quite compete with the excitement level that had been generated by the skeleton's discovery, but it came a very close second. Mysteries, it would seem, are more gripping than solutions.

That evening the conversation in Bar del Bigot centred exclusively on the murder perpetrated by 'este maldito Aleman', and there were ferocious arguments over who remembered him best and what he had looked like, some even outrageously suggesting that they had harboured suspicions about him all along! He had been too tall, too blond, too northern, and too good looking to be anything but out and out wicked!

If his had been an honest, impulsive 'crimen apasionado' they might have harboured mild admiration. But clearly he was not at all the ardent lover who had killed Marte's husband in uncontrollable jealousy, for if he had *really* loved her, how could he possibly ditch her and decamp to India a mere six months later? Oh no; the facts actually suggested that he might not have cared a hoot for Marte, might even have actually hand-picked her as an easy, gullible prey to gain him a new and better identity, made vastly more attractive by the very decent regular monthly allowance that came with it.

He had - not so entirely dissimilar to Colin's fictional tale - followed Tomas out of the party, partly because he needed a van to get him to Villahermosa to buy leather and sniff out the scene there, partly because he was curious to see just how humble and obliging Tomas could be. In those days it went against the grain to say 'No'. Showed you up as negative, small-minded, full of 'hang ups'. 'Yes' was expansive and acceptably bold.

"Hey man, can you lend me your van tomorrow?" Manfred asked a dejected looking Tomas (in German of course) when he caught up with him in the almond grove, having been slowed down by the mud-suction from the recent rains tugging at the soles of his fashionably unlaced Doc Martin boots.

Tomas lessened his pace, weighing up this audacious request. Manfred had already stolen his wife and made mincemeat of his plans, for what would Tomas do in Morocco on his own? All he had left was his van.

"No," he answered, his unreposessing chin jutting defiantly. "Anyone can have Marte, and quite a few have. But the van's *mine*."

Manfred had not intended to kill him then and there. At that point his fantasies of swiping Tomas' identity plus all its ancillary bonuses was only a very fledgeling idea, a mental game to toy with when bored, and still needing rigorous planning if he seriously meant to put it into execution. He had in any case been fully expecting him to agree to loan the van, not enthusiastically, but certainly without too obvious a show of reluctance. He had read Tomas as a cringer, more of a would-be hippie than the real thing, so all the more likely to conform to the mould. And in Manfred's experience women always gave in to him, while men gave way - or gave up.

It was therefore a genuinely impulsive flash of anger that guided his hand towards a sharp rock lying conveniently beside the roots of an almond tree, innocently placed there by Eulogio years ago when the land was still his to provide a counterweight and discourage the sapling from growing crooked.

Tomas politely waited for him during their brief conversation, but once his defiant 'nein' brought an end to their exchange he headed straight for the camino. It was his last moment of consciousness. The sudden blow to the back of his head was struck with horrific force. It shattered his skull on impact so that he fell in his tracks, as limp and silent as an empty glove puppet.

Manfred suspected the blow might have killed him for he heard the skull bone splintering - even above the sound of his own anger sizzling in his ears. Two metres in front of them was a convenient three metres drop of terrace wall, and a crumpled body at the foot of that would engender no surprise. Anyone leaving a party on a moonless night could so easily trip up, especially after the amounts of dynamite hash and cheap local wine they would find in Tomas' blood - *if* they even bothered with an autopsy. It was not the ideal scenario, because a Tomas known to be dead would put a stop to the allowance, but at least *he* would not be done for murder.

Manfred barely broke sweat, either from fear or exertion, as he easily lifted Tomas' inert body and slung it over the edge. It could have struck against a protruding stone, or it might have been because Manfred's heavy boots sunk deep into the raindrenched earth forcing the top rows of stones to bulge outwards, but whatever the cause the wall had already been so distorted by the torrential rains it needed little encouragement to collapse. And it did so with such immediacy Manfred had to scramble back with alacrity and without his boots, which had stuck fast in the mud as if encased in hardening toffee, when the section nearest to him came tumbling, thundering down. He dared not risk peering over the drop to see how successfully the avalanche had buried the body for fear of dislodging more of the wall, so instead he sauntered casually back to the party scene and resumed his merrymaking.

It was only when he left with his arms amorously entwined around Marte, about two hours later, that he noticed (with a convincing pretence of shock and awe) the volume of the landslide he had triggered. Tomas' body lay buried deeper than in any standard grave, and with all that density of rock and saturated earth on top of him not even the sweet smells of its decaying would give it away! He smiled at the sheer smoothness of the operation, and affectionately fondled the van key he had thoughtfully extracted from Tomas' pocket before slinging his body away.

It was a key not merely to a doddery old van with a dodgy back-axle, but to a whole new rose-tinted future...

The van was effectively a mobile home, where trusting Tomas kept everything of importance in a small cupboard to the right of the camping stove where Marte had previously cooked their simple vegan meals. Marte had even inadvertently told Manfred this, whilst blaming Tomas' boring, orderly tendencies for ruining their spiritual rapport. She must also have told him of Tomas parents' disgust at their marriage and their intention of going to such a poor country as Morocco, for if Manfred had thought Tomas had loving, considerate, caring parents who would continue to be concerned about his future whereabouts he would not have been such a perfect victim. Certainly he seemed to know that no-one would miss Tomas if he did disappear, and that the allowance would keep on coming despite the parental disapproval, being the income on a trust fund from the estate of a rich spinster aunt.

One can only imagine him licking his evil lips (a touch on the thin side, and in the current newspaper photo at the time of his arrest hidden behind a rakish moustache) when he found everything neatly laid out as if waiting for him: ID, passport, social security pass, cheque book, birth certificate, University degree certificate, car papers, insurance papers and quantities of letters which suggested the added bonus of a future inheritance if he played his cards well. Man, he was made!

He drove the van to Villahermosa, opened a bank account in his new name (ie. Tomas'), arranged for 'his' German bank to transfer the monthly allowance there (until further notice) and seamlessly took over Tomas' identity. He tidied away the traces by part-exchanging the van with a used car dealer (the chances of Marte seeing it with a FOR SALE sign in an out of the way garage forecourt in a Villhermosa suburb were negligeable) for a fat wad of pesetas and a humbler Citroen 'Dos Cavallos', and by getting a new passport with his handsome photo alongside his lucrative new name. All that remained then was to skillfully dispose of his old identity.

To this end he simply drove a few kilometres north along the coast to a picturesque rocky headland shielding a sandy crescent beach, since for someone of his impeccable taste death (albeit a fake one) would never occur somewhere ugly. He efficiently stripped off the clothes he was wearing, *Manfred's* clothes, took off his watch, an eighteenth birthday present from his parents - just to rub it in for them, the boring middle class fossils, and shoved these belongings along with his old 'Manfred' passport and some small change into his green rucksack. This he left secreted in a hollow cleft on a large rock at the sea's edge while he indulged in a brief swim.

Just exactly as he had planned the rucksack was recovered several weeks later, and this, along with his failure to return home after his parents had sent him the money to do so (which had actually bought the land where Marte still lived), gave credence to his status as 'Missing, feared dead'.


Marte questioned very little in those days. Life was simple and plans were fluid, spontaneously made and as easily broken. The overall aim was to live as fully as possible in the present and 'Be Here Now' were the golden watchwords. So there was really nothing to have aroused her suspicion. Manfred looked, talked and acted like a benign and genuine hippie, so why would she have supposed that he did not really think or emote like one? There was also nothing unusual in Tomas disappearing from view without a word to anyone because people did that all the time. In the jargon of that era they showed up, hung out, then split. It was the way of life all over the States, Europe and on the road east to India.

Nor did she question Manfred's story of needing to stay on the coast for a few days to buy his Dos Cavallos and check out the price of leather, in case he fancied making belts to sell in the local markets; nor wonder how he got the money for the car. His parents of course - hadn't they just obligingly sent him the money to buy the land? Nor did she query the monthly allowance. Tomas had one and any man useful and attractive to her was unlikely to be stony broke. They seemed the perfect, colourfully attractive hippie couple; Marte and Manfred, die zwei 'M'.


Only the one thing troubled Manfred: his old name. He had successfully assumed Tomas' identity in every way, and took money regularly out of Tomas' account without problems because Marte never came with him. But, indifferent to paperwork and the official sides of life as she was, he could not risk her ostrich attitude for ever. One day she might idly look in his passport and find his photo with Tomas' name and particulars, or she might insist on coming to the bank, or he might fall off a ladder and need to have a broken leg set in hospital, or be stopped on the road and have to show his driving licence. He knew perfectly well that there were innumerable risks to being known by everyone as 'Manfred', yet having the official identity of Tomas, the lawful husband of Marte. *Only* if he were to leave Marte and Milagra for good, could he hope to finally shed his old 'Manfred' label and the attendant risks it carried.

Marte therefore received an unpleasant shock when he announced, completely unexpectedly, that he was off to Poona the following day. Other people had got themselves caught up in 'Rajneeshfever' and were frantically saving up for the journey to India, dyeing their clothes orange and swooning at taped samples of the master's voice, but she had never dreamed Manfred would fall for it. He was so cynical, considered himself absolutely no-one's inferior, and in fact, very late at night, had even confused himself with God on more than one occasion. What was more, he had not thought to consult her at all, just egotistically used up their entire month's money on a single plane ticket just for himself!

But in those days it was essential to be cool, so it was unthinkable that she complain or scream or cry or show emotion like some pathetic conventional wife. She had to appear serenely unfazed. Thus she simply shrugged her shoulders. She might come out to Poona later if the mood took her, but on the other hand she might not...


Manfred was therefore finally and deliriously free, on a decent fixed income, and without any history to restrict him. He arrived in Poona both officially and unofficially as Tomas. And he had cunningly chosen the one place in the world where he did not have to go around calling himself by that awful, boring name, because one of the very first initiation ceremonies (along with all the rampant sex orgies and naked Tai Chi) was the renaming by the great guru, Rajneesh himself. He could say goodbye to Tomas and be hailed by his new name, Swami Dayan Yogi. Success at last! How he must have gloried in the temerity of the ingenious stunt he had pulled off...

# 30

The first residents of Holidaylandia were moving in. She could see a daffodil yellow removal lorry parked in the street at right angles to her camino. A powder blue three piece suite wrapped in plastic was being carried in as she watched, and last night she had overheard the clinking of glasses as the first families toasted their success in discovering 'unspoilt Spain'. The shrill yapping of a matching pair of off-white poodles now clashed discordantly with the growlier sounds of the rottweilers' barking, from down in the guard dog compound.

Andres reacted by flooding the earth beneath the newly planted cypresses.

"They'll have to grow fast," he said, studying their green tips impatiently, "I'll buy more manure."

"They'll screen out the eyesore of the buildings, but what about the sound? I never realised how clearly it travels, I can even hear individual words!" she moaned. "It must be an acoustic trick of the mountains."

"It'll be better when they're all talking at once, and not just in English. A babble of German, Dutch, Swedish and English might blend into something almost musical," he suggested, ever the optimist. "And Marco's your secret weapon. He can out-talk the lot of them."

They assumed a lightheartness, but beneath the surface they both knew that the intrusion of Holidaylandia was just one more nail in the coffin of her future life in Spain. The deep attachment she had for the house, the plants, the birdsong, the smells of the different seasons and the landscape, all of them relatively unchanged since her early childhood, was about to be irredeemably broken by the insertion of a hideous housing scheme and hundreds of strange new neighbours, none of whom would remotely understand what damage they had done. Julia could not put her finger on the overall effect, but it was the equivalent of banishing God from the landscape - and yet she was not a believer. So not God, but a sense of mystery, of spirituality, of the power of nature. All gone. Two thousand year old olive trees uprooted, terrace walls dating back to Moorish times bulldozed, wildlife escaped or perished, and the style of housing imposed not even remotely Spanish. A row of cypress trees was no real defense against all that.

Her heart ached for many reasons. Andres had warned her not to look ahead, but she could sense an ominous foreboding.

"I don't have to go for this audition," she said, bringing rich dark earth from beneath the carob tree to feed his floodwater under the cypresses. "I could find work here I guess, if I tried. I could give dance classes in Montejoven or Villahermosa."

"No you couldn't." He was emphatic. "You need to perform or you'd always regret your missed opportunity. Think of Alex and Marco - are they cut out for village school in Milagra, any more than you were?"

"But I don't want to go! I was born here, my roots are here...I don't want to go now, Andres, because of you..."

She cursed herself, having meant to avoid all pressure. She had persuaded herself to let things drift, knowing that she had agonised so long over the past that the worst possible strategy was to channel that same apprehensive intensity into the future.

She sighed, "Perhaps I should go as soon as possible, before it gets more difficult."

"Don't look at it in such absolute terms. I'm not a tree that's rooted here - the flight only takes two hours. I'll come to London whenever I can, and sometimes you can come here. See it positively. Please."

"OK," she tried to sound convinced.


She let her mind play over the prospect of weekends spent together and weekdays apart, an intermittent kind of relationship. It would be compartmentalised very differently to the one her mother and father had had, but it might also be unpalatably similar. A dual life. A fractured life.

"Andres I want to know your personal circumstances. You've guarded them close to your chest long enough."

"I think you'll find," he leapt swiftly to his defense, "we were of necessity focussed on you. *I* wasn't the subject of a police investigation, with a skeleton on my land. My life's been unimportant..." He was trying to make light of it, or else delaying the inevitable.

"Not to me. I need to know Andres, even if...it's worse than I think."

"Well...I was married, and I'm separated now. I did tell you that."

"But *how* separated are you?"

She felt torn; ignorance was not bliss but it might be more comforting in its deluded way. Did she really want to know about Andres' life outside the realm of their shared experiences? At this moment in time she desperately wanted to know, but ten minutes later, or even after a deep breath, who knows, she might feel less urgent and fall back into the pattern of before.

Perhaps a greater independence was even preferable. But despite her misgivings she continued to probe.

"D'you still see each other? And do you...have children?"

He hesitated. And when he spoke his voice was stretched with reluctance, "Yes, I have a child, a little daughter called Claudia who'll be two this August. I see my wife whenever I go to see Claudia, which isn't as often as it should be. I've not been for five months, not since I moved from Sevilla to Villahermosa to create some space between us."

"Might you... go back to them?

"I won't go back in that way, no. But I shan't abandon Claudia. It's difficult for me Julia. If it wasn't difficult I'd have told you before - believe me."

"I'm trying to."

She smiled wanly and lent against him, and could gauge from his breathing that he felt both sadness and relief to have unburdened himself a little, although she was realistic enough to sense that a lot still remained unspoken. Suddenly she remembered Reggie with a lurch of guilt.

"D'you think he's alright? He was extremely close to Colin and my mother, and he has no shoulder to lean on."

"I'm sure he's OK. He looked tough to me. He'll have found the bar - but why don't you phone him? Perhaps I don't feel enough sympathy when it comes to old goats who secretly...fancy you."

She laughed and shook her head at Andres, only to discover his assessment remarkably accurate. For Reggie's speech was indeed slightly slurred, but still coherent enough that he managed to communicate the key facts in the story buzzing round the bar - and the background noise to their conversation showed the bar to be truly and energetically buzzing. That was how they learnt that Manfred had already been picked up in Frankfurt, (although of course that was not the name he had been using or was known by). Otto was also in the bar, hence the news would reach Marte and Lise soon enough. She thought - but could not be certain - that she could overhear the cockatiel's strident tones declaiming 'Que fuerte la muerte' above the excited babble of conversations.

"There's not the remotest possibility Alex'll be suspected of being the informant," Andres reassured her, "but I think I'd better have a word with him all the same."

Marco joined her in the kitchen. His offended expression testified to his certain suspicion that Andres had given him the brush off to impart something secret to Alex.

"Since you're now so masterful with the superglue, how about sticking the handles back on those mugs?"

"Sure." He brightened visibly, but when he'd finished he turned pensive again. "If I hadn't taken away the skeleton's teeth would…would Colin still be alive?"

"Marco it had nothing to do with that. Colin knew they'd find out sooner or later that he hadn't killed the skele…Tomas, teeth or no teeth. You're in *no way* responsible."

She heard a faint expulsion of air, like the sharp release of pressure from a tyre valve. She hugged him close, feeling immediately conscious of her own hypocrisy in deliberately hiding from him the real reason for Colin's suicide. Nor did she want to tell Alex, or not yet, since he was already burdened enough by his own duplicity. She wondered how Alex would have coped without Andres to confide in. Would she manage to cope, without Andres? She closed her eyes; stop thinking ahead, stop it - take life as it comes. Count yourself lucky. If there'd never been a skeleton you'd never have met Andres anyway.


Her thoughts drifted to Marte. Andres plainly failed to understand the degree of self-induced euphoria which was most hippies' consciousness in those days, not just from drugs but also indoctrination. Marte used to scatter her hill with psilocybin spores and eat the mushrooms for breakfast, and back then she was a staunch believer in the essential goodness of mankind. She would have been deceived by Manfred very easily. And after all the help and support Marte had given her recently, she surely owed her some sympathy. She must go and see her.

"Tomorrow," Andres insisted, "not tonight. Let the enormity of it sink in, so you time your help for when it's most needed."

"You're cruel Andres! You don't want the misery preempted, do you? You want it to sink in deep."

He remained silent for a while. "You might be right. I guess I must be identifying with her poor dead discarded husband. But you should see her more dispassionately for what she really is. Self-serving, self-centred, self-obsessed. And I should know" he smiled at Julia, "because she's an old goatess who…fancies me!"

"I know," she smiled. But the laughter in her eyes was clouded with anxiety.

"She may have been duped by a ruthless man, but her own attitude also helped to kill her husband. There's no need to feel extra sorry, just because you're more beautiful, younger and talented. Don't feel guilt about the ways in which you *are* lucky Julia, because I know you do."

She blushed. "It's not that. My guilt is I used her in some vague way in my battles with Frances. I can't remember exactly how, but I know I said things, I got her on my side - it was never very hard to canvas support against Frances."

"No more past," he gave a gentle reminder. "We have so little time left..." and aware that he was wading into depressing waters with such words he steered them instead into an expression of body and soul, in which - apart from the first time - there had never been misunderstandings between them.


Julia was deeply, peacefully asleep when suddenly she jerked awake. She studied the reflected pattern of leaves moving restlesslessly within their framed rectangle of moonlight projected onto the far wall, and heard the triumphant cry of an owl as it swooped on some succulent prey. She closed her eyes, not wanting to lie awake in the small hours because then she would begin to think, begin to worry. She eased herself closer to Andres, gently so as not to disturb him. But instead of his usual comforting warmth his back was drenched in cold sweat.

"You awake?" his voice sounded strained, "I just had a nightmare."

"You're soaking!" She brought a towel from the bathroom, "It's the full moon and the restlessness in this house. It sometimes happens to me."

"It was my own terrors. To do with you - not the house."

"Tell me."

"No. It's too sick... Just hold me, and I'll soon recover."

She felt faint tinges of warmth gradually return to his body. He turned towards her as if about to say something, before abruptly sitting up. Then she was aware of him running towards the bathroom, and next she heard him vomiting; mingled sounds of coughing, wretching and the gurgling of water. When he came back he looked empty and as pale as the moonlight. He curled up against her and stroked her hair.

"I'm sorry - that was my retribution. I deserved to be sick."

He fell asleep almost immediately yet his body still felt chilled, even though she lay against it to suffuse it with her sleepy warmth. It seemed only fair that she absorb his coldness, considering how much of her difficulties he had taken on, and how much she had stolen his strength in the sense of taking it for granted.

In the morning he had to go to Villahermosa so Julia danced; they would visit Marte together later. Her audition was only three days away now, so she threw her body - if not her heart - into a long, energetic workout, willing the sweat to purge her in the way Andres claimed he had been purged, but without the weakening effect. Marco had gone hunting with Alex for the right colour and width of stalks to replace the two teeth prised from his collage, and they returned with news of a toad sighting. A toad. But not necessarily *the* toad. She was to be the judge of that.

They approached the Fuente in stealth and silence. The toad obligingly stood its ground, squatting contemplatively on a grey rock sheltered by a natural parasol of overhanging leaves, staring unblinkingly in their direction. Its hind leg (the injured one on 'their' toad) was unfortunately hidden from view, for that would have been conclusive evidence - unless it had already fully healed. Julia could understand their problem immediately; this toad seemed simultaneously familiar and unfamiliar. It was the same size, had the same presence (personality was too strong a word), but there was something altered - or forgotten - about its colour and markings. This one appeared faded, was more beige than the original shadowy green-grey, and seemed to have more speckles. Had she only imagined warts on the original toad? This one had none.

"We ought to have taken a photo, then we'd know," Alex regretted.

"P'raps that's why they're called 'Familiars', Marco suggested, " 'cause they are - yet they're not."

"Back to joke school Marco! Hey, could it be Toad's wife?"

"Maybe." Marco perused its face more intimately "We didn't see much of her 'cos they did it in the missionary position, so she was underneath."

"Oh Marco," Alex sighed at such ignorance, "missionary position's with the woman on her back. Those missionaries sure behaved like dogs but they didn't fuck like 'em!"

"Oh," Marco sounded chastened.

"Is this how you normally talk?" Julia asked, mildly surprised.

"Sometimes," Alex conceded. "Oh come on mum, you'd seen far more of that by the time you were Marco's age than he'll ever see!"

Marco sighed at the prospect of his deprived life. Then inspiration struck. "Hey!" he shouted, so loudly that the toad flinched, "Maybe it's Coli..."

Alex's darting foot caught him a sharp blow to the back of the knee, and his legs buckled so that he almost knelt on the toad, who sensibly retreated inside the fissure of rock to whatever mountain kingdom lay behind that narrow entrance. Either a cold blooded reptilian world or hell itself.

"Maybe it's colic" Marco said in a subdued voice. "Andres looked pale like that this morning. He said he'd had colic and spewed up in the night."

Alex's look of anger subsided in a flicker of admiration. "Could be," he agreed readily, "or maybe they shed their skins like lizards 'n snakes, and this is its summer skin."


It took a long time to walk to Marte's, since it was a pathway up memory lane. Julia had not wanted to revive the past, but the boys took over and showed Andres not only their memorable spots but also hers; where she almost shot Eulogio with her bow and arrow, where her wigwam had been pitched, and where Frances caught up with her and spanked her once when she did something too awful to be told.

"I think we should hurry," Julia interrupted agitatedly, "I'm concerned about Marte."

Alex's face clouded. "Oh - I've just remembered. I was gonna go to Arturo's, I've gotta finish something." He turned back abruptly.

"D'you want me to collect you?"

He shook his head. "I'll walk home. I'll be back by eight, I promise I won't be late *this* time." He gave a faint, pained smile.

Marco took over as guide, and Julia noticed that he grasped Andres' hand as they neared the dark, musty smelling section of the pine forest.

"This is the wolf's lair," he announced. "But none've been sighted since Eulogio was a kid."

Andres looked suitably impressed, "There are wolves in the Pyrenees," he said, "and because the farmers get compensation for every sheep mauled by a wolf, there are more wolves than sheep these days."

Marco laughed, then suddenly became mournful. "I'm the black sheep of this family."

"Huh, why's that?"

"Dunno. Just everybody prefers Alex, that's all. I know you do."

Julia held her breath, on tenterhooks as to how Andres would extract himself.

"What nonsense!" Andres pulled him round to face into his eyes, "Alex is my favourite thirteen year old, of course. But you are far and away my favourite eight year old. And that's the absolute truth."

Marco sighed and squeezed Andres' hand, and there was a jauntiness to the way he capered ahead into the clearing leading to Marte's hut.

Going inside was to enter a perfumed steam broth, a sudden immersion in the thick atmosphere of hippie homesteading melded with the heady flavours of a Moroccan souk. Incense sticks burned on ledges wafting spirals of blue smoke, a stew of aromatic leaves seethed inside a heavy copper urn while a clay pot with coucous was suspended above it, making use of the steam. A copper samovar sweated with hot mint tea, and several wasps were stickily drowning in a pot of honey. Ant trails meandered across the floor, and feverish ant labour seemed to be engaged in ferrying away as much of a spilt packet of henna to their nest in the river stone patio as they possibly could before their theft was discovered. The contents of the house had been piled in various corners of the room, and had still not been tidied back to their places after the fruitless search for the wedding certificate had come to such an unrewarded end. The general disorder, however, was carefully camouflaged by screens and curtains of colourful silk cloth, some of it embroidered with fine gold thread.

The haunting melodies of an oud accompanied the faint and ever fainter buzzing from the dying wasps, and Julia imagined she actually heard high pitched squeaks of jollity from the thieving ants. They stopped to listen, hoping to locate sounds of human habitation, for the silk screens wafted in the light breeze and made it impossible to see if any occupants were at home. The door had finally been taken off its hinges, perhaps with the idea of repair, but if it had been sent to Emilio Fuster it would be unlikely to return before Autumn. They had entered via a heavy woollen kelim hung over the entrance, but since that could not be locked it gave no clue to whether the occupants were in or out. Julia did not want to call out; any sound would break the mysterious atmosphere of enchantment.

Eventually Andres raised an eyebrow at a peacock blue silk float, and behind it they found a bubble world of modernity - Otto crouched inside a smaller version of his plastic capsule. He stared at them long and hard before deciding they were real visitors, not cyberspace clones.

"Ha! Good to see you," he said, heaving himself to his feet.

"This is Andres," she said, "and this Otto," and she giggled because it seemed - and sounded - so ridiculous.

"I've heard a lot about you." Otto parked his laptop on a flimsy ledge out of Marte's reach, and gave Andres a gruff but friendly cuff over the shoulders. "When she gets jealous of my internet relationships she winds me up wiz your charms."

Andres looked Otto in the eye and Julia could see an instant rapport. "I'm sorry about that, it's some older woman thing…" he paused, "Julia said you were writing a book."

"Your verb tense is sehr accurate. Now I am hooked to the internet, and I probe all ze alternative stories to the stuff we're fed by mass media. I have my own website." He probed his shirt sleeve for a recent card, which described him as a Professor of History. "You're a lawyer, I hear, so you deal with injustice too?"

"It's what led me into criminal law, yes. I work for the legal aid program, so," he smiled "make little money and even less impact. But I manage to retain *some* sense of justice in what I do."

Julia had talked to Andres only briefly about his work, so this shamed her yet again for the excessive demands she had made on his time. It was refreshing to hear Andres and Otto talk about objective realities, about the world outside Milagra; in fact she dreaded the necessary progression to Marte's problems for it would confirm the self-centredness of women for her; emoting, stressing, attention seeking, demanding, - thank God she had had sons!

"As a German," Otto was saying, "I had to question how and why ze people are so easily duped, that's what led me into it. But Julia here has always believed I had a speck of sanity, on ze Zionist conspiracy front at least."

"I read a book, about the systematic ethnic cleansing of the Palestinians in 1948, and on and on, and still on. That's what opened my eyes," she said. "But I'm afraid I don't do anything - just carry on leading my selfish life." She swallowed uncomfortably.

Andres placed his hand caressingly on her arm. "Not everyone can. If mothers deserted their kids - what then?"

"He's zer right you know," Otto insisted, "my mother won't speak to me no more zese days - what a bitch! Ah! I guess you've come to speak wiz Marte. She is behind ze green cloth." Then he whispered, "She is experiencing an alternative past, in which she got to Morocco wiz Tomas." He shrugged, "I guess it helps."

Behind the green cloth was another inner world. Marte was its centre piece, and she appeared to be embalmed. Julia was wrong to assume those ants had purloined the lion's share of the henna, for most of it had gone on Marte; her hair had not one glimmer of grey, it was a shining mane of copper and burnt sienna, spread carefully like an open fan upon a lime green cushion. Her body was wrapped in many metres of emerald green silk sari, but without the modesty of the little bodice so that her ample bosoms flopped loose. All visible stretches of skin - upper torso, neck, arms, ankles and feet - were decorated with mendi. She had, in fact, transformed into a priceless work of art. So, lucky for her Otto was no hard bitten conceptual artist's agent, or he would have sold her already!

Julia stood aghast for a moment, wondering if Marte had truly died of remorse because her stillness was so complete. Then she twitched her toes where a fly had impertinently landed, and the silver anklets chimed their miniature rows of bells.

"Marte?" Julia murmured softly.

Marte's eyes fluttered, then closed again. Evidently she was not yet ready for a return to the present. Julia glanced at Andres who was hovering by the green curtain, none too willing to commit himself to the inner sanctum.

He gave a mischievous smile and mouthed a word that she lipread as 'Cleopatra', - but she could hardly press for corroboration so simply returned a conspiratorial wink. There was indeed a jar of milk white liquid on a Moroccan silver tray near Marte's outstetched arm, but its label read not 'Asses' Milk' but 'Milk of Magnesia' which struck a childhood chord; a remedy for indigestion or constipation, Julia had forgotten which. The enveloping silence of the false past was finally broken by Marco, who began to sing his latest favourite pop single from the swing in the pine copse.

"Julia?" Marte's lips gleamed with a beeswax shine, and her breath smelled sweetly of honey. She eased herself up to lean on one hennaed elbow. "I was escaping," she whispered, "now I can face facts. Oof, I have lost faith in myself." Then she noticed Andres. "Mein Gott, I am not dressed right, Julia, what are you thinking? Quick, hand me a cloth."

"What colour?" There was a waist high pile of different shades of silk and cotton to choose from, but Marte had strong views on mood to colour relationships.

"Blue," Marte snapped, such was her impatience to tie up her drooping breasts.

Julia struggled with the unfamiliar figure-of-eight loops and fishermen's knots, her fingers enfeebled by her efforts to suppress the giggles. 'Büstenhalter' was such an evocative German word for 'bra', reminding her of similar monstrous words like 'blunderbuss' and 'boobytrap' (which probably had no German origins at all), yet what she was concocting truly was some form of matronly halter. She yanked at the knot in a last desperate flurry of strength, and swallowed her laughter. Marte did not notice her confusion, because once her front was decent she was too busy confronting Andres with large, mournful cow's eyes. The effect was enhanced by an artful shadowing of kohl.

"Up 'till now," she sighed tragically, "I trusted my judgment of people. Not politics or history," her eyes flitted vaguely Otto's way, "but *normal* people. I thought I could suss zem immediately. How could I get it so wrong in ze case of Manfred?" She gave a heavier sigh. Then, recovering, she coyly studied Andres, "I sink I was blinded by his beauty. What a rat!"

"A strange metaphor," Andres answered harshly. "for someone who murders your husband in such a horrific way...or are you more concerned with how he treated you?"

"Zere are different metaphors in different languages. In German 'rat' is OK," she said tetchily. "*Poor* Tomas!" She looked at Andres enquiringly, "What must I do now? Will ze Guardia come to question me?"

"Yes. You'll need to convince them that *not* worrying when you husband disappeared without trace, then having *no* interest in his whereabouts, was normal or innocent behaviour. Women from your country usually want a divorce – that you didn't will also strike them as suspicious."

"You mean..." her hennaed hand leapt to her mouth, "you mean zey will suspect *I* had a part in it?! How can zey think that, when Manfred escaped from me, and I knew nothing - nor ever touched - ze money?!"

Andres' relented somewhat. He sounded almost sympathetic. "Of course your later behaviour suggests you knew nothing. But I'm sure Manfred will, unless he's a changed character, attempt to implicate you. So you must be prepared for the 'weaknesses' - for want of a better word - in your story. They'll be certain to question you soon. And obviously you'll be a witness at his trial."

"Oh Gott, Oh Gott!" she cried, her hands twitching at the cloth that now cruelly pinched her breasts. "I hate to go to court! Is zere no other way?"

Andres shook his head, and Julia asked, "Where's Lise? How has she taken it?"

Marte sniffed disconsolately. "With her friends. She took it not so bad. She said," and a glint of satisfaction entered Marte's eyes " 'I'm like Alex now, I'm gonna say I have no father'. - She never knew him after all."

"I'm going to check on Marco," Julia spoke abruptly, "I'll be right back." The green curtain twitched as she disappeared.

"So," Marte looked curiously at Andres, "you who are so critical, are also hypocritical. You have disappeared from your own wife. Is it not so?" and she stared again at his ring finger, where the ring no longer was.

"My wife, though it's not your business, is happily alive. Don't you dare drag us into your quicksand, especially Julia. If it weren't for her I certainly wouldn't have come here."

"Ooh...touchy! I think I know Julia better than you. My judgment was rotten with Manfred - OK, but I'm older and wiser now. I can see from those dark, dark shadows under your eyes and from your skin, which was *so* beautiful before, that you're falling ill. Dehydration." She smiled. "She will suck you dry, my friend. She's *exactly* like her mother."

"*You* should act more like a mother to her! You know something of what she's been through... How *can* you twitch your butt and wave your breasts at me, and kid yourself you're turning me on? What makes you even want to *try*?"

Andres' voice was deathly quiet because Otto, who was fluent enough in Castellano, was but metres away, separated by mere gossamer-thin folds of silk. Also, his upbringing had instilled him with a respect for elders and a reverence for mothers. He felt disproportionately angry with Julia for insisting he see Marte. She did not know how closely Marte resembled his stepmother, admittedly, but she *did* know Marte's methods. Yet she had walked out, deliberately leaving them alone!


Julia returned to a scene of turbulence. In imitation of Marte's product label, Andres was a fighting bull, hyperventilating, pawing the ground, with Marte the bright red drape goading him on. Julia silently cursed herself for dragging him into Marte's mess; he had been sick the night before and needed rest, not Marte. She looked at him with concern, and was about to speak when Marte's sudden sobbing distracted her.

"Men are all ze same! Und Spain is such a horrible, macho country! Go back to England Julia. You are wasted here." She sat up tearfully, the kohl now smudging her cheeks. "Even Otto has some stupid lover on the internet, some kindred conspirator. Ze 'Net Fairy'. Neocons, fundies, Zionists, Fairies..." She smiled feebly at Julia, "You'd better take your lover home before he smashes me in ze mouth. He is *so* like Manfred, only darker of course."

Julia's heart pounded as they walked - or marched - in silence. She had never seen Andres so angry before and it was alarming, so much so that it had even silenced Marco and that was no easy feat. His anger was not violent but he had retreated into some heavily guarded cell of pent up energy, somewhere she did not know how to reach, and she sensed that in some obscure way she was the cause. Perhaps he had simply had a surfeit of emotion, like a goose forcibly fattened for pâté de foie gras. He had been sick. That was the physical manifestation. Now he was going through the psychological rejection of everything to do with her.

Oh well, she thought, I'm seeing an unknown side to him. He's not the calm, rational lawyer with words to cover every problem that I first met. He's like a dragon, his fiery breath is scorching the hillside and he has an inner rage that burns as fiercely as - dare I say it - Frances!

# 31

It was Marco who broke the spell. When they reached home and Julia fumbled for the key, he stared fixedly at the carved wooden door from Toledo, which even in normal times resembled a fortress door.

"Oh well," he said fatalistically, "guess I'm back to being the black sheep again."

"How can you be?" She was surprised that her tongue wrapped itself round words at all. Her voice shook, "*You've* done nothing wrong."

"No," Andres said, "I have. I'm definitely the black sheep today," and he picked Marco up and ran with all the enthusiasm of a young boy trying to launch a kite, so that she felt he must have needed to break the barrier of touch as well as speech. Both were laughing when they returned, and the dark foreboding clouds had vanished.


Vanished, but not without trace. She wondered what might have happened had Marco not been there. Would it have been the end? Was their relationship truly that fragile? With Frances, once a wedge had levered a point of separation, it signified the end for her. The problem for perfectionists lies presumably in surviving the first major down, quarrel, difficulty, whatever you call it. It is similar to cutting the umbiblical cord yet still retaining the bond of love; once you have done it the first time it can be done again because the knowledge of how to do it - or the belief that this is possible - is retained. She noticed that Andres and Marco had grown closer, so perhaps he too had recognised the acuteness of that danger point, or else Marco's charms had finally filtered properly through.

"Would you like me to stay with Alex and Marco while you're away for the audition?" he suggested later that evening.

"Are you sure? You're not compromising work are you? I would love that Andres, and so would they. But Reggie can cope otherwise."

"I wouldn't offer if I couldn't. I can consult by phone. You know Reggie wouldn't easily cope and you'll be needing all your confidence intact for the audition."

"I'm glad you've finally said that because it's not certain I'll audition well. Sometimes you make it sound like I have the part already - but they'll be wary of me, after such a long gap. I'll have to dance exceptionally."

Andres looked at her but said nothing.

She bit her lip "I don't know why I'm doing it sometimes, it's such a...useless, pointless way of life. So privileged and vacuous. What good does it do? Dance isn't like any other art form. You look at a painting, it has a presence and makes you think; you read a book and hold it in your hands, and words have meanings; film and theatre - they tell a story and help us understand more about life and other people. Music lifts the spirits, and you can listen to it again and again. But dance," she snorted derisively, "just fluff, something that stirs the air for a moment, a kick and a flounce, then it's vanished into thin air - unless someone bothered to film it and then who would watch it anyway? It's not even independent - without music it doesn't work. And I've spent *nineteen whole years* on it, solidly, from the age of eleven, day after day, devoting my energy to nothing! And meanwhile, in the real world, people are living, working and dying... Oh Andres what have I done?"

He could not think of anything to say at first, her outburst had taken him by surprise, and perhaps he secretly agreed with her. It wasn't an original condemnation, in that the gist of those arguments - certainly the 'privileged', bourgeois and out of touch elements were from time to time used against both ballet and opera whenever the subject of Arts Council funding was debated, although it was different in Spain where dance was more central to the culture. In Spain dance was gregarious, an essential socialising part of all fiestas, and a visual and percussive element of Flamenco. He put his arm around her.

"Sometimes there's no easy answer. I can only say that ever since humans have inhabited the earth they've danced. Every single ancient festival celebrated with dancing; it's like music, a spontaneous expression of emotion and something more deeply spiritual. When people watch it or join in it - it moves them. I can't come up with anything more adequate than that."

She kissed him. "Thank you," she said, "that helps more than you imagine." Then her voice became a shade less steady, "Can you tell me then why I'm allowing this happy, spiritual expression to separate us, when it's so obvious that that won't make us happy. Neither of us - nor Alex or Marco?"

"I'm trying to see it this way; that we won't be separated for long. It's not the fifteenth century, Julia, it only takes a few hours door to door. I can do a lot of work by phone," he smiled, wrily, "that's why I'm busily practicing. Maybe my English will get so good I can handle international cases - who knows? And you'll come to Spain sometimes won't you?"

"Yes. But none of that is as easy as it sounds."

"I don't want to talk about it," he was suddenly brusque. "It'll be hell. I'll go there when I die, so why now?" and he stared at her with something very close to hatred, as if he were damning her for opening the topic.

She felt pathetically tearful on her solitary journey to London. She could not convince herself of the validity of what she was doing despite the reasssurances he had given. Partly it was generalised human contrariness, the grass is greener syndrome, or whatever tick we have that deflates distant dreams into something anticlimactic when you appoach them. She had long been tainted by this virus: while Frances was alive she had wished her dead, when she died she wished they had been closer in those final years and parted on a friendly note. When trapped by the skeleton she wished to be back in England and able to dance, when she had first known Andres she had wanted his commitment - not to feel she was his bit on the side, when he got bored with his wife. Then she wanted his love, wanted to love him...and *now* what? She did not know. She wanted their relationship to continue, but if she gave up everything else for it she had the premonition that it would never work. Did that mean it only worked *because* of the emotional stress it engendered, and if everything became simple and easy they would realise that the emotion was not love, but love compounded with a love of stress? She used to want to dance more than anything in the world, but did she still? Would she grow to resent dancing if it destroyed her relationship with Andres? Would she grow to resent Andres if being with him stopped her dancing? Would screaming or crying help to clear her mind of all this confusion? How could she hope to audition well in this frame of mind?

She telephoned Carmen from the airport, whilst waiting in the departure lounge for her flight to be called. She felt guilty about it, knowing it was a kind of underhand snooping on Andres.

"Hola, Julia."

"I'm about to fly to London. I wish you were on the plane with me. It's come full circle, but I need you to talk to even more this time!"

"Are your kids with you? Are you finally going back?"

"No, I'm alone. The kids are with Andres - oh, it's so difficult Carmen, I seem to have fallen in love with him..."

There was a moment of silence. Like an electric shock to Julia. "You're not... not his wife, are you?" she asked in terror.

"Of course not! You know I have no kids, I told you so! I...do know his wife though." Was there less warmth in her voice now, or was it simply a reluctance because of the awkward situation?

"Is she a close friend? Oh I know I shouldn't ask you…but…what's she like?"

Again a fractional hesitation. "She's very nice, intelligent, sensitive - what d'you want me to say Julia? This is something you should talk to Andres about. It's difficult for me - I don't want to be caught in between."

"No, I'm sorry. I know that - I shouldn't have called, I knew it anyway. I - could you do me one favour?"

"What's that?" again a hint of reluctance.

"Please don't tell Andres I called."

But she would, probably. Even as she berated herself for her clumsy stupidity it occurred to her that, like the worm in the perfect apple, she might have subconsciously done it deliberately. She must have wanted to play with fire, to plant the seed of their destruction, for once Andres knew she had gone behind his back and phoned Carmen to ask about his wife he would see it as some kind of betrayal of trust. And the words 'intelligent, sensitive' dug into her, and of course 'beautiful, erotic, sensual' which Carmen had been too tactful to add swirled through her thoughts and wittled away at her confidence. Knowing she was possessive and easily jealous, why had she set her own trap and then dived into it, an arrow seeking the bullseye? For the first time she almost believed in that hippie doctrine of predeterminism or whatever it should be called - the one where they assumed babies chose their parents on the grounds of suitability (perhaps it was an offshoot of the reincarnation theory). Anyway, she had done brilliantly with Frances, just the sort of difficult, destructive mother a masochist like her would drool over.

Next morning she arrived at the audition looking outwardly calm, but inwardly she was in turmoil. She missed Andres unimaginably, and her blue eyes had doubtless turned green like Frances' after a sleepless night imagining him making endless passionate love to his 'intelligent, sensitive, erotic, beautiful' and ultimately unleavable wife, for of course their relationship would be immeasurably strengthened by the brief threat she had posed it. Perhaps they had needed danger to spice it up for them, to stop them becoming complacent. In her vision his angelic little daughter gurgled happily in the background, intuitively aware of the powerful rapprochement between her parents. Julia, the minx, the temptress, the dancer - she could almost manage a wan smile at the irony by which in the nineteenth century all those English aristocrats fashionably had their affairs with Spanish dancers, and she had managed a kind of parody-reversal of this cliché!

Waiting in the wings, limbering up, she pondered again the relevance of dance in a world hellbent on wars, the war in Iraq, the endless war over Israel's endless appropriation of Palestine, and now the threat of more wars - Iran,

Syria, Lebanon. Her dancing or not dancing would really make a difference, wouldn't it, to the world? Trivial, frivolous, pointless; almost as meaningful as putting broken pots back together again when you come to think of it. No, in fact Frances had found a far more purposeful use for her life by doing that. She had at least restored a solid object of beauty, which informed us man had been 'civilised' for millennium, and that was surely better than being a dancer.

It was a breath of fresh air to dance, when her time came. It banished thoughts and thinking, it released all the pent up emotions and particularly purged her of jealousy. It had all the excitable pleasure of rushing downhill through the snow on a tobaggan, and all the exhilaration of sailing into the wind with sea water flecking her face, with all the precision and perfection of a solo climb without a rope up a sheer rock face - and the terror of death if you fall. She remembered reading some climber's autobiography, not a particularly memorable book, written by one of the many who had died near to the summit in an attempt on Mount Everest. He described a moment when he had bivouacked alone on the north face of the Matterhorn (or was it the Eiger?), one stormy February night, so it was a midwinter ascent, the most dangerous. He spent the night frozen in his inadequate arctic sleeping bag clinging to a narrow ledge, listening to the music and merriment of après-ski partying wafting up from St. Moritz. And he thought 'Why can't I be like them? Why can't I just enjoy life? Why do I have to set myself these tasks, risk death, trying to climb to the peaks of mountains that have anyway already been climbed before?' Of course no answer came to explain his obsession, just the realisation that he had to. He was not fully alive unless he did that.

Julia, as she danced, felt something similar. All the criticisms she had heaped on it might well be valid and her desire to do it had maybe very little justification - simply, she had to do it. She knew it clearly aged ten and eleven and had not questioned it. It satisfied some inner core of her being that nothing else did.

Flying back she had a window seat so she could feel physically, and psychologically, on top of the world. She got a crick in her neck from spending so much time looking out of the window, watching the rear blade of the wing and the layers of cloud scattering into wisps and finally evaporating the further south they flew. The late spring snowfall still frosted the Pyrenees, even thickly coating the higher peaks towards the centre of the chain where visibility faded into a violet murkiness, and you could see very clearly the narrow rock wall they formed dividing France from Spain. When you are on the ground and you see a plane in the sky, you are aware of the physical presence of the plane but unaware of the interior, all the rows of seats with people sitting reading onflight magazines, listening to ipods, worrying about the landing. Conversely when you are in a plane you relate only to the people and the interior, not the shape of the plane thrusting forward through the air; while the earth below seems rock and earth, grass and trees, houses and roads - but without real people. That was her thought, but she could make no ultimate sense of it, draw no philosophical conclusions. It was something related to the gap between consciousness and reality, the inability to see more than one or two facets of anything at any one time, the limitations to our perception and understanding.

Similar thoughts ran through her mind as she drove from the airport. She had only yesterday driven this same route in reverse, yet the two journeys had almost nothing in common. The landmarks were different, every roadside sight was new and unfamiliar - merely the patterns of poor driving were almost comfortingly consistent! Yesterday she felt so nervous. Today she felt elated and full of herself. But she must not be too full of herself, for that would be offensive to Andres.

Unfamiliarity pursued her, even to her own doorstep. Three strangers came to meet her and she felt suddenly shy.

Alex - how had he grown so tall? He was close to her height now, he had crept upwards in the night, and Marco's old skinny, fragile look had vanished without trace, he had strength, confidence and an enormous grin. But Andres, a little behind them because dignity prevented him running, and anyway they should hug her first and then leave him some space, she saw him with fresh eyes and he took her breath away. There was an urgent question in his eyes for she had not phoned after the audition, but the spring in her step and the elation in her eyes answered it, and a cloud crossed his face and he made an almost imperceptible sign of the cross against his chest - a gesture she had never seen him do before - and it sent a chill of fear through her.

"OK boys," he said with such easy rapport, "I want a chance to be alone with your mother now."

They went upstairs. There had been twenty four hour gaps in their cohabitation before yet no discernible distancing, the threads picked up exactly where they were left off. Did flying three thousand miles disturb one's consciousness? Was it simply jet lag? While she undressed, she tried to rid herself of this strange feeling of shyness, awkwardness, embarrassment even. As if she were a young virgin with a crush on him, who had never been naked in his presence before and did not know his body, or what to do with it, how to excite it. A novice who had pretended an experience she did not have and was about to be found out, someone who had never explored her own arousal with a man before. The same body that had earlier that morning danced with such grace, fluidity and confidence felt gawky and awkward. She could even see goose pimples sprouting all over her skin.

"I'm scared Andres - I don't understand it!"

"That's why we have to be together straight away, to get to know each other again."

She remained tentative, hanging back, and then familiarity of him flooded through her and she remembered everything. Except that she was drawing not on conscious knowledge but subconscious impulses; smells and tastes of skin and hair and warmth and movement, excitement, pleasure, sounds; a little far away voice in the back of her mind did remind her at one point that the boys might well be listening, but she ignored it for she did not care. Eventually they lay quietly in each others' arms.

"Why was I frightened? - I've only been away for thirty four hours!"

"Those hours were very long. And this bed was terrible to sleep in alone."

She wondered yet again how they would manage soon, but could not bring herself to tell him they had only five more days.

He propped himself on one elbow and looked into her eyes. "Julia..."

"Um?"

"You called Carmen from the airport...Why?"

Her hand whipped across her mouth, instinctively trying too late to stem the words that were already spoken. "I'm sorry, I was...desperate in a different way - or nearly the same. I know I shouldn't have. I did ask her not to tell you."

"She didn't tell *me*, but she told Isabel. My wife."

She looked at him in horror, "I thought she knew about us! You lying bastard - you said you'd told her!"

"Of course I did, that's not the problem. What upset her was to find out I had time to look after Alex and Marco, but none to visit Claudia, my own daughter." He glanced sadly out the window, "She's absolutely right, I should have gone at some point. I know."

"Andres I have to be in London by this weekend." Her voice grew husky, "Can't you see her...after that?"

"No. It's not fair that my seeing her depends on your timetable, don't you understand? I'm going tomorrow, and I want you to come with me."

His face had such determination she could only manage a feeble, "But what about Alex and Marco?"

328

"Reggie'll manage." Finally he grinned, "Forget what I said before, you know he can cope. We'll be back by late evening, if we start really early in the morning. You owe it to me Julia."

Alex and Marco were curious about her trip to London but she gave only sketchy replies, conscious that Andres would feel excluded if they chatted about people and places he did not know. Their excitement at an imminent return was obvious though. She deflected it by demanding to know what they did in her absence.

"Football. Break dancing. This and that - and we went to Frances' grave" Marco told her.

"What!"

"...and planted something."

"We suggested poisoned ivy," Alex chipped in, "or brambles, or prickly pear, deadly nightshade or toadstools - something suitable, but Andres wouldn't agree. He's a sentimental old fool really." Alex looked challengingly at Andres but in a manner that was transparently light-hearted, "He chose honeysuckle for God's sake!"

Julia laughed initially before glancing accusingly at Andres. "Have you become my conscience? You're trying to rub my nose in my neglect, aren't you?"

"Not at all! Going there was Marco's idea and then, because it looked bare and forlorn, I planted something symbolic for me. If it survives it'll be an easy way to recognise where she's entombed, in case you've forgotten."

She accepted the criticism with better grace this time, "I suppose I should go. The trouble is I don't believe she's there - if you see what I mean."

"She was a mean old ratbag, always vicious to Julia," Alex came to her defence. "She doesn't deserve a visit."

"You saw the worst of her, Alex. When she was younger, she was miles better."

"What's the worst thing she ever did or said?" Marco lent forward eagerly.

"Marco..." Julia sighed "another time OK? I'm feeling guilty now. I've been feeling that way since Andres reassured me that dancing was worthwhile because I never respected what she did."

"What? The pots, or the sex?"

"Alex! The pots - and that's how dismissive *I* was, because they weren't 'pots' but amphora, remarkably old and beautiful... Once, after a scene, I hurled one of her favourite bowls, one that she'd made herself, across the room. Then I yelled 'Don't worry! Some fool like you two thousand years from now will pick up those ugly pieces and put it all back together'. She didn't say a word. She very deliberately gathered the pieces and left them in a plastic bag in the cupboard." A look of desolation crossed her face. "They're still there. I came across them when I was sorting through," and she buried her face in her hands.

Marco scampered off to the cupboard and after some scuffling noises returned triumphantly with the bagfull of broken ceramic pieces. " 'Cause I've finished my mural masterpiece and still got some glue, I think I rather fancy having a go at this tomorrow!"

Julia's face reappeared, looking at him in undisguised horror.

Alex patted her reassuringly on the back, "No worries. It's like a puzzle for him - he won't turn into Frances! You can't object anyway, because I love dancing but it doesn't change me into you."


It was an agreable experience being driven by Andres and being able to talk about externalities, to be liberated from the personal, to absorb the lines of mountains on the horizon and the speed with which the immediate landscape confronted them, and then retreated behind them. They deliberately focused on the present, the past, the history of Sevilla, Andres' antecedants and anything that came into their heads so long as it was unrelated to their future. Apart from that first meeting in a seafront bar in Villahermosa and the excitement of Carocaballo, and of course the tension of her interview in the Cuartel, she had spent no time with Andres outside the confines of her own house, incredible though that seemed, which made it doubly refreshing. It was only when they reached the outskirts of Sevilla that apprehension surfaced.

"I don't want to meet Isabel, Andres. It'll put flesh on my horrid imaginings, I can't face it. Please let me wait somewhere while you fetch Claudia."

"OK." She could see the tension mounting in his face too, more than the sudden complication of heavy city traffic would explain.

Sevilla was stunningly beautiful in a friendly, colourful way, with tall town houses gleaming in the sunshine, elegant colonnaded squares with fountains, and occasional flashes of beautiful blue, white or green ceramic tiles that would have attracted Frances. It had a southern, warm, alluring Moorish quality to it, with little of the severe austerity of a northern city, and it was not self-consciously Roman Catholic despite its vast cathedral. The streets were lined with orange or tangerine trees and profusions of potted flowers hung off balconies. With its easy combination of music, plant life, water and buildings she could feel its Arabic heritage. She wished they had the time and the serenity to visit the striking beauty of the Giralda, but they had not come as tourists.

If she did not feel so nervous she would have enjoyed waiting for Andres on the street corner where he dropped her off, but as it was after ten minutes she began to feel a rising panic. What if he left her there? Her passport and money were locked in the boot of his car and he had the key, and she had no idea where he had parked it. She was effectively stranded - without even a mobile phone to warn Reggie!

At last her antennae trembled to see him coming towards her, familiar and yet frighteningly unfamiliar for a little stranger child with wavy, fluffy dark brown hair was in his arms, and neither of them looked quite natural to be so close to each other.

He smiled at Julia sheepishly, knowing full well that he held Claudia awkwardly, and she leaned stiffly backwards away from him in slight rebellion at her capture, looking at him with puzzlement, suspicion even, although there was a hint of recognition struggling in her eyes. Big brown eyes, Andres' eyes - maybe she could recognise them in his face although they were not quite the same for hers were rounder and more babylike.

"At first she wouldn't come with me," he said apologetically in explanation of the delay, "and I wasn't allowed the buggy - God knows why. Probably I'm meant to experience the full weight of her," he added, a touch bitterly. "Let's go to the Park."

Julia could not always walk beside them because the pavements were crowded, and every so often cyclists or skate boarders zoomed along the curbside so close that they skimmed her elbow, so mostly she walked behind in their wake. She could tell that Claudia remained stiff and unrelaxed from the way that her head dipped and rose jerkily to his stride. She rather admired her spirit, for she was not crying, but certainly letting him know he was a stranger. At last they reached the park and he gently lowered her to the ground, keeping firm hold of her hand.

"God," he said, "it's like carrying a twenty kilo sack of potatoes! How do women do it with such effortless ease?"

"When they're relaxed it's twice as easy. I used to carry them on my hip or shoulders, or in a special pouch thing when they were little. But if they're tense it's a dead weight, especially if they deliberately lean the wrong way." She couldn't help smiling at his mild exasperation.

"Well *you* can carry her back."

"Andres, she doesn't know me at all."

But she was staring at Julia curiously, then looking from Andres to Julia, not fearing that she had been kidnapped exactly but a little perplexed at the novelty. Andres found a bench and sat down, lifting Claudia astride his legs and tentatively becoming a horse.

"Papa," she said, smacking him on the nose, "Papa?"

"Soy tu papa," he said, relieved they were getting somewhere at last. But Claudia continued to attack his nose, so he lifted her onto Julia's lap. "You take her a moment Julia, she's still furious with me."

It was too late for Julia to object, but the sudden close contact produced a current of alarm, almost an aversion.

Alex and Marco had felt so close and cuddly, as babies they had melted into her body and even smelt of her own milk; yet this one was strange, with the smell of starch or something unfamiliar on her dress and flavoured yoghurt on her breath, another, unknown woman's child. She could not bring herself to contact her skin and felt her hands turn stiff with rejection; all she could do was look into her eyes, curious eyes, reminding her of Andres. Then she felt tears unexpectedly streaming down her face - she would not have been able to explain why, but Claudia was immediately fascinated by them. At last she relaxed, trampled happily on Julia's thighs and wiped her finger in the wet tears.

"Ow," she said.

"No," Julia said, and slapped her own thigh, "that's 'ow'! These" and she wiped her tears away "are just tears."

She found she could now stroke Claudia's hair without revulsion. It was soft like dandelion fluff, and with its chestnut highlights it was many shades lighter than Andres', so her mother might even be blonde. She wondered if Andres had mainly been attracted to her because she reminded him of Isabel.

They found a small children's playground with bright coloured swings, slides and roundabouts, and Andres finally managed to make Claudia laugh when they shared the see-saw because he was too big and had to counterbalance her weight with only half a leg. The best amusement was the fountain though, catching the water in their hands, funneling it with long leaves and Julia became a lizard with her tongue, flicking it out and stabbing the fine spray of the fountain so that it deflected off course.

"Don't you do it Claudia, only me" she said, suddenly realising that the water was probably far from safe for drinking. "Let's hope I'm not sick in your car on the way back," she warned Andres.

Andres looked exhausted when he rejoined her after returning Claudia home. Julia suspected he had had the brunt of further bitter words, which had doubtless sunk in deeper due to his weakened state, because she could tell he was saddened by his restrained rapport with Claudia. She tried to cheer him up; when you are only twenty months old and have not seen someone for five months, even though they are your dad, it is a very long time - longer than all but buried memory. All the wisdom and understanding he had shown towards her and her life somehow evaporated when directed back on himself, and he failed to see that he had set himself up for disappointment. He had wanted too much: to have Claudia fall into his arms, head over heels in love with him; to adopt him and Julia immediately as alternative parents; for Julia to love her as a mother would. Claudia had felt unfamiliar even to him although he had known her and loved her as a baby; also he had subconsciously compared her to Alex and Marco, who could relate by talking, sharing jokes and booting a football at him. All these things she tried to tell him, and he listened but could not shake his sadness off. He had wanted to show her some of his favourite haunts, but in the end he did not have the heart.

"We'll just drive past the family house, but not get out," he said.

So all she had was an infinitesmally brief glimpse of a large imposing town house set in a walled garden behind high wrought iron gates, a flash of flame colour from bougainvilla and African tiger lilies, and tall, sombre trees hiding behind a thick cypress hedge. Fortunately it was too brief to feel the chilling presence of any demonic stepmother that might lurk inside the nobly proportioned reception room facing the garden, where Julia saw a light was on - the glinting crystal lozenges from an ornate chandelier.

"That's why I planted your cypresses," he told her, managing the vestige of a smile, "I remembered how well they cut out the sound of traffic even in a busy city."

She rested her head against his shoulder, gently so as not to interfere with his ability to drive, "Andres please don't feel so sad. It's always painful to revisit the past like this, and even worse if you're worrying about its effect on me. Your sadness is filling the car."

"I'll try my best," he promised, but his voice was grey, flat and lifeless.


He recovered a little after locking horns with another driver who attempted to cut him up twice at successive traffic lights, because he finally outwitted the man in their deadly war of nerves and it seemed to reawaken a need to assert himself. Perhaps it reminded him of something he had told her about his schooldays; act like a loser and you invite male aggression and female derision - something like that, but it sounded much better in Spanish..

"That building's where they have the major dance and music events," he explained moments later, "Sevilla's a very cultural city."

Some time later, as they drove through a darkening landscape of long brooding shadows where the distant hills formed deep purple silhouettes - yet with a faint mistiness, like the bloom on a grape - against the almost luminous quality of evening aquamarine fading to lemon yellow, and she was wondering what created that clarity of colour since it could not be the sun, he broke the moment of peaceful silence.

"How did you like Sevilla?" It was a question full of hidden charge.

"It's a beautiful city, on brief first impressions. Frances took me to Granada and Cordoba but somehow we never made it to Sevilla. Maybe she hated the marmalade."

"I don't mean for visiting... I mean as a place to live."

A feeling of horror slipped into her throat, so sharp that she had to place her hand there to ensure no knife had sliced through the skin, and was almost surprised when her retracted fingers were free of blood. It took time to find her voice.

"You mean...go back to Isabel? Is that why we went to see Claudia? Was it some kind of a test?"

"Are you crazy! Of course not that, I don't know how many times I have to tell you the same thing, that I'll never go back. But I...I do have to make a confession to you..."

"What is it?"

"When I stayed the night while you were in London I realised that I couldn't wait for six whole years - that's how long you said your performing career would last, you in England, me in Spain except for weekends and holidays. I can't do it Julia, it's impossible for me. So I...you're not going to like this..."

"Andres could we stop a moment, park in a lay-by. You're weaving about, trying to look at me instead of the road, and I get nervous after my mother's accident."

So he concentrated fully on the road, and since they were travelling at high speed along a major route, an autovia, there were no convenient stopping places for several kilometres, or if there were they saw them too late to risk being shunted from behind by the usual trail of tailgaters who were gathered behind them, snorting, jeering and snapping impatiently at their heels since Andres had reduced his speed. It was a long five minutes for Julia. Her insides seemed to have been stripped away and her unblinking eyes remained uncomfortably rivetted to the approaching headlights, any one of which might have been a Colin coming to dazzle and kill. At last Andres found a dirt track at right angles to the road, on a bleak hillside in the middle of nowhere.

"Don't look at me like that Julia. This will make you angry with me, nothing else."

"Please get on with it..."

"OK. While you were in England, I...I'm afraid I snooped through your mother's desk, late at night after I couldn't sleep and the boys had gone to bed. Don't worry, they didn't see me. I felt ashamed about doing it - I didn't know what I would find, maybe things that would feed my jealousy, maybe things that no outsider should ever see. I knew absolutely that it was wrong, but I emptied all the drawers out. Everything. I found a lot of old photographs of you as a child - that was very emotional. I did take one of them. I read some of your letters to your mother, and guessed from them that there were many more that you'd destroyed, not wanting to be reminded. Anyway - I should move on. I found some reviews of your dancing, showing you have so much more of a glowing reputation than you pretend. I also found a copy of your CV, an older one, and since the boys had let me in on the password earlier in the evening when we played computer games, I turned it on and accessed your up-to-date version and printed out a copy. Please let me finish, I'm afraid there's worse to come... Remember my state of mind Julia, before you judge me too harshly. It's four or five in the morning, I haven't slept and I'm cold, I'm guilty of an unforgivable breach of trust and I feel physically sick - much worse than the night when I was sick - because I know that you're going to go back to England and I also know now what I chose to disbelieve before - that I can't actually manage without you. That's my state of mind. I'm trying to speed this up for you - so we get to the crux. OK, so I pore over your CV and it's enormously impressive, and the fact that you're so good at tap, as well as classical dance and all your other skills, and that's quite rare, and you know a fair bit about Flamenco...it set me thinking. I know dancers do exchanges, go on loan - that sort of thing, and I think: of course! Any Spanish Dance Company would leap at the chance of having her for a year, perhaps as an exchange, who knows? So in the morning I phone the two main Companies, one in Madrid and one in Sevilla. It was incredibly easy - I pretend to be your agent of course - and I basically more or less get it wrapped up. Both are wagging their tails with tongues drooling out at the idea, they've both heard of you anyway because of something at the Barbican two years ago. I pride myself I handled it rather well, although I know I shouldn't take pride in anything, considering what I've done. Anyway, they were desperately eager, and on the money front generous as well, and they'll both be sending someone to watch you perform, one on

335

the opening night I think it was, so's to discuss the future - they do know you're contracted 'till the end of the summer, I did at least get that right."

He had been staring out of the dark, blank windscreen most of the time, giving her only occasional glances, but now he turned to face her, although it was so incredibly dark she only knew it instinctively.

"The worst thing for me now, since I always knew you would find it hard to trust me, is to know that although you probably at last trust that I love you - for why the hell else would I do what I've done? - You'll now never trust me fully in other ways. I was desperate Julia! Otherwise I'd never have done it."

The silence between them, as with the silence all around them, on the rutted dirt track on that desolate hillside in the middle of nowhere, was immense. The imprint of all the onrushing headlights still replayed on her retina, so that although her eyes would normally have adapted to the dark by now, this time they failed to. She could hear him breathing but couldn't see him at all. Blindness.

"Please say something, even ..."

"I can't think what to say Andres, because I don't know what I think. I have three different thoughts; one is I don't control my life anymore because you've taken it over. You decided when we should start a sexual relationship even though I didn't want one. Now you're directing my future and where I should live, regardless of us - me and the kids I mean, for their lives are of course affected. That's the first thought. The second is picturing me doing as a child exactly what you did; I went hunting through that same old desk looking for secrets, for love letters, for traces of my father; her underwear drawers too - for anything embarrassing or sexual. I even snipped a hole in her diaphragm to get a brother or sister, so I'd have an ally and a friend, but it was so big she spotted it. So what *can* I say without being a hypocrite? - Except of course I was only little and had some sort of family right to snoop." She paused for breath, a long pause. Then she suddenly leant against him almost roughly, "And the third is what the hell, I was so dreading being without you, maybe what you've done is a stroke of genius and I'd never have thought of it. It gives us something to work towards that's not so far into the future that it might as well not be there. And yet I hate how you did it - why the hell couldn't you have asked me instead of sneaking behind my back? And how did you dare make me feel guilty for phoning Carmen when you'd done something a thousand times worse?"

"I didn't plan to do it, Julia. I did it because I couldn't help myself, and once I got started I couldn't stop. Then of course I didn't know how to tell you, so I did...plan our going to Sevilla. But I still didn't know how, or when, I'd be able to confess. That's why I've been feeling so bad, I'm not proud of my deception..."

He rested his head wearily against hers and they absorbed the strangeness of their situation, the confusions of right and wrong, of love and possessiveness, of lying and subterfuge, of the jealousies of that day and days before and doubtless days to come, all the time watching the moving ribbon of lights along the road which cut a slice through the dark wilderness. Eventually she stirred and poked him into life.

"Are you alright to drive? If not I can, because we'd better get going. Who knows, Reggie might be rifling through that desk right now and plotting. I've always suspected he fancied getting his hands on my mother's house!"

"Julia! You can't make a joke of it!"

"Oh yes I most certainly can. You'd better not start telling me when I can joke and when I can't, how I should speak and when I shouldn't. That's taking your new role of control freak one step too far."

He knew she spoke in humour but simultaneously recognised his new vulnerability. He could sense only too clearly that although his betrayal of trust and his audacity had in many ways been forgiven it would not be forgotten, and thus she had gained the absolute right to use it for her amusement or to her advantage if ever she so wished.


They arrived back just after midnight, but the lights were still blazing and it was obvious no-one had gone to bed. The living room had transformed into an embryonic casino: packs of cards, humble piles of euro coins and taller ones of centimos, the chess board out and the computer on, with the fan surging showing it had clearly been working hard for many hours. Alex and Marco greeted them at the doorway, the light of illicit revelry shining in their eyes, falling over themselves to be solicitous about their journey so as to deflect criticism from their own midnight gambling.

"We had to stay up in any case," Alex explained, "to babysit Reggie." He waved vaguely in the direction of the sagging old armchair, where Reggie was slumped fast asleep, his chin resting on his chest.

"We tired him out," Marco added gleefully. "He's honestly far too old to manage us all day long. It was the football that did for him."

"No Marco, actually it was the whisky," and this time Alex's finger homed in on an empty bottle of malt. He lowered his voice, "He got a bit emotional, I'm afraid to say. All Marco's fault of course. Whilst glueing up that broken bowl he kept pursing his lips, apparently just like Frances used to," and Alex rolled his eyes for dramatic effect. "So I'm sorry to say it's a bit like 'Frances is dead, long live Frances!' " and he gave Marco a hefty whack on the back.

"Have you been drinking?" Julia asked suspiciously, with the shadow of a smile.

"Jusht a shoupçon" he said, deliberately slurring and exaggerating the sibilance.


They went into the kitchen so as not to disturb Reggie, and Julia made a camomile tea. She decided their ebullient mood was perfect for what ought to be shared, and that it would be much better to tell them immediately instead of allowing time to brew and breed anxieties within her.

"Andres will come with us to London this weekend, so as to help us settle in. Then of course he has to come back here for his work. And we can't expect Jan to move out instantly - she only knew about our returning on the day of my audition - so you'll have to share a room for a little while. OK?"

They both groaned theatrically.

"And," she hesitated, looking at Andres who was drumming nervously on the table, "We might well be coming back to Spain in the Autumn, to live in Sevilla for a year. That's the plan anyway - although you never know what'll happen." She smiled wistfully, "It all depends on how well Andres and I get on, over the summer."

"Oh well," Alex said off-handedly "can't count on it then." But when he saw the depth of emotion on Andres' face he took a firm grip on his inebriated levity. "I'm sorry - I actually can't think of anything better," and he threw a somewhat unco-ordinated arm around Andres' shoulder.

"Awesome," murmured Marco.


Or at least they all three thought that he did. But when they looked more closely at him they realised that they must, purely through wishful thinking, have imagined it. For even though he was still sitting upright in his chair he proved to be already deeply asleep, his eyes closed and his breathing slow and regular. However the faint ghost of a smile that hovered on his half-closed lips suggested a state of peacefully contented oblivion.